Based in Scotland and drawing on the author's many years as a criminal defence lawyer, the Best Defence Series of legal thrillers feature defence lawyer Robbie Munro, and in which William McIntyre turns fact into fiction. Described as an antidote to maverick cops chasing serial killers, the series emphasises that justice is not only about convicting the guilty, but also about acquitting the innocent.

The Best Defence Series

GOOD NEWS
BAD NEWS

#8 in the Best Defence Series

William McIntyre

1

The most common question asked of a criminal defence lawyer is: how can you possibly defend someone you think is guilty?

Top answer, most people think, is money, and it does definitely help. However, the fact is that most defence lawyers are interested in justice, and most clients have the decency not to say if they are guilty. Often it's the guilty ones who sound the most innocent and come up with the best lines of defence. Some of them have had a lot of practice. What's important for defence agents is not to prejudge the issue; there are enough people doing that already.

So I like to respond to that question with another question. How is it that a prosecutor can seek to convict someone he or she may think, and indeed, must presume by law, to be innocent? That was a question you heard asked about as often as you heard Sheriff Albert Brechin putting 'not' and 'guilty' together in the same sentence.

'It was an assault, Mr Munro. Plain and simple. Did you not hear the evidence of the two witnesses? Are you deaf as well as...'

'As well as what, M'Lord?'

Sheriff Brechin put a hand under the front of his yellowed, horse-hair wig, scratched whatever it was that lived under there, and looked down at me from the Bench. 'As well as extremely stubborn. When will you realise that it doesn't matter how long you stand there addressing me, the facts of the case remain unalterable. Your client struck—'

'Slapped.'

'There you have it then! You admit it yourself.'

'A slap from my client does not necessarily amount to an assault.'

The Sheriff sat up straight, raised his right eyebrow an inch and his voice an octave. 'Really? Since when?' The day Bert Brechin was appointed Sheriff of the Sheriffdom of Lothian & Borders, was the day the theatre world missed out on a fine pantomime dame. 'Has someone changed the definition of assault and not told me? It is still defined as an attack by one individual upon another with evil intent, is it not?' Brechin glanced around, as though some legal messenger might arrive hotfoot from Parliament House with news of a change to the law.

'Yes, it's still the same,' I said, 'and that's why I'm certain your Lordship will take my point.'

'Point?' Brechin's left eyebrow caught up with the right, both threatening to disappear somewhere under the fringe of his wig. 'Point? I didn't realise you had a point, Mr Munro. It's most unlike you.'

'My point, M'Lord, is evil intent and the distinct absence of it in this case.' I stepped to the side to allow the Sheriff a better look at the young woman in the dock. Heather Somerville was a student teacher, one week off her twenty-third birthday, two away from graduation and six from her wedding. One Saturday afternoon, a couple of months previously, Heather had arranged to meet her fiancé and go shopping. When he hadn't shown up at the allotted time she'd gone looking for him, and, with her woman's intuition requiring only to be placed on a low setting, had tracked him to the pub where he was watching a game of football with his mates. There had been an argument. He'd called her a nag. She'd slapped his face. The barmaid had ejected the pair of them and phoned the police.

Subsequently, and on him apologising to her, the two had kissed, made up and considered the matter closed. Not so the Scottish Justice System. It was clearly an act of domestic violence. As such it fell to be dealt with under the prevailing zero tolerance policy on such matters.

Heather Somerville had been arrested and held in custody. After a weekend pacing a police cell, she had appeared in court late on the Monday afternoon. A conviction for assault would spell disaster for her future career as a primary school teacher, and so on my advice she'd pled not guilty and opted to take her chances at trial.

Unfortunately, Heather's boyfriend had been extremely helpful to the prosecution. That was the problem with dragging nice, law-abiding people to court. If you asked them to put their right hand up to God and swear an oath, they had the annoying habit of telling the truth, even if they'd rather not. Had her boyfriend been one of my regulars, asked to testify against his girl, there would have been a sudden and violent onset of amnesia at the mere sight of the witness box.

Of course, while it was bad news for some that the Crown insisted on prosecuting even the most trivial of relationship spats, there was good news for others. The silver lining to the leaden cloud of zero tolerance was an increase in prosecutions, and more prosecutions meant more work for me. No matter how much I despised zero tolerance policies, eventually I came to view them the way dentists viewed bags of boiled sweets: dead against them in principle; happy for the business.

I carried on. 'M'Lord, the complainer, if you can call him that because he never actually complained about what happened, may have given evidence to say that he was slapped...'

Brechin snorted. 'No may about it. He did say that. Precisely that.'

'But he also said that he deserved it.'

'No-one deserves to be slapped, Mr Munro.'

I could think of a few who did. One of them was sitting ten feet away, keen to uphold some twenty-first-century, politically correct notion of justice, while frowning at me from under the type of hairpiece made popular circa the mid-eighteen-hundreds. 'Surely, your Lordship will agree that some people deserve the occasional slap?'

'Such as whom?'

'Such as errant boyfriends who don't show up when they say they will and are then rude to their partners.' If not, what was the world coming to? What would Mae West, Rita Hayworth and just about every Hollywood leading lady of yesteryear have done if they kept being hauled off to chokey every time they gave Jimmy Cagney a drink in the face or John Wayne a scud on the jaw?

'And what about errant girlfriends, Mr Munro? Do they deserve the occasional slap too?'

It was a neat switcheroo, I'd give the old devil that

much. 'Vive la différence, M'Lord. As I say, my submission is that the complainer—'

'The victim.'

'The fiancé saw the slap as less of an assault and more of a correctional aid. However, if, as you say, it was an assault, it was justifiable. How about we call it reasonable chastisement?'

Brechin smiled like a gutted fish, cheery at the imminent prospect of ruining some young person's career over a lover's tiff. 'How about we don't? How about we call it what it was – an assault.'

'But—'

'But nothing. I'll decide who deserves to be slapped, Mr Munro. Not you, not your client and not even the young man who was unfortunate enough to have been on the receiving end of this vicious attack. Now, are you quite finished?'

I'd been presenting my closing submission for half an hour. Hugh Ogilvie, the Procurator Fiscal, had done his in thirty seconds, pushing at a door to a conviction that was not so much open as falling off its hinges. Clearly Brechin was satisfied that the slap comprised the necessary wicked intent. It was time for a change of tack. 'If your Lordship is not with me when it comes to the mens rea, is this not perhaps a case where the Court could consider these proceedings to be de minimis?' Latin often helped when dealing with sheriffs as well as impressing the hell out of clients.

Brechin looked at me as though I was speaking an alien language as opposed to his favourite dead one. 'De minimis?'

That the law did not concern itself with trivialities was a well-established rule and set out, as every law student knew, in limerick form.

> *There was a young lawyer named Rex,*
> *With a very small organ of sex,*
> *When charged with exposure,*
> *He said with composure,*
> *'De minimis non curat lex.'*

I didn't think a recital would help. Nonetheless, for some sheriffs, those with a shred of humanity, to find the incident de minimis would have been a way out. All Brechin had to do was accept that while, legally speaking, there had been an assault, the whole matter was so trivial that there need not be a conviction. His brother Sheriff, Larry Dalrymple, Livingston Sheriff Court's Yin to Bert Brechin's Yang, would have seized the opportunity with both hands. The most annoying thing about it all was that the trial had originally been set down for Dalrymple's court because Brechin was supposed to be on vacation. Sheriffs were allowed an inordinate number of holidays. Bert Brechin took far too few. On this occasion, for some unknown reason, he'd returned early from a two-week bird-watching expedition on Madeira and volunteered to do the trials' court. It meant that on this, the first day of May, when I should have been giving my face a wash in the morning dew, I was instead getting a hosing from the Bench.

'Your client is guilty, Mr Munro.' The Sheriff had heard enough of my legal argument. 'Stand up,' he ordered the accused, his words accompanied by wails of grief from my client's mother in the public benches. 'Miss Somerville, I fine you four hundred pounds. Do you require time to pay?'

10

She did. Twenty-eight days to pay the fine. The rest of her life to pay for the conviction.

2

Tuesday afternoon. I was back from court, stomping about the office and restocking the swear box while Grace-Mary battered out some letters and otherwise did her best to ignore me. It was basically business as usual.

The phone rang. 'That'll be Ellen Fletcher again,' she said, not looking up from her typing. 'She's been calling all morning. You're going to have to speak to her sometime.'

'What's she stolen now? Doesn't that woman ever buy anything? Tell her to call back later and make an appointment with...' I nearly said 'with Joanna'. But Joanna Jordan no longer graced the halls of Messrs. R.A. Munro & Co., Linlithgow's premier criminal defence firm — Linlithgow's only criminal defence firm.

It hadn't taken my former legal assistant long to come to the conclusion that she had a choice to make: either to continue our business partnership or our romantic one. Running both in tandem was apparently not an option.

Though there was no hiding my hurt feelings, Grace- Mary was less than sympathetic. 'You men are fine in small doses,' was my secretary's take on the issue. I preferred the, 'You can have too much of a good thing,' line that Joanna had spun me, before, once more, succumbing to the lure of Her Majesty's civil service.

It had long been my opinion that the Crown Office

and Procurator Fiscal Service was no place for a woman with a mind of her own but, apparently, Joanna's departure to the dark side made a lot of sense. At least, it did to Grace-Mary, who could usually be relied on to back any line of argument that was contrary to my own. Nine to five, proper holidays, a pension. She'll even be allowed to be sick occasionally.

Grace-Mary held the receiver out to me. 'Great to be popular, isn't it?'

Back in the days when they actually prosecuted folk for shoplifting, I wouldn't have minded how often Ellen was caught. These days the courts were cluttered with more hi-tech criminals, like those who'd posted offensive tweets or sent snapshots of their genitalia to people who really wished they hadn't taken the trouble. A good old- fashioned shoplifter was less likely to see the inside of a court than be handed a fixed penalty or a warning letter asking them politely to stop stealing stuff. Ellen could have papered her living room walls with those. 'Ellen, I'm really busy...'

'I know, Robbie, and thanks for speaking to me, it's so good to hear your voice again.' Ellen's smooth and sensual tones oozed their way down the line. I was impervious to her charms.

'Nice to hear from you, too,' I said, 'but I'm in the middle of something at the moment. How about if—'

'Look, Robbie, I'm really sorry for bothering you,' Ellen continued, 'I just don't know who else I can turn to.'

'I'm sorry too, Ellen, but I really have to go.'

'Robbie, I've won the lottery.'

'That's fine, I'll hand you back to Grace-Mary and she'll fit you in sometime mutually convenient.' I put a hand over the mouthpiece and held the handset out to my secretary. 'Give Mrs Fletcher an appointment, will you? Never is good for me.'

'Did you hear what I said, Robbie?'

I thought I had, but it must have been a fault on the line. 'I said I've won the lottery.'

As I slowly returned the receiver to my ear, I could feel my previous imperviousness dissolving like a body in a barrel of hydrofluoric acid. 'The lottery? You're kidding. How much?'

'Enough to last me the rest of my life.'

'And your problem is what?' I asked after the several seconds it took me to assimilate the information. 'You need help spending it?'

'No, spending the money is something I can manage.' Ellen laughed again. I supposed lottery-winners saw the funny side to a lot of things. 'Listen, I can't talk on the phone. Why don't you come and see me tonight? I'm staying at the Balmoral Hotel. Yeah, the big fancy one at Waverley Station. We'll have a few drinks and I'll tell you all about it.'

It sounded good to me, until I remembered. 'Sorry, Ellen. I can't make it tonight.'

'Oh, well, if you really are too busy, I suppose there are other lawyers who—'

'However...I think I may be free on Friday afternoon.'

'You're not,' Grace-Mary said.

'How would that do? Say about three o'clock? Just let me check my diary.'

Grace-Mary threw open the big appointments diary. 'You're busy all of –'

'Yes, I'm definitely free.'

'Great,' Ellen said. 'Three o'clock, Friday it is. Oh, and Robbie,' she added in honeyed tones, as if the sound of her voice could have been any the sweeter, 'you'll not need to bring any of those nasty Legal Aid forms with you.'

3

It was a rainy night in George Street, Edinburgh.

'The things I do for love,' I said, holding the umbrella over Joanna while she clamped a hand on top of her head, trying to keep her hair in place. The hair was one of the reasons we were late. Up or down had been something of a dilemma. Then there was our slow pace caused by Joanna's new shoes, shoes she defended on the basis that they looked great and were actually very comfortable — unless you had to walk anywhere in them. The main hold-up, however, had been down to the fact she had nothing suitable to wear. Though, when I say nothing, of the two dresses auditioning for the part, I'd been unable to identify a problem with either. They were little and black and Joanna looked sensational in both of them.

With time marching on there had been an urgent need for someone to make an executive decision, and so I'd come out strongly in favour of the first black dress because I liked its little sparkly bits. Joanna's expression told me she didn't agree. Not to worry. The flow and how to go with it was something I'd been practising since Joanna had moved in with me. With the effortless efficiency of a precision instrument, I'd recalibrated my opinion and decided that, no, upon reflection, the sparkly bits might not be appropriate, and the other black dress did have the advantage of frilly bits that, while decorative, were less glitzy and perhaps more suitable for such a formal occasion. Even then, with me having expressed a clear and unambiguous preference for both frocks, Joanna's look of dissatisfaction remained unchanged. What did she want me to say? It had to be one dress or the other. I suggested we flip a coin. That's when the third dress appeared. A red one. I hadn't seen it before. That was because it was new. Joanna had bought it earlier that day on the spur of the moment. It was way too expensive, and she'd been fully intending to take it back, hadn't even been going to take it out of the bag when she got home but, seeing as we both agreed the little black numbers were quite clearly out of the question, what else was there for it?

'Quit moaning and keep walking,' Joanna said. 'It's one dinner. I've not asked you to pull me out of a burning building.' She stopped under the portico outside the Assembly Rooms, the crowd parting around us, rocks in a river of black suits and evening dresses.

'Come here.' Taking me by the shoulders, she squared me up and straightened my bow-tie with a couple of swift tugs. Joanna had binned the clip-on job that had served well for many a year and bought me a proper one that I'd had to learn how to tie. The dinner suit was also new. According to Joanna, borrowing my brother's tuxedo and Wonder-Webbing the hems of the trouser legs was no longer an option.

'Right,' she said, giving me a helpful shove in the back, 'shut up, get in there and smile.'

The Scotia Law Awards Dinner was an annual event, which in previous years I'd had little difficulty avoiding. For one thing I'd never been in the running, for another the tickets were one hundred and fifty a head.

'So, how do you win one of these awards?' I asked. 'I don't remember ever being asked to vote for anyone. Do you?'

'Seriously?' Joanna said, divesting herself of her coat and handing it to me. 'You really think there are lawyers out there who would vote for other lawyers to receive an award?' My wife-to-be was definitely in the running for most cynical lawyer of the year, and, it seemed, if there was a prize for the most gullible I'd be sole nominee. 'I think that's why I love you, Robbie. You always try and see the best in everyone.'

I did. Well, almost everyone. Obviously, exceptions had to be made in the case of certain politicians, most sheriffs and all but the very latest recruit to the Procurator Fiscal Service.

'The way these things work is that Firms vote for them- selves. They apply, saying why they should receive the award, and the organisers consider the written submissions very carefully along with the number of tables each firm is taking at the dinner. Book enough tables at fifteen hundred a go and they might even tailor an award especially for you.'

'Most dashingly handsome. Something like that, you mean?'

Joanna took my chin in her hand and kissed me. 'Yes, if it was me who handed out the awards.'

'And if it wasn't?'

'I don't think they have that many tables.'

I checked in our coats and brolly and once more we entered the stream of diners coursing towards the ballroom. The place was buzzing. Crystal ware and silver cutlery twinkled and glinted on fifty or so large round tables. Everywhere people mingled, laughed, sipped fizzy wine and generally looked very much like what they were: a bunch of lawyers who needed to get out of the office more often. I was cornering a tray of canapés that had foolishly strayed into range, when Joanna took my hand and dragged me towards an arm that was waving in the distance.

The arm, like the rest of the tall, lean body to which it was attached, belonged to Joanna's Uncle Ted. Ted Hawke was Joanna's mother's brother and a partner in Fraser Forrest & Hawke. I'd only met him once, fleetingly. 'Ted's an insolvency specialist,' Joanna said. 'If you get stuck for conversation you can always talk about the law.' That was all very well, but what did insolvency practitioners actually do? Years ago I'd lost track of what those other lawyers, the ones who didn't stand up in court and argue for a living, did to make ends meet.

'He oversees the restructuring and trading of distressed debt.' Was there any other kind of debt? 'Just don't get involved in courtroom chat. The people at our table will be proper lawyers.' By which Joanna meant not the type of lawyers who spent their days shouting at hostile witnesses and arguing the toss with uninterested sheriffs. Or maybe it was the other way around.

'Ah, the guests of honour have arrived.' Ted gave his niece a peck on the cheek and me a hearty slap on the back. 'Good of you to join us last minute.' Clearly, the years spent dealing with all that distressed debt hadn't rubbed off on Uncle T financially. His fifty-something frame was covered with an evening suit that unlike mine hadn't been pulled off a peg, and beneath it was a shirt so startlingly white it was sore on the eyes.

'No, thank you for asking us,' Joanna said, multi-tasking with a gentle dig in my ribs.

'Yes, very kind of you, Ted,' I said.

Our expressions of gratitude were dismissed with a friendly wave of his hand. 'It's nothing. We always take four tables at the Scotias. It's something of a standing order, and this year we had a few last-minute call-offs. I'm only glad you could make it on such short notice. We're up for a few gongs, and it doesn't look good if our tables are half empty.' He pulled out a chair for Joanna, and the other dinner suits at the table, recognising the relationship between the boss and my fiancée, rose while she took her seat.

Leaning over us, Ted rested a hand on Joanna's and my shoulders. 'Now that we have two of our criminal law contingent here, let me introduce you to the person I hope will be the star of tonight's show.' He gestured to a sturdy young woman sitting directly across from us. 'Joanna, Robbie, this is Antonia. She's the daughter of a very good friend of mine and the best legal trainee we've ever employed at F, F and H. Present company excepted, of course.' He smiled at the other faces around the table, some of which looked like they were sucking the lime from their gin and tonics.

Antonia stood, reached across and shook our hands. She had a cute little smile, but you wouldn't have wanted to arm-wrestle her for a pint.

'And that's why,' Ted continued, 'Antonia has been nominated for Legal Trainee of the Year.'

'Well done,' Joanna said. This from the woman who five minutes ago had told me what a fake the whole award ceremony was.

The young woman treated Joanna to her lovely smile. 'We've met before, you and I,' she said. 'It was two years ago when I was doing the Diploma and you came to Edinburgh Uni for a mock trial. You were the Procurator Fiscal, I was the complainer. My imaginary shop had been robbed.'

Joanna's half-open mouth, wide eyes and slow-motion nod of recognition told me she had no idea who the girl was. 'Of course. Remind me. How did I do?'

'You won. Guilty as libelled,' Antonia said. 'I think it was my identification evidence that swung it.'

I didn't know why, but there was something in the way she said 'guilty'. It made me feel not so much that someone was walking across my grave, more like they were bouncing all over it on a pogo stick.

Ted shook his head. 'Crime, eh? All the young lawyers want to do it. All the smart ones know it doesn't pay. No offence, Robbie.' He laughed and threw an arm over my shoulder. I'd liked Ted from the word go. 'Let me buy you a drink.' I was a good judge of character. 'I hear tell you're fond of the uisge beatha.'

'I'd rather have a whisky if you don't mind,' I said. Ted looked at me for a moment. It was a look that said, "This guy is a criminal lawyer. Not only that, he's a Legal Aid lawyer. Yes, he really could be that stupid."

I smiled to show I was kidding, and he smiled too. With a wave of his magic arm, there was a waiter at our table in an instant, and a round of drinks swiftly followed.

As I sipped at what I hoped would be the first of many single malts, I began to think that perhaps it might not turn out to be such a bad evening after all. That was until I heard a horribly familiar voice behind me, and the exclamation, 'Granddad!'

Antonia stood and skipped around the table towards us.

'Am I the last?' said a voice. It couldn't be.

'I'm afraid I was guilty of thinking it would be easy to find a taxi on a wet Thursday night in Edinburgh.'

It was. There was no mistaking the 'guilty' in that sentence. Not when I heard the word on so frequent a basis. I turned slowly in my seat. The late arrival was clad in tartan trews, an Argyll jacket secured midriff by a single square silver button. He had more hair than I thought, but then it was always covered when I saw him. Sheriff Albert Brechin gave Joanna a stiff little nod of the head. 'Miss Jordan, how nice to see you. I hadn't realised you and Mr Munro would be coming tonight.' He snapped me off a brittle smile that I was unable to return.

'Likewise,' I said.

4

Antonia Brechin was called to the stage to be crowned
Legal Trainee of the Year, shortly after Uncle Ted had
narrowly missed out on the Managing Partner award,
and before a group from another city Firm was given
the accolade of Public Law Sector Team of the Year, an
area of law with which I was unfamiliar, and probably
as boring as the title suggested. The whole presentation
ceremony seemed to go on forever, with speeches,
photo- graphs and a big screen Twitter feed for lawyers
to send gloating messages to other lawyers who hadn't
voted for themselves or bought enough tables.

I tried to drink my way through the boredom, but
even half a bottle of wine and a few single malt
digestifs couldn't exorcise the ghost at the feast. Now I
knew why Brechin had come back early from his
holiday in Madeira. Not only to convict my boyfriend-
slapping client, but also to share in his granddaughter's
moment of glory. How could it be that he acted so
normally in company, almost like a human? Everyone
else seemed to find the old git thoroughly charming.

Ted, for one, was finding the Sheriff's conversation
particularly stimulating. Was it only me who could
sense his malevolent spirit?

'You know what I've always wondered about
criminal lawyers, Bert?' he said. 'How anyone can stand
up in court and defend a person they think is guilty?'

'Good question,' Brechin said, 'but one I think better

directed at Mr Munro. Defending the guilty is something he's made a career of.'

Laughing, Ted turned to me. 'Is that right, Robbie? How can you do it?'

'I do it because some of those people are actually innocent, and someone has to stand up for the wrongly accused.'

Ted swirled the last of the red wine in his glass and threw it back. 'Sounds like one of those dirty jobs that someone's got to do. Joanna tells me you've had a few famous victories in your time.'

It was meant as a compliment, and I would have accepted it and left things at that, but for the sarcastic snort from across the table. I'd heard that snort so often in court that I didn't have to turn my head to establish the origin.

'Not so many victories as I'd have liked,' I said, aware of the steely grip Joanna had taken on my thigh. 'Or should have had. You see, while it's my job to defend the wrongly accused, it's the job of others to judge them. Unfortunately...' I continued, ignoring the introduction of Joanna's nails into the gripping process, 'some of those whose job it is to judge guilt and innocence, wouldn't know an innocent person if they stood right in front of them.' I turned my head to look Brechin straight in his oyster eyes, adding for clarification, though by his beet- root face none was required, 'In the dock of the Sheriff Court.'

When the Sheriff spoke, his lips scarcely moved. 'If you are insinuating that I am an unfair judge—'

'I'm not insinuating anything,' I said. 'I'm stating that there are too many people who think that the definition of justice is a finding of guilt, and yet the last time I looked, Lady Justice had two pans in her set of scales.'

'Leave it, Robbie,' Joanna said, placing a hand over the top of the wine glass that her uncle was determined to refill.

Brechin agreed. 'Yes, Mr Munro. Don't say something you may later regret.'

The others at our table had stopped chatting and were leaning in, lapping it up, and, by the expression on his face, Uncle Ted was beginning to think that maybe the price of my ticket had been worth it after all.

'Come now, Joanna, Bert, let the man speak,' he said. 'We're all friends here. I'm sure no-one is going to take offence at a little after-dinner legal debate.'

I didn't need any encouragement. 'Antonia, how old are you?'

Confused, the young woman looked at her grandfather and then back at me. 'Twenty-three.'

'And with your whole career ahead of you. Did you know that earlier today your grandfather convicted a woman, not much younger than you, of assault, all because she'd slapped her boyfriend on the face during a row? A young woman whose career in teaching is now over before it's even had a chance to begin.'

It was unfair of me to bring Antonia into it. I knew that as soon as I had spoken the words. She blushed with embarrassment and played with the gold chain around her neck.

'That's quite enough,' Brechin snarled across the table at me. 'It is no good repeating your argument from earlier today. I had to listen to it for quite long enough as it was. Your client committed an assault, plain and simple. I am very sorry if the law of Scotland doesn't meet with your warped sense of justice. Unfortunately, it is the job of some of us to apply it, not twist it to suit our own ends.'

'No matter if the consequences far outweigh the offence? That's not justice.'

'Perhaps not. But it is the law.'

'No, it's not,' I said. 'The law does not concern itself with trivialities. It's only because the Lord Advocate's zero tolerance policy dictates that every row between a man and woman must equate to domestic abuse that the case ever made it to court.'

Ted caught a passing waiter by the sleeve. 'What if it had been the other way about?' he asked, after ordering up another round of drinks, rehearsing the line put to me by Brechin in court. 'What if this girl's boyfriend had slapped her?'

'That would be different,' I said.

Ted pointed his finger. 'Aha, got you there, Robbie. Equal rights. What's sauce for the goose...'

'Not when the gander is six foot two and built like a brick chicken house and the goose is five foot one and eight stones soaking wet,' I said. 'If she'd shot him or stabbed him, fair enough, but a slap? Come on.'

'An assault is an assault.' Brechin was intent on having the last word. Nothing unusual there. 'My verdict might have seemed like an injustice to you and your client, Mr Munro, but I'd sooner resign my position than bend the law. To quote Oliver Wendell Holmes Junior, I preside over a court of law and not a court of justice.'

Trust Sheriff Brechin to take literally a tongue-in-cheek obiter remark, just so long as in his twisted mind it justified a conviction.

'Very good, Bert. Very good,' Ted said, enjoying every minute of it. 'What do you think about it all, Joanna? You're probably best placed to give a balanced view, having worked both sides, prosecution and defence.'

Joanna smiled diplomatically. 'Just like you say, Ted. I can see both sides of the argument.'

'Come on, Jo-Jo, don't be shy,' Ted said. 'We're all lawyers here. Pick a side and argue your case.'

The waiter arrived with a tray, noticeably absent of further refreshments. He whispered something to Ted, and the inclination of his head was followed by everyone at the table to a clot of blue uniforms standing on the other side of the ballroom.

Brechin couldn't resist. 'Looks like there may be some business for you, Mr Munro. Nothing too de minimis, I hope.'

He smiled at Ted. Ted didn't smile back. Two evening dresses stood up at nearby tables. Slowly they began to float across the room to the awaiting police officers.

As I was trying to think up some caustic remark to throw back at Brechin, I couldn't fail to notice that the colour had drained from his granddaughter's previously flushed face.

That and the fact that she too was rising slowly to her feet.

5

I hadn't known Ellen Fletcher in her younger days. I'd first acted for her only a year or so before, when she'd lost her husband, fallen on hard times and embarked on a career as an inept shoplifter-slash-credit-card-fraudster. Though she'd often been caught, she'd had only the one small taste of prison, a week's remand before a successful bail appeal. I'd been recommended to her by Jake Turpie, my former landlord, who'd known Ellen forever. She came from Croy originally, a small town, third stop on the train line from Linlithgow to Glasgow. A town where a lot of people got on and even more people didn't want to get off.

Apparently, Ellen had been a real looker back in the day. Ellen of Croy, the face that launched a thousand pub fights. But if her face had once been her fortune, these days it was accruing less interest. Or perhaps I was being unfair. Whenever I saw Ellen she was dressed down and in her working clothes. No make-up, no hair-do, just another woman doing the shopping. Someone not out to attract attention. Not while she was filling her tinfoil-lined carrier bag with anything from packs of razor blades to jars of coffee to designer labels. However, on this Friday afternoon Ellen was almost unrecognisable. Hair up high, the neckline of her evening gown down low, she looked more like the madam of a Texas cathouse than a recently retired shoplifter.

Ellen had taken a suite on the top floor of the Balmoral, and we sat in comfortable armchairs in the sitting room, chatting and polishing off what was left of the bottle of champagne she'd been drinking upon my arrival. When Ellen rang for room service it took three porters to deliver another, which had nothing to do with the logistics of the exercise and everything to do with her tendency to tip like a lorry at a landfill.

Ellen closed the door, put her purse back into a big pink handbag and handed me the bottle to pop. 'I like it here,' she said. It certainly had prison beaten hands down.

'You mentioned something about having a problem?' I said, peeling the gold foil from the bottle, and thinking it was about time we came to the reason I'd been summoned.

'I'm dying,' she said.

That was certainly a problem, if not the one I'd expected. I didn't know what to say. I poured and waited for the foam in our glasses to settle.

'Yep, life is a real comedian.' Ellen snatched up her drink and took a long pull at it, leaving bright red lipstick around the rim. 'Ellen, I've got good news and I've got bad news. The good news is that you've won the lottery. The bad news is that you'd better spend it fast because you'll be dead in three months.'

'What's the matter?' I asked.

'Blood cancer. The bad kind.'

'And they've only given you three months?'

'Three good months or twelve bad months with treatment, and I'm not spending a year traipsing back and forward to a cancer ward, being pumped full of chemo, no hair and plenty spewing. I'm going out with style and I have the money to do it.'

She took another sip and set her drink down again on the glass table between us. As she leaned back she winced, and pressed a hand to her side.

'Are you okay?'

She waved away my concerns, and, as though on cue, the bedroom door opened and a woman entered the room. She was tall with beautiful auburn hair, her slim figure and long legs covered by an all-in-one, light green trouser-suit that had a small white logo with a red cross embroidered on one of the collars. She gave me a polite smile before turning her attention to Ellen. 'Mrs Fletcher, I hope you're not overdoing it,' she said, with a pointed stare at the bottle of champagne. 'It's four o'clock and time for your nap.'

'I'm fine,' Ellen said. 'I'll sleep plenty when I'm dead.'

'Come on now, Mrs Fletcher. I think forty-winks would be just the thing.'

Ellen reached for the champagne bottle and poured herself some more bubbly. 'Away and stop treating me like a child.'

The nurse paid her no heed. 'I'm going to turn your bed down, and if you're not through in ten minutes I'll be back.' The severity of her tone was mitigated by the wink she gave me as she returned from whence she'd come.

'You've not got much time,' I said, adding hurriedly, 'I mean, not much time to tell me why I'm here.'

'Freddy,' she said.

Freddy Fletcher, Ellen's spouse, had been a well-known conman. In the conning business that's the worst type of conman. Ideally, the mark should never see you coming. Freddy had tended to arrive with all the surreptitiousness of a cruise-liner sailing down the Forth and Clyde Canal.

'What about him?'

'I want to see him.'

It seemed to me that, assuming Ellen's prognosis correct, she'd be seeing her husband soon enough, for Freddy Fletcher had gone missing over a year ago. Disappeared, as I recalled, owing Jake Turpie a large sum of money and in the process breaking Jake's first commandment, "Thou shalt not bump me." It was a law that was not so much written in stone as set in concrete – a bit like everyone suspected Freddy was.

'And how are you going to do that?' I asked.

'I want you to find him.'

It was sad. It's said that every wife takes her husband as she finds him and then spends the rest of her life trying to change him. Ellen had married Freddy in the hope she could reform him, and every time he'd gone to prison she'd waited for him to come out so that she could try again.

'I want you to find him and bring him home to me,' she said. It had to be the fizzy wine talking.

There weren't too many ways of saying it. 'Freddy's...well, he's dead. Isn't he?'

'That's what I thought.' Ellen knocked back her flute glass in one swift movement and set it down on the low table. 'Until last week.'

I took a sip of champagne. It was good. Not as good as whisky, but with some practice you could get used to it and I was prepared to put in the hours.

'I know what you're thinking.' She was right. 'But Freddy doesn't know about me winning the lottery.

No-one does. Just you. I was strictly no publicity.'

'Ellen, there are bound to be people working on the inside who leak that sort of information. Do you think Freddy was the only conman out there? Who told you he's alive? Has he been in touch? Don't tell me. Someone has said they'll find him for you for a small fee. Is that it? Can't you see it's a scam?'

'It's not a scam. I'm telling you. He's alive.'

I didn't like to argue with a sick woman, especially not one who was paying privately for my services, and with fine champagne thrown in, but surely she had to see the bigger picture? She had to realise she was the target of a con. How could I put it delicately? 'So, to recap. Freddy, having conned Jake Turpie out of...how much money?'

'A lot.'

'Runs away, without telling you, his wife, where he's going, and, after a year of complete radio silence, by sheer coincidence, happens to appear back on the radar straight after you've won—?'

'Half a million. But it's not like that.'

'Yes, it is. It's exactly like that. Can't you see what's happening here?'

But Ellen wasn't listening. She laughed. 'When I think of the names I called Jake Turpie, accusing him of murdering Freddy, and he just kept denying it.' The laugh developed into a cough. She clutched her side. 'Turns out he was telling the truth.'

There was a first time for everything. I didn't think this was it. 'So, where is Freddy?'

'Prague.'

'Then let me guess. This person who told you that Freddy is in the Czech Republic would like you to go over there and visit him?'

'No, I'm not going away over there,' she said. At least she wasn't completely stupid. 'You are.'

'Me? Go to Prague? To do what? Say hello to the conman who's pretending to be your husband?'

'I've told you. It's not a conman. It's Freddy.'

I knew what she meant, even though the two terms were not mutually exclusive.

'And you, Robbie,' she said, 'are going to bring him back here. Don't worry, I'll cover all your costs.'

I replenished our empty glasses. 'Okay. Let's say I do go and bring Freddy back. Won't Jake find out?' If Jake Turpie had missed Freddy the first time around, it was very unlikely he'd be so careless given a second chance.

'That's why, before you go, I want you to go see Jake. Don't let on to him that Freddy's alive. Just sound him out, you know... hypodermically.'

'Hypothetically?'

'I don't care how you do it. Just find out what it would take to sort things between him and Freddy. It'll come down to money. Everything does with Jake. Find out how much he wants and then bring Freddy back to me.'

'If you're so sure it's Freddy, why don't you go and see him yourself? It's only a three-hour flight. You could travel first class. Take your nurse with you.'

'No, it's better if you go and tell him things have been cleared with Jake. He'll believe you.'

'Why would he believe me? He knows I'm Jake's lawyer.'

'That's why he will believe you. Come on, Robbie. I'm offering an all-expenses-paid trip to Prague. Make a holiday out of it. The only thing I ask is that you bring my husband back so that I can spend my last days with him.'

'You want to spend them with the man who's not bothered to contact you for the last twelve months? If he

does come back, it will only be for your money.'

Ellen lifted her newly filled glass, watched the bubbles for a moment, and then tossed it down her throat in a oner. 'I don't care if he just wants my money. I'm going to leave it to him anyway, and I'm going to need a lawyer to draw up the papers. So there will be more legal work for you.'

'Ellen, I'm not that kind of lawyer.'

'You've got a law degree, haven't you?'

'Yes...I suppose...but...'

The woman in the light green trouser-suit appeared at the bedroom door. Ellen smiled, reached across and took my hands in hers. 'I need a lawyer and I want the best. In my book that's you.'

Even I couldn't argue with that.

6

'Prague? You don't go to Prague for a honeymoon.'
Joanna's Uncle Ted might have been a posh lawyer, but
her dad, my father-in-law-in-waiting, was as down to
earth as a planet-killing meteorite. Jim Jordan was a
builder. He had his own small construction company.
As a wedding gift he'd offered to build his daughter
and new son-in-law a house. He just needed some land
to put it on. That's where my own dad came in. When
he'd bought his cottage on the outskirts of Linlithgow,
it had arrived with an acre and a half of land. Part of it
he'd fenced off to form what he laughingly referred to
as a lawn: a patch of scrub grass that he tried to keep in
check and where he practised the deadly art of chip-
ping, something that along with a highly imaginative
handicap had won him many a golf game. The rest of
the land was left to run wild. It was ours if we wanted
it. We did. Meantime, Joanna had sold her flat and was
now sharing my room in my dad's cottage. Outline
planning permission having been granted, Saturday
morning, Jim had called out to show me the detailed
drawings he was about to submit. Joanna and her mum
had taken my daughter Tina swimming. Malky, my
brother, was eating toast.

'It's not a honeymoon,' I said. 'We're just going
away for a few days. It's a city break.' I was beginning
to wish I'd never mentioned it.

Jim spread the drawings for the new house across

my dad's kitchen table with a hand the size of a frying pan.

Malky came over, munching and staring down at the blueprints as though he knew what it all meant.

'Prague's a great place for a stag night,' he said. 'Full of strip joints and—'

'What I think you mean, Malky,' Jim said, brushing crumbs from the blueprints, 'is that Prague is a great place for a stag night for men who are not marrying my daughter. I mean, what's wrong with Paris or Rome or Venice? Somewhere romantic, with a bit of culture.'

'Me and your mum went to Aviemore for our honey- moon.' My dad stared out of the window and into the distance. 'Bloody freezing it was. We went ice-skating and she got a blister, so we tried skiing and I fell and broke my ankle. He blinked a few times and smoothed his moustache with thumb and index finger. 'Happy times.'

'How often have I got to tell you?' I said. 'It's not a honeymoon or a stag night. It's just a short break to a city of culture. There's tons to see and do in Prague and spring is the best time to go, before it gets too full of tourists.'

'I don't know why the pair of you don't wait and go somewhere straight after the wedding. That's what you're supposed to do,' Jim said.

My dad was straight in there. 'Oh, don't you know, Jim? The week after the wedding, Robbie has a really important case only he can do. Don't you, son?'

'There's an element of delectus personae,' I said, hoping that Latin would slam a lid on his sarcasm. It didn't.

'Deflect us what? Save the lingo for talking to dead

Romans. You know fine well you could have someone else do the case. Stop mollycoddling your criminals.'

'Leave him, Alex,' Jim said. 'He's like Joanna. They think they're indispensable.'

'Aye, well, the cemeteries are full of indispensable folk,' my dad said. 'I don't see what the big fuss is. I'm sure another lawyer could get his client the jail just as easily.'

'Well, you see, Dad, if my client had wanted a different lawyer, he wouldn't have instructed me. And, anyway, Joanna won't be able to get the time off right after the wedding because she's starting her new job. Not only that, but we have a lot of saving-up to do for the new house. I can't thank you and Jim enough but we've all the fixtures and fittings, kitchen appliances, furniture and all that sort of stuff to get. It adds up, and an exotic honeymoon, just like a big lavish wedding, is an unnecessary expense.'

'Don't, Robbie. You're making my heart go all fluttery with your romantic notions,' Jim said.

There had been a few awkward discussions with my in-laws-to-be about the wedding. Joanna's older sister had married a year or so earlier with all the frills and tassels. Joanna's parents had not been hugely happy at our decision to go for a much smaller affair, one we insisted on paying for ourselves.

'Look, what the pair of you are doing for us far outweighs a one-day extravaganza. You're giving Joanna, Tina and me a home.'

That settled for the umpteenth time, I stuck the kettle on.

'Uh, and I was supposed to tell you that Ted was on the phone to Joanna's mum this morning,' Jim said.

'She told him I was seeing you today and I've been asked to find out if you know what's going on with Annie Brechin. I think that was the name.'

'Annie who?' my dad asked.

'I think Jim means Antonia Brechin,' I said. 'She's a young lawyer who works for Joanna's Uncle Ted. She was arrested at the awards dinner the other night.'

'I've been at a few dos like that,' Malky said. 'Do you mind when I won player of the year after my first season with the Rose?' On that occasion a few of my brother's more experienced Linlithgow Rose F.C. teammates hadn't been too chuffed about a seventeen-year-old beating them to the annual prize. Things had become slightly heated and there had followed an impromptu re-arrangement of furniture, most of which had not been aeronautically designed.

'Aye, I remember it,' my dad said. 'Someone would have phoned the cops if I hadn't been there already.'

'Any message I should pass on to Ted?' Jim asked me. 'The girl's not been in touch with him, and he thought that you or Joanna might know something.'

Each time I thought back to Thursday night I had conflicting emotions. I felt sorry for the young trainee of the year, but the look on Brechin's face as the handcuffs snapped around the wrists of his darling granddaughter had sent a sadistic thrill through me and I hated myself for it.

'Oh, I've got a message all right,' I said. 'Tell him the last person Sheriff Albert Brechin would ever let his granddaughter take legal advice from is Robbie Munro.'

'Robbie!' Joanna's voice from the front door. Why was she back so soon? Had there been an accident? I

38

sprinted from the kitchen to see her standing in the living room. By her side, dressed more casually today in jeans, a shapeless burgundy sweater and a pair of serious walking boots, was Antonia Brechin. Her hair was tied back and held in a clasp. She didn't look like she'd seen much sleep recently. 'Antonia called me when I was on the way to the sports centre,' Joanna said.

'I'm really sorry to bother you on a Saturday, Mr Munro,' Antonia said. 'It's about what happened on Thursday night. I'm in need of some advice.'

7

It was one of those fresh, spring mornings that Scotland does best. Sun shining, distant hills etched against a bright blue sky, wisps of cloud drifting here and there and the soft scent of green barley carried on a gentle breeze that was cold enough to strip the flesh from your bones.

Once we'd established that I was Robbie and that Mr Munro was the puzzled face staring out at us from the kitchen window, I decided to come straight to the most important point. 'Does your grandfather know that you're here?' I took her screwed-up face as a no. 'Then, I think I should tell you, in case you hadn't noticed, that the little disagreement we had the other night...it wasn't down to too much drink. We do sincerely hate each other.'

Antonia sighed. 'The only lawyers I know deal with corporate tax, finance and banking, competition law, that sort of thing. I don't know who to turn to, Robbie. I'm in trouble. Really big trouble. Well, not big trouble, I mean it might not seem all that big to you. I haven't murdered anyone or anything like that, but—'

'Before we come onto your life of crime,' I said, 'can I ask you what your grandfather is saying about all of this?' We walked down the garden path at the back of the cottage to a makeshift gate. The latch was a piece of orange twine, hooked over a wooden fence post. I lifted it off and opened the gate to let Antonia through onto a rough track that wound its way between two walls with fields either side.

'He's not saying anything,' she said. 'I haven't spoken to him since I was released yesterday afternoon.'

'Then there isn't much point you speaking to me. Your grandfather is going to have his own ideas, especially about which lawyer to instruct. I'm probably...no, not probably, I'm definitely the last person he'd want you to take legal advice from.'

My phone buzzed. I excused myself and extracted it from the pocket of my jeans. A text message from Joanna. I opened it. Stop being awkward. Help her.

frowny face Were all women psychic? It would certainly explain a lot.

'Listen, Antonia. It's not that I don't want to help. But you've got to see how things are between me and that old...I'm sorry, I mean your grandfather. I'd be more than happy to recommend you to another lawyer. Someone he might actually approve of. Just about anyone apart from me should fit the bill.' I tried a little laugh. Antonia didn't follow my lead. Instead she stopped and dug a hole in the dirt with the toe of a hiking boot.

'I know what my granddad is like,' she said. 'I shadowed him for a week when I was a student and saw him in action. He's quite tough.'

If by 'quite tough' she meant mercilessly brutal, she'd hear no opposing argument from me.

Antonia fixed me with determined eyes. 'All I know is that the defence lawyer he complains about the most is you. I only realised your first name was Robbie when I met you on Thursday. Up until then I thought it was

Bloody, as in *that Bloody Munro has appealed me again!'* This time she did laugh, though it would have been easy to miss.

'And how do you think he would react if you told him I was your lawyer?' I asked.

'I don't care.'

'You have to care. We've only just met. Your grandfather has known me for years. Maybe he's right about me. A lot of people would agree with him.'

Antonia toe-ended a small boulder. 'Well I hope he is right about one thing,' she said, watching the stone skip and bump its way down the track before it dived into a clump of scrub grass at the edge.

'And what would that be?' I asked, and then wished I hadn't.

'That you've made a career out of defending people you knew were guilty.'

'Well, I don't know if you are guilty and I don't want to know.'

'Too bad, I'm telling you. I am guilty and I just want to plead guilty and get this whole thing over and done with. My career is finished. I know that. I just don't want to go to prison.'

In criminal defence work, intermittent deafness isn't a disability, it's a necessity. 'Sorry, I didn't catch any of that,' I said. 'But there's no need to repeat it. You can tell it to your lawyer, when you instruct one.' I walked on further down the track.

The phone in my pocket buzzed again. I didn't look. It would be Joanna checking up on me. If I didn't help Antonia she'd want to know why not.

Antonia trotted after me, scuffing the soles of her boots in the dirt. 'Don't you even want to know what

42

I'm accused of?'

'Not really.'

'Cocaine.'

She was persistent, I'd give her that. 'How much?'

'I don't know exactly. It didn't look like a lot. It was the first time I'd ever bought drugs. I didn't even pay for them, they were given to me.'

What should I do? A client was a client. On top of that, I had to take into account how much it would annoy Brechin if I took on his granddaughter's case. I think that's what swung it for me.

'So, you've been found in possession of a few flakes of snow. Big deal.'

'It's a big deal for me.'

I hadn't meant to trivialise things, only to try and cheer her up and put things into perspective.

Antonia took a swing at another rock and missed. 'It's a big deal for all three of us—'

'Three of you?'

'My flatmates are lawyers too. We've all been charged and we're—'

'Innocent,' I said, not looking around. 'No, I've just told you—'

'What you've told me,' I said, turning to come face to face with her, 'is that there are three of you all charged with possession of cocaine. If you're going to be my client, you should take my advice.'

'And that is?'

'That every snowflake in an avalanche pleads not guilty.'

8

'Falkirk? They're moving me to Falkirk?'

Sunday morning, Tina and my dad were in the back garden building a rabbit hutch. I was in bed with a book. Joanna was pacing the room in her dressing gown, reading yesterday's mail that had fallen through the letter box and got itself temporarily lost in the confusion of shoes and wellies inside the front porch. 'I thought they'd just shunt me to Edinburgh out of the way, but Falkirk? It's not even in the same Sheriffdom.'

'No,' I said, 'but it's a lot closer to here. Fifteen minutes in the car in the morning, door to door. You can park right outside.'

'I've got friends in the Fiscal's office in Edinburgh. I don't know anyone in Falkirk.' Joanna crumpled the letter from COPFS HQ and bounced it off my head as though it were all my fault, which in a way it was. She was only having to move from Livingston because I was marrying her. Justice had to be seen to be done, and the idea of a wife prosecuting a case in which her husband was defending, was not something that could be countenanced by the authorities, even though I was sure it would only have made competition all the fiercer.

'Falkirk's a great court,' I said, 'and the real bonus is that there's no Albert Brechin.'

'What are you talking about, Robbie? For a PF Bert Brechin is probably the best thing that ever happened to the Crown Office and Procurator Fiscal Service. Now I'm going to have to actually do some work to get guilty verdicts.' She picked up the crumpled ball of paper again and tossed it carelessly from hand to hand. 'Talking of Sheriff Brechin...'

I didn't say anything, just returned to my book.

'Go on, Robbie. I'll not say a word to another living soul.'

I flicked to the next page. 'How many times do I have to tell you? It's confidential.'

'I'm going to be your wife.'

'And Antonia Brechin already is my client.'

'I don't see why you have to be so mysterious. You know I'll find out. A couple of phone calls tomorrow morning is all it will take.'

'Then don't be so impatient.'

'Maybe I can help.'

'And maybe you can stop trying to have me disclose confidential information to a member of Her Majesty's prosecution service.'

'Oh, I see. So that's how it is. You don't trust me.'

'It's got nothing to do with trust, and everything to do with professionalism,' I said.

Joanna sighed. 'Oh, well, that's that then. With Tina and your dad away nailing lumps of wood together, I was thinking about coming back to bed...' She followed the sigh with a yawn, and the yawn with a stretch that somehow caused the dressing gown to slip from her shoulders and onto the floor in a puddle of silk. She stood there for a moment, naked, then turned and opened the door of the wardrobe. 'Now, what shall I put on?'

It was true. We had the cottage to ourselves and had

to be looking at around ten minutes' complete peace until my dad came in with a DIY wound or Tina needed refuel- ling. I tossed the book aside. 'Then again, we are both professional people...'

Joanna came over to the bed and pulled back the corner of the duvet. 'And?'

'And I suppose there would be no harm approaching things on a hypothetical basis.'

'If you did, then, hypothetically, we could have sex.' I patted the mattress. She didn't move.

'Okay,' I said, 'hypothetically, there was this girl—'

'Did she hypothetically happen to be Scots Legal Trainee of the Year, whose hypothetical grandfather was a sheriff, and who, having been hypothetically arrested at an awards dinner, is hypothetically now on police bail?'

'That's her.'

'Get on with it then.'

'Drugs,' I said.

'Really?' Joanna climbed into bed beside me. 'I thought it would be something white-collar, like corporate fraud or insider trading. What kind of drugs and how much are we talking about?'

'Just a few grams of coke, hypothetically.'

'You can stop saying hypothetically now.'

'Okay, this girl, whoever she may be, and her two flatmates, were all lawyers in the running for the Trainee of the Year award, and agreed between themselves that the winner would celebrate by bringing Charlie with them to a party at the weekend. Someone we know was tipped off that she'd won and invited Chico well in advance.'

'So why the big show of force by the police at the

awards ceremony, then?'

'Same reason the cops arrest celebrities at six in the morning with a TV camera crew, I suppose: maximum embarrassment.'

'Stupid of her. If she's convicted that'll be her career over, don't you think?'

'It's hypothetically possible.'

Joanna squirmed a little closer, put her arms around me. 'I hope she gets off.'

'Can I remind you that you are a prosecutor? You're not supposed to hope accused people get off. That's my job.'

'But she's such a nice person. Just how strong is the evidence against her?'

'Just how hypothetical is this sex?'

The bedroom door crashed open and Tina leapt onto the bed. She'd been attacked by nettles and my dad was busy hunting the garden for dock leaves to rub the stings with.

Joanna gave me a peck on the cheek and sat up, the duvet wrapped tightly about her. 'Extremely.'

9

May Monday might have been a holiday everywhere else, but there were no slackers at the home of Turpie (International) Salvage Ltd, where even the rats wore boiler suits. Forklifts and low-loaders rumbled about the yard, and everywhere the crunch of glass and metal as car after car met the jaws of the crusher. Now that he was no longer my landlord, I saw very little of Jake Turpie - which was fine by me. Occasionally I'd be called into action when one of his boys was lifted, but, other than that I was happy if contact between us was kept to a minimum.

'What do you want?' he asked, prowling the perimeter of a six-year-old Mazda hatchback, kicking its tyres.

Jake had made his money from scrap and unlicensed money-lending. Not that you'd have noticed his wealth from the oil-stained boiler suit that was his chosen form of everyday wear, or by the dented white Transit van his muscle-bound business associate, Deek Pudney, chauffeured him around in. A few years back Jake had added another division to the company, a new venture called JT Motors Ltd. Selling second-hand cars had been a clean start for Jake. So clean, even the profits were laundered.

The business model was simple, but ingenious. When someone came to Jake for a loan, instead of the usual handshake and associated death threat, he signed them up for the sale of a car. The car was usually only worth scrap value, but whether it could actually be driven wasn't really the point. The point was that Jake then had the person signed up on a valid car purchase contract for an amount that included his ridiculous interest rates. If the instalments weren't paid, the customer received a visit from Deek. If the customer complained to the law that Jake was a loan shark, then, on the face of it, all the authorities could see was a perfectly sound car purchase agreement that someone was trying to weasel out of.

Obviously, I couldn't come right out and say that I was there because Ellen Fletcher wanted me to find a way to resolve the differences between Jake and her husband. If the missing conman was indeed alive, Jake's idea of a satisfactory resolution would probably have involved an industrial wood-chipper and Freddy's amputated body parts. Nor did I want to give Jake grounds to suspect that I knew where Freddy was. He had ways of making people talk - usually after they'd finished screaming.

'I'm looking for a new car,' I said, knowing that Jake did keep one or two reasonable motors around, although they were mostly for show. 'Something a bit bigger with four doors, now that I'm going to be a family man.'

Jake gave one of the tyres a final tap with the heavy end of a steel toecap boot and looked up at me. He prob- ably thought he was smiling. 'Oh, aye. I forgot. You're marrying your wee understudy.'

'She's not my understudy, Jake. And she's not working with me anymore. She's gone back to being a Fiscal.'

'Has she now?' He winked. 'Smart move. Someone on the inside. Bound to come in handy.' Jake made the holy bonds of matrimony sound like the acquisition of a business asset.

'What have you got for sale around the two-grand mark that won't break down at the first set of lights?' I asked. Jake thought about it. 'I've an oh-six Beamer, two-litre, automatic. I could let you have it for three if you trade in that heap you're driving the now.' I made a face.

'It's a nice motor. One owner. A man of the cloth.'

I didn't doubt it. He probably wore the cloth over his head when he was robbing banks. 'How many miles has it done?'

'How many do you want it to have done?'

'Colour?'

'Green.' I pursed my lips and sucked in.

'What's wrong with green?'

'Hard to resell.'

'You've not bought it yet, and a lot of folk think green's a lucky colour.'

It wasn't much of an opening, but I shoved a crowbar in and wiggled it about. 'Didn't Freddy what's-his-name drive a green BMW?' Freddy Fletcher could have driven a coach and horses for all I knew.

'Freddy who?'

'Fletcher. He used to drive a green Beamer, didn't he?

Or was it a Jag? Or a Ford?'

Jake looked at me as though I'd just spat on his mother's grave. Not that I knew if his mother was dead. Or if he'd had one. 'What's Freddy Fletcher got to do with anything?'

'Nothing. Just that you said green cars were lucky and...well...Freddy's wasn't lucky for him, was it?' Jake eyed me suspiciously.

'I was just thinking about him because I happened to bump into his wife the other day,' I said casually.

'You saw Ellen?' Just for a moment I thought I saw a spark of humanity flare in Jakes eyes, and then, just as quickly, it was gone. He cleared his throat. 'Do you want to see this motor or not?'

'What was the big problem between you and Freddy, anyway?' I asked, as he marched off, me following. 'You ever hear from him these days?'

'Why should I?'

'Just wondering.'

Jake led me to the far side of the compound where a recently polished, racing-green BMW stood, chrome trim glinting in the morning sunshine. Whoever'd done the detailing had been meticulous but, then, I imagined Jake had his own employee incentive scheme. One on each foot. He buffed up a wing mirror unnecessarily with the sleeve of his boiler suit. 'You another one that thinks I done him in?'

'The thought had crossed my mind,' I said, feeling obliged to kick a tyre as I did.

Jake opened the driver's door and allowed me to look inside. By the time I'd re-emerged he was already at the rear of the vehicle opening the boot.

'Very nice,' I said. 'What were you saying about Freddy?'

Jake slammed the boot shut. 'What's this about? What's it to you what happened to Fletcher?'

'I told you. I just happened to bump into Ellen and it got me thinking.'

Jake opened the passenger door. 'Let's go for a test drive.' I'd never driven an automatic before. It was easy. I took it gently down the rough track leading from Jake's yard and onto a minor road that wound its way east. After we'd gone a mile or so I was wondering why they even bothered to make cars with manual transmissions. It couldn't be just so that your left foot didn't get bored.

'Take a next left,' Jake said.

I did, and after another mile he told me to stop along- side a ragged hawthorn hedge that stretched off into the distance. We got out and each rested a foot on a dilapidated five-bar wooden gate, looking into a field that was a thick carpet of wild grass and bramble tangles, speckled by the vivid yellow blooms on tall stalks of ragwort. In the distance was a small cottage, its grey slate roof sagging slightly in the centre.

'All this is mine,' Jake said. 'Freddy Fletcher told me I should buy it and develop it.'

'Must be at least an acre.'

'One and a half if you count that row of trees at the far end,' Jake said.

'When did this happen?'

'Last year.'

I had a slight inkling as to where this might be going. With Linlithgow three miles to the west, Bo'ness the same to the south and Edinburgh twenty minutes east by motorway, the land was perfect for a spot of property developing, apart from one thing. 'It's all green belt round here, isn't it?'

'That's what I thought when Freddy told me to buy it. Said he'd checked it out with the head of the planning department. She told him the land had once been set aside for a travellers' site. Something to do with making sure the Pikeys had somewhere to live, but not close enough to town so that they could nick the washing off folks' lines. They were going to install water and electricity and it was taken off the green belt register and given permission for residential use. After that there was too many complaints and the site was closed. There's not been a single Pikey on here, but no-one ever thought to change it back. At least that's what Freddy told me.'

If Freddy Fletcher had told me there were fillings in my back teeth, I'd have asked for a mirror and a magnet.

Jake opened the gate and we walked into the field. It was a teardrop-shaped piece of ground and we were standing at the fat end. Looking to our left, the ground rose in the centre and then tapered off to a copse of spindly birch trees on the far side that straggled its way past the cottage to the road.

'So, anyway,' Jake continued, 'Freddy got talking to the owner, an old guy who lived in the cottage over there. He didn't know what the land was worth. Even if he did, he never had the money to develop it.'

'Why didn't Freddy buy it?'

'He was skint an' all.'

'It's a good chunk of land,' I said. 'You could probably build five—'

'Six, big, detached houses with gardens.' Jake had obviously given the matter much thought. 'Build them for a hundred grand each, sell them for three times that, easy. I was looking at –'

'One point two million profit.'

'Not as much,' he said. 'I'd have needed to put in an

access road, then there's all the services, drainage, footpaths, communal ground, lawyers and everything. But I had to be looking at the thick end of three-quarters, maybe a million clear.'

'So what went wrong?' I asked, fairly certain that something had indeed gone wrong, since I was standing on a bunch of weeds and not in someone's front garden. 'The owner got wind that I was going to develop the land. He wanted half a million for it. It put me off. Freddy said he knew a way I could get it for half that.'

'But you did know that Freddy was a conman?'

'That's why I believed him when he said he knew a way to con the owner.'

That and the fact that only someone with a death wish would try and con Jake Turpie out of money.

'Freddy told me to put in an offer for the full half million and make it subject to planning permission. Freddy said the woman from the planning department would knock back the application and say the place was green belt.'

'I thought you said it wasn't?'

'I know, but she was going to say it was and then change her mind later after I'd bought it. I spoke to her personally. It was all sorted.'

I could see where this was going. A land transaction involving Flim-Flam Freddy Fletcher? It must have been the pound signs that blinded Jake to the obvious.

'Once the owner was told the place couldn't be developed, I hit him with a new offer. Seventy-five grand. We settled for a hundred and I gave Freddy fifty for a finder's fee on top.' We had reached the centre of the field. Jake turned and looked back the way we'd come. It was a pleasant enough afternoon, the sun stripteasing behind thin veils of cloud, and only the lightest breeze disturbing the expanse of long grass and weeds as we walked through it. 'After that, I thought all I had to do was fire in a fresh application to the Council and start building houses.'

I'd already guessed the rest, although Jake told me it anyway as we made the walk back to the car.

'The woman from the Council's planning department came to see me again. She said she'd been overruled at a high level and the decision was made that the land should be declared green belt.'

'And Freddy? What was he declared? Dead?'

'No. Missing. Before I could get a grip of him.'

'What about the owner?'

'Gone. I asked about. Someone told me he was Freddy's uncle. Now I'm stuck with a dilapidated cottage and a lot of weeds in the middle of nowhere. I can't even rent the field out for grazing because these yellow buggers poison the horses,' he said, swinging a boot at an impertinent clump of ragwort.

The visit didn't help Jake's mood, the default setting of which was usually best described as perilously unstable. I drove us back to the yard making complimentary remarks about the car as we went along, desperately trying to think of non-inflammatory ways to bring up the subject of Freddy Fletcher again, whether he was still on this earthly plane and what it would cost to keep him here should Jake discover his whereabouts.

'What do you think, then?' Jake asked, after we'd bounced our way along the potholed road to his yard and I'd brought the BMW to a halt in the compound adjacent to his company headquarters: premises easily mistaken for a rickety old prefabricated hut with some dodgy wooden steps leading up to them, because that's what they were. 'I like it,' I said. 'But three thousand is a bit more than I'd been thinking of paying.'

'It's a solid motor. But if you want to drive the wife and wean around in a cheap rattly old death trap, that's up to you.'

'And I felt the brakes were soft.'

'I can have one of the boys check the fluid level.'

'Let me think about it.' I handed Jake back the keys and was making my way across the potholes back to my own car when he called to me.

'Hey, Baw Heid. If you see Ellen again – tell her I was asking for her.'

10

'Jake Turpie was asking after you.'

Ellen Fletcher removed the cotton wool discs from her eyes, fluttered her lashes a few times and stared up at me. She was enveloped in a white robe, a white towel wrapped around her head, white slippers on her feet and reclining on a white sun lounger. The only thing not white about her was her lipstick and the liquid inside the margarita glass. They were both red. She took a sip before replying. 'You've seen him then?'

'This morning.' I pulled up the adjacent lounger and sat side-saddle. 'He was telling me the story about how Freddy swindled him.'

'Anything else?'

'Yes, he denies killing your husband, but only because he hasn't managed to find him yet. He was so suspicious at me turning up out of the blue asking about Freddy, I nearly had to buy a car from him.'

Two young women who'd been lying on the loungers to our left got up, slipped out of their robes and into the pool where they began a lazy breaststroke, barely disturbing the viscous, azure depths. I was so busy watching I didn't notice another young woman, dressed in a white smock and trousers, approach us until she'd arrived at our side. Clearing her throat, she looked me up and down before suggesting to Ellen that it might be more convenient if we took our conversation through the glass doors behind us and outside onto the patio. I gathered she'd been sent by the three women perched on stools at the small bar at the far end of the pool, who were sipping cocktails and staring hard at the strange man in his outdoor clothes.

Ellen knocked back her red drink, dug a hand into the pocket of her robe and fished out a couple of fifties. 'Thanks, but we're fine here,' she said, thrusting the cash and empty margarita glass at the attendant. 'I'll have another one of those and get my lawyer what he wants.'

'A beer is fine for me,' I said. 'Anything cold.'

The attendant stared down uncertainly at the money and glass she now held in either hand.

'The money's for you, dear,' Ellen said to her. 'Put the drinks on my room. Mrs Fletcher, the penthouse suite.'

Any uncertainty evaporated and the attendant scurried off to fetch our drinks.

'I suppose it does look like Freddy's alive,' I said, lowering my voice. 'That's something.'

'Aye, something not very much. I told you he was alive. I wanted you to find out how much Jake would take to leave him alone.'

'Freddy conned Jake out of a hundred and fifty thou- sand pounds.'

'Was it that much?'

'Yes, and each one of those pounds was Jake's personal friend. At the very least he's going to want them all back. Then there's the interest.'

'What's a year's interest come to? Can't be that much.'

'Jake's not a building society, he's an illegal money-lender. The interest will be huge.'

Ellen looked away. 'Just tell him I'll pay him off if he leaves Freddy alone.'

'He'll want to know how you're going to do that, and I'm not starting off negotiations by asking him how much he wants and, by the way, Ellen's won the lottery.'

'Then don't mention me or the lottery,' Ellen said. 'Just tell him that Freddy's scraped enough cash together to pay him back and see what he says.'

'I'd rather we sounded out this Freddy guy first.'

'I've told you. There is no Freddy guy. There is only Freddy.'

'But you haven't actually seen him?'

Our drinks arrived. Ellen's in a margarita glass, my beer in a precariously tall tumbler with a slice of lime jammed onto the rim. Ellen absorbed some red liquid and placed the glass on the small wooden table by her side. 'I know you think I'm being conned. That's why I've brought you in. I can trust you. Go see Freddy. Satisfy yourself it's really him, and then you can take the money to Jake. If it worries you so much, there's no need for Freddy even to see the money. After Jake's been paid off, and then when I'm...' Her voice faltered. 'When I'm...gone, Freddy can have what's left.' She lifted her glass and toasted me. 'I'm not planning on leaving that much behind.'

I still didn't like it. 'So, you're saying that Freddy has been gone for over a year, never sent you so much as a postcard from sunny Prague and yet you want to leave him your money? There are bound to be more deserving causes than him.'

'Like you?'

I laughed. 'No, I mean like charities, children's

homes, hospices. Not some clapped-out con-artist who ditched you as soon as he laid his hands on a decent score.'

'Freddy's my husband.'

'Big deal. It's not like you owe him anything.'

'That's where you're wrong.' She picked up the glass, drank what was left and waved to the attendant for another. 'It was my fault he left.'

11

Antonia Brechin's case was called on Tuesday in front of a visiting sheriff who'd been brought in especially. I met her in the lobby outside court where she was anxiously pacing up and down, clutching the summary complaint that had been served on her by one of the court cops.

Across the lobby, the two young women, one blonde, one brunette, whom I took to be Antonia's co-accused, were each deep in conversation with their own solicitors while friends and family members orbited.

'How's it looking?' Antonia's mum, clothes by Burberry, figure by Cadbury, had a broad freckly face that was unnaturally pale and gaunt that morning. She'd been sitting on one of the public benches and came over when she saw me arrive. 'Is it serious? Is Antonia going to prison?'

For simple possession of cocaine, I thought her daughter would be looking at a fine or a spot of unpaid work in the community. That was the good news. The bad news concerned her future in the law.

'No,' I said, 'she's not going to prison.'

'But she'll lose her job, won't she? They'll strike her off.'

'I'm sorry,' I said, 'but we're at way too early a stage in proceedings for me to say what might happen down the line. Right now my only thought is to try and have Antonia acquitted.'

'Acquitted?' Mrs Brechin looked at me as though I were mad. 'You mean get her off with it? How can you get her off with it? She's guilty.'

Antonia tried to lead her mum away, but the woman was not for budging. 'Antonia is taking a few days off and then having a meeting with Mr Jordan about her job. You're married to his niece, aren't you?'

'Not yet,' I said, 'but I'm sure he'll be fine about every- thing. Innocent until proven guilty after all.'

'But what happens when she's found guilty?' Mrs Brechin's mouth got small and tight. 'What then? Her grandfather says—'

'Mum,' Antonia placed an arm around her mother. 'At least let Mr Munro read the charge sheet and then he'll tell us what he thinks.'

Mrs Brechin shrugged off the arm and returned to the bench with a departing accusatory glance at me as if I were in some way responsible for her daughter's illegal recreational activities.

I took the charge sheet from my new client. As I'd thought, the allegation was straightforward enough: a contravention of section 5(2) of the Misuse of Drugs Act 1971. I turned to the summary of evidence and read that the police had received an anonymous tip-off, obtained a warrant and, on the evening of the first of May, crashed through the door of the flat in Linlithgow that Antonia shared with two others.

According to the summary of evidence, a wrap of cocaine had been found inside a small wooden box on a coffee table in the living room.

'How bad is it?' Antonia asked when I looked up from the papers. I could see her mother pretending not to listen in. 'What's the worst-case scenario?'

Clients always want to know the worst-case scenario. Ever since we'd stopped killing criminals in Scotland back in 1963, the worst-case scenario was prison, but clients didn't want to hear that. Clients wanted their lawyers to say that everything was going to be okay. I'd found the pessimistic approach, or even the honest one, was a sure-fire way to send a client off in search of a lawyer with a more cheerful worst-case scenario; a bit like watching all the news channels until you found a weather forecast you liked. It was easier just to tell clients that everything would be fine. That helped keep them on-board and, if not exactly happy, at least with some hope to cling onto. If, at the end of it all things did go disaster-movie, well, so long as I'd tried my best, I could always console myself with the fact it wasn't me going to prison.

'It's early days yet,' I said, cheerfully, 'but, trust me, there's definitely scope for optimism.'

Antonia's lovely smile threatened to break out, but disappeared at the sound of a court officer calling to me from the top of the stairs. It was Eleanor Hammond the Sheriff Clerk, Bert Brechin's right-hand woman. I walked over to see what she wanted.

'Sheriff Brechin would like to see you and his daughter- in-law in chambers,' she said, meeting me halfway.

I went back down the stairs and over to the now slightly less disconsolate figure on the public bench. 'Mrs Brechin, your father-in-law would like to see you in chambers. I take it you know the way. I'll wait here with Antonia.'

There was no danger of me going in for a quiet chat with Sheriff Brechin. He'd only demand I hand in my marching papers, and, tempting though it was to be shot of the case, the certain knowledge that my involvement would annoy him, somehow, made all the hassle worthwhile.

With her mother away, Antonia wanted me to give her my real opinion. 'Did you mean that? Are you really optimistic or was that for the benefit of my mum?'

'You made no comment when interviewed by the police, so that's good. Now I need to find out what the other two have said. If they've also kept quiet, then all the police have is some drugs in a box on a table in a flat. How can they prove who had the necessary knowledge and control to constitute possession? Worst case, I think I can do a deal with the PF so that one person pleads and the others have their not-guilty pleas accepted.'

'And who would that one person be?'

'Let's put it this way, if I'm doing the dealing it's not going to be you.'

She did smile this time, and I remembered the pretty young woman I'd first met at the awards dinner, her face flushed with excitement and pride. The smile slowly dimmed. 'But why does anyone have to plead guilty? I thought you said every snowflake in an avalanche pleads not guilty?'

I looked across the lobby at the other two snowflakes. If no-one pled guilty the case would go to trial and anything could happen. We needed a sacrificial lamb. Someone for the Crown to lay on the altar to the God of conviction statistics. Both of Antonia's co-accused were young women. Each had a defence solicitor with them. I recognised their lawyers.

Gail Paton, hair scraped back and too much make-up. She'd been around the legal block so often they probably had a street named after her. I'd never persuade her to sell her client down the river.

The other lawyer was Andy Imray, my former assistant, clad in a pristine black gown that put my tattered, bullet- holed one to shame. Andy, never the most confident of young men, looked more worried than his client, an attractive blonde girl whom I recognised from the Awards Dinner.

I gave him a friendly wave. Our paths hadn't crossed in a while and on the last occasion we hadn't parted on the best of terms. I'd heard Andy had forsaken crime, gone off to Edinburgh and joined one of the big corporate firms, operating in some field of law I knew very little about; there were acres of those. I was sure that if my ex-employee had any recent experience of litigation, it would be instructing counsel in the rarefied climes of the Court of Session and not rolling around in the blood and sawdust down at the Sheriff Court. Ten minutes alone with him and I'd have him loading his own grandmother onto a cattle truck.

'That's true, Antonia, I did say that. But sometimes it's best if one of the snowflakes takes the fall so that the others can simply melt away.'

12

'I wondered when you'd show face,' was Hugh Ogilvie's welcoming remark to me as I walked through the side door into Courtroom 4. The Procurator Fiscal was standing at the table in the well of the court sorting his case files. The only other person present was a Bar Officer sitting in a corner reading a paperback. 'Can we make this quick? I want to make a start and put a few cases through before lunch.'

I could make it very quick. 'Antonia Brechin and chums,' I said. 'You know you're never going to prove a possession charge against them all.'

'Do I? How's that then?'

'Because no-one's admitted to knowledge of the drugs.'

'They're the tenants of the property. The drugs were in a box on a coffee table slap-bang in the middle of the sitting room.'

'I thought you wanted to make this quick, Hugh?'

'Try me.'

'One out of three would do for you, wouldn't it?' Ogilvie looked at his watch and nodded to the Bar Officer who folded down the corner of a page, closed his book and went off to open the doors to the public. It was about as exciting as the life of a Bar Officer got.

'No.' Ogilvie donned the black gown that was draped over the back of his chair. 'I want them all to plead guilty to the charge as libelled.'

I laughed. 'Of course you do, Hugh, and it's good to have dreams and ambitions, but we all know that's not going to happen. These are young lawyers. They're still training. A conviction for possession of cocaine could see them struck off. They'll certainly lose their jobs, and finding another won't be easy with that on the old CV. They might have to stop being lawyers and go out and actually work for a living.'

'Then your client and her pals should have thought about that before they started getting themselves involved with Class A drugs.'

'Did you mark this prosecution?' I asked.

'I did.'

'Then you'll know the relationship between my client and Sheriff Brechin?'

'Of course I do. Why on earth has she instructed you?'

'Long story. But how do you think Brechin is going to react if word happens to filter back that you wouldn't cut

his granddaughter a break?'

'You mean when you tell him?'

'He'll find out without me having to say a word, and I wouldn't like to be you when he does. He might even stop prosecuting cases from the bench and start coming up with reasonable doubts. Maybe you should have thought about that before you started prosecuting his granddaughter for the sake of a few grams of coke.'

'I did think about it. Very hard.'

'So let's get this straight,' I said, 'just in case Brechin should ask. You're insisting she pleads guilty, no matter what?'

Ogilvie straightened the stack of files that lay on the table before him. 'It's a waste of time threatening me, if that's what you're trying to do. I happen to have spoken with Sheriff Brechin off the record. There was enough cocaine found to constitute a dealer's quantity. Those three are lucky they're not on petition for intent to supply. Then it would be prison and not just some employment problems they'd be facing. They've got yours truly to thank for it being kept at simple possession. Bert Brechin knows that and he's not expecting any more favours from me.'

'Come on, Hugh. You don't really believe him, do you? He's just saying that. He's got to, to keep face. Read between the lines.'

One or two lawyers had drifted into court and the public benches were starting to fill. Out of the corner of my eye, I saw Andy and Gail homing in on us. I would be wasting my time with Gail, but Andy was different, pliable. I'd given him a start in the law. It was payback time. 'Tell you what, Hugh. Give me ten minutes to talk things over with my colleagues, and after that one of the accused will plead - if you let the others take a walk. How's that sound?'

'And I suppose that happy band of walkers would include your client in its number?'

'That's something us defence agents would have to discuss...'

'With you in charge of the thumbscrews?'

'What's it matter to you? You get a conviction, my client and one of her friends go back to being proper lawyers and Sheriff Brechin ends up forever in your debt. Everyone's happy.'

'Not everyone.'

He could be pedantic at times. 'Okay, not absolutely everyone, just the important people, namely, my client, Sheriff Brechin...' Time to twist the knife. 'And you, if you ever want a reference from him.'

As a Procurator Fiscal it was hard not to be elevated to the Bench. The Judicial Appointments Board loved a prosecutor. But you still needed three sound references and one had to come from a sheriff familiar with your work. Hugh Ogilvie would be banking on Brechin doing him the honours in due course.

'Robbie...' Ogilvie rubbed a hand over the shininess of his scalp and grimaced. 'Go away.'

Eleanor, the Sheriff Clerk, arrived with a big bundle of papers and sent the Bar Officer to bring the Sheriff on. Some of the other lawyers were now jostling me, trying to speak to the PF in order to negotiate last-minute pleas. Eventually, I was forced to give way. I backed off, climbed into my gown and in the process bumped into Gail Paton. 'The PF's being difficult,' I said. 'He wants them all to plead.'

'What's your client doing?' Gail asked.

'Nothing for it. We'll need to all plead not guilty and let the heat die down. With a bit of luck we'll get a more reasonable Fiscal at the intermediate diet.'

'And then what?'

'And then we toss a coin and someone pleads to let the other two out.'

'A coin has only two sides,' Gail said. 'Let me guess, you were thinking I could be heads and Andy here would be tails, with you doing the coin-flipping?'

Andy, who was standing nearby, came over when he heard his name mentioned. 'My client is pleading guilty.'

'That's my boy,' I said, 'except, hold off for just now.

There's no point rushing into this. Let's wait and keep our powder dry.'

'No, she's pleading guilty today.' He seemed very confident for someone who'd only recently exchanged nappies for a court gown.

'Listen, Andy, we need to think strategically.'

'I am.' By the firm line of his mouth, he had already made up his mind. 'That's why my client is pleading guilty at the very earliest opportunity. That way, she'll receive the maximum sentencing discount.'

Did he really believe all that sentence-discount crap that was put about in the hope that it would save time and make life easier for judges? All that happened in reality was that the starting point of the sentence was increased and then reduced to what would have been imposed anyway.

'The sentence isn't the issue, here,' I said, 'it's the conviction. All our clients can handle a fine or a spot of extra-curricular gardening. Who cares if it's a hundred pounds more or a few hours longer? If your client wants to be noble and take the blame, that's great. But ask her to do it later when her sacrifice might let her friends walk and keep their jobs.'

'Sorry,' Andy said, not sounding it. 'These women are all going to end up in front of the Scottish Solicitors Disciplinary Tribunal. Admitting guilt at the first chance is going to look much better than trying to squirm out of something later and failing.'

'He's got a point,' Gail said.

The Sheriff came on and ours was the first case to call. The three accused made their way forward to take up position in the dock.

'Stick with a not guilty,' I whispered to Gail. 'Let's call Ogilvie's bluff. If Andy pleads his client guilty, that might be enough for the Crown. Why would they bother going to trial on a simple possession charge against our two when someone's already pled to it?'

Gail didn't look convinced.

The accused were identified by the Sheriff Clerk. Gail's client was first accused.

'Miss Paton, how does your client plead?' the Sheriff enquired.

Gail hesitated for a second, and, with a sigh and a final sidelong glance at me, said, 'Not guilty, M'Lord.'

I was next up. Before I could say anything, Antonia beckoned me over to the dock. 'I want to plead guilty.'

'I don't think that's a good idea,' I said. 'But, I—'

'You're pleading not guilty.'

'Mr Munro?' the Sheriff enquired.

'Miss Brechin is pleading not guilty,' I said, and sat down in the well of the court.

'And Mr...?'

'Imray,' Andy said. 'Your Lordship will find my client pleads guilty as libelled.'

The Sheriff confirmed the plea with Andy's client. 'Is that correct? You plead guilty that on first May this year at Royal Terrace, Linlithgow you did have in your possession a quantity of cocaine in contravention of section five subsection two of the Misuse of Drugs Act nineteen seventy-one?'

The young woman nodded her head, not looking at the bench.

'What was that?'

'Yes,' she said.

The Sheriff looked down to his right. 'Are those pleas acceptable, Mr Fiscal?'

Ogilvie stood. 'Only the third accused's plea, M'Lord. Would your Lordship's clerk please fix trial and inter- mediate diets for the first and second accused and defer sentence on the third so that all three may be dealt with together?'

Thereafter, as requested, dates were set and the three young women released on bail.

I met Antonia's mother outside in the corridor. 'Why didn't Antonia plead guilty too?' she demanded. 'I heard that other solicitor say it would be better in the long run.'

'Antonia didn't plead guilty,' I said, 'because I'm a defence lawyer and, call me old-fashioned, I'm trying to

have your daughter acquitted.'

'But she doesn't have a defence. She's guilty. You must know that. Her own grandfather says she should plead guilty.'

'Antonia's grandfather thinks everyone should plead guilty.'

'You do the crime and you take what's coming to you.

That's justice.'

'No, Mrs Brechin,' I said. 'That's the law. Justice is something completely different.'

13

'Why didn't you tell me about this?' Joanna held up the sheaf of papers I'd given her and waved them at me. She didn't start her new job until the following Monday and, while I'd been at court that Tuesday morning, she'd been at the office working with Grace-Mary to tidy up a few things and clear the way for her imminent departure.

'It's supposed to be a surprise,' I said. 'More like a shock.'

This was the thanks I got. 'A few days in Prague in a five-star hotel. What's shocking about that?'

'Four whole days in Prague with you, Robbie. It's enough to make a girl's head spin.' Grace-Mary had decided to enter the discussion.

I ignored her like I did most of my secretary's interventions. 'The Czech Republic is a beautiful country.'

'When it's not being invaded by the Nazis or Soviets,' Grace-Mary muttered. 'And it's not the Czech Republic anymore, it's called Czechia now.'

I put my hands on Joanna's shoulders. 'Don't listen to her. The Panzers rolled out years ago. These days Prague is a lovely place for a holiday.'

'Why? Have they moved it closer to the sea?' Joanna asked, opening the envelope again and checking, just in case the reservations had magically changed to somewhere sunny with sand and surf. 'And where are we getting the money from for this trip? I thought we were ploughing every spare penny into the new house?'

Every relationship needed its secrets. Other than admit- ting that the Czech Republic was indeed still landlocked, I didn't mention that I was going for work purposes, or that the trip was being funded by a client. What lottery- winning Ellen wanted me to do, could be done in a morning or an afternoon. I could explain it all to Joanna once we were safely in Bohemia. For now, it was too good an opportunity for killing two birds with the one stone.

'And it's a bit short notice,' she said. 'I've nothing to wear.'

'Think of it as a honeymoon rehearsal. Clothes are optional.'

Joanna looked at the tickets again. 'Prague? Whatever made you decide on Prague? What's the weather like in May?'

'I'd pack my woollies if I were you,' Grace-Mary said, as though I was about to strap my fiancée to a sledge, and set off across the North-West Passage, rather than take her on a pleasant trip to the crossroads of Europe.

I was having none of my secretary's negativity. 'It'll be a lot hotter than Scotland, and we're not going for the beach. We're going for the culture, the history —'

'The cheap beer?' Grace-Mary lifted a bundle of mail from the wire basket on my desk and leaned in close to Joanna. 'I suppose you should just be thankful he's taking any time off at all.'

I'd run out of argument. All I had left was a hurt expression. Joanna came over, lifted her face to mine and kissed me. 'Prague will be great. We'll go somewhere warmer in the summer. Me, you and Tina.'

'Two holidays in the same decade? You'll be lucky,' was Grace-Mary's parting shot. She tapped the bundle of paper on the desk a few times to square it up, and then carried it through to reception. She was back two minutes later. 'That's your first appointment in. Heather Somerville. She wants to appeal her conviction.'

Joanna winced. I'd told her all about the boyfriend-slapping case. 'I'll leave you to it. I'm more or less finished here. I'll go home and see how the rabbit hutch is doing. You do know that when it's finished we'll actually have to put a rabbit in the thing?'

'Then that'll be another vegetarian to keep you company,' I said, ushering my fiancée out and my client in, the latter with her partner in tow.

'I don't understand,' said the boyfriend, after I'd explained the summary appeal process for the third time. 'How could he find Heather guilty? You told the judge that Heather didn't mean to hit me. How's that an assault?'

'Okay,' I said. 'Let's take this step by step. First of all, Heather did mean to hit you. Didn't you, Heather?'

The young woman stared down at her hands, thumbs pressed tightly against each other, and nodded.

The boyfriend started up again. Suddenly, I could understand my client's need to administer him the occasional slap. 'But you said —'

'I say a lot of things in court when I'm trying to win a case. It doesn't mean they're necessarily true.'

'But you said the case was too trivial to bother with. If you send in an appeal won't the appeal judges see it the same way?'

I doubted it. When it came to matters jurisprudential, my mind and that of the Appeal Court were seldom in the same orchestra pit, far less in tune.

'But it's not fair,' he whined.

'No, you're right, it's not. But it is the law. Best not to get the two mixed up.'

'And she didn't hit me that hard. I hardly felt it.'

That was a mistake I wouldn't make if he didn't quit moaning. 'Maybe not, but legally speaking the Sheriff was entitled to hold it was an assault.' I hated taking Bert Brechin's side; nonetheless, I had to get across the fact that an appeal was a waste of time. Furthermore, as I explained, presumably to dissuade people from contesting wrongful verdicts and excessive sentences, Legal Aid rates for appeals hadn't risen in twenty-six years and I'd be losing money by doing it.

'So that's what it's about, is it? Money?' Boyfriend removed his wallet and started counting out notes onto my desk. Strange how you could grow to like even the most annoying people.

Before I could get my paws on the cash, my client's tiny hand clamped down onto her partner's and pinned it to the pile. 'Don't, Bobby. Didn't you hear Mr Munro? There's no point in appealing.'

Boyfriend Bobby wrenched his hand away and began stuffing the money back into his wallet, like he was stuffing a cushion. 'I told you, you should have got a better lawyer.'

Just as I stood up for her in court, my client now stood up for me. Sort of.

'I wouldn't have needed a better lawyer if you'd been a better witness! How many times did Mr Munro ask you if you could have been mistaken about the slap? All you had to do was agree with him and say the barmaid was wrong and that I'd reached up and stroked your face to calm you down after you'd shouted at me. But oh, no...' she crossed her eyes and stuck her tongue in her cheek and said in a low, gormless voice, 'No, she definitely slapped me on the face, your Honour.'

'But you did slap me.'

My client looked down at her boyfriend and then at me, shaking her head. 'You see what I've got to put up with?'

'He is right about one thing, though,' I said. 'You didn't hit him hard enough.'

Two of us in the room saw the funny side, the other jumped out of his chair, face ablaze. 'Listen—'

'No, you shut up and listen.' My client stuck a finger in his face and slowly Bobby the boyfriend resumed his seat. 'Right,' she said, once he'd settled himself again. 'The truth of the matter is that I've only got myself to blame, and, if Mr Munro says an appeal is a waste of time and money, we need to take his advice. After all, he's the lawyer. If I'm not going to have a job when I graduate, there isn't going to be much money available for legal expenses. Now what have you got to say to Mr Munro, Bobby?'

After her boyfriend had mumbled an apology in my direction, she reached out and shook my hand. The teaching profession was about to lose an excellent disciplinarian.

'I suppose there'd be no harm firing in an appeal,' I said. 'I can't see how it can possibly work, but then the Appeal Court's decisions are usually a mystery anyway, so who knows?'

'You really think there might be a chance?' There was a flicker of hope in the young woman's eye that I could not bring myself to extinguish.

'Only one thing's certain,' I said, with a shrug. 'If you don't buy a ticket you can't win the raffle.'

My client managed a faint smile. 'Did you hear that, Bobby? Get your wallet out.'

14

We arrived in Prague shortly before noon after an early start and a three-hour flight. The Hotel Jalta was a five-star establishment built during the Cold War and came complete with its own fall-out shelter in the basement. Once popular with the leaders of Soviet Bloc countries, it was now on the UNESCO World Heritage list and described as an almost perfect example of socialist realism architecture, whatever that was. It looked like just another splendid building to me. Prague was full of them.

The lift in the lobby took us to a two-room suite on the fourth floor. Ellen had spared no expense. We checked the bedroom first. The bed was ridiculously large and comfortable and we tried it out, though we weren't particularly tired.

'The best thing about this holiday is that we don't have to queue for the toilet,' Joanna said, when I emerged from the bathroom, one towel around my waist, and giving my hair a rub with another. 'Or listen to your dad's daily commentary on his bowel movements.' She had already showered and dressed and was sitting on the small sofa in the sitting room, eating red grapes from a complimentary bowl of fruit. 'So, then? Who or what is the second bird?' she asked.

Joanna popped a final grape in her mouth, stood and walked to the doors leading to the balcony. She stepped out intending me to follow, which I did, warily. How or why or in what way I didn't know, but I'd definitely been rumbled. 'What do you mean, "second bird"?'

Joanna leaned on the balcony railing and gazed down the length of St Wenceslas Square. 'That's what this trip is about, isn't it? Two birds, one stone?'

If I'd been one of my own clients, my advice to myself would be to say nothing in case I incriminated myself. My clients didn't have to encounter Joanna, arms folded, turning and staring them straight in the eyes. 'Okay, how do you know?'

'Robbie...' It seemed an effort for her to find the right words. 'This hotel for a start...It's five-star, it's luxurious, we have a suite with a balcony overlooking one of Europe's most prestigious thoroughfares.'

Even I'd noticed that. 'So?'

'So, it's not a standard room with a view of a wall, and...well...it's not like you to go to this sort of expense.'

'Are you calling your husband-to-be a cheapskate?'

She wrinkled her nose. 'Let's say I'm marrying a man who is cautious with money. Especially his own.'

'I don't have my own money,' I said. 'We have our money. We opened a joint account, remember?'

'And you're careful with it. That's good. Usually.'

'So what are you trying to say?'

'That there is not a chance you'd lash out on a four-day excursion to Prague and a stay in the best suite in a five- star luxury boutique hotel.'

'But it's our trial honeymoon.'

'No, Robbie, not even for our actual honeymoon.'

'Why wouldn't I?'

'Because if this had really been your idea of a trial honeymoon, you'd have done the sums, worked out that for the same money, me, you and Tina could have all gone somewhere sunny for a fortnight.'

'Don't you like it here?'

'No, I do. I love it. What I'm saying is that I might only have got engaged to you four months ago, but I've known you for nearly seven years and we've worked together for at least three of those. I know you, and I know that by whisking me off on a romantic city-break-slash-trial- honeymoon, you'll be thinking you've killed one bird. What I want to know is what's the second bird and who paid for the stone?'

I had wondered about telling Joanna the true reason behind the Prague visit; perhaps over dinner, after she'd been mellowed by a couple of glasses of wine. Not when I was standing inches away from a five-storey drop.

'Great view from here, isn't it?' I eased past her and gazed to my left along the bustling street below to the immense statue of Prague's patron saint, guarding the way to the National Museum. 'Now you can say you've looked out onto good King Wenceslas. Instead of the other way around.'

'Robbie...'

'You know, like in the Christmas carol?'

'Robbie...'

'There's some great shops too. Maybe we should have a quick look in some of them while we're here.'

Joanna didn't so much as flinch. 'Robbie. Seriously. I'm warning you.'

If the prospect of retail therapy couldn't side-track her, I was a man running fast out of ideas. 'Look, there's a pigeon on the next balcony.' Joanna took my bicep in a loving but viciously tight grip. 'Okay, okay,' I said, 'let's go out and explore. I'll explain everything.

You'll laugh when I tell you.'

She let go my arm. 'I'd better.'

We left the hotel, took a right and strolled down Wenceslas Square towards the Old Town, cutting in and out of a maze of side streets, stopping now and again to look in shop windows.

'You know, you'd make a hopeless witness,' Joanna said, when we'd walked and talked and ended up, as most tourists do, in the Old Town Square, where we formed part of a crowd that had gathered to watch the Astronomical Clock strike the hour. 'You crack under pressure.'

'I didn't crack. I was going to tell you anyway. I was just waiting for the right moment.'

And talking about right moments, we'd arrived just in time to see the old clock in action. Joanna had been reading all about it, as well as some of Prague's other tourist attractions, on the flight over. The ancient mechanism was apparently a fascinating piece of six-hundred- year-old chronometric kit. Certainly it was way too complicated for me to work out what was happening.

'You see the twenty-four numerals in gothic script around the perimeter?' Joanna said. She was standing in front of me, head tilted so that the back of it rested against my chest, pointing up at the clock tower of the Old Town Hall. 'It indicates the approach of sunset, depending on the time of year. Twenty-four is sunset. All the others are the hours before or after sunset. 'And you see those four colourful statues?' She had to shout in order to be heard above the excited chattering of those gathered about us. 'There are two either side of the clock face. One of them represents vanity. That's him holding a mirror. The one next to him is a miser with a bag of gold and across from those two there's a man dressed in fine clothes and playing a stringed instrument. He stands for lust and earthly pleasures.'

I didn't need any help with the fourth and final figure. Death was a skeleton and at precisely three o'clock he struck the time by pulling a cord and ringing a bell. As he did so, the other figures shook their heads, supposedly signifying their unreadiness to go with him.

The show was over in a matter of seconds and the crowd began to disperse, many of the clock-watchers making their way to the crowded restaurants, cafés and hot food stalls all around the square. Joanna put her arm through mine.

'Come on, we've got to have a look in there,' she said, leading me towards the nightmarish spires of the Church of Our Lady before Týn. It was good to have brought my very own tour guide along with me, but right at that moment I'd have preferred someone with more knowledge on Pilsner Urquell, Budvar and Staropramen and less about the Hussites, counter-Reformation and ornate, baroque altarpieces.

'Air travel can be very dehydrating,' I said, as we passed fellow clock-watchers now sitting at tables and being brought amber liquid in tall glasses. 'It said so in the in-flight magazine.'

'You can borrow my moisturiser later.' Joanna was unrelenting in her march towards the cathedral. She was either really keen on turning this trip into an exploration of Bohemian history and cultural identity, or just trying to annoy me.

I was looking for a suitable cobble on which to twist an ankle when Joanna said, 'When have you arranged to see this Freddy guy?'

'I haven't quite finalised arrangements,' I said. 'There are still a few loose ends to tie up.'

'How loose?'

I had to admit the ends were hanging pretty freely at that precise moment.

Joanna stopped and stood in front of me. 'But you do have an address for him?'

'No...not as such...I thought I could go out looking for him tomorrow morning. You can have a long lie, order room service and, when I come back, we'll go somewhere nice for lunch. After that we'll have the rest of the week to ourselves. Assuming I can find him. How does that sound for a plan?' I asked.

'Not as good as mine,' she said.

15

Joanna's plan, which I was strenuously encouraged to adopt, was to find Freddy Fletcher, get the business with him out of the way and then get on with our holiday. I knew he lived somewhere in Prague, but it was a big place, and Ellen hadn't been able to narrow it down that much for me. All she knew was that her estranged husband had a souvenir stall on Charles Bridge. Presented with an all-expenses-paid trip, that information had seemed sufficient for me to go on at the time. After all, how hard could it be to find a man on a bridge? The Freddy I knew was a tall and solidly-built individual with a loud voice, even louder clothes and a full head of disobedient brown hair. Once seen, never forgotten. I reckoned that if he was standing on a bridge selling souvenirs I couldn't miss him. But I did. At least I did on my first two sorties.

On the short walk from the town square, Joanna, my tour guide, explained that the bridge spanning the Vltava River was the main pedestrian passage between the Old Town and the Prague Castle complex, so I expected it to be fairly busy. I didn't expect a five-hundred-metre fairground along which an army of tourists ran a gauntlet of buskers and hawkers. It looked not so much like an excellent place to find a long-lost husband, as for an about-to-be husband to lose a wallet. To save time, I stopped to speak to one of the caricaturists. He seemed helpful enough initially, but the more questions I asked about Freddy Fletcher, the less English he understood.

It was on our third stroll along the fourteenth-century bridge that I spied him. The brown hair was gone, trans- planted from his now shaved head to a splendid Van Dyke with moustaches that curled up at the ends. He'd lost several stones in weight which made him look even taller, the vibrant clothing was gone, replaced by a jumper and jeans and the only remnant of his previous flamboyance was a pink cravat knotted at the neck. So different was he to my mental image that the only reason he caught my eye at all was because, out of all the other street vendors, he was the one not actively seeking to attract my attention to a display of paintings, jewellery and fridge magnets. But for this abnormal reticence I could have walked up and down the bridge all day and not recognised him. Ironic, that by trying to remain inconspicuous, he'd only made himself stand out from the crowd.

Without making eye contact, but aware that I was being watched, not breaking stride, I continued my stroll, hand in hand with Joanna, back along towards the Old Town side of the bridge until, swallowed up by the crowds, I was certain I was out of sight. Then I doubled back, leaving Joanna to study the statue of St Jan of Nepomuk, the most visited of the thirty religious monuments lining the bridge. St Jan, so tradition had it, had been a priest unwilling to disclose to King Wenceslas IV the confession of his queen whom he suspected of adultery. For that he'd been thrown off the Charles Bridge. Most historians thought the actual reason for his execution had less to do with a strict adherence to the confessional and more to do with politics and an allegiance to the wrong Pope, there being two at the time; whichever, martyrdom made for a better story. It also made Jan the patron saint of the drowned. Rubbing the bronze plaque beneath his statue was said to bring you whatever you wished for within one year and a day. I was wishing for a fat payday from Ellen Fletcher and didn't want to wait that long to collect.

'Hi Freddy,' I said, approaching him from the rear. His stall was one of the last at the far end of the bridge, nearest the road leading to the Lesser Town and onwards up the winding cobbled street to the Castle. I guessed he was in his early fifties, but the years seemed to be piling on him by the second. He stared at me, puzzled, before saying something in a language I took to be Czech. I wasn't to be put off. 'How you doing? It's me, Robbie...Robbie Munro.' I held his stare. I could tell by the look in his eyes that he was considering keeping up the pretence of being someone else. 'You've really picked up the language,' I said, before he could continue his confused foreigner routine. 'How long have you been out here now? Got to be a good few months. I like the beard.'

Freddy had assessed his options and decided the mistaken identity route wasn't going to work. 'Mr Munro,' he smiled, 'good to see you. What brings you here?'

'I'm on holiday.'

'Well, enjoy yourself. It's a great town.' He bent to rummage around in a cardboard box full of trinkets.

'Also, I've been asked to bring you a message,' I said. He straightened. The corners the moustache drooped slightly. 'I'm busy. How's about we catch up later?'

'I'd rather do it now,' I said. 'It won't take long. Can you take a ten-minute break or something?'

Freddy looked from side to side. 'Sure.' The mouth amidst the facial hair was smiling, but the eyes weren't joining in. 'I'll go and ask one of the other chaps to mind the stall. Wait here,' he said, and was gone.

The speed at which he departed took me by surprise, and left me in little doubt that he wasn't planning on coming back anytime soon. Jostling and zig-zagging my way through the throng I set off after him, spurred on by the occasional glimpse of a bald head, bobbing up and down just a few yards ahead, separated always from me by the mass of tourists. When I passed the halfway mark of the bridge I'd made up very little ground if any. The archway of the Gothic tower on the Old Town side loomed before me. If Freddy made it through that to the maze of side streets beyond, I'd never see him again. My chances of catching him were even more reduced when a group of giggling Japanese girls stopped for a photo-shoot, blocking my way. I dodged through them, jinking this way and that, bumping into people, shouting apologies over my shoulder, all the time watching the head in the distance bob up and down like a boiled egg on a trampoline, putting more distance between us with every step. I'd more or less given up hope, when in front of me the crowd suddenly parted and people backed away to either side of the bridge, leaving a gap in the centre. I drew to a halt. There in front of me Freddy Fletcher was sprawled on the cobbles being helped to his feet by a profusely apologetic Joanna. I took a hold of him by the arm. 'Freddy, are you okay?'

'No, I'm not okay.' He tried to pull free, but I wasn't letting him get away again. 'This wee bitch tripped me up. I take it she's with you?'

'Firstly, the wee bitch is my fiancée, so watch it. Secondly, I only want to talk.'

'I know what you want.'

'I don't think you do.'

He grabbed my hand, twisting my fingers, loosening my grip. 'Here's the cops coming. You ever seen the inside of a Czech prison?'

A couple of police officers, one male, one female, wearing peaked caps, pale blue shirts, grey trousers and expressions of faint interest, made their way over to us. The female clearly worked out and was slim and athletic looking. The male looked like he'd worked out where to insert doughnuts and decided to leave it at that.

'No, and he's not going to,' Joanna said. She turned to Freddy. 'What's the penalty here for trying to dip a tourist's handbag?'

The female cop wandered over to check that everything was all right. 'Dobre?' she enquired.

Freddy stepped forward to meet her and give his assurance that things were extremely, dobre. Satisfied at the three happy faces in front of her, with a smile and a nod the policewoman re-joined her colleague to continue their patrol of the bridge.

'Let's go for a chat,' I said, not letting go of Freddy's upper arm.

'What about my stall?'

'How much is the stock worth?'

'A few hundred.'

'Then leave it,' I said.

He looked worried. 'I'm not going back to Scotland, if that's what you think.'

'What I think is that you'll change your mind when you hear my news.'

'And that is?'

'Well, Freddy,' I said, releasing my grip, and instead throwing a friendly arm around his shoulder. 'There's good news and there's bad news.'

16

We let Freddy take us to a small restaurant in the Jewish Quarter where we sat outside on high stools around a circular table. I ordered the fallow deer meatloaf with dumplings and gravy, and a pint of home-brewed dark beer.

'There's always lots of game on the menu in Prague,' Freddy said. 'The Czechs love to hunt. The guy who owns this place doesn't only brew his own beer, he probably shot what you're going to eat too.'

Sounded good to me.

'So long as you realise that could be Bambi's mum you're about to eat,' Joanna said. She'd opted for one of the few vegetarian dishes on the menu, a frighteningly healthy-sounding vegetable-steak tartare and less health- conscious glass of fizzy wine.

Freddy ordered his food in a language I didn't under- stand. There were a lot of those in the world. He had relaxed somewhat after I'd assured him I hadn't been sent by Jake Turpie, and the presence of Joanna helped, even though he hadn't completely forgiven her for his tumble. He reached under the table and rubbed his knee. 'Those cobbles were bloody hard.'

'It'll heal,' I said. 'A bruised knee is worth what I have to tell you.'

'Go on then. Give us the good news first. Jake Turpie die, did he?'

Suddenly, I felt guilty about being so cheery. The

good news I had to impart was conditional on the imminent death of Freddy's wife, albeit they'd been estranged for a year.

'Let's go with the bad news first,' I said. 'It's about Ellen. She's the reason I'm here. She has cancer. It's terminal. She wants to see you, before...You know...'

There was an awkward silence until the food arrived. Mine consisted of four thick slices of meatloaf, three fluffy dumplings, all swimming in gravy, and a small dish of cranberry jam on the side. Freddy was served a glass of mineral water and an extremely pale omelette laced with grey slithers of mushroom. He started in on it straightaway. News of his wife's imminent demise didn't seem to have spoiled his appetite. Not that a fluffy omelette was going to put much meat on his emaciated frame. He looked more like a cancer victim than his wife did. If it was all part of his disguise, he had taken things to extremes.

I waited for Joanna's vegetable burger thing to arrive and the waiter to depart. 'Why did you leave her, Freddy?' Ellen had told me it was her fault in some way, but nothing more. 'I know that you conned Jake out of a lot of money. Everyone knows that. Just like everyone thought they knew Jake had...' I made a slashing motion with my knife in front of my neck. Not close enough to touch my neck, but close enough for meatloaf gravy to splash onto my shirt.

Joanna dipped the corner of her napkin in her wine and dabbed the stain. 'I told you to bring more shirts.'

'So what did happen between you and Ellen?' I asked, once Joanna had finished dabbing.

Freddy stopped mid-chew and looked up from his plate. 'You'll have to ask Ellen that.' He sliced into his food again, impaled a portion of omelette and held his fork up to his face. 'Great things, mushrooms. Low in carbohydrates and fat-free, they're high in fibre and protein, stuffed full of vitamins and virtually no calories.'

'Not much fun, though,' I said, sticking my own fork into a doughball and rolling it around on the plate, mopping up gravy.

Freddy popped the morsel in his mouth and chewed as he spoke. 'I've got IBS. It's brought on by stress, the doctors say. Thanks to Jake Turpie, I'm nothing but skin and bone. No deer hunting for me. The only thing I hunt are mushrooms, and an omelette is about as much fun as it gets.'

'You and Ellen...' Joanna intervened on our food talk. 'Why don't you tell us what happened.'

'Why should I tell you anything? You—'

'I know, I know, I tripped you up. You're making it difficult for me to forget. But I'm here on holiday and it starts for real after your business with Robbie is finished, so start talking.'

'It's a long, complicated story.'

'Then,' Joanna reached out and took hold of the hand that was raising another forkful of omelette, 'how about you give us the quick and simple version?'

Freddy set down his cutlery, looked at Joanna and then at me. 'Okay,' he said, finally. 'Ellen cheated on me. I left her. Simple enough for you? I'm sorry she's dying, but I'm not going back, even if she wants to beg my forgiveness.'

'She wants to leave you money in her will too,' I said. 'Whatever she's got, tell her to keep it.' Freddy picked up his weaponry and shoved omelette into his mouth.

I followed suit. The meatloaf was delicious and no meal was ever the worse for gravy and a doughball or two.

Joanna ignored her own food, keen to have everything tied up before we moved onto the coffee and little biscuits. 'So she cheated on you. What was it? A one-night stand? Every woman can make a mistake.'

'Wait a minute,' I said. 'No they can't. Not every woman.' My further protests were stifled by a swift kick from under the table.

'What I mean,' Joanna continued, 'is that maybe Ellen did make a mistake. A big mistake—'

'That some men...' I paused, to give Joanna what I hoped was a meaningful stare, 'could never forgive.' I turned back to Freddy who was stoking his face with omelette, while the gravy on my meatloaf grew cold and began to congeal at the edges.

Joanna took up the reins of the conversation once more. 'Freddy, Ellen's dying. She just wants to spend some time with you and say goodbye.'

'I said goodbye to her the night she cheated on me.'

'But surely you can't deprive your wife of her dying wish?'

'You don't think so? Then just watch me.' He halved his final piece of omelette with a decisive swish of his knife, like an old-school surgeon who thought keyhole surgery was for wimps. He poked egg into his face, allowing us to spectate as he spoke. 'She screwed Jake Turpie...' Freddy paused to take a drink of water and then inserted the final morsel of his meal. 'And so I screwed him and left her.'

'I'm sure she's sorry,' Joanna said.

'If she's sorry, then she has no-one to blame but herself.'

'And she wants to leave you her estate.'

'If she expects me to forgive her just because she's going to leave me a few quid—'

'Half a million,' I said. 'She won the lottery.'

Freddy stopped chewing, mouth wide open. He closed it eventually, which came as a relief to those of us forced to witness the early stages of his digestive process. A sudden difficulty swallowing was only overcome by a pull on my glass of dark ale.

I put a hand inside my jacket, took out an envelope and shoved it across the table at him. 'That's two thousand euros. Get yourself on a flight back to Edinburgh, book into a hotel and give me a call when you're settled.'

'But not too soon,' Joanna said. 'First of all, we have some sightseeing to do.'

17

And we did. We saw a great deal of Prague over the next three days, and a fair amount of our hotel bedroom as well. The following Monday it was business as usual. Joanna started her new job at the PF's office in Falkirk, and I was face to face with Sheriff Albert Brechin for the first time since the arrest of his granddaughter.

'The court will rise and sit again at eleven thirty,' the Clerk announced, after I'd finished my final plea in mitigation that morning. Surprisingly no-one had gone to jail yet. 'Sheriff Brechin would like a word with you before you go,' the clerk whispered to me, a look of apology on her face. Eleanor Hammond had been a Clerk of Court as long as I'd been in business, possibly since I'd left school, possibly since I'd started school. She'd been the mainstay of the court forever, initially when it was based in Linlithgow and then after it had been relocated ten miles south to Livingston.

Eleanor had summoned me to Sheriff Brechin's chambers on many occasions over the years, usually to discuss procedural problems that had arisen during the course of a trial; today it was for something else.

'I see you've appealed me,' Brechin said, leaning back in his chair. 'Again.'

I sat down on the other side of the extremely neat and tidy desk from him. There was a small pile of papers in a wire tray to his left, a larger pile in the tray to his right, a pen-holder, and two silver-framed photographs. One of the photos was a black and white shot of a young man in a Scots Guards' uniform, whom I took to be Brechin back in the day, the other, a more recent coloured photo, was taken shortly after he'd departed Crown Office to take up the post of sheriff, when he'd switched from prosecutor to persecutor in one swift donning of a horsehair wig. Eleanor having shown me through to chambers, was dismissed by a wave of the shrieval hand.

'I'll be waiting outside,' she said, with the reassuring smile of a zookeeper who's just put a visitor in charge of the tiger enclosure while she nips around the corner for a smoke. Brechin leaned forward. With an effort he lifted a few sheets of paper from a leather-bound, green blotter that was situated front and centre on his desk. He held them up to me. 'No reasonable Sheriff, you say, would have reached the verdict I did in Miss Somerville's case.' For obvious reasons, the no reasonable Sheriff ground of appeal was particularly disliked by sheriffs and one usually given short-shrift by their brothers and sisters sitting in the Appeal Court; however, as, technically, Brechin had not erred in law, I could see no other avenue. 'I can go over my de minimis argument again if you like,' I said.

'I'd rather you didn't, Mr Munro. I heard quite enough at the trial.'

'If you're not prepared to concede the point, then why am I here?'

Brechin tossed the papers to one side. He'd had enough of smiling. 'Why didn't my granddaughter plead guilty?'

'We defence lawyers call it the presumption of innocence. You may have heard of it.'

That didn't provoke quite the explosive result that I thought it might.

'I'm not asking you as a sheriff. I'm asking you as her grandfather. If Antonia had pled guilty at the earliest stage it would have gone much better, both sentence-wise and when she came before the disciplinary tribunal.'

'Can I refer you back to my early comment about the presumption of innocence?'

'But there is no presumption of innocence here.' He leaned forward and thumped a fist on the blotter, driving his point home like he was driving a nail into my head. 'The girl is guilty. She's told me as much. I know she will have told you too, and yet you have pled her not guilty, no doubt expecting a larger fee the longer you can spin—'

'I'm a defence lawyer. Presenting defences is my job and

in my opinion a plea of not guilty is best.'

'Best for your business, perhaps, while Antonia's career sails off down the river.'

I'd had enough. It wasn't his insults. I was used to those. And I could understand his role as the concerned grandfather. Antonia was his flesh and blood and he'd want what was best for her. What I wasn't prepared to accept was advice from someone who'd shown scant interest in the well-being of any other client I'd had up until then.

'I think I should go,' I said.

He wasn't listening, but at least the fist-banging had stopped. 'By dragging this whole sorry process out you are only maximising the embarrassment to everyone.'

I stopped halfway out of my seat and sat down

again.

'Is that what this is really all about, minimising embarrassment? To Antonia or to you?'

The anticipated detonation might very well have taken place there and then, but for a light knock on the door. Eleanor poked her head into the room. 'Are you going to be long, Sheriff? We've still the court to finish and there's a police officer here looking to have a search warrant executed.'

Brechin beckoned her in, dipped a hand into the wire tray to his left and removed a single pre-signed sheet of paper. 'Give him this.' The clerk came over and took the piece of paper from him. 'Tell the Procurator Fiscal that I'll sit again in five minutes.' When she was gone he turned his attention once more to me. His temper seemed some- what defused, no longer a UXB with corroded wiring. He took off his wig, set it down on the desk and stared at it. Suddenly, I felt sorry for him. Almost.

'I'm going to do my best for Antonia,' I said.

'You'd better.' Not looking up, he stroked the roughness of the wig, lovingly, like it was a pet cat, albeit one in need of a hot-oil conditioning treatment. 'I strongly believe she should have pled guilty when she had the chance.'

'With the greatest of respect, Sheriff,' I said, which is legalese for, "listen up dunder-heid," 'when have you ever not thought it best that someone should plead guilty, and the sooner the better?'

He stopped stroking the wig, placed it on his head and stood up.

I wasn't finished. 'Another thing—'

'Thank you, that will be all.'

But it wasn't all. Not for me. I remained seated and stared up at him as he came around the desk, walked to the door and held it open for me. Eleanor had sent a bar officer who was waiting patiently in the corridor, ready to lead the Sheriff back onto the bench. 'Why should Antonia opt for the worst-case scenario? Plead guilty and the only result is a conviction. With a plea of not guilty there's always hope.'

'Put off the evil day, you mean. Let you rack up the fees.'

'The longer we hold out, the more chance there is of the PF dropping the charge. After all it's only a single wrap of cocaine.'

'Really? How likely is it that the proceedings will be discontinued? The case against my granddaughter is more open and shut than this door.' He pushed the door to his chambers, slamming it against the frame. 'She should have pled guilty and you should have put forward mitigation and begged the court for leniency.'

Mitigation? Leniency? Brechin was finding a whole new vocabulary.

'This is a prosecution under summary procedure,' I felt it necessary to remind him. 'There are lots of things that can go wrong with the Crown case.'

'And you're the very man to capitalise on any mistakes.

Is that it?'

'You're a judge. I'm a defence lawyer. Each to his own.'

'Well, if there is a chink in the Crown's armour you'd better find it.'

'I'll do my best,' I said. 'At least there is one major problem I won't come up against.'

'And that is?'

I opened the door for him. 'You.'

18

Freddy Fletcher was taking no chances. He called me while I was still at court on Monday morning to say that he'd booked into a hotel, the name of which he was not prepared to divulge. We arranged to meet in Edinburgh at one thirty at a café on the corner of West Richmond Street and The Pleasance, looking onto the Deaconess Gardens, where, on a reasonably warm May afternoon, the cherry trees still hung on bravely to a few clumps of blossom, and students sprawled on the grass amidst scattered text books pretending to study.

Directly across the road was the murder locus of Lord Darnley, Mary Queen of Scots' second husband. The main suspect, James Hepburn, fourth Earl of Bothwell, having been tried and acquitted, promptly married Mary three months later. On the site now stood the Kirk O'Fields, the point of its red spire stabbing the cloudless blue sky like a bloody dagger.

But it wasn't for reasons of horticulture or history that Freddy Fletcher had chosen our meeting place. That had more to do with the public setting and the fact that St Leonard's Police Station was but a truncheon-throw away.

Not renowned for my punctuality, I was nonetheless first to arrive. I pulled up a bamboo chair at one of several small round tables on the wide pavement and ordered myself an Americano and a sausage sandwich. I was becoming better acquainted with the latter when

Freddy appeared from behind the red telephone box to my right only twenty or so metres away. He was looking more like how I remembered him, dressed in a heavy-weave, tobacco-brown suit and yellow shirt, his bearded chin resting gently on a bright, multi-coloured cravat. Perhaps in August, during the Festival, he'd have blended in more, but for a man trying not to draw attention to himself he was about as inconspicuous as the seagull perched on the adjacent table that was eyeing up my sausage sandwich with evil intent.

'I sincerely hope this is not a set-up, Robbie,' were his opening remarks as he shook my hand using his fingertips as though trying to avoid contaminating himself in the process.

I pushed a chair at him with the sole of my shoe and looked around for the waitress, while Freddy studied the occupants of nearby tables for potential assailants. The only possible suspect I could see was the seagull. 'Stop worrying and sit down.' I took out my mobile phone and laid it on the table between us. 'Ellen isn't far away. She can be here in five or ten minutes. She's just waiting for my call.'

'Why is she not here herself? What has any of this got to do with you?' Freddy took out a paper pack of foreign cigarettes, and offered it to me. I declined. He shook one out, tapped the end of it on the table and put it in his mouth. 'Why...' He lit the cigarette with a cheap disposable lighter and puffed. 'Why does Ellen need you here if she just wants to meet me?'

'Two reasons,' I said. 'Firstly, she wants me to ensure your safety. After all there is Jake Turpie to think about. We wouldn't want you ending up inside a crushed vehicle on the back of one of his low-loaders would we?' Freddy started looking around again, as though Jake might jump out of one of the cars parked nearby or from behind the red and yellow plastic dumpster at the side of the building. 'I really wish you wouldn't say things like that, Robbie.' He took a restorative puff and blew smoke out of the side of his mouth. 'It's upsetting.'

When the waitress arrived, Freddy sent her off in search of a double espresso as I munched the final bite of my sandwich. 'Ever think that maybe caffeine and nicotine are the cause of your irritable bowel and not Jake Turpie?'

'I see you've added a medical degree to your LLB since I've been away,' Freddy replied. 'How about I deal with my eating disorder the way I see fit and you don't speak with your mouth full?' This from the man whose mushroom-omelette-coated tongue and tonsils formed a mental image it had not been easy to dispel. 'What's the other reason Ellen wants you involved?'

I chewed, swallowed and wiped my mouth with a paper napkin that was already slightly damp from some spilt coffee. 'She wants me to break the news of your return to Jake and square him up for the money you stole — without any loss of blood. Your blood.'

The waitress hove into view with Freddy's coffee. 'And you and Ellen think that's possible?' he asked, squashing his cigarette into a small tin ashtray.

I picked up my phone. 'Let's find out, shall we?'

Freddy was stirring a heaped teaspoonful of sugar into his second double espresso and I was peeling the foil from a can of San Pellegrino when a taxi pulled into the kerb. The red-headed nurse with the legs and light green trouser-suit got out, opened the rear nearside door and helped her charge onto the pavement. Ellen came across to where we were seated.

'Hello, Freddy,' she said.

'Ellen,' Freddy grunted, stirring his coffee and not looking up. Ellen sent her companion off inside the café and stood gazing down awkwardly at her husband. I pulled over a chair for her.

'What can I get you?' I asked.

'A glass of water is fine,' she replied, and I conveyed this to the waitress who was collecting empty cups and saucers from a nearby table.

'I've just been telling Freddy that we'll have to tread cautiously with Jake Turpie,' I said, when it became apparent that neither of the two was going to break the silence.

Freddy pulled another cigarette from the packet, lit it, inhaled deeply and let the smoke out in a long, extended stream straight at his wife.

Ellen sat there for a moment, tendrils of smoke winding themselves around her recently coiffured hair, and then she snatched the cigarette from Freddy's lips and threw it into the street. 'I get it. I get that you're angry with me for what happened. Sorry. Unfortunately, I can't turn the clock back. In fact, there aren't that many hours left on my clock.'

Freddy raised his tiny coffee cup to his nose and gave it a sniff. Apparently satisfied at its aroma, he drank the contents with one deft flick of the wrist. 'I suppose,' he said, with a sniff, drawing a crooked forefinger across his moustache, 'it is good to see you, Ellen, and I'm sorry to hear about your...your predicament.'

'Can it,' Ellen said. 'I don't need any fake sympathy

from you. You decided you could do without me and even though you made that decision, without giving me the chance to explain—'

'Explain what?' Freddy set down the tiny coffee cup. 'That you didn't have sex with Jake Turpie?'

Freddy's voice was raised, and one or two tables were now beginning to take an interest in the real-life soap opera unfolding in front of them.

'Maybe we should continue this discussion somewhere more private,' I said. 'How about we go back to your hotel, Ellen?'

Freddy shook his head. 'No, I like it here fine. I'm not going to any hotel room with people I don't trust.'

I didn't know if Freddy Fletcher's new life in the Czech Republic centred entirely around selling tat to tourists, but until he'd disappeared off the radar, his main goal in life had been to make as much money as possible, by conning as many people as possible. Now he was being handed a fortune on a plate and seemed intent on throwing it away. 'Let's all calm down,' I said. 'I'm sure there was fault on either side and that both of you are sorry for what happened. I glanced from one to the other. Neither seemed particularly repentant. 'Now, we all know why you're here, Freddy.'

'Do we? Tell me, Ellen. Why am I here?'

Ellen reached out to take his hand. Freddy tried to pull it away, but wasn't fast enough. She took a firm grip. 'I may have no future, but I do have a past and that's you. We've no children and, like you, I've no family. All I have is money, and I can't take it with me. However, if you don't want—'

'No, no,' Freddy protested. At long last a degree of sanity was being restored to the proceedings. 'It's not that I'm not...'

Ellen assisted his search for the right word. 'Grateful?'

Freddy dragged the words out of his throat like a sick man dragging himself out of bed. 'Yes, I am grateful.'

'Then show it.'

He placed his other hand on top of hers and squeezed. 'Thank you, Ellen.'

The waitress returned with a bottle of mineral water and a tall glass with ice and a slice. Ellen extracted her hand from Freddy's grip.

'Good. Then I'll let you go for now,' she said to him. 'I'll stay here with Robbie. We have some legal formalities to talk over. Give him your phone number so he can keep in touch.'

It took a few moments for Freddy to realise he'd been dismissed. I wrote down his mobile number, and, without another word, he stood and began to walk towards The Pleasance. Then he changed his mind and instead walked back up West Richmond Street.

Ellen watched him go. 'Boy, he hasn't half lost weight,' she said.

'It's all the worry, apparently. Maybe he'll relax a little when he gets his hands on your money.'

'Ah, yes. My money.' Ellen poured the contents of the bottle into her glass. 'I think there's maybe something I should tell you about that.'

19

'She doesn't have any!' Joanna stopped stirring the pot. Tina was sitting at the kitchen table, bowl and spoon at the ready, all set to do damage to the loaf of bread and a pat of butter in the centre of the big wooden table. First of all, the soup had to arrive.

'No, she has some money,' I said. 'But she didn't win the lottery?'

'No, she did win the lottery. Just not all that much.'

'I thought you told me it was five hundred thousand.'

'I did. That was wrong.'

'How wrong?'

'It was nearer fifty thousand.'

'How much nearer?'

'Exactly nearer.'

Joanna turned off the gas, took the pot and ladle over to the table and served up a large helping. Tuesday night was Tina's weekly golf lesson at the nearby Kingsfield driving range, and my dad's turn to take her, just as it was Joanna's turn to make the tea, a duty that seemed to fall to her a lot these days as my dad came up with more and more excuses.

The old man entered the kitchen tightening his belt, folded newspaper under his arm, look of satisfaction in his face. 'I'm thinking maybe I should alert the coastguard,' he said, taking a seat at the table next to his granddaughter. 'That one I've just flushed could be a danger to shipping.' From somewhere deep in Joanna's throat came a low rumbling sound. I put an arm around her. I whispered in her ear. 'Keep calm. It's only until we have our own place.' She tried to pull away. I held on, pinning her arms to her side, the ladle in her hand dripping soup onto the floor.

'I don't like nippy carrot,' Tina said, staring down at the faintly orange gloop in her bowl.

'I've got to say, Joanna, I'm not all that keen on it either,' my dad said. 'No offence or nothing, but you do remember the last time?'

'It's not nippy,' Joanna said. I let her go and she shoved the ladle back into the pot. 'It's not even carrot! And I only added some chilli the last time to liven it up, because you, Alex...' she dished my dad up a big bowl of orange gloop, 'told me the time before, that I should have left the wooden spoon in to lend a bit more flavour.'

Tina picked up a spoonful and let it drop from six inches. Some of it landed back in her soup bowl. 'What is it, then? It looks like nippy carrot.'

'It's butternut squash and sweet potato.'

'Mmm. Looks great,' I said. 'Makes me wish I hadn't had something to eat earlier.'

'Butternut squash?' My dad stared into the murky depths of the bowl. 'Was that what that thing in the vegetable rack was? Looked to me like one of those pods from that film we saw the other night: Invasion of the Bodysnatchers. I don't suppose there'll be any meat in it?'

'No.' Joanna replied, through teeth firmly clenched, pot in one hand, ladle still gripped tightly in the other. 'That's because, unlike the Alex Munro vegetarian soup recipe, I don't make mine with a chicken.' The vegetarian debate was one we'd had several times since Joanna had moved in. To be fair, when it was her turn to cook she had no problem preparing meat dishes for the rest of us. 'You know it is possible, just occasionally, to have a meal that doesn't involve something dying. But don't worry. This soup is only to keep you going until you get back. I'll slam a piece of dead animal in the oven for later.'

Joanna rattled the pot back onto the stove, chucked the ladle in after it and marched through to the living room.

'It's not for much longer,' I called after her.

'It better not be!' she called back. 'Two months it's been, and no remission for good behaviour.'

I turned to the two diners. 'I really wish you two would stop complaining about the food. Joanna's doing her best. Today was her first day back at work and to hear the pair of you, you'd think you were expecting her to come home and whip-up a quick paupiette of guinea fowl in a wild mushroom mousseline.'

'What's a pappoo...?' Tina began.

'Never mind,' I said. 'It's just me being funny.'

'Oh,' she said. That apparently explained everything. My dad gave the soup a few tentative slurps. 'Actually, it's not all that bad. Quite good really.'

'Not bad? Quite good? Go easy on the extravagant praise, won't you?'

'No, I mean it. You might have the makings of a good wee cook there, Robbie.'

'Well, it would be nice if you tell her that,' I said. 'Just don't make it sound quite so patronising when

110

you do. You know what patronising means, don't you?'

'You're a funny man.' My dad helped himself to some bread and butter. I noticed that Tina was now also digging in and seemingly enjoying the sludge. 'What I will say is that this soup's a lot better than your last attempt, Robbie. Remember that, Tina? What was it supposed to be? Pea and ham? Tasted more like pee and poo.'

I left the two of them spluttering over their soup bowls, to join Joanna in the living room.

'Just what does she think she's playing at?' Joanna asked, when I sat down beside her on the sofa.

'Don't listen to her. Tina's loving your soup.'

'I'm not talking about Tina. I'm talking about Ellen Fletcher. What's she up to?'

'She has a plan.'

'And that is?'

'To insure her life.'

'But she's dying.'

'Best time to get life insurance, wouldn't you say?'

'She'll never get it. No insurance company is going to insure her when it finds out...' It was taking some time, but Joanna was getting there. 'She isn't going to disclose her illness? But that's fraud!'

'Yes,' I said, 'that's what I told her...' I walked over and shut the kitchen door. 'Just not quite so loudly as that.'

'How much is she going to insure herself for?'

'I don't know exactly, but definitely a lot.'

'Then you are definitely having nothing more to do with her. Is that clear?'

Joanna's enunciation was as ever crystalline. I didn't

really need the accompanying pokes in the chest to under- stand what she was saying. I took hold of the finger that was doing all the poking. 'It's all right. I've told Ellen I'm not getting involved. I've returned Freddy to her. My work is done.'

'It had better be.' Joanna flopped back on the sofa. 'I still don't get all the fuss about bringing him home.'

'Ellen's got this crazy notion that by dying she can pay off Jake and save Freddy's life. I suppose it would be nice for her to know she's not dying in vain.' I said. 'You'd do the same for me, wouldn't you?'

'What? Commit a major fraud?'

'Well...Yes. To save my life.'

The question went unanswered. Tina burst through the door and hurled herself onto the sofa between us. 'I like butter, nuts and squash soup!'

I lifted her up and plonked her on my knee. 'That's good because it's what all the best golfers eat before they practise. Butternut squash soup and bread, especially the crusts. Did you eat your crusts?'

My dad walked in. 'Of course she ate her crusts.'

'And I won't find them forming a neat little circle under her soup bowl, like the last time?' Joanna asked.

Tina was saying nothing that might incriminate herself. My dad scooped her off my knee and up into his arms. 'Come on or we'll be late. It's only a half-hour lesson, and if you're good we'll go to Sandy's for ice cream afterwards.'

Sandy's café lay claim not only to the world's finest bacon roll, but, when it came to homemade ice cream, it was pointless for others to compete.

'I want a black man!' Tina yelled, jumping down from my dad's arms and running off to fetch her coat.

'Alex, she's learned that from you. I've told you not to let Tina hear you call them that.' Joanna followed the pair of them into the hall and called out of the front door after them, 'It's not a black man! It's a nougat wafer!' She returned to the living room and dropped onto the sofa beside me. 'We've really, really got to find our own place. If it's not black men, it's Chinky carry-outs and Paki shops. That man's going to end up getting his grand- daughter arrested for making racist remarks.'

She stretched out on the couch, her legs across my knees. Somehow I knew what she was going to say next. 'Talking about granddaughters and crime, what's happening with Antonia Brechin?'

I slipped an arm around Joanna and pulled her towards me. We had at least an hour to ourselves.

'What's she going to do, Robbie? Are you really taking it to trial? What's the plan?'

I had absolutely no idea.

'Then, you'd better come up with one.' She snuggled into me. 'But then you usually do.'

I hoped she was right, but, for the moment, I didn't care. We had an hour.

20

Joanna's faith in me was touching; however, it was exactly one week before I could think of something, anything, that might help resolve Antonia Brechin's plight. Even then, what I eventually came up with was less of a long shot and more of a punt for goal from the halfway line.

'Oh no, it's you.'

Ogilvie, white vest, white trackies, red towel draped around his scrawny neck, was putting his lanky body through a series of painful looking stretches and bends.

'Evening, Hugh,' I said. 'This is a coincidence.'

'Is it?'

Not unless coincidences could be bought it wasn't. I'd had to pay nineteen-ninety-nine for a temporary gym membership that I was never going to use again.

'Joanna says I've put on a little weight.' I patted the Boca Juniors home strip that I reserved for Friday night five-a-sides.

Ogilvie shook his head, sadly. 'Joanna Jordan. How on earth did you manage to talk her into marrying you? She has got one thing right though.' He took the towel from his neck and flicked my stomach with it.

I caught the end and threw it back at him. Yes, it was true that when I took off my shirt they didn't issue a missing person's alert, but I didn't see my fuller physique being in urgent need of reduction. 'Never mind my figure, how about we take this opportunity to have a serious word about Antonia Brechin's case?'

'How about we don't?' Ogilvie glimpsed someone alighting from a running machine and leapt on to it before I could stop him.

I tried some limbering-up exercises myself, one leg over the other, touching my toes, or very nearly, anywhere south of the knees was pretty good for me, and followed that with a few lunges, which were possibly inadvisable since, like the football top, my shorts seemed to have shrunk since they were last on; nonetheless, the exercise did help me manoeuvre closer to the PF's running machine.

'The only serious thing I'm here to do,' he said, raising his voice along with the speed of the conveyor belt beneath his feet, 'is train for a half-marathon at the end of the month.'

I could think of nothing worse than running a half-marathon, unless it was running a whole marathon. Why did people do it to themselves? Running was all very well in its place: good for catching buses and trains, chasing footballs, stuff like that, but running for no reason? I could never understand it. Indeed, I was at odds with the whole notion of exercise for exercise sake. It was fine if you were enjoying yourself by playing a game. Football, golf, even tennis, if you were that way inclined, or cricket. Well...maybe not cricket, but most games. They were called games for a reason: you had fun playing them. Fun and games went together like fun and gym didn't. What Hugh Ogilvie was doing, picking up his size nines and slapping them down again on a rolling rubber mat - that wasn't fun. He was on a treadmill, an item historically used as an instrument of torture. I didn't like to think of all the wasted heartbeats. They only gave you so many and then you died. Why use them up doing something that made you look like Ogilvie did right then? With his red face and white sports gear, he reminded me of an unused match. The man should have been grateful when I pulled the little green safety cord and the running machine carried out an emergency stop.

'What did you do that for?' Ogilvie demanded, after he'd regained his balance.

I picked up a couple of loose weights that were lying nearby and began some casual bicep curls. 'Do yourself a favour, Hugh, we both know how Antonia Brechin's case is going to pan out.'

'Yes, it's going to pan out with her being convicted. Now goodbye.'

'Oh, well, if you're going to be like that—'

'I am.'

'Towards a fellow professional. A brother in law, so to speak.'

'You're no relative of mine professionally or by any other connection, thankfully. You're a chancer who thinks that by stalking and harassing me I'll change my mind and drop the charge against his client.'

'Will you?'

'No!' He became aware of raising his voice and looked around. 'Why you even thought we could discuss business here, I don't know,' he hissed. 'It's a public place.'

Around about then I thought my biceps sufficiently curled, especially the left one which wasn't as keen on curling as the right and had started to complain. I set the weights down at my feet, whipped Ogilvie's towel out of his hand and wiped my face with it. 'Five minutes and I'll go and never mention the case to you again. Ever.'

Ogilvie grabbed back the towel. 'Promise?'

I took him by the arm and led him over to a water cooler situated near a rack of brightly coloured kettle bells, their cheery hues a cunning attempt to conceal how alarmingly heavy they were. 'Right,' I said, 'we both know that drug reports are never available for the trial first time around.' Ogilvie draped the towel across a shoulder and helped himself to a paper cone of chilled H2O. 'I'll admit there are occasional delays at the moment due to government cuts.'

'And if there is no forensic drug report, there's no proof that what my client is said to have possessed —'

'Make that, did possess.'

'...was actually an illegal substance. No proof, no conviction.'

Ogilvie threw his head back and poured the water down his throat. 'Robbie...' He wiped his mouth with a corner of the red towel. 'You do know that I am the Procurator Fiscal, don't you?'

I was prepared to concede the reality of his elevated status, if not that he deserved it.

He wagged the little paper cone at me. 'Then I think it's also safe for you to assume that I know how one goes about establishing the proof of controlled substances in a drugs trial.'

'Good, then let's also assume that the forensic report won't arrive in time for the trial —'

'In which case I would move to adjourn.'

'Precisely.' My turn to drink some water. 'But the way I see it happening, is that you move to adjourn in such a half-hearted, pathetic manner that the Sheriff refuses the motion, bingo the case is deserted and my client takes a walk.'

'O-kay...' Ogilvie said. 'I see only three problems with that scenario.' He needed to rehydrate some more before he could get to the first. 'One. What if I don't want to make a pathetic, half-hearted motion to adjourn?'

'Just be yourself and you'll do fine.'

'Two. Why would any sheriff refuse a motion to adjourn at the first calling of a trial?'

'Because whatever sheriff they bring in will be bending over backwards to do Brechin a favour.'

'You don't know that. Sheriffs are only human.' I'd certainly heard they started out that way. 'You could easily get a sheriff who doesn't like Bert Brechin, holds a grudge or something. It's not only you defence lawyers he's rubbed up the wrong way over the years.'

I disagreed. A sheriff was a sheriff. Male or female, young or old, their brains all came out of the same bucket. 'Sorry, Hugh. Trust me on this. Whoever they rope in to do the trial will be only too happy to have a senior Sheriff like Albert Brechin indebted to them. And what easier and more face-saving way to ingratiate themselves than to let his granddaughter off on a technicality? Who could criticise them for strictly applying the rules of procedure?'

I thought Ogilvie might mull that over for a little longer than the time it took him to crumple his paper cup.

'Three,' he said. 'I've already got the forensic report and it says cocaine. Fifty grams of it.'

'Fifty!' I tried not to say out loud, but couldn't help it. He lobbed the crushed cone into the little blue plastic bin at my side. 'Oh, yes. And every one of those fifty grams is as pure as the driven snow.'

21

Fifty grams of coke? Street value two and a half grand. The rates of pay for young lawyers must have increased significantly since I was a legal trainee. It would have been one hell of a party if the cops hadn't gate-crashed it before it had even started. Hugh Ogilvie was right. Antonia had been extremely lucky not to be charged with being concerned in the supply. That would have been a whole different ball game.

But Antonia Brechin wasn't the only damsel in distress on my mind that Monday night. I hadn't lied to Joanna. Not exactly. I had no intention of assisting Ellen Fletcher with her life insurance scam, but neither did I want her husband's death on my conscience, not after being partly responsible for putting him back in Jake Turpie's firing line. If I wasn't prepared to help, I thought I knew a man who might. I just had to find him.

My first port of call was St John's Hospital in Livingston. Not being as young as he once was, Sammy Veitch didn't chase ambulances these days; he preferred for them to come to him. Usually he could be found whiling away the hours between accident victims reading the latest legal thriller in the warmth of the A&E waiting room. Unfortunately, not on this particular evening. Instead, I had to journey a further six miles west and traverse the Bathgate hills to the home town of James Young Simpson, the man who discovered the anaesthetic qualities of chloroform. There I found a man who was setting out to rediscover the anaesthetic qualities of single malt whisky. 'It's yourself, Robbie,' Sammy said, seeing me alight from my car and walk across the street towards him. The wearing of the kilt was not something Sammy did for show. He wasn't one of those folk who donned the eight yards of plaid only when attending weddings or ceremonies. For Sammy it was his daily attire, be it work or leisure. Why he wanted to go around dressed as the Victorian idea of a Scotsman, I didn't know, just as I didn't know, and didn't want to know, what he wore under it. All I knew, as I walked up Bathgate Main Street on an early May evening, with a star-studded sky and a chill wind blowing, was that he was a braver man than I. 'To what do I owe the pleasure?' he said. 'You didn't come all this way just to buy an old lawyer a drink, did you?'

'If there were any old lawyers about, I might.'

He laughed. 'I'll take it that as a compliment to my youthful appearance and not a criticism of my legal expertise.'

'It's your legal expertise I've come about,' I said. 'Would you be interested in taking on a spot of business that I can't handle?'

'Can't handle or don't want to handle?' There were no flies on Sammy that hadn't had their passports stamped.

'A little of both.'

We walked a short way further down the street to his local where the barman had a double whisky and a small jug of water set up in the time it took us to make the trip from front door to the counter.

'Better make it a ginger beer for me,' I said. 'I'm driving.'

'SNP tossers,' Sammy said. There weren't too many people in Bathgate, far less habitual kilt-wearers, who weren't nationalists, but lowering the drink-drive limit had tested a few resolves. 'It's getting that you can't suck a wine gum without breaking the law.' Being a personal injury lawyer, it was possible Sammy's dislike for the lowering of the drink-drive limit was more professionally based than anything else. He waited until my drink was poured and half a dozen ice-cubes added before clinking his glass with mine. 'So what's this piece of business you'd like to put my way?'

'It's a financial matter and a wee bit tricky,' I said. 'Let me ask you a question. What if—'

'What if? Is it that kind of business?' Sammy tapped the side of his nose twice and winked. 'Carry on.'

'What if someone was sick?'

'How sick?'

'Dying.'

'That's the worst kind of sick.'

'And she wanted to leave some money behind for her next of kin to remember her by?'

'Just how much does she want to be remembered?'

'Let's say about half a million pounds' worth.'

Sammy took a sip of whisky before adding a drop of water. 'I always taste it first just in case there's water in it already, if you know what I mean. Sometimes I think the bottles in here don't get lower...' He put a hand to the side of his mouth as a barrier in case the barman could lip-read, but spoke the words loud enough for him to hear. 'They just get paler.' He stretched, straightened his back and relaxed again.

'Those chairs in A&E been giving you gip?' I asked. 'Old age, Robbie.' He rolled his head, loosening the

tension in his neck muscles. 'It doesn't come by itself. I had to stop doing school nights up at St John's a while ago. Sometimes I'll go up for an hour or two on a Saturday if the wife's watching that dancing show on telly, just to get away from it, but Friday night's where it's at.' He rubbed the small of his back. 'Anyway, it's nothing a wee dram won't cure.' He finished his drink and raised a finger to the barman who was already at the optics, glass in hand. 'Same again, Robbie?' Sammy asked, looking at my full tumbler. I declined and we took our drinks over to a table. 'Half a mill. Let me see.' Sammy strummed his bottom lip with a finger. 'It's going to have to be a term insurance policy of some kind.'

'I don't want to land you with something you'd rather not get involved in,' I said.

He shook his head. 'Are you kidding? It's nice to get some proper business for a change. I've not had a serious accident in ages. It's been all crappy wee trips and slips. Now this...' he lowered his voice. 'This insurance thing. This is more like it. This is right up my street. I used to do a lot of it in the eighties with the AIDS boys. I had a contact with some gay guys through in Edinburgh. First sign of anything wrong and they'd come to see me before they went anywhere near a doctor. If it was a false alarm, great, they just stopped paying the premiums. If it wasn't, then their next-of-kin cashed in.' Sammy took the whisky for a stroll around the glass, studying its legs. 'Then they went and found a cure.' He took a sip to console himself. 'I don't think they've found an actual cure for AIDS,' I said.

'Aye, well, they don't die the same as they used to.'

'Does that mean you can arrange something for my client and her husband?'

'No problem.'

'But it's a lot of money. She's only got three months to live. Won't there be an investigation?'

'If there is, what will they find? Woman gets ill and dies. Happens all the time.' He got up and covered the few metres to the bar with a new spring in his step and a certain swish to his kilt. 'If it didn't,' he said on his return with a replenished glass, and a smile, 'we wouldn't need life insurance companies.'

'But half a million. For that kind of money won't there need to be a medical?'

Sammy wafted a hand at me. 'They might write to your girl's GP and ask if there's anything dodgy on her records.' Sammy looked worried for a moment. 'There's nothing on them about the Big C is there? I take it that's what we're talking about?'

'That's right. According to Ellen...'

'Ellen?'

'That's the client's name, Ellen Fletcher, do you know her?'

'Of course I know her, and her illustrious husband, by reputation if nothing else. What was his name again?'

I'd hardly touched my ginger beer. The ice had almost all melted and it scarcely tinkled as I lifted the glass to my lips and took a drink before answering. 'His name was Freddy. It still is.'

'That a fact?'

'You're not the only one who's surprised.'

'I heard about that thing with Jake Turpie and him a

while back and just assumed...'

'A lot of people did.'

'So he's alive and Ellen's on the way out? Pity it wasn't the other way around, but there you are.'

'She says she started feeling not well around the time she came into some money, so she went private.'

'How private?'

'Harley Street.'

Sammy grinned. 'Nothing of concern there then. That lot are about as likely to breach patient confidentiality as a Swiss Bank will give back its Nazi gold.'

'How much is this going to cost?'

'One and a half ridiculously measly percent. Up front, of course. Cash. You can sort your own commission out with the client.'

I made a face. Sammy didn't understand. I had to clarify. 'I'm not wanting involved. At all.'

'Don't want to get your hands dirty, eh?'

'It's not so much my hands, Sammy. It's the rest of me too. It doesn't want to do a six stretch for a half-million- pound insurance fraud.'

He laughed, knocked back his dram and rattled the base of the glass on the table for the barman to hear. 'Have it your way.'

'No, really, Sammy. I feel bad about passing this onto you. If I'm not prepared to do it, I don't see why you—'

'Whoah there, Trigger. I'm more than happy to do it. But if you want to stay squeaky and still cash in, why don't you do the wills?'

'What wills?'

'They'll both need wills, and if I'm doing the

insurance for fifteen grand--'

'Both? Why both? And fifteen thousand? The last time I checked one and a half per cent of half a million was seven and a half.'

Sammy patted my cheek. 'Think about it. If you've got a man and wife and it's only the one who's taken out life insurance that happens to croak before the ink's dry on the policy, then it's bound to raise a few eyebrows.' The barman came over with a bottle and filled Sammy's glass. 'Raised eyebrows are what you try to avoid in this game,' Sammy said, after he'd gone. 'And...' Apparently there was more to it. 'They'll also have to make up some reason why they're taking out a term policy so that it looks legit — a mortgage, something like that.' He took a sip of his drink and smacked his lips. 'You see?'

I was beginning to.

'As for the wills, they'll make for less paperwork and less paperwork means fewer awkward questions later. Come the day, it should just be a case of having hubby appointed executor, lodging a claim, sitting back and waiting for the cheque to arrive.

He made serious fraud sound so simple. 'Simple is best,' Sammy said.

'I suppose I could bash out a couple of wills.' Where was the harm? I was a lawyer, and if clients asked me to draft wills for them, it would be unprofessional to say no. 'That's the spirit.' Sammy raised his glass to me and I joined him in a toast. 'Ellen might not be able to take her money with her, but we can see that she leaves some of it behind for us.'

22

'Say one for me when you're down there.' I was on my knees in the corner of the room raking about in the bottom drawer of a filing cabinet when Grace-Mary came in with the files for a long court day ahead.

'I'm looking for a style,' I said.

'Well you know what they say about style. You've either got it or you haven't, and, I hate to tell you—'

'A style for a will. I had a whole stack of them in my old trusts and executry lecture notes from uni.'

'What? Those ancient things? They're long gone.'

I stopped rummaging and stood up. 'Gone? You threw them out?'

'Ages ago, when I was having a clear-out. You never used them. Most weren't even in your handwriting, and those that were, were illegible. What's come over you? Feeling all grown up and responsible now you're going to be a married man and want to make out a will for the distribution of your estate? That's not going to take you long once you decide who's getting left the PlayStation. You can leave me Tina if you like.'

'If I do I'll have to leave you my dad as well.'

'No thanks, I can only manage one child at a time.' Grace-Mary thumped the files down on my desk. 'By the way, you're late for court.'

I filled my briefcase with the case files and picked up my car keys. 'Grace-Mary, any chance you could—'

'I'll see what I can do.'

'Thanks. I've got Ellen Fletcher coming in at three to make a will. When they get here, don't put them in the waiting room, bring them straight through to my room.'

'They?'

'She's bringing her husband, and I'm not wanting him on display to the public just yet.'

Grace-Mary, who had almost made it to the door, stopped and about-turned. 'Ellen Fletcher's re-married?'

'Not a new husband - the old one.'

'You want me to rustle you up an Ouija board as well?'

'No,' I said, taking my briefcase and edging past her out of the door, 'a style for a standard, no-frills will should suffice. Four o'clock.'

And at four o'clock I returned to find, on my computer screen, a simple enough looking template that would only need a few tweaks here and there to form the last will and testaments of Mr and Mrs Frederick Fletcher.

Ellen arrived bang on time and alone. It gave us time to talk.

'I'd rather it was you doing the insurance for us, Robbie,' she said.

'I don't want involved. Speak to Sammy Veitch.'

'But you said you'd help.'

'No, you said I'd help. I said I'd think about it and I have and I don't like it.'

'Robbie...'

'I'm not doing it, Ellen. If you want help, Sammy will do the business for you. You don't even need a lawyer to take out a life policy.'

She reached out across the desk and took hold of my hands. 'But I do need a lawyer. And not Sammy. A lawyer I can trust. If it's about the size of your fee...'

'It's not always about money,' I heard myself say, as though from a distance. 'I don't mind doing a couple of wills. Sammy says it'll make things easier, but I'm not assisting in a large-scale fraud just so that your waster of a husband can have an easy life after you're gone.'

Ellen yanked her hands away. 'This is not about giving Freddy an easy life and you know it. It's about giving him back his life. He can't stay in Scotland. Not while Jake Turpie's alive.'

'Freddy's made a pretty good job of staying hidden for the past year. He can keep doing it.'

'Come on, Robbie. It's not like these big insurance companies can't afford it. And it's not really all that risky for you. How would anyone find out you knew I was dying? I won't be around to tell them, and there's no chance Freddy would say anything. I'll bet if I was leaving the money to you, you wouldn't mind so much.'

There was a knock at the door and Grace-Mary showed Freddy into the room.

'Sorry I'm late,' he said, 'the train I went for left without me.' Nothing was ever Freddy's fault.

I squared up the keyboard, one finger on each hand poised and ready to type. 'Okay, let's get started. First of all, Ellen, I'm going to need your full name and an address, and then you'll have to decide who's going to be your executor.'

'What's an executor?'

'It's the person who engathers your estate and pays it out in accordance with the will.'

'Probably best if you do that, Robbie,' Ellen said. 'If it's not too much trouble, that is.'

I ignored her sarcasm. After that it was more or less a case of filling in the blanks so that Ellen left her entire estate to Freddy.

As Sammy had recommended, for the sake of appearances, I rattled off a mirror will for Freddy. 'All done. You can sign them now with Grace-Mary as a witness if you like.'

'Is that it?' Ellen said. 'There wasn't much to it, was there?'

'What you don't see,' I said, 'is the hours of work I've done beforehand, tailoring this legal document to your specific requirements. This here...' I tapped the computer screen. 'This is years of university studies and legal experience condensed into a few pages.' I emailed the will through to Grace-Mary for her to print off. A few minutes later, when I was wondering what was taking so long, Grace-Mary walked in and put the document on my desk. 'Can you squeeze in another appointment?'

'When?'

'Now. Mr Turpie phoned to say he was on his way, so I'm guessing he'll be here any moment.'

Jake wasn't a man to follow the normal rules of professional etiquette such as making appointments or even checking into reception when he arrived. He'd barge straight into my office and let any other client with whom I might be engaged take the hint that it was time for them to leave. He would only have phoned to make sure I was in.

When Freddy heard the news of Jake's imminent arrival, he jumped out of his seat like it had been plugged

into the mains. He pushed past Grace-Mary and out of the door. 'I'll call you!' His yell was swiftly followed by the sound of clattering feet on the stone steps to the front door. I went to the window and saw him exit the close, turn left and try to blend in with those few pedestrians on the High Street. He had only walked twenty metres or so when a familiarly grubby Transit van pulled up on the double-yellows outside.

'I'll leave you to it,' Grace-Mary said, making a tactical withdrawal to reception.

Seconds later Jake marched into my office clad in his usual oil-stained boiler suit and steelies and smelling strongly of eau de diesel oil. He was about to say something when he noticed my remaining client and came to an abrupt halt. 'Ellen?'

'Hello Jake.'

'What are you doing here?'

I was about to tell him it was none of his business, but Ellen was in first. 'I'm seeing my lawyer about something.' Jake could probably have worked that one out for himself, but he seemed satisfied by the answer, subdued by it almost. 'All right then. I'll...away and leave you to it.' He backed towards the door, pointing at me. 'I'll see you later, Robbie,' he said, almost politely and was gone.

'What just happened?' I asked.

Ellen joined me at the window and we both stared down at the street where Jake was climbing back into the white van. With the rattle of a dodgy exhaust it pulled out into traffic and headed east.

'Me and Jake go back a long way,' she said. 'What do you think he wanted?'

'Does Jake know that Freddy's in Scotland?'

'Not unless you've told him,' she said.

I hadn't, though maybe I'd raised his suspicions. Anyway, back to business. I asked Grace-Mary to come through, and after Ellen had signed the will on each page my secretary adhibited her own signature on the last.

'I'll take this and put a testing clause on it,' Grace-Mary said. 'Would you like me to send you out a copy, Mrs Fletcher?'

Ellen didn't think it necessary. 'How much do I owe you?' she asked, opening her big, pink handbag once Grace-Mary had left. 'For the wills and for bringing Freddy back?'

I looked at her. Hard to think that she'd be dead inside three months. Fifty thousand pounds wasn't a big lottery win. Not if you needed the money to fulfil your bucket list and had chosen to spend your last weeks in a suite at a five-star hotel.

'Joanna and I had a nice time in Prague,' I said. 'Let's call it quits.'

Ellen shrugged. She stood up and I walked her to the door, where she turned to face me. 'If Freddy stays alive long enough for you to see him again, tell him I'm alive too, and that I want him to pay me some attention.' She smiled bravely. 'Tell him I still have enough strength to tear up a will. That should do it.'

23

Freddy was in touch a lot sooner than expected. I was on the High Street, locking the front door to the office, when he appeared from under a bus shelter and fell in beside me as I walked to my car.

'I need to tell you something,' he said.

My car was parked outside Sandy's café. I suggested we go in there to talk.

'No, too many eyes. I'd feel a lot safer if we went for a drive.'

It was only the back of five. If I went home too early I might be roped into making the tea. 'Where are you staying?' I asked. He didn't answer. 'I don't need an address. How about we start with a town or a city or even a point on the compass?'

'East,' he said. 'Edinburgh.'

'I'll drop you at the West End, Haymarket or somewhere around there,' I told him, once we were in the car and I was trying to find a gap in the traffic to squeeze into. 'That should give you plenty of time to tell me whatever it is you think I should know.'

Freddy acquiesced with a shrug and a grunt. We were onto the M90 east-bound before he communicated again. 'I want to go back to Prague.'

'You can't.'

'Who's going to stop me?'

'No-one. By all means, catch the next flight. The turn off for Edinburgh airport is only a few miles further down the road, but be aware it's not what Ellen wants and it's not hard to change a will.'

'I've been thinking about that. I'm her husband. I'll still get something when she dies. I know my rights.'

Freddy had obviously been reading up on the law. Not a good idea if he'd been doing it via the Internet, where a distinction between English and Scots law was seldom made.

'It's true, you might get something. Or, then again, you might not,' I said.

'I'd be entitled to half her lottery money for a start.'

'I've got some bad news for you, Freddy. Ellen never won the lottery. Well, she did but not half a million.'

'How much?'

'Fifty grand.'

'What!'

'And I'm guessing she's spent most of it or she will do over the next few months.'

Freddy bashed the dash with a fist and threw himself back in his seat. 'I knew it. All that nonsense about leaving me half a million.'

'Oh, she's going to leave you the money.'

'How's that, then?'

'Life insurance.'

'She's insured?'

'Not yet. But she intends to be. The policy will be valueless until Ellen dies and only worth anything to you if she doesn't stop paying the premiums or assign it to someone else.'

'Like who?'

'Like a charity.'

'Or her favourite lawyer?'

'Let's just say there are plenty of ways she can make sure you go back to Prague with nothing but a bottle of duty-free whisky and some Edinburgh rock.'

'And you're going to tell me what I should do, are you?' I took the slip road at the Newbridge roundabout, hoping that from my failure to reply Freddy would reasonably infer that I didn't care that much what he did.

He pulled out a pack of cigarettes. 'Mind if I smoke?' I did.

He knocked a cigarette out of the pack onto his hand and placed it between his lips.

'No, really,' I said. 'Don't smoke. I don't like it.'

With a show of effort Freddy returned the cigarette to the pack. 'What am I supposed to do?'

'You'll just have to wait until I drop you off.'

'No, I mean about Ellen. Listen, Robbie, you're a man of the world. You don't think I've spent all that time abroad without attracting some interest from the opposite sex, do you?'

It wasn't a problem I'd been wrestling with. Freddy was a middle-aged man with odd facial hair, a weird taste in clothes, and who made a living selling fridge magnets on a bridge. I didn't think it impossible that the women-folk of the Czech Republic might have found the necessary willpower to resist.

'I've a woman. We live on the outskirts of Prague. I can't just leave her to fend for herself while I wait months for Ellen to die. What if she drags it out?'

'Drags it out? Drags out dying?' I pulled in at the side of the road and switched on my emergency indicators. We had just passed the turn-off for Edinburgh Airport and were nearly at Gogarburn Golf

135

Club. 'You know what, Freddy? I think this is far enough. You want my advice? Stay in Scotland. Pay attention to Ellen, who is still your wife after all, make her last days happy and collect your money. Alternatively, and personally I'd prefer it if you did this, bugger off back to Prague and I'll make sure that every last penny Ellen leaves goes to the nearest orphanage.'

'And if I stay, what happens if Jake catches up with me? That was a near miss today. If I'm seen strolling around with Ellen he's bound to find out.'

'Freddy, I'm not your life coach. You've got a tough decision to make, and only yourself to blame. What made you con Jake Turpie of all people? I thought you grifters researched your marks before pulling a stroke. It wouldn't have taken much investigation to realise that Jake wasn't a man to forgive and forget and chalk the loss of a hundred and fifty thousand pounds down to experience.'

'He didn't lose a hundred and fifty grand. He got a cottage out of it.' Freddy reached for his cigarettes again and then remembered my no smoking policy.

'That's not the way he sees it.'

'Would you believe I never intended to roll Jake?'

'Come off it.'

'You don't even know what happened.'

'Yes I do. Jake told me. You talked him into buying a piece of land and received a whacking great finder's fee after telling him it was suitable for development.'

'That's how Jake sees it.'

'What other way is there to see it?'

'The correct way.'

I switched off the emergency indicators. This I had

to hear. 'Okay, I'm dropping you off in Corstorphine, but no further. You can make your way back to wherever you're going from there.' I pulled out into traffic again. 'So what is the correct way to look at it?'

Freddy produced the pack of cigarettes again, pulled one out and held it up to me.

'All right, but open a window,' I said.

He lit up and took a deep drag. Blue smoke curled up his nostrils. 'It's like this. The head of the planning department owed me a favour. She tipped me off about a mix-up that meant the land was no longer green belt. It was just sitting there ready for someone to build houses on it. I told Jake my idea of tricking the old guy who owned the place.'

'You mean your uncle?' Freddy smiled. 'You got me.'

'Any chance you could just tell me the truth?'

Freddy thought about that as though it were an interesting concept he'd never considered before.

I had no time to tip-toe through his tulip field of lies. 'So long story short, you conned Jake and left for the Czech Republic taking his money. Why not take Ellen with you?'

In reply, Freddy drew on the cigarette and flicked ash out of the window.

'You could have contacted her,' I said. 'Let her know what was going on, given her the chance of joining you in Prague. You've made a good enough job of staying hidden. What was Jake going to do? He gets a nose bleed if he leaves West Lothian.'

Freddy sucked in more smoke and studied the glowing end of his cigarette. 'If I tell you something you promise you won't mention it to Ellen? Ever?'

I promised. I didn't expect to see Ellen again.

'My woman in Prague didn't always live there. She came with me from here.'

'From Scotland?' He nodded.

'You're telling me that you ripped off Jake Turpie so that you could make a new life for yourself in Prague with some other woman?'

Freddy took two rapid puffs and pinged what was left out onto the A8. 'So, you see, taking Ellen with me was the one thing I couldn't do.'

24

Hugh Ogilvie was a man who liked to smile every morning just to get it out of the way. It seemed I was to be the victim of his grin for the day.

'I've got some good news for you.'

Words I'd never heard him say before. We were standing in the corridor outside Sheriff Brechin's chambers. What exactly the good news might be I'd have to wait to find out, because just then the door opened and Eleanor, the Sheriff Clerk, ushered us in for the adjustment hearing on Heather Somerville's appeal.

Summary appeals were dealt with by a process known as Stated Case, probably the most inefficient and unfair method of reviewing a possible miscarriage of justice ever invented. With no audio or video record of the evidence, everything was based on the presiding Sheriff's recollection of the evidence, and some sheriffs were excellent at re-writing history to suit their verdict. After Heather Somerville's stated case was finalised, it would be signed and sent to the Appeal Court for consideration. If it was thought to have merit, a date would be fixed for a formal hearing. I wasn't keeping a space free in my diary.

We were shown to a couple of chairs in front of the Sheriff's desk, Ogilvie smiling smugly as Brechin poured scorn on each of my proposed adjustments. Since the only argument I could put forward was Bert Brechin's unreasonableness in rejecting the notion that a wee girl slapping her big boyfriend was too trivial a matter for the law of Scotland to concern itself with, I'd not anticipated a hearty welcome; however, the temperature in the room was a few degrees cooler than expected, and our backsides hadn't warmed the seats before we were out in the corridor once again, where Hugh Ogilvie was still exercising those under-developed smile muscles of his.

'Well, are you going to tell me this good news?' I asked.

'Buy me a cup of tea first.'

Buy the Procurator Fiscal a cup of tea? I'd thought about pouring a hot drink over his head many a time, but pay for one and let him drink it? 'You know, Hugh...' I said, after the several seconds it took my brain to accommodate the suggestion, 'I think I'll have to decline. I wouldn't like to leave you open to accusations of accepting bribes.'

He tugged me by the arm. 'I'll take my chances. Now, do you want to hear the good news or not?'

'Teaspoon? Or am I supposed to rely on Brownian motion?' Ogilvie enquired, when I brought one mug of coffee, a cup of tea and a tiny jug of milk back to the round metal table where he was making himself comfortable.

'This good news really better be brilliant news,' I said on my next return from the counter, rattling a teaspoon into his saucer.

'Did they run out of biscuits?'

'You're in training for a half-marathon, remember?' I said. 'Now, let's have it, what's the good news?'

Ogilvie poured milk into his tea and watched it swirl

around, before giving it a stir. 'Antonia Brechin,' he said, taking a sip.

'What about her.'

'A decision has been made to drop the possession charge.'

Perhaps he did deserve a chocolate biscuit. 'I thought you told me you couldn't do that.'

'I couldn't. It wasn't my decision.'

'Whose was it?'

'Because the three accused are trainee-solicitors, the case should have been run past Crown counsel before I marked it for prosecution.' Ogilvie drank some more milky tea. 'When someone on high heard about it, they called for the papers to be sent through to Edinburgh to be reviewed there.'

I could hardly believe it. Someone in Crown Office had done Brechin a good turn, either an old pal doing him a favour or a new one looking to be owed one. I didn't care. A touch of spin here and there and I'd be modestly accepting all the credit from my client and her mum, along with payment of a fee note that reflected such a great success.

We were drinking our drinks and discussing the case and other matters in an almost civil manner, when I became aware of a shadow looming over me. It was Gail Paton looking decidedly unhappy about something.

'Does Gail know the good news?' I asked Ogilvie. 'Oh, I know all right,' Gail said. She slapped a familiar type of document down on the table beside my almost empty coffee mug. It was a service-copy indictment.

Ogilvie knocked back the last of his tea and stood

up. 'Well, thanks for the cuppa, Robbie...'

I picked up the papers and read: 'Her Majesty's Advocate against...Antonia Brechin!'

'Yes,' Ogilvie said. 'Sorry about that. I gave you the good news, and never got around to telling you the bad. Anyway, Miss Paton will fill you in on the details, got to dash.'

By the look on Gail's face, she was going to fill me in all right. I flicked to the next page. The charge was similar to the previous one, except now the allegation of possession of cocaine had been altered by the addition of the words 'with intent to supply.' We'd gone from a contravention of section 5(2) to a breach of 5(3). It was a minor amendment with major consequences.

Gail snatched the indictment from me and made as though to hit me over the head with it. 'I told you we should have pled guilty. Now we're looking at a jury trial and a solemn conviction. That's definitely striking-off material for our clients. Maybe even the jail. Meanwhile young Andy's client gets a slap on the wrist for simple possession and brownie points for pleading at the earliest opportunity.'

No wonder Brechin had been even more frozen-faced than usual. What would my client say? I'd gone against her express instructions to plead guilty. Even worse, what would Joanna say?

'Well?' Gail demanded. She sat down opposite me in the seat vacated by the PF. 'Any more bright ideas? While you're thinking one up, I'll have a milky coffee and a KitKat.'

'It's easily fixed,' I said on my return, bearing Gail's refreshments. A few minutes standing in the queue was all it had taken for me to come up with a cunning plan.

It was a gift I had. 'We go to trial and get Andy's client to give evidence and say the drugs were hers. She's bomb-proof. The Crown has accepted her guilty plea to simple possession, it's too late to amend it to an intent to supply charge for her.'

Gail thought that over as she dunked a chocolate finger into her coffee and took a bite out of it. 'She'll never go for it.'

'Of course she will. They're all pals, aren't they? Three girls who share a flat, chat about boys, discuss colours of nail varnish, share clothes, they probably have bedtime pillow fights when no-one's looking.'

'Perhaps in your feverish imaginings, Robbie.' Gail wiped crumbs from her lipstick. 'But I reckon there's about as much chance of Andy's client taking all the blame as there is of her climbing into a wee frilly nightie and beating her co-accused about the head with a sack full of feathers.'

I dismissed her fears almost as quickly as I nicked one of her KitKat fingers. 'I doubt very much if Andy's client will need to go anywhere near the witness box. As soon as the Crown gets word of what's going to happen, they'll pull the plug on the whole proceedings. Why go to the expense of a jury trial when the result is a foregone conclusion? Waste of time if they've already got a guilty plea from Andy's client, even if it's only to possession.'

Gail carried out the same old routine with her next piece of KitKat and washed it down with another gulp of coffee. She looked at her watch. 'Got to go, I've a case calling in five minutes. Who's going to speak to Andy about this?'

'Leave it to me,' I said. 'I'll charge through to

143

Edinburgh and have a face to face with him.'

Gail stood. She looked marginally happier than she had previously, although that may have been down to the chocolate rather than her faith in me to resolve matters for our respective clients.

'Do that,' she said. 'I want some kind of a game plan in place before I present my client with this.' She folded the copy indictment lengthways and flapped it in my face. 'Don't worry,' I said. 'Leave everything to me. Andy's my former trainee. I taught him everything he knows.

He'd do anything for me.'

25

'Not a chance, Robbie.'

I'd had Grace-Mary track down Andy's new employers. The Linkwood Rattray Law Group operated from several floors of glass and steel up at Quartermile. It looked like the sort of place that had an employee dress code, made sure no-one left the building until they'd squeezed every second out of every billable hour and bought lots of tables at legal awards dinners.

Andy agreed to meet me over lunch, something he was in the habit of eating al fresco, and well away from his office. Or maybe that was only when his old boss came a calling. We bought sandwiches at a nearby delicatessen and took them for a stroll in The Meadows, a large green space that was good for picnics, dog walking and impromptu games of football during the day, and an excellent place to get mugged at night.

'If you think I'm going to ask my client to stand up in court and take the rap for this, you've got a second think coming,' Andy added, for the avoidance of doubt.

We paused the conversation to take bites from our sandwiches. Mine was Italian meatball. It tasted just like any other meatball sandwich to me, but I supposed there was only so much a cook could do with ball-shaped meat no matter from which country it was said to originate.

Unlike my relatively simple sandwich, Andy had taken an option that contained way too many fillings.

He jumped back, stomach arched, as a red, slimy object slid out and splatted onto the path.

'What I don't get is that you actually think I'd sell out my client,' he said, kicking the fallen foodstuff into the grass at the side, in case the woman heading towards us pushing a pram hit it and went into an uncontrolled skid.

'Oh, I see,' I said. 'This is the gratitude I get? I take the boy off the street, teach him everything I know, release him into the world of...what is it you do here?'

'We call it the law, Robbie. You should try it sometime. And if there is one thing you did teach me, it was never to sell out a client. "Always do what you think is best for the client and never mind what anyone else says." That's what you told me.'

It certainly sounded like me, but I would have been talking about not selling out Munro & Co. clients. Andy didn't work for me anymore. I didn't mind him selling out other people's clients if it helped mine.

'It's not a case of selling anyone out, Andy. Your client has pled guilty. No-one can change that, not even the Crown, that's what's so beautiful about this arrangement. Everyone's a winner. Your client will still have the benefit of her early plea, all she has to do is go into the witness box and say the cocaine was hers and that the others had nothing to do with it.'

'But that wouldn't be the truth.' Some things never changed about Andy.

'The truth? That's what you're worried about? This is the law. What is—'

'Don't bother giving me your Pontius Pilate, quid est veritas? speech, Robbie. The truth is the truth.'

'Okay, let's suppose it is.'

'How can we suppose it isn't?'

'Would you shut up for a moment and listen? What does the truth matter?' Andy almost dropped the rest of his sandwich. I waited for him to reassemble it before continuing. 'In the general context of this case, who cares what the truth is? These girls were going to have a party with some recreational drugs. They weren't planning to blow up Linlithgow Palace.'

'You say recreational drugs, Robbie, I say cocaine: a class A controlled substance that's illegal to possess in this country.'

'And don't you think all three girls have learned their lesson? Why does my client have to lose her career over it? Has it made her any worse a lawyer? Don't you think there are High Court judges who know how to roll a five-skin spliff or snort a line of coke occasionally?'

'If you do the crime, you do the time.'

'You mean if you get caught doing the crime.'

'Okay, maybe I do. Maybe lawyers who are stupid enough to get caught aren't smart enough to be lawyers and should take the consequences.'

'I know you don't mean that,' I said. 'The consequences for Antonia Brechin far outweigh the crime.'

'Drugs are harmful.'

'So are rugby, hillwalking and drawing cartoons of prophets.'

'And you're all for the legalisation of drugs are you, Robbie?'

I munched thoughtfully on a bite of meatball sandwich.

'I don't think I could afford the downturn in

business.'

'Money. Is that the only reason?'

'Well, there are all those drug enforcement officers. They'd lose their jobs. And what about the gangsters in organised crime? The ones who keep the retail economy alive? Who's going to buy all the bling and fast cars if there's no drug money to throw about?'

'If you're not going to take this conversation seriously, there's no point in discussing it any further,' Andy said, taking another tentative nibble.

I came to a halt at a green iron bench, polished off the final portion of bread and meatball, wiped my mouth with the paper wrapper and tossed it into a nearby waste bucket.

'Sit down,' I said, and we did. 'I didn't come here for a debate on the war on drugs. I came here to ask you to persuade your client...What's her name again?'

'Freya. Freya Linkwood.'

'Well, why can't Freya, who has already pled guilty on your advice, do her pals a favour? What difference will it make to her?'

Andy was still struggling with his sandwich. If I'd thought keeping meatballs in situ between two slices of bread was tricky, goats cheese, sun-dried tomato, roasted peppers, pesto, rocket and olives took things to a whole different level. Eventually he gave up. After one final swift bite, he dropped what was left into the bucket. Chewing, he looked at his watch, then up at me and swallowed. 'This is not about saving your client's career, is it? This is about saving your own skin.'

I cracked open a can of Irn Bru, took a swig, nearly stifled a burp, and pretended not to understand.

'You should have pled guilty to the lesser charge

when you had the chance, Robbie. I heard your client tell you to plead when she was in the dock, but you ignored her direct instructions. Now if she's done for dealing drugs, and struck off by the Law Society or, worse, sent to prison, who do you think will be to blame for that?' He twisted the top off a plastic bottle of mineral water. 'It's as clear-cut a case of defective representation as I've ever heard of.'

I was beginning to wish he hadn't finished his messy sandwich, because I could have taken it from him and rubbed it in his hair. 'The decision to plead not guilty was tactical and based on my legal expertise and experience of court practice and procedure. What's the point of hiring a defence lawyer if you're not going to follow his advice?'

'Even if that advice is hopelessly misguided?'

My tactics were only misguided because Andy had refused to let his client play ball. If all three girls had hung tough the Crown would have had major problems attributing blame. I tried a smile. The friendly approach was more likely to succeed than would a war of words. 'Andy, listen to me. If your girl—'

'Freya.'

'How hard would it be for her to say the stuff was hers and that the others knew nothing about it? I'll bet she wouldn't even need to give evidence. All you have to do is provide me with an affidavit. I'll run it past the Crown and they'll probably ditch the whole thing in five seconds flat.'

Andy's mumbled reply was drowned by an almost simultaneous swig from his plastic bottle.

'Sorry, I didn't catch that.'

He took another drink and screwed the cap back on

tight. 'The Crown has already asked Freya to give an affidavit.'

I felt the retreating Italian meatballs threaten to about- turn in my stomach and mount an attack on my throat. 'Saying what?'

'That Freya knew about the cocaine in the flat, and so was technically guilty of possession, but that Antonia Brechin was the buyer and was intending to supply it.'

I slumped, shoulder blades thumping against the bench's metal-slatted backrest, and gazed up through the crooked branches of an ancient elm tree into a sky that was clouding over about as fast as Antonia Brechin's hopes of a legal career. 'I don't understand. Why would you do such a thing?'

Andy was up on his feet again, staring down at me. 'Because it's the truth.'

'Don't give me that. The truth is that you're sticking the knife into my client, probably because of all the hard times Bert Brechin used to give you in court when you were training. You need to remember that it's not him who's going to be booted out of the law, it's his granddaughter.'

'Is that what you really think?' Andy turned and started walking back the way we'd come. 'Have you any idea who Freya's father is?' he asked, once I'd caught up with him.

I knew that, mythologically speaking, Freya was a Norse goddess.

'He's Russell Linkwood, the senior partner of The Linkwood Rattray Law Group.'

'He's not Odin, ruler of Asgard, then?'

'Njördr was Freya's father in Norse mythology, but

Russell Linkwood might as well be a god so far as my future career is concerned. When his daughter was arrested, he didn't know what to do other than he wanted the whole thing dealt with in-house, and with as little publicity as possible. It turns out that of the hundreds of lawyers he has working for him, I'm the only one who's actually appeared in a criminal court.'

'Another thing you have to thank me for,' I said. 'Yeah.' He held up the bottle of water. 'Cheers.'

'So you're under a little pressure,' I said, while he took a drink. 'I can understand that.'

'A little pressure!' he spluttered.

'Yes, but it's no excuse to have your client grass on her mates.'

Andy replaced the cap on the bottle and gave it a final tap with the flat of his hand. 'She's giving an affidavit to the Crown, Robbie, whether you like it or not. And if she is called to the witness box, her evidence will be entirely in keeping with it. If not, she'll be guilty of perjury, one way or another.'

'Thanks, Andy, I know how it works. What's the deal?'

'What do you mean?'

'She must be getting something in return. You're not telling me she's going to swear an affidavit that sticks her friends right in it without expecting something in return.'

Andy cleared his throat and looked straight ahead. 'If the case goes well...'

'You mean if her friends are convicted?'

'Freya will be given a letter from the Lord Advocate's office saying that she fully co-operated with the Crown.'

'And I suppose that will iron out any little wrinkles she may later have with the Solicitors Disciplinary Tribunal?'

'Combined with her early plea of guilty, yes. And before you say anything, don't blame me for getting the best possible result for my client.'

'No, Andy, there was a better possible result.'

'Try for a not guilty?'

'There were three girls in that flat. Who was to say who was really to blame?'

'Every snowflake? Too risky. Do you know what I do at Linkwood Rattray, at least when I'm not being forced to roll around in the dirt of the Sheriff Court? Alternative dispute resolution, that's what. And if I've learned anything from my time spent mediating, it's this - never take risks. There is always a safer middle ground.'

And perhaps he was right. Maybe there was an easier, less risky way. But where was the fun in that?

26

Joanna was late home that evening and caught me in the kitchen slaving over a hot stove. Before they'd gone into the garden to continue construction of the world's largest rabbit hutch, I'd served Tina and my dad fish fingers, boiled potatoes and peas. Now I was in the process of creating a Spanish omelette using my daughter's untouched vegetables.

Joanna slapped my backside and gave one of my bum cheeks a squeeze. 'That's what I like to see, my man in the kitchen making me nice things to eat.' She stared down into the bowl I was stirring. 'Is it supposed to look like that?' She gave me a kiss on one of my higher-up cheeks. 'I was on the phone to my dad at lunch time. Do you want to hear the good news?'

'Is it going to be followed by bad news?' I asked.

'How did you know?'

'It's been one of those good news, terrible news days.'

'Tell me yours,' she said.

'No, you first.'

'All right. The good news is that we've got detailed planning permission for our new house.'

'And the bad?'

'It's going to cost at least three hundred thousand pounds to build.'

'Three hundred thousand! How can it possibly cost three hundred thousand pounds? I've seen the plans.

It's a three-bedroom cottage, it's not the Taj Mahal.'

Joanna left to take off her coat. 'And that's not counting all the work my dad and his men would do for free,' she said on her return. 'The Council want a new private access road put in. They say that your dad's service road is inadequate if there's going to be more than one car coming in and out onto an unclassified road that's near to a bend. Then there's the drainage system and water supply, they both need to be completely upgraded and new pipes laid, and there's also a problem with the electricity. They were going to take a spur off your dad's supply, but that's not going to be good enough for Scottish Energy. I think they'd prefer it if we installed our own nuclear power station and linked it up to the National Grid.'

I was glad Joanna could still see the funny side of things. The thought of an indefinite spell living in my dad's back pocket wasn't a pleasant one.

I poured the eggy mixture into a sizzling hot frying pan. Joanna sat down at the table and propped her head on the heel of a hand. 'What are we going to do? I'll never get a mortgage that size on a PF depute's salary and as for you...'

'I know, I know.' A self-employed, Legal Aid lawyer with an overdraft, looking to build his own house in the country, wasn't the sort of business the banks were after. 'What if we asked my dad to extend this place? He could add a couple of rooms and give us all a bit more space.'

'This is no time for sick jokes,' Joanna said. 'Anyway, what's your good news, bad news story?'

'It'll wait. Let's eat first,' I said, prising the edges of the omelette up around the circumference, letting the uncooked egg flow underneath.

'No, it can't be that bad. Come on, tell me now.'

'It's to do with Antonia Brechin's case.'

'What about it?'

'They've dropped the summary complaint.'

'Okay, that's good news. And the bad?'

'They've amended the charge to intent to supply and put her on an indictment.'

'I see.' Joanna left it at that.

I took the frying pan off the hob and stuck it under the grill to finish off with some slices of cheese on top. After that I dished it up and had just taken my first mouthful, when Tina crashed through the back door. 'The hutch is finished!'

The hutch and the promised acquisition of a rabbit were the result of two previous pet disasters. First there had been Goldie the goldfish, who'd contracted an ailment so severe that even a teaspoonful of single malt to the gills couldn't resuscitate it, followed shortly thereafter by Hammy the hamster, who my dad had put outside for a breath of fresh air, forgotten about and found the next morning, ice-welded to the bars of its cage after a shower of rain and a particularly sharp frost.

'Do you see this, Tina?' my dad said, clumping into the kitchen and setting a collection of tools down on the draining board. 'Your dad makes us do with fishy fingers, boiled spuds and peas while he dines on only the finest...' He came over to the table, looked at my plate and recoiled. 'What is that thing?'

It was true the omelette had neither folded over properly nor slid off the frying pan quite how I'd intended, still, I felt it was vaguely discernible as a

155

Spanish omelette. 'An omelette, eh? They tell me they're not all they're cracked up to be,' he said, and Tina joined in enthusiastically with her grandpa's uproarious laughter, not sure what was so funny and not caring. 'We've put the roof on the hutch and now we're going to Sandy's for ice cream to celebrate.'

'Sit down and have a break, Alex,' Joanna said. 'Robbie, your dad's bound to be tired looking after Tina all day. Why don't you and her go and get us all ice cream?'

Joanna was either being considerate to my old man or intent on disposing of her share of the omelette in my absence. I noticed she hadn't actually eaten any of it yet, just given it a tour of her plate. Whichever, no sooner had I finished my meal than I was bundled into the car along with my daughter. Half a mile or so down the road the red oil light on the dashboard came on. I pulled into the side.

'What's the matter, Dad?'

'The car's run out of oil and I don't want to drive any further in case it breaks the engine.'

Tina was keen to see what an engine looked like, so I popped the bonnet and let her peer inside while I phoned Jake Turpie to have him send someone with a tin of oil. Jake always expected me to be available when one of his mob was lifted, which they were, frequently, and usually at very unsociable hours, so I saw no reason why he shouldn't reciprocate; nonetheless, I was surprised when the man himself turned up in a tow truck ten minutes later.

'It's knackered,' he said, after a couple of seconds under the bonnet. 'It's probably been pissing oil for days.'

'Has it, Dad?' Tina asked. 'Has it been pissing oil for days?'

'Try not to be quite so technical in front of my daughter, Jake,' I said, not replying to Tina's question and hoping she'd just forget the word, or think it was something to do with car engines and not bring it up a lot during polite conversation. 'What's wrong with it?'

Jake looked up into the sky that had started to spit rain. 'You really want me to tell you?'

'It might help.'

Actually, it didn't. Piston rings and valves I'd heard of. By the time he'd gone on to crankshaft case covers, I was beginning to wonder if he was taking the Mickey and making up names. 'I see. Sounds like it's definitely knackered, then,' I said, once he'd explained his diagnosis. I helped him connect my car to the tow truck and we drove back to his yard, Tina sitting between us, high up in the cab and enjoying every minute of it.

By sheer coincidence, or more likely not, a certain green BMW was waiting for us, sitting front and centre on the Tarmac forecourt. Jake slapped its off-side wing. 'Three grand and she's yours.'

I needed a car for work. I could ask Joanna to take the train now that she was working in Falkirk, but that would mean me driving her pride and joy Mercedes SL. The thing was a flying machine. I'd have no licence by the end of the month. Jake sensed my hesitation. 'I'll throw in a set of car mats. Nearly new. Well, nearly, nearly new.'

'Okay,' I said, taking a grip of Jake's oil-stained hand.

'Two and a half, it is.'

Jake squeezed. 'It's three, and I'll take your motor

for scrap too.'

We left Tina outside while I went into Jake's HQ to fill out some paperwork. Jake's previous guard dog, whose life's ambition it had always been to tear off one of my legs and gnaw on the juicy end, had gone. The replacement was little more than a puppy, of equally ambiguous parentage, but seemingly a lot less homicidal. It took a shine to Tina from the word go, wriggling about on its back, tongue lolling wildly while she rubbed its stomach. 'That daft wee dug's way too friendly with folk,' Jake said. 'I'll need to knock that out of it.'

'What happened to the old one?'

'It got a big lump on its neck and I had to put it down.' I noted he didn't say he'd had it put down. No, I fancied Jake would have saved on veterinary fees and self-prescribed the application of a length of scaffolding pole to the skull. 'Done all right though. Lasted me ten years. Good animal. This new one's too soft. I'm going to need to learn it a few lessons.'

I didn't like to think how you transformed a friendly, child-loving puppy into an irritable, human-hating, hellhound. Knowing Jake, I assumed it involved a regime short on rations and long on beatings. Judging by the way this wee dog was happily bouncing about trying to lick Tina's face, it was a slow learner.

Deal done, no money was exchanged for the car. Jake knew I knew what happened to people who bumped him. That was what made me think back to Freddy's visit and his sharp exit from my office at the mention of Jake's imminent arrival.

'Why were you at my office yesterday?' I asked, once the logbook was signed over to me.

158

'Oh, aye,' he said. 'I nearly forgot. I was coming to see you about this.' He pulled open a drawer and took out a summary complaint made out to his foreman, credit-controller and resident-bone-breaker, Derek Pudney. Big Deek collected criminal charges like Jake's late-payers collected compound fractures. 'Take care of that, will you?'

I turned the page and read the libel, a straightforward enough charge of assault. The chances of any witnesses turning up for the trial weren't good. The chance of any witnesses who did turn up, speaking up, even worse. I told Jake I'd take care of it and enter a plea of not guilty at the first calling. Deek didn't need to appear. We walked down the steps together.

'What was Ellen Fletcher seeing you about?' he asked. Telling Jake that it was a confidential solicitor/client discussion and, therefore, none of his business, wouldn't have stopped him wanting to know. Even though I'd washed my hands of Ellen's life insurance scam, I did feel sorry for her and thought I'd try and use Jake's query to her advantage. 'She came to see me about Freddy.'

'You still think I killed him?'

'I know you didn't.'

'How's that?'

'Because he's alive.'

'You've seen him?'

'Before you start, I don't know where he is. You asked me why Ellen came to see me. She came because she's scared.'

'Scared of what?'

'Scared of you.'

'Ellen's scared of me?'

'Scared for Freddy. She thinks you'll do him harm.'

'Well, she's right. I will.' Jake hunkered down beside his mutt to unhook the chain that was a lot sturdier than the wooden railing to which it was attached. He gave the end to Tina. 'Take it for a walk while I talk to your dad.'

'What's its name?' Tina asked.

Jake didn't have an answer for that.

'It's not a pet. It's a guard dog,' I told her. 'It's here to keep all the bad men away.'

'Aye,' Jake said, 'you know, like a bouncer outside a nightclub,' as though, after her warm milk and bedtime story, my five-year-old daughter liked to climb out of the window and go clubbing.

Still, it was a good enough answer for Tina. 'Come on, Bouncer,' she yelled, and the three of us set off down an avenue of crushed vehicles, Jake's trainee guard dog leading the way, tugging my daughter after it.

'Freddy Fletcher owes me a lot of money,' Jake said, as though I was unaware of the situation.

'I know. That's why he's been living abroad. Ellen wants you to cut him a break. He'll only be here for a few months at most and then he'll be gone for good. Call it a truce.'

Jake said nothing, and we continued tramping our way along a path of orange shale punctuated by potholes filled either with muddy water or a shovelful of grey hard core. When we'd reached the end of the path it opened out into a large, irregular area of waste ground enclosed by a dishevelled perimeter of gorse bushes. Clumps of scrub grass and thistles fought through the hard ground and tangles of weeds

160

wrapped themselves around scattered piles of discarded metal objects, corroded beyond recognition. Jake whistled through his teeth and the dog bounded towards us, dragging Tina along. He released the chain from around its neck, picked up an old wooden chair leg that had teeth marks along its length and threw it. The dog scampered off. 'You give it a try,' he said. Tina didn't have to be asked twice and charged off after the animal.

'Call Freddy's visit compassionate leave,' I said, still trying to think of ways to sell Jake the novel idea of not killing the man who'd conned him.

'Why do you care so much about what happens to Freddy?'

'It's not just him...It's Ellen.'

'What about her?'

It was easily forty-five minutes since I'd left home for ice cream. I hadn't brought my mobile phone and Joanna and my dad would be wondering where we'd got to. Meanwhile Tina was running around shards of rusty metal, chasing after a scrapyard mutt. I'd be lucky to get her home without stopping off at A&E for a tetanus jab.

'Ellen's not well,' I said.

'How do you mean? What's Ellen not being well got to do with Freddy?'

There was what I could only describe as a note of concern in Jake's voice. It took me by surprise, as did his firm grip on a left bicep that hadn't fully recovered from the curls it had been forced to endure during my recent trip to the gym.

'She's got cancer, Jake. Is it too much to ask that she gets to spend her last few weeks with Freddy without you—'

'Weeks!'

'Three months, she says.'

'Ellen's dying?' Jake looked at me bewildered, uncomprehending. Were those tears welling up in his eyes? The grip on my arm loosened as his face paled. He lowered his head and stared at the ground. 'She can't be dying.' It was an emotional side of Jake I'd never witnessed before. I thought about maybe giving him a comforting pat on the back, and had decided against it when he looked up at me, face contorted, less in grief than in anger. He grabbed hold of the front of my shirt. 'I lent her fifty grand. How am I going to get it back?'

27

'Dad's car has been pissing oil for days and so he had to buy a new one,' was how Tina explained our delayed return. The ice cream probably helped, but Joanna was surprisingly fine about me lashing out three thousand on a car when we were busy saving to live somewhere, anywhere, that wasn't already occupied by my dad. I was pleased about that and yet at the same time worried that it suggested she had given up on our plans to build a cottage.

I left her and my dad discussing Tina's growing vocabulary while I whisked the girl off for a bedtime story. By the time I was back in the living room, the old man was already asleep in his armchair, an empty whisky tumbler held loosely in his right hand.

It was a lovely evening so Joanna and I went for a walk that took us down past the proposed site of our new home. The air was still and warm, the only sounds breaking the silence the distant rumble of trains on the Edinburgh to Glasgow line and the cooing of wood pigeons.

Two lawyers out for a stroll: it was difficult not to talk about work. Inevitably the subject of Antonia Brechin came up.

'I don't know why you're so bothered,' I said. 'There are plenty of other victims of the criminal justice system requiring your sympathy. Antonia has only got herself to blame for the mess she's in.'

Joanna didn't reply at first, but I knew she was going to. 'Except...'

'Except what?'

'Except the mess she's in now didn't have to be quite so messy. Did it?'

'How was I to know the Crown would upgrade the charge?'

Joanna took my hand in hers. 'You weren't, but you did know that she told you to plead guilty when the charge was only for simple possession. I'm more worried about you than I am about her. What if she makes a complaint of defective legal representation?'

I didn't say anything. The thought had crossed my mind more than once since Andy had raised the subject.

'The way I see it, you've got two choices,' Joanna said. 'One, you withdraw from acting...'

'From which it could be inferred I'd done something wrong.'

'That's because you have done something wrong,' she reminded me. 'Two...You persuade the PF to drop the charge to possession again, and this time do what your client tells you and plead guilty.'

'That's not going to happen. Hugh Ogilvie will never override a decision of Crown Office. How about option three, where I take the case to trial and secure a famous victory?'

Joanna tilted her head and gave me a look. 'Need I rehearse the evidence?'

'Okay, run number two past me again. Why would the Crown agree to reduce a charge they've already increased?'

'Easy. You get Antonia to give them the name of her supplier.'

'You want me to turn her into some kind of supergrass?'

'I'm a prosecutor. I know what prosecutors want. We
would rather catch big fish than plankton.'

'So you think the Crown would do Antonia a favour if she squealed on whoever gave her the drugs?'

'It would be another rung up the drugs ladder. The higher the Crown climbs in drugs cases, the better they like the view.'

'It'll be hard for Antonia to climb with no kneecaps.'

'Her supplier won't necessarily have been a gangster.'

'This is illegal drugs we're talking about, Jo. There's always a gangster.'

'At the very top, yes. Not necessarily near the bottom.'

'You really think that would work?'

'If Andy's client can save her own skin by testifying against Antonia, I don't see why she can't do something similar.'

I mulled that over as we walked along, until Joanna pointed out the area of ground where our dream house would have stood had we the money.

'Talking of money,' I said. 'Guess who didn't win the lottery?'

'You already told me: Ellen Fletcher.'

'No, I told you she didn't win half a million. Now I'm telling you she didn't win anything.'

'Not even fifty thousand? Why did she tell you she had, then?'

That was a very good question. 'All I know is that she borrowed 50k from Jake Turpie and that she's using it to see herself through her last few months and go out in style.'

'That was nice of Jake...' Joanna, who had been pacing out the dimensions of our living room on the grass, stopped. 'Wait a minute. Nice of Jake Turpie? What am I saying? Does Jake know Ellen is terminally ill?'

'He does now.'

'You didn't tell him?'

'How was I supposed to know she'd borrowed money from him? She told me she'd won the lottery.'

'How's she going to pay him back?'

'This would make a good spot for a bedroom, right here,' was my less than seamless segue to take us off topic. 'We could have a big window with a view across the fields all the way down to the Forth. You can just about see Blackness Castle.' I hunkered down and patted the ground. 'You know the grass is quite dry.' I looked around. 'And it's very secluded here.'

Joanna helped me to an upright position with the aid of my left ear lobe. 'Robbie, if you've landed that woman in trouble with Jake Turpie, you're going to have to warn her.'

'Okay, okay, I will.' I removed Joanna's hand from my ear, put my arm around her and led her on a few metres. 'Where will we put the garden? I've heard it's not a good idea to have one that's too big for your wife to look after.' Joanna pulled away. 'We're not going to be living here, remember? And stop trying to change the subject. If Ellen has conned Jake out of money, then someone is going to end up paying. You know that.'

'I know, I know. I'll warn her about Jake and about my mistake.'

'About your big mouth, you mean.'

'I've done what she asked me to do. I brought her husband back. If she's got herself into money trouble with Jake then that's her problem.'

'And you don't care what happens to her?'

'Look, I've said I'll tell her, okay? After that my involvement with Ellen will be over.'

'It's not all that will be over for Ellen.'

'That's no longer my business and it's definitely none of yours.'

'Listen to yourself, Robbie. She's your client.'

'So is Jake Turpie.'

'Which is why you know what he's like.' Joanna was correct of course. We both knew exactly what Jake was capable of. Ellen might have a short life expectancy, but Jake could make what was left even shorter and a lot more painful. 'If you've landed Ellen in trouble by breaching her confidence, then you owe it to her to get her out of it.'

'And, any ideas how I do that?'

'No, it's none of my business. Remember?' She put her arm through mine. 'But you'd better make it yours or whatever happens to that woman will be on your conscience.'

28

Under his Firm's disciplinary procedures, Ted Hawke, managing partner of Fraser Forrest & Hawke, had no option other than to suspend Scotland's Legal Trainee of the Year from work, pending the outcome of court proceedings. The Crown had accelerated matters by early service of an indictment and the trial was set to take place in four weeks' time with a First Diet fixed for Tuesday the following week. At the First Diet Antonia would be asked to plead guilty or not guilty to the new, more serious charge of possessing cocaine with the intent to supply.

The speed of the prosecution was surprising in some ways. In other ways it wasn't. With such a shooty-in of a case, why wait? Two young women found in possession of cocaine, all the Crown required to lead was evidence of the drugs found in the search and an expert to say there was too much for personal use. Freya Linkwood testifying against her flatmates was merely the icing on an already well-decorated Prosecution cake. The trial wouldn't last more than a day or two.

Whatever the timescales involved, unable to work at the moment, Antonia Brechin was a woman with time on her hands. She insisted on spending some of that time with me, a lot of it on Thursday afternoon.

I had just returned to the office, fresh from a post-court sortie with a bacon roll at Sandy's café, when

Antonia's presence, and that of her parents, was brought to my attention by Grace-Mary who intercepted me in the corridor outside reception.

'Why are you so late? The Brechins are here in force. When they called this morning I told them you'd be back by half-one, two o'clock at the latest.'

I knew I'd have to confront Antonia Brechin's family eventually to set out a line of defence. I just hadn't expected the meeting would be so soon.

'Why didn't you tell them I was busy?' I hissed.
'Because you're not.'

'Then you could have warned me and I'd have made myself busy.'

'I sent you a text about half-eleven when they called to make the appointment. You never replied.'

I vaguely remembered a faint buzzing coming from my jacket pocket sometime during my cross-examination of a ridiculously young police officer. 'All right, listen, stall them for another fifteen minutes and then show—'

'Fifteen minutes? They've already been here nearly half an hour. I'll give you two minutes and then I'm bringing them through, ready or not. Now, what will I say to them about you being late?'

There was no point arguing. Grace-Mary was right. The Brechins would be upset enough without being asked to sit any longer in my closet of a waiting room. 'Tell them I was held up in an important consultation.'

Grace-Mary tugged a crumpled tissue from the sleeve of her cardigan. 'Okay, just let me wipe some of that important consultation brown sauce from the corner of your mouth.'

I intercepted her hand, took the tissue and returned

to my room. This was not going to be pleasant.

'So what's the plan of attack or, should I say, defence?' Antonia's father, Quentin, was not at all what I'd imagined. This was the son of Sheriff Albert Brechin? He was a tall, gangly man with lots of hair and teeth and a set of large friendly features that put me more in mind of Jake Turpie's reluctant guard dog than his father's bulldog appearance. I'd half expected him to come marching in demanding to know what I was playing at and screaming threats of reporting me to the Law Society for ignoring his daughter's direct instructions, but from his cheerful demeanour and opening remarks, you could have been mistaken for thinking we had gathered to organise a trip to the seaside. Unfortunately, neither his daughter nor his wife – especially not his wife — looked anywhere near as happy. 'It's very early days,' I said.

Mrs Brechin was straight in there. 'Early days? What do you mean, early days? Antonia is due up in court next Tuesday.'

'Yes,' I said, 'for a First Diet. It's only to confirm her plea of not guilty and deal with any procedural matters that need to be tidied up before the trial. At the moment there isn't much I can do because I'm still awaiting disclosure of evidence from the Crown. That's why I think it would be best all round if we waited for the witness statements to arrive before we had a meeting to discuss the defence in any detail.'

'But Antonia is due in court next week,' Mrs Brechin repeated, speaking slowly, enunciating each word, like a Briton abroad who assumes everyone understands English if it's spoken loudly and clearly enough.

'And if the Crown has not fulfilled its duty to

disclose the evidence by then, the proceedings will be continued until it has,' I said. 'The whole trial may have to be adjourned to a later date. The court can't expect us to be ready before we've seen the evidence.'

Mrs Brechin sat back heavily in her chair, unable to look at me.

Her husband stood and put out a hand to shake mine. 'There we are then. No point getting worked up about things until we know all the facts, eh?' He looked from wife to daughter. Neither met his eye. 'You'll be sure to give us a call when you have everything, Mr Munro? We can come through to see you whenever you're—'

His words were interrupted by a light knock at the door and Grace-Mary entered carrying a brown folder. 'I thought you'd need this.'

'Thank you,' I said, loudly, hoping to drown out the rest of her words and failing.

'It's the Crown disclosure in Miss Brechin's case.' With that and a sympathetic smile at the client and her mum, my secretary withdrew. Everyone stared at the folder.

'Well, well. Here it is, hot off the presses,' I said, with a light little laugh, placing a hand on the folder and lifting it off again quickly. 'Ouch. Why don't I read this through thoroughly and then we'll set up a meeting for, say, the day before the First Diet? How would that suit?'

It wouldn't suit, at least not Mrs Brechin. 'There doesn't seem to be much to it. Is there any reason why we can't go over it now?' she asked, staring fixedly at the thin cardboard folder.

There wasn't any reason, other than I didn't want to

tell them the bad news of the Crown case, because they'd be expecting me to come up with some good news for the defence and there wasn't any. Slowly, I flicked through the various papers explaining what each was as I went. Mrs Brechin was quite correct: there wasn't much to it. I'd seen the same type of evidence hundreds of times before. Acting on information received, the police obtain a search warrant, carry out a search, find drugs, arrest and inter- view the suspects and then charge them. That took care of the bulk of the disclosure statements and left only the three Crown productions: a forensic report confirming that what had been found in the search was, indeed, fifty grams of high-quality cocaine; a drug expert's opinion that the quantity was too great to be consistent with personal use, and so therefore the person in possession must have intended to supply to others; and, finally, a search warrant.

Drug search warrants were fairly simple, largely pro forma documents. The only essential additions required were the address of the premises to be searched and the date. Occasionally some cop mucked up the address, perhaps put down the wrong number of a flat in a tenement block. Not on this occasion. It was bang on. Same with the date: Friday 27 April. A warrant obtained under section 23 of the Misuse of Drugs Act required to be acted upon within one month of signing. The one in my hand had been signed only three or four days before the search on first May.

There was absolutely nothing untoward about any of the evidence. It was all simple and routine and as effective as a knot in a noose.

'Well, then...' Mr Brechin clapped his hands

together.

'Now that you have the information, we'd better give you some time to think on where we go from here.' He put an arm around his daughter. 'It's not the end of the world, Toni. What's really important is that we're all fit and healthy. If things don't work out for the best, so be it. No need for everyone to worry themselves to death over it.'

He rose from his chair and encouraged Antonia from hers. Mrs Brechin remained seated. 'Quentin, why don't you take Antonia for a breath of fresh air while I speak to Mr Munro in private?'

Mr Brechin hesitated for a second and then reached out and shook my hand again. 'Nice meeting you, Mr Munro. I think we'll go for a wander up to the Palace. Haven't been there in ages.' He leaned down and gave his wife a peck on the cheek. 'See you back at the car in ten minutes, dear.'

Mrs Brechin sat there, eyes fixed on mine. When she spoke I hardly saw her lips move. 'Better make it twenty. I have a few things I'd like to explain to Mr Munro.'

29

When it came to explaining things, Mrs Brechin didn't go in much for bullet points. Nineteen of those twenty minutes later she was still very much in my office and still very much talking. I hadn't asked for a potted history of the Brechin family, but she served me up one anyway.

Quentin Brechin had been his father's pride and joy. As Dux of the High School and president of the debating society, twenty-five years ago he'd sailed into Law at Edinburgh University towing a raft of top grades and high hopes behind him. Hopes that were sunk mid-way through the second year of his studies when he met, and promptly impregnated, the now Mrs Quentin Brechin. Their respective families had urged them to consider a termination or adoption. To his credit Quentin would countenance neither; however, with a further three and a half years of study in front of him, followed by a two-year, low-paid legal traineeship, he'd worked out that his child would be donning her first school uniform before he came close to being able to adequately support a family. So he'd quit. A move that had almost killed his father. I dispelled any uncharitable thoughts I might have on that front, and listened to how, in an effort to support his family, young Quentin had entered the employment limbo where many University drop-outs found themselves: over-qualified for apprenticeships, underqualified for graduate posts. Undeterred, he'd taken on a series of unskilled jobs, labouring on building sites and dockyards, shelf-stacking and warehousing. He'd been hopeless at them all. So he'd become a house-husband while his wife went out to work, spending his days child-minding and doing domestic chores, washing, cleaning and ironing, most of which had to be redone properly by Mrs Brechin when she came home from work. In his free moments he indulged in his favourite pastime: art, and sculpting in particular.

Mrs Brechin sat back in her chair and relaxed for the first time since she entered the room. 'For years no-one was interested in Quentin's pieces. He made a few sympathy sales to friends and family, just pocket money really but it wasn't until quite recently that things took off. Quentin found himself an investor and put that money and all our savings into casting bronze sculptures. He sold his first bronze to an old school chum who put it on display in his office. A rich client noticed it and wanted to know where he could buy one. From there word spread and nowadays there's barely time for the metal to cool before his latest work is sold. He's exhibited all over Europe: Paris, Bruges, Berlin, Vienna, even though he hates travelling. If Quentin had his way he'd live in his studio. Sometimes...' Mrs Brechin got out of her chair, walked to the window and looked down on the High Street. 'Sometimes I think he never wanted to do law. That I was a get-out clause in a contract his father had written for him at birth.'

'He's a man doing for a living the job that he loves. Isn't that what everyone dreams of?' Saying that made me think. What did I love doing most? What were my hobbies? Golf, football, whisky-drinking. Not recreational pursuits that were ever going to make me rich, and none that could match standing up in front of a jury or getting stuck into a lying, recalcitrant witness. Had I found my niche? Was I doing what I loved?

Mrs Brechin turned from the window. 'My father-in-law is a difficult man to get along with. You think he gives you a hard time? Try being me, twenty odd years ago. For years he refused to even speak to me...' Like a proctologist with a full clinic, I could tell there was a 'but' coming. 'But he's always been there for Antonia. Right from her birth he has supported her financially. He paid for holidays, clothes, sent her to the best schools and paid all the fees. When Antonia was accepted into law at Edinburgh, he almost exploded with joy.'

I had never imagined there was any news capable of detonating an explosion of joy in Sheriff Albert Brechin, unless perhaps it was news of my retirement or the reintroduction of capital punishment.

'You already know that he cut short his holiday to Madeira when he heard she was in the running for Legal Trainee of the Year, don't you?'

'Mrs Brechin, I know how important the case is to your father-in-law, and to you, and especially to Antonia. But defending people against criminal charges is my job. It's what I do for a living. I've been doing it for years, even if Bert Brechin wishes I was the one who'd dropped out of law school. I don't need an incentive to do my best for a client, whoever's grandchild they happen to be.'

'Good...' Mrs Brechin smiled a smile I didn't like the look of. 'Because I want to make something extremely clear.' She wasn't a small woman, and when, with her back to the window, she walked over and planted her hands on the desk, the better to lean across at me, she blocked out a good portion of daylight. 'When my husband said there was no need for everyone to worry themselves to death over Antonia's plight, please do not assume those words extended to absolutely everyone. I want one person to be extremely worried.' The expression on her face avoided the need for further clarification as to who that person might be. 'You completely disregarded Antonia's instructions. You can't possibly deny it.' Mrs B obviously didn't know me that well; denying stuff was my stock in trade. I let her continue. 'I told my father-in-law and he believes that fact alone would be a solid ground on which to make a complaint to the Law Society that would see you struck off.'

It had taken far longer than the promised twenty minutes, but now at last we were getting to the point. She was threatening me. Well, I didn't have to sit there and take it. I could stand, and anyway, bullying me was Grace-Mary's job.

I pushed back my chair and stood up. She was a tall woman, but I still had an inch or two on her. 'I did what in my professional opinion I thought would be best in the long run. If Antonia wanted a lawyer to stand up, say sorry and let her face the consequences, she shouldn't have instructed me.'

'Believe me, Mr Munro, I really wish she hadn't.'

I came around the other side of the desk, walked to the door and opened it. 'In that case, I'll make this easy. You let me know who you think should represent your daughter and I'll be more than happy to forward the papers.' I never liked to see business slip through my fingers, but this was a piece of work I hadn't wanted to take on in the first place. I was relieved that the poisoned chalice would soon pass from my hands to those of another. I marched over to my desk, snatched up Antonia Brechin's case file and held it out. 'Why don't you take the stuff with you right now and it'll save me a stamp? Don't worry, I won't be charging a fee for the work to date.'

Mrs Brechin ignored the case file I was holding, gathered her handbag and strode to the door. 'I'm not worried about your costs. I'm not the person meeting them.'

'Then tell Antonia, or her dad—'

'They're not paying your bill either. Your fee will be settled by the same person who demands that you continue to act.' She pushed her big, red face closer to mine. 'But I'm warning you, you'd better live up to my father-in- law's great expectations or I'll see that they never let you near a courtroom again - unless it's in the dock.'

30

The discovery that Sheriff Albert Brechin was not only funding his granddaughter's legal fees, but insisting I act in her defence was as confusing as it was alarming. He either had great faith in my abilities or else he didn't want any debate as to who to blame when she was convicted and struck off. I pondered my predicament the next day on the drive back to the office, but things were no clearer as I pulled into my usual parking spot outside Sandy's café. My mobile buzzed. It was a message from Ellen. She was with Jake Turpie in the Red Corner Bar and needed to speak to me urgently.

Lunchtime was always the same at the Red Corner so far as food was concerned. There wasn't any. Not unless you classed SPAM rolls sweating in cling film as a foodstuff.

'This is a pub. You're here to drink not eat,' was Brendan the barman's reply to my sarcastic 'what's on the menu today?' enquiry. He slung a small bag of peanuts at me, and I took it and my ginger beer on the rocks over to where Jake and Ellen were deep in discussion.

'I hear you shared my bad news with Jake,' Ellen said, budging along a bit so that I could drag a low stool over and squeeze in beside her at a small wooden table. I placed my drink down on the sticky surface beside a pint of heavy and a tulip glass in which a ring of lemon was cast adrift on a sea of red.

There was no note of criticism in Ellen's voice, and yet I knew I should never have mentioned her private affairs to anyone. The state of her health was her own business, and not for me to go bandying about with the likes of Jake Turpie. If I'd known she owed Jake money I definitely would never have mentioned it. Then again, if she had been straight with me from the start I wouldn't be here making do with peanuts for lunch when I could be at Sandy's café laying waste to a crispy bacon roll.

'So what are you going to do?' Jake asked me before I had a chance to say anything by way of apology.

'What am I going to do?'

'Aye, Ellen's borrowed fifty grand off me and she says she's spent it.'

I was still trying to work out where I fitted into all of this when Ellen spoke up, giving me a chance to crack open my bag of peanuts.

'I'm sorry, Jake. I needed the money to try and bring Freddy over here so I could see him before… before I…'

Jake turned his head and studied the demented fruit machine that was flashing and bleeping away to itself in a darkened corner of the bar. Ellen reached out, took hold of one of his hands with two of hers and squeezed. 'When I first found out I wasn't well, I think I went a bit crazy. I really am sorry, Jake. I should have told you I couldn't pay it back.'

"Sorry, Jake?" The woman was into him for fifty large, with no means of repaying, and the best she could come up with was, "Sorry, Jake." The most bizarre part of it all was that Jake seemed to be accepting the situation. How come? There were people with body parts broken or missing because they owed Jake a fraction of that amount or had been a day or two late in their weekly instalment plan.

'It's going to be okay.' Ellen patted his hand like he was a brave wee boy in the dentist's waiting room. 'Robbie will work something out for me. Leave it to him. He'll get you your money back.' She got up from the table, leaving her red drink undrunk. 'I'm going to leave now,' she said. 'I know you two boys will have a lot to talk about.'

The brief ray of sunshine that sliced through the door and split the dimly lit bar seemed to rouse Jake from his contemplations.

'Well?' he said.

I dropped a few peanuts into my mouth and chewed. 'Well what?'

Jake looked at me like I was stupid. 'My money? What are you going to do about getting it back?'

I palmed some more nuts, dusting the salt off onto a floor that wouldn't notice the difference. 'You know, Jake, Ellen has obviously lost the plot, but I think you're losing it too. First of all you let yourself be conned by Freddy Fletcher, the world's worst conman, then you give his dying wife fifty K, and now, suddenly, you expect me to do something about it?'

Jake swiped the packet of peanuts from my hand, sending it across the bar. Individual nuts scattered like shrapnel, striking one or two of the less nimble patrons.

Brendan 'The Linlithgow Lion' Patterson, proprietor of the Red Corner Bar, was an ex-boxer who'd won medals for punching people on the head until they fell over. He kept in practice with awkward customers but, despite this outburst, he just stood there polishing a beer tumbler with a grubby tea towel as though nothing had happened.

'You better do what Ellen says and sort this, Robbie,' Jake growled. 'I want the money I'm due back from her...' He stabbed a finger at the door. 'And I want the money I'm due from her man or else I'm having someone's head on a plate, you understand?'

To be honest, I didn't. In fact, I was having great difficulty understanding my role in any of it. 'You don't think you're being at all unreasonable, Jake?' I said. 'Considering the mess you're in has got bugger all to do with me.' There were a few spilled peanuts lying on the table top, and it was still lunchtime. I picked one up. Jake jumped to his feet, put a hand under the table and hurled the whole lot, drinks and all, across the room, leaving me sitting on a small, isolated stool, holding a single peanut halfway to my mouth, while glass and beer splintered and sprayed about me. A soggy slice of lemon came out of orbit and touched down on my right knee. I brushed it away and stood up. Even in the dim light of the bar I was aware of a shadow falling over me. I turned around to see the immense object that was Deek Pudney. He must have been sitting in a corner making himself inconspicuous. How was that even possible?

'Tell me again how unreasonable I'm being...' Jake said, his words accompanied by the weight of one of Deek's boxing-glove-sized hands resting on my shoulder. 'And we'll see if I'm losing the plot.'

I didn't feel any pressing need to repeat myself. I preferred just to sit down again and say nothing.

Once Jake and Deek had gone, Brendan finished polishing the beer tumbler, came from behind the bar with a brush and shovel and started to sweep up around me. 'Bad news, Robbie?'

I could sense the eyes of the other patrons on me. I'd represented many of them over the years, and hoped to again in the future. It wasn't good publicity to show that I'd been at all fazed by the skirmish with Jake.

'You could say that, Brendan,' I said, tossing the remaining peanut into the air and catching it in my mouth. 'But then again, if there was no bad news in the world, I'd be out of business.'

31

Friday night. Joanna was out with friends and my dad had gone down to the Red Corner Bar. Tina was bathed, in her pyjamas and on the sofa engaging me in a no-holds-barred game of dominoes. I was wondering when she'd notice that I hadn't played the double-blank, but another domino turned upside down, when Malky walked through the front door carrying a small cardboard box and looking pleased about something.

'Close your eyes,' he said to Tina, setting the box down on the coffee table and knocking some of the domino pieces onto the floor. 'Right, now you can open them.'

'What is it?' Tina asked, excitedly. The box started to move. She jumped back, and then, very slowly, bent closer.

Malky lifted the lid off the box, put a hand in and brought out a furry, grey object. 'It's a rabbit for your new hutch!'

Tina screamed with joy as my brother placed the animal in her lap. Surprisingly, the rodent seemed pretty okay with the swift transition from the relative safety of a cardboard box to the more uncertain care of a five-year- old, and sat there twitching its nose.

'She can live in the new hutch you and Gramps made,' Malky said, rather obviously. 'I've got sawdust and wood shavings and a wee thing for it to drink from and everything.'

Tina wanted to know if it was a boy or a girl rabbit because she wanted to call it Rosie, and Rosie wouldn't really do if it was a boy rabbit.

Malky turned to me for gender advice.

To my knowledge, the only sure way to tell the sex of a rabbit involved the introduction of another rabbit, standing back and waiting to see what happened next.

Malky took that opinion and applied his own logic. 'And so, seeing how you've only got the one rabbit, no-one knows if it's a boy or a girl so you can call it whatever you like.'

I was about to suggest she call it Schrödinger, but Tina was already demanding more information on my two- rabbit gender test, so I didn't think the introduction of theories on quantum physics would assist matters. When Malky changed the subject and suggested we go looking for dandelions, I slipped out of the back door, walked around the side of the cottage and climbed into my new car.

The difficulty between Jake and Ellen, that I'd been ordered to sort out, was a tricky one raising all sorts of legal issues, and although there were people to whom I could turn for advice on tricky legal matters, there was really only one person I could rely on to advise on tricky illegal matters. This being Friday night, that particular person's be-kilted behind would be resting on a seat in A&E.

'What's the news?' I asked, strolling into a large, harshly lit room where the casualties of a West Lothian Friday night were scattered around on the orange plastic bucket seats awaiting triage.

'Pretty good, as a matter of fact,' Sammy said, slipping a paperback into his jacket pocket. 'There was a nice wee smash on the B8046, down by Ecclesmachan. Some eejit took a bend too fast, went through a hedge and into a field. There were three passengers, all teenagers. I've already spoken to their parents about making a claim. There's no-one to blame but the driver. I've got one of them signed up already, so I reckon the others will follow.'

'And the bad news?' I asked.

'Bad news? No, Robbie, there's no bad news. The whole lot of them are properly injured. One's quite serious.' He rubbed his hands together. 'Anyway, what brings you here?' I glanced around and lowered my voice. 'You remember what we were talking about the other night? I've been giving it some more thought.'

Sammy's turn to check around. He stood up. 'Not here.' He pinched the sleeve of my jumper between thumb and forefinger and gently tugged me towards a snack- vending machine situated in a region of the waiting room populated only by a couple of jakeys, one pressing a piece of white gauze against a head wound, the other sprawled across two chairs singing Roy Orbison.

'Can I take it there have been some developments?' Sammy let go of me, reached into his sporran and began feeding coins into the machine.

It had been obvious to me since being tasked by Jake to 'get things sorted', that the only way Ellen and Freddy could pay back the money they were due was to adopt the original life insurance plan, but it would need to be tweaked.

'Things have become slightly more complicated,' I said. 'There's another party involved.'

Sammy pressed a few numbers on the keypad. A

bag of crisps took a nose-dive from the top rack and landed in the tray at the bottom. He stooped to collect it.

'And I take it this third party would like a share?' he asked, after he'd straightened again, pulling the bag open.

'Bang on.'

'What do you want?'

'To have nothing to do with it.'

'That can be arranged, but I was meaning do you want crisps or a Mars bar or something?'

I didn't. All I wanted was to leave the problem with him and hope that he could come up with an arrangement to keep everyone happy and me out of it.

'And this third party. Anyone I know?' he asked, delving into the packet, pulling out a large crisp and stuffing it into his mouth.

I could see no obvious path around it. I'd have to tell him. 'It's Jake Turpie.'

Sammy stopped chewing, looked at the floor for a moment and then up at me, swallowing hard. 'You don't half know how to make life difficult, Robbie. Why on earth would Ellen Fletcher want to do business with Jake Turpie?'

Why would anyone? I was going to ask, until I recalled that I'd just bought a car from him, even though I was yet to part with the money.

'I wouldn't have thought that pair would be on speaking terms, considering,' Sammy said.

'Considering the difficulty with Freddy, you mean?'

'Definitely that, and there was also that difficulty with Ellen's brother, way back.'

I knew nothing about any such difficulty, mainly

187

because I didn't know Ellen had a brother. When preparing her will, I'd been told she had no next of kin.

'He's dead,' Sammy said.

'So, what's difficult about that?'

From the waiting room entrance door someone called, 'Mr Veitch? Could we have a word with you, please?' A nurse in a pale blue uniform was standing next to an older man and woman, who themselves were standing either side of a teenager wearing a big black rubber boot and propped up on crutches. There was a little white ladder of paper stitches across one of the youth's eyebrows and a plaster over the bridge of his nose.

'Sorry, Robbie,' Sammy said, 'duty calls.'

He made to go, but I pulled him back by the arm. 'What's the difficulty with Ellen's dead brother?'

'Not now, Robbie.'

'Yes, now.'

Sammy shook his head and sighed. 'It happened a long, long time ago. Jake and Ellen were going out with each other back then, they were just kids. Someone noised-up Ellen's brother, Eric, at the dancing. He was a nice enough lad, not a fighter, but he'd gone through to Glasgow and chatted up someone else's burd.' Sammy smiled and waved to the group at the entrance door. 'He was a good- looking boy, Eric. The girls loved him. Knocked one of them up and came to see me about having to pay child maintenance. I think it was a wee girl he had. Could have been a boy. It was one or the other, I can't remember all the details. All I know is that Jake, being Jake, and no doubt wanting to show off to Ellen, went through to see this other guy, taking Eric with him. Things didn't go too well.' Which was

Sammy's way of saying that Jake had kicked off a fight with a group of neds, during which young Eric had been stabbed through the heart with a carving knife and died.

'Ellen always blamed Jake for Eric's death. If she's prepared to do business with him now, it must be because she's got no other option.'

More calls from the entrance as the group grew impatient.

'Listen, Robbie, it's no problem for me to set up a term insurance policy to cover the three lives. The problem is that the three lives belong to three of the dodgiest individuals in West Lothian. If we're going to—'

'If you're going to.'

The voices from the entrance door were growing more irritated and irritating by the second.

'Okay, if I'm going to,' Sammy said. 'And if I'm going to do it right, so that there is no chance of a comeback, I'll have to put in place some kind of business transaction involving all three, so it looks like there's actually a reason for them to be insuring each other.'

'Finding a good reason won't be easy,' I said.

'Don't worry.' Sammy shoved the packet of salt & vinegar crisps at me. 'I've got to do something to earn my money, and, anyway, I don't need a good reason. A bad reason will do just as well.'

32

Inspiration often springs from the most unexpected of sources. I'd never thought it would issue forth from Stan Blandy, a long-time client of mine who dabbled in drugs in much the same way as Adolf Hitler used to dabble in European politics.

Stan Blandy was a man low on educational qualifications, high on street smarts. He'd left school at fifteen when his father died in a prison fight, and found himself head of the family. By the time he was seventeen he was a forklift driver working chiefly at Grangemouth docks and other ports along the Firth of Forth. For the next ten years young Stan lifted heavy pallets and lightweight pay-packets, watching as others with exam passes and University degrees climbed over him up the career ladder and into cushy well-paid managerial positions.

That was why Stan eventually came to the conclusion that if he was ever going to make it he'd have to do it himself and set up his own business. How hard could it be? The secret to a successful retail enterprise boiled down to an efficient workforce selling quality merchandise to a loyal customer base. So Stan set up his own import company. His years on the docks hadn't been wasted. He'd formed friendships, made contacts, and knew the best methods of importing goods - including those goods that should never have been exported in the first place. All he needed was a commodity to specialise in, and it didn't escape his attention that the market for illegal drugs was an especially buoyant one. But what kind of drug should he deal in? As a product, marijuana was bulky to import and growing your own involved too much outlay on people and equipment.

Heroin was out of the question too. It wasn't the product, it was the customers. You could trust a junkie about as far as you could stick a used syringe into a collapsed vein. Careless to an alarming degree, easy for the cops to spot, everyone knew that when the average smack-head was arrested he sang like a canary on a TV talent show, prepared to grass on anyone if it meant getting back on the street in search of the next needle.

Cocaine and ecstasy were the preferred options. Both readily available to those who knew how to import goods from abroad, and a little went a long way. All Stan needed to do was ensure a good quality product that would keep a good quality clientele happy. A clientele that, unlike heroin addicts, didn't hang around street corners looking like the living dead. Stan's customers were responsible people in responsible jobs; people who seldom came into contact with the police; people careful with everything except their money, for whom spending a couple of hundred pounds on a few grams of coke or some quality disco-biscuits at the weekend was just so much loose change; people who didn't need to run the risk of shop- lifting jars of coffee or packs of bacon to score their next tenner bag.

Product and clientele sorted, that left human resources. Just as a port's chief operating officer never toted a bale on the waterfront, Stan had no wish to dirty his own hands, and, because his staff were the only link between him and his product, he realised he needed to instil loyalty in his workforce for those times when things didn't go quite according to plan. That was why he made sure his personnel were hand-picked, well-paid and shit-scared of him.

For Stan it was a business strategy that worked. Since starting off in business in the eighties, he had never been so much as questioned by the police, far less arrested or charged. The same couldn't be said for certain members of his staff nearer the base of the company pyramid. Whenever one of the delivery team was arrested, I was given a call. Stan paid for my services generously and in cash. So far as I and the shoebox under my bed were concerned, his personnel didn't get caught nearly enough. On the rare occasions I met with Stan, it was never at my office. This Saturday afternoon we were at the football. Stan wasn't a football fan, but his workers were and so he had corporate hospitality at various stadiums. It was all part of his employee incentive scheme. Today we were at Hampden for the Scottish Cup Final.

Stan had no family, didn't use drugs, take a drink or chase women. He didn't listen to music, never read books or watched TV. Once when asked to name his favourite film he'd answered, 'cling.' No, Stan's only interest outside business was gambling. Perhaps he was keen on it as a leisure activity because he was otherwise so risk averse.

Stan had a thousand on the favourites to win by two goals or more. He was getting even-money. Just to be sociable, I'd put ten pounds on their opponents to lift the trophy after penalties at odds of eight-to-one.

Our padded seats were a lot wider than those available in the less salubrious parts of the ground, but Stan still had some difficulty cramming his bulk into the one next to me. We hadn't discussed any business over pre-match food and drinks, Stan preferring to do his talking in the privacy of fifty thousand or so noisy football fans.

'One of my boys was delivering a message for me yesterday,' Stan said, as the match kicked off and the crowd roared in anticipation. 'He was headed for St Andrews, and told to take the coast road to keep out of the way. I've not heard from him.'

The favourites had launched an early attack and a speculative long shot was tipped over the bar for a corner kick. Stan emitted a small grunt of approval at his chosen team's early signs of intent. The noise of the crowd around us lowered and it wasn't until the set-piece was cleared, allowing play to break down the right wing, that the volume increased sufficiently for Stan to continue, his mouth close to my ear. 'It can mean only one thing. He's been lifted.'

There was no more talk for a while as we watched the match. It was a good game. Most underdogs tended to park the bus, employing two ranks of four defenders, a number ten rattling around in middle-field and a lone striker hoping for a breakaway. Today's minnows were clearly under instructions to go for it, and their have-a-go tactics paid off when they took the lead with a strike on the half hour mark. It was only a controversial penalty kick on the stroke of half-time that saw the teams go in at the interval with the score level at one apiece. With a grand riding on them to score two more without reply, Stan seemed neither up nor down.

Meanwhile my tenner bet was looking good.

When the referee blew for the interval, Stan and I, along with the rest of the suits and ties, shuffled off to our lounges for sandwiches and another quick beer, leaving the masses to their Scotch pies and beef tea.

'How big a message was it?' I asked, eyeing up a cute little steak pie, one of a number reclining on a silver tray, all vying for my attention.

'Just a couple of bricks.'

Perhaps in Stan's world, two kilos of cocaine wasn't much but, if it had been seized, the Crown's PR department would value it as a £100,000 drugs haul.

The mini steak pie never stood a chance. I washed it down with a swig of beer, and picked up a couple more. 'What do you want me to do?'

Stan devoured several prawn pastries and then led me back outside to the now deserted directors' box. There was a half-time penalty shoot-out taking place between two youth teams, each successful strike eliciting a smattering of applause and half-hearted cheers from the pie and Bovril brigade.

'I don't want any unwanted attention,' he said. 'Of course not.'

'I mean it, Robbie. He'll know he's looking at a decent stretch, so I don't want him trying for a better deal by being all co-operative. If he's done out the park, he'll just have to plead and take what's coming. Tell him you'll go and see the Fiscal and fire in an early plea, get him a reduced sentence or something. I'll see that he's all right for money when he's inside and I'll square him up when he gets out.' Stan stared at me unblinkingly, smiling as though to do so was hurting him. 'Just so long as he keeps his trap shut.'

Knowing Stan's unforgiving employment disciplinary policy, I don't know why I bothered to ask if it was his delivery boy's first time in bother, but I did and remark- ably it wasn't.

'Do you not remember him, Robbie? Toffee McCowan. You acted for him the last time he was in bother. Wee wrinkly old guy. Face like a chewed-up—'

'Toffee?'

'Aye that's him. He was done for the same thing about eight year ago. He was a first offender then and you got him fifteen month. I should have cut him loose.' Stan shrugged his massive shoulders. 'But you know me. I'm a big softy.' About as soft as the blue tint on armour-plating. 'Aye, Toffee's all right. Old school. Not like most of them these days who can't keep their hands off the stuff. The only bump Toffee's after comes out of a rum bottle.'

The seats around us began to fill. Ballboys ran down the tunnel, dispersing in all directions, followed at a trot by the two teams of players and finally the match officials walking after them. I didn't really care who won but, such was the intensity of the atmosphere, even I was excited.

That's when inspiration struck, as did the underdogs. An early shot from the edge of the box was deflected off a defender's heel. It spiralled in the opposite direction leaving the wrong-footed keeper with nothing to do except watch it squirm agonisingly over the goal line.

It turned out to be the winner. That's why I seldom gambled. I felt worse having thrown away a tenner than I'd have felt good about winning eighty. Stan didn't even mention his wager. To him a thousand-pound loss was probably the same as losing ten pounds was to me.

We left the ground and arrived at the point where we were to part company, jubilant fans, shouting and singing, jostling and bumping their way past us.

'Thanks very much for that, Stan.' I said, 'It was a good game.'

'Not a problem. Glad you enjoyed yourself. Let me know how things go for Toffee on Monday.'

'About that...' I said. 'I was wondering...' I wasn't entirely sure how to present my idea. 'What if when I see Toffee I do a wee deal with him that would help me out with another case I have on the go? Wouldn't affect you too much.'

Stan frowned.

'Not at all, actually.'

That hurried assurance didn't lift the frown. 'You should have mentioned it earlier, Robbie. I've no time right now. How about we meet up later and talk about it?'

Given the infrequency of my meetings with Stan, such a discussion was unlikely to happen inside the timeframe I had in mind.

'It's okay, Stan. Leave it to me. I'll take care of every-thing. It'll be fine.'

He was still frowning.

I laughed. 'What's wrong? Don't you trust me?'

'Trust you? Of course I trust you. I trust everyone who

works for me or they wouldn't work for me.' He reached out and gave me a not-so-friendly thump on the back that sent a flotilla of mini steak pies surfing my stomach on a wave of lager. 'And I definitely know I can trust you, because you know what happens to people who abuse that trust.'

33

'It didn't take you long to break your promise.'

The voice on the other end of the phone came quick and breathless.

'I'm holding our previous contract null and void,' I said, propping myself up on a couple of pillows.

'Careful, Robbie. Don't start bandying about legal words you can't back up with actual legal knowledge.'

'You know very well what I mean, Hugh. Just because I might have said—'

'No, you definitely did say.'

'That I would never talk to you again about Antonia Brechin's case, that was before the charge was upgraded from simple possession to supply.'

'Which, may I remind you, had nothing whatsoever to do with me.'

I had to make this quick. Joanna was in the shower. If she overheard she'd want to know what was going on. 'Let me spell it out for you in great detail.'

Ogilvie capitulated with a groan. 'Just tell me what it is you want.'

The plan was a simple one and went something like this. Joanna had already told me that there might be a chance of the charge against Antonia being reduced to simple possession again, just so long as Antonia gave the Crown the name of her dealer. Very few people charged with possession ever did, on the basis that what the court could do to them was significantly less painful than what their dealer definitely would do if they squealed. I'd found a way of neutralising that problem. With two kilos of Bolivian Marching Dust in the boot of his car, and a previous conviction for precisely the same thing, Toffee McCowan was staring down the barrel of a long sentence anyway. An extra conviction for supplying Antonia with the fifty grams she'd had in her possession wouldn't add a day to his release date.

'Think of it Hugh. I hand you her dealer on a plate and you've still got Antonia Brechin pleading guilty to possession.' Ogilvie made no sound of approval, but neither did he put the phone down. 'Not only that, but you can tell Bert Brechin that the decision to save his granddaughter's career, by reducing the charge, was all down to you. It's like your birthday and Christmas rolled into one.' I skipped the part about Toffee already being in police custody. Best to leave that out and lean more heavily on my promise to have Toffee confess to supplying my client.

'And how exactly are you going to persuade this drug dealer to confess?' I could hear a note of suspicion in Ogilvie's voice, but mostly a lot of heavy breathing. 'You going to phone him on a Sunday morning and annoy him until he cracks, like you're trying to do with me?'

'Never mind how I'm going to do it,' I said. 'All I want to know from you is if we have a deal or not. Then I can let you go back to doing whatever you were doing with Mrs Ogilvie.'

'I'm not doing anything with Mrs Ogilvie. Mrs Ogilvie doesn't...Look never mind, I'm out running and it's hard enough getting up this hill without you—'

'Deal or no deal?'

'Deal,' he panted. 'The moment you let me have your man's written confession to the supply, I'll reduce the charge against Miss Brechin to simple possession.'

In for a penny, I thought I might as well get back in Gail Paton's good books. 'And her co-accused too?'

'Okay, but you'd better get a move on. The First Diet is the day after tomorrow.'

An hour later, after breakfast and a shower, I was outside in the garden with Tina and Joanna. What had been a pleasant enough Sunday morning was deteriorating into a wet and drizzly mid-morning, not that a patch of rain was going to deter my daughter from poking dandelion leaves through the chicken-wire of the hutch door at the fluffy bundle inside.

'So, what do you think of that for a plan?' So pleased had I been with the deal I'd struck I thought I'd share it with Joanna after all.

'You can't do it, Robbie.' She seemed quite certain about that, which was surprising because I was equally certain that I could; however, like a politician, I was prepared to engage in a consultation process before doing things exactly the way I'd intended to do them in the first place.

'Why not?' I asked.

'Do we know if this guy Toffee did supply the cocaine to Antonia?'

'No, but you can't have everything.'

'Then it's illegal.'

'What else?'

'What else? Is the fact that your plan is based on a lie—'

'Possibly a lie.'

'And therefore a crime, not enough?'

'A crime...?' I stooped to pluck a handful of dandelions. There was an abundance of them at the hutch end of the garden and running along the line of the fence. So many, that I was fast coming to the conclusion that my dad's idea of building the hutch had less to do with acquiring a pet for Tina, and more to do with us weeding the garden for him. I held up the leaves clenched in my fist. 'I'm probably committing a crime picking wildflowers.'

'You're not.'

'Uprooting wildflowers is an offence, isn't it?'

'Not when they're weeds in your dad's back garden it isn't. Stop trying to justify your actions. You know perfectly well you're in the wrong and are just blinding yourself to the truth.'

I stroked a strand of damp hair that had fallen across Joanna's face and softened my words. 'All right, maybe pulling weeds isn't the perfect analogy, but I'm trying to explain to you that there's no harm done by a crime like the one I have in mind. Surely you see that?'

Joanna jerked her head away. 'Robbie, when it comes to interpretation of the law, not many people see things the same way as you.'

'Do you ever think that it might be those people who are wrong? Why does it have to be me?'

'Because it is.' Joanna seemed definite about that too. 'It's all about you being wrong. Having someone who's got absolutely nothing to do with Antonia Brechin's case, take the blame for it is...It's just not on.'

'Not on? When did just not on become the test for justice?'

'I'm warning you, Robbie...'

'The man's a drug dealer. He's in custody for drug dealing. All he does is confess that he supplied some of those drugs to Antonia. Hugh Ogilvie says thanks very much for the conviction, reduces the charge against Antonia, she pleads guilty to possession just like she's always wanted to do, and everyone's happy. Especially me when I send Bert Brechin my bill.'

'And this guy in Dundee. He's agreeable to this, is he?'

'He will be. It's just another charge that's going to make no difference to his sentence.'

Joanna took the dandelion leaves from me and handed them to Tina. 'I still don't like it. You're trying to make a man confess to a crime he's innocent of.'

'Innocent? He's a drug runner. He's probably done it hundreds of times. So what, he takes the blame for the one time he didn't do it? That'll make up for all the others he has done and got away with. It's justice.' I took her hands in mine. 'How about you stop being a Fiscal for a moment? Did all those lectures on jurisprudence mean nothing to you?'

'Robbie, everyone knows that jurisprudence means whatever you want it to mean. I'm more interested in what is legal and what isn't.'

'You want what's legal more than what's just?'

'Without laws, justice is entirely abstract. What is legal is indisputable. It's the law and we're lawyers.'

So engrossed in our conversation was I, that I didn't notice the rabbit had buzzed through the stack of dandelions, or that Tina had gone inside and was now returning with a selection of vegetables I was pretty sure were the ingredients for Joanna's next batch of soup.

'Those aren't for the rabbit,' I said. 'They're for us. The rabbit has got its own special food to eat and it's had loads of dandelions. It'll be full up.'

Tina pulled away, brows lowered, bottom lip protruding. I tried to take the vegetables from her, but she clung to them tightly.

Joanna knelt down beside her. 'Tina, you've got to be careful what you feed Rosie. Some food is poisonous to animals. Did you know that if dogs eat chocolate or onions they can die?'

Tina could understand the problem with onions, especially if they were cut too chunky and in mince, but life without chocolate?

Joanna gently relieved her of the armful of vegetables. 'You have to be careful. We'll need to go and make sure that all these things are safe for Rosie to eat.'

I could only admire Joanna's handling of the situation. It was both well-reasoned and informative, if not quite as much fun as my idea of tickling Tina until she dropped the stuff.

I took one of the smaller carrots from Joanna and gave it to Tina. 'Here, this'll be safe enough. Never did Bugs Bunny any harm.'

The rain had become more persistent. I left Tina with instructions to come inside once the carrot was finished, and Joanna and I made our way back down the garden to the cottage.

'So, Antonia Brechin losing her career, me possibly losing mine, that's okay because it's the law?'

'Robbie, you are not going to wear me down with your puerile arguments. What you are planning to do is illegal, plain and simple.'

'It is justice, though.'

'No, it's your idea of justice. There's a reason we have laws. It's so that we know what justice is, otherwise justice would be a purely subjective concept. You must see that.'

'Here, let me help you with those.' I relieved Joanna of some of the vegetables. 'After all, we wouldn't want a rogue courgette falling into the wrong hands.'

Joanna gave me a wry smile. 'You do understand, don't you, Robbie?'

I smiled and nodded. I found it to be the quickest and easiest way to ignore what people I didn't agree with had to say.

'If there was no framework of laws, we'd be left with everyone thinking their idea of justice was the best.'

'You're right, Jo. It would be wrong for someone to bend the law just to make it suit their idea of justice.'

Wrong for someone, but not for me, and not if the law-bending was for the benefit of one of my clients.

34

As it turned out, there was no need for me to drag my weary Monday-morning butt fifty miles north across the silvery Tay. My latest client was not in Dundee, nor due to appear in any other court within the Sheriffdom of Tayside, Central and Fife. Grace-Mary had tracked him down to the cells at Edinburgh Sheriff Court.

Colin 'Toffee' McCowan didn't look like a drugs courier, which was probably why he'd been chosen to be a drugs courier. He was a spritely sixty-something with a perma-tan and a weather-beaten face to show for his time served before the mast as a merchant seaman.

It was around eight years since I'd last met Toffee. That had been in the cells at Stirling Sheriff Court after his then unblemished record, combined with a heart-rending plea in mitigation by yours truly, had secured him a sentence of fifteen months' imprisonment for couriering a kilo of Stan Blandy's merchandise.

As he came walking though the court's revolving door and across the courtyard towards me, he looked a lot happier than I remembered. Probably because he was a lot less in jail.

He didn't notice me at first. Not until I stepped in front of him to bar his way.

'Mr Munro. How you doing? What's up?'

'It's not a case of what's up,' I said, 'it's a case of who's out and why.'

'Come again?' He slipped a Rizla paper from its slim

green packet and held a corner between his lips while he took a tin from his pocket and teased out a pinch of tobacco.

'I heard you'd been caught with a car-boot-full of coke.' Toffee replaced the tin in his jacket pocket and fashioned himself a rollie, deftly for a man who had two deformed fingers on his left hand. He twisted an end and stuck the other in his mouth, face crinkling into a smile, tanned features contrasting with the white cigarette

paper. 'You heard wrong.'

'Really? So why are you here?'

'There was a misunderstanding.' He sparked a match, put it to the end of his rollie, took a deep drag and exhaled. 'Looks like I done a weekender for nothing.'

I didn't think so. People with a couple of kilos of cocaine in the boot of their car didn't collect get-out-of-jail-free cards, not unless they had been helping the police with their inquiries, and Toffee's boss was a man who did not like being inquired into.

Toffee looked down at the black gown I had draped over my left arm. 'You've not come for me, have you? Did big Stan send you?'

We were standing in the courtyard outside the Sheriff Court. There were lawyers, witnesses, accused persons, all coming and going. A police car pulled up on the double- yellows on Chambers Street to drop off a couple of cops. They alighted and looked to be heading our way.

'Not here,' I said. 'Let's walk.'

Toffee didn't move. He took the smouldering rollie from his mouth. The wrinkles in his face had ironed themselves out and their colour had noticeably paled. 'Does Stan know I was lifted?'

I walked on. Toffee caught up with me as I took a right onto George IV Bridge, the statue of Greyfriars Bobby across the street to my left. Some vandals had painted the wee dog's head orange. Or perhaps it had been students, in which case it wasn't vandalism, it was high-jinks and over-exuberance. I continued walking, heading towards the High Street. From there I could meander down to Waverley Station and catch the train back to Linlithgow.

Toffee fell in step beside me.

'Stan doesn't need to know about this, does he?'

'About what?'

'About me being here - in Edinburgh.'

'Why would he care where you were? You're a free man, aren't you? Unless, of course, you're free for a reason, in which case you may want to stow away on the next cargo ship bound for the Far East. And I don't mean North Berwick.'

He thrust a folded sheet of paper at me. I took a look at it. It was a bail undertaking to return to court in three weeks, by which time the Crown would have decided whether to prosecute. Why wouldn't they? What was there to think about? People caught with two kilos of cocaine didn't receive bail undertakings and those with a previous analogous conviction were ineligible for bail, presumption of innocence or not.

'What did you tell them?'

Toffee jerked his head back as though he'd been hit in the face by a stiff south-westerly. 'Me? Nothing.'

'I really hope you haven't done anything stupid.'

'You think I'd grass on big Stan?'

I waved the bail undertaking sheet under his nose. 'Two kilos and you get this?'

Toffee stopped and pulled me back by the shoulder.

I turned to face him. 'Stan didn't know which court you were in. He told me you must have been lifted on the way to St Andrews. I'm pleased for you that you're out, but how you did it, and why you did it, and what Stan will think about it all, that's no business of mine.'

'But what if he asks you what happened?'

'I don't know what happened. You'll need to tell him.'

'And what will I say about me being in Edinburgh?'

I waited until we had walked past a queue of people at a bus stop. 'Tell him you got lost on the way to Fife. What difference does it make?'

I didn't know why, but it seemed to make a big difference to Toffee. For an ancient mariner, he now had the ghastly complexion of someone with terminal sea-sickness. He pointed ahead to the end of the street. 'How about we nick into Deacon Brodie's for a wee rum to settle my stomach?'

It was ten o'clock in the morning and I had better things to do than sit in a boozer discussing the finer points of cocaine trafficking with a wizened, old, rum-soaked salt. Both reasons for my meeting with Toffee had evaporated. Firstly, his court proceedings had been postponed, which meant I was not being paid, and, secondly, there was now no possibility of him agreeing to take the blame for supplying Antonia Brechin.

'It's important,' Toffee said. 'I need your help.'

What Stan Blandy and his cohorts did for a living, or how they went about it, was nothing to do with me. I only took to do with it if things went wrong. Up until that point, I preferred to stay well clear. 'I'm going to the station. If you've got something you want to tell me, you'll need to do it on the way.'

We walked on without talking, up to the Royal Mile and down the side of the High Court, coming to a halt at the top of the News Steps where there was no-one else around.

Toffee took a final draw on the few millimetres of rollie that remained and flicked it into the gutter. 'Stan can't find out about today.'

'Nothing to do with me,' I said.

'If he asks, I want you to tell him it was all a mistake.'

'Was it?'

Toffee rammed a hand into his trouser pocket and brought out a couple of crumpled twenties that he forced on me. 'Aye,' he said, 'it was.'

'What happened?' I asked him. He didn't answer.

'If you want my help, you'll need to tell me what the problem is.'

'And whatever I say, it stays between us? You'll not tell big Stan?'

My turn to hesitate. Toffee put his hand back into his pocket and rummaged around. I took hold of his elbow. 'I'm your lawyer. What you tell me is confidential. Stan knows you were arrested. That's why he sent me. It's only a matter of time until he finds out that you're a free man, and he might think what's good news for you is bad news for him, which could quickly turn into extremely bad news for you.'

I looked at my watch. The Linlithgow train ran every half-hour. It was five minutes until the next one and I was approximately four minutes away from the station.

'I'll need to go,' I said, handing him his money back. 'I'll not speak to Stan today, even if he calls me. You'd better make your mind up about what you want to tell him. But whatever he is, he's not daft, and if you being in Edinburgh is a problem...'

My phone buzzed. It was Ellen. 'Did you know?' She sounded upset.

'Ellen, I'm right in the middle of something and trying to catch a train at the same time.'

'Did you know about Freddy and that other woman!' she shrieked down the phone.

'I'll call you back,' I said.

'No, I want to see you now. I'm changing my will.'

'Where are you?'

'I'm still at the Balmoral.'

From the top of the steps I could see the hotel standing proudly on the other side of Waverley station, at the corner of Princes Street and South Bridge. Formerly the North British Railway Hotel, the hotel's famous clock, an Edinburgh landmark, had since 1902 been set three minutes fast to make sure travellers were in time for their trains. Even with that chronological safety net, I wasn't making mine.

'I'll be there in half an hour,' I said, and hung up before she could shriek at me anymore.

'Okay, Toffee. I'll give you ten minutes. What do you want to tell me?'

'Fancy a rum?' he asked, pressing the notes into my hand again and nodding his head back the way we'd come, to where Deacon Brodie's pub was perched at the top of the mound.

'No,' I said, 'I've a better idea.'

35

We found a corner table at the café on St Giles Street, next door to the High Court. It was quiet on a Monday morning. Apart from a few lawyers who were killing time for their case to call next door, it was just me, the old sea dog and his tale of woe.

'You know the procedure, don't you?' Toffee asked. Empty of rum, he was sipping miserably from a mug of tea he wished was distilled molasses.

'No,' I said, 'not in detail. Do I really need to?' Apparently I did.

'The stuff comes into Antwerp...'

I knew from past experience that the Belgian port of Antwerp was Europe's second busiest, handling hundreds of millions of tons of cargo each year and serving ships from hundreds of worldwide destinations. The operation was on such a massive scale that it was almost impossible to police and security was lax.

'Could you speed it up, because once I've finished this bacon roll I'm out of here,' I said, bringing about no noticeable change in the pace of Toffee's narration.

'From there Stan brings it into a Scottish port, could be anywhere, but it's usually along the Forth. I pick it up, make the delivery, collect the cash and drop it off. I never see Stan at any stage. Not unless there's been a mistake.' He laid his left hand flat on the small wooden table. The pinkie and ring finger were twisted and shrivelled. Did you think all I got the last time for getting caught was fifteen months?'

'Why do you work for him?'

'The money. Pure and simple.'

'If that's what happens to your hand when you make a mistake, what do you think's going to happen to the rest of you once he finds out you've grassed?'

'Would you stop saying that?' Toffee hissed, looking about as though Stan Blandy might emerge from behind the serving counter clutching a two-pound mash hammer.

'If you didn't grass, what's the big problem?'

'This is between you and me, understand?'

I was really wishing he'd get on with it. Those two twenties in my pocket were counting down.

'I picked the stuff up like he wanted. No bother. I always do a run to St Andrews this time of year. The last exams are next week and it'll be one big party. Anyway, then I was supposed to take the money to the drop-off point. It's a big safe in a warehouse in the middle of nowhere that Stan owns.'

'And you got caught?'

'No. I'm in Edinburgh, remember? I made the delivery. I just haven't dropped the money off yet.'

'You weren't thinking of bumping him, were you?'

'Naw, of course not, the money's stashed back at my place and I'll drop it off later today or the morn.'

So far, I couldn't see any misdemeanour that would necessitate Stan getting out the hardware. Drugs delivered, cash collected and about to be dropped off. 'What's the problem?'

I had time to take two bites from my bacon roll before Toffee replied. 'I kept a wee bit of the stuff back for myself.'

'How much?'

It was a simple enough question, but it set Toffee into plea in mitigation mode. 'They posh students have more money than sense. They couldnae tell quality gear from a bag of sweets.'

It was Toffee's way of saying that he'd skimmed some cocaine off the top and bulked what was left with glucose or some other cutting agent.

'How much?' I repeated.

'Never more than fifty grams. Maybe a hundred now and again.'

'This wasn't the first time, then?'

He shrugged. 'I've got a few regular customers of my own.'

I made the last of my roll disappear. 'How about you just tell me why the police arrested you in Edinburgh?'

'I had a blow-out on the Queensferry Road. I was causing an obstruction. The cops turfed up when I was changing the wheel. They were trying to help.'

'And they found something?'

'Aye, it was in the wee toolbox thing. I was keeping the stuff in there inside one of those re-sealable sandwich bags. I never had a chance to move it because they sneaked up on me.'

'What did you tell them?'

'That I'd only had the car a couple of months and never used the toolkit before. They arrested me anyway, but the PF released me to make further enquiries. They'll probably go and see the last guy who owned the motor. They'll have problems with that. He's dead. I bought it off his missus. I don't know if they'll come back to me or not. It was only fifty grams.'

'Enough to put you inside again.' I finished my coffee, wiped my hands on a paper napkin and stood up. 'Don't worry. I'll say nothing to Stan. Why's he going to be bothered if the delivery was made and he's getting his money?'

'Stan is a very cautious man. If he knows I was lifted, he's bound to ask what happened. Will you back me up if I tell him I was lifted for a breach of the peace in the pub or something?'

I looked down at Toffee's twisted fingers. Stan Blandy had contacts everywhere. If he was really interested, he'd find out what Toffee had been questioned about. 'No, your best bet is to tell him the truth,' I said. 'Or as near as you can.'

'I can't tell him about the...you-know-what.'

'Then don't, not exactly. The stuff will have been presumptively tested, but will be away to the forensic lab by now for a proper report. That'll take months. If Stan checks, all he'll find out is that you were found in possession of an unspecified quantity. Tell him the police must have found traces that leaked out before you made the delivery.'

Toffee seemed unconvinced. That was too bad. I had more important things to do than devise ways for him to cheat his boss. I left him one of his twenties to cover the bill and was in the foyer of the Balmoral inside ten minutes. I was about to ask reception to put a call up to Ellen's suite, when the woman herself approached me, dark glasses not hiding the black streaks of her tears.

'You knew.'

'Knew what?'

'Don't act all innocent. You knew Freddy had

another woman.'

'How would I know that?' Come to think of it, how did Ellen know?

Ellen's long-legged nurse was not dressed in her usual trouser-suit uniform today, and more casually attired in neat-fitting jeans and a sweatshirt. She put a hand on her charge's shoulder.

Ellen shook it off and thumped her fists on my chest. 'Why didn't you tell me?' Over her shoulder I could see the doorman, all top hat, tails and tartan trews, eyeing us up. Slowly he made his way from the revolving doors to stand under the ornate golden chandelier, not looking at us, but making it very clear that he was.

I took hold of Ellen's wrists. 'Let's go for a walk.'

'No, I'm wanting you to cut that cheating bastard out of my will, right now.'

What did she want me to do? Whip out pen and paper and jot down a quick codicil? Maybe the doorman could witness it before he frog-marched us off the premises.

'Calm down. We need to talk this through.'

'No, we don't. He's not getting my money.'

The doorman cleared his throat and took a couple of discreet yet meaningful steps in our direction. Now wasn't the time to remind Ellen that she didn't have any money. She wasn't actually a lottery winner. She was living off a loan she'd somehow managed to wangle out of Jake Turpie. A loan she'd have to repay one way or another.

'Come on,' I said, gently tugging her towards the door. 'Let's go for a walk and talk this over.'

Ellen wasn't for moving. The doorman came over. I looked up at him. He wasn't as tall as the Scott

Monument but looked to be built out of a similar material. I guessed he wasn't there just to give guests directions to Edinburgh Castle.

'Sir?' he enquired.

'Just leaving,' I said.

36

I was intercepted as I walked through the sliding doors of the Civic Centre on my way to court the next morning.

'What's new, Robbie?' Kaye Mitchell's voice was way too casual. 'Anything interesting on today?'

In the world of journalism, "interesting" translates as salacious or scandalous. As editor-in-chief of the Linlithgowshire Journal & Gazette, Kaye didn't normally do her own court reporting and so I knew there must have been a special reason for her to be there that Tuesday morning.

'Nothing particularly fruity,' I said, walking on, hoping I might shake her off and knowing I wouldn't.

'No special clients up today then? Just the same old faces, is it?'

I stopped. I could see Antonia and her mother on the top landing of the stairs leading to the court. I didn't want them to see me talking to the press. 'I'm sure you know very well that Sheriff Brechin's granddaughter is appearing today.'

'Just an in-out procedural diet, is it?'

'There's going to be no plea of guilty if that's what you mean.'

Kaye pursed her lips and nodded her head a few times. 'So, I might as well not be here?'

'That's entirely a matter for you.'

'Going to be pretty embarrassing for Bert Brechin,

wouldn't you say?'

Antonia had gone through the door, but her mother remained resolute at the top landing staring down at me. 'These things happen,' I said. 'She's not the first grand- child to have experimented with drugs and won't be the last. See you later.'

'I wasn't talking about the drugs, Robbie!' Kaye called after me.

I stopped, turned and walked back to where she was standing, looking pretty smug about something. 'Okay, let's have it.'

'You mean you don't know?' Kaye picked at a thumb- nail. 'Maybe it's not true then. A little bird told me...' She looked up. 'Actually it was a great big one in plain clothes.'

'Don't tell me, Dougie Fleming?' Over my career I'd had many a run-in with Detective Inspector Douglas Fleming, usually in connection with his notebook. Dougie Fleming was a cop who believed confession was good for the soul — and his conviction statistics.

'You know I can't disclose my sources,' Kaye said with a smile that confirmed my guess.

'And you would believe a word Fleming said? Talk about journalistic licence? Have you seen the admissions in his notebook? He makes up better stories than you do.'

'So you don't know?'

'What don't I know?'

'Where would you like me to start?'

'Kaye...'

'Sorry, my lips are sealed.'

Mrs Brechin's eyes were laser beams. I suggested Kaye and I meet at Sandy's later for a coffee.

'Will there be cake?' Kaye asked.

'There could be, but you'd have to unseal your lips to eat it.'

I could tell Kaye had milked the suspense as much as she could and was dying to tell me. 'The search warrant,' she said.

'The one in Antonia's Brechin's case?' She nodded.

'What about it?'

'Guess who signed it?'

'Oh, let me see. I'm guessing it was a sheriff?' I reined in my sarcasm. 'Wait...not...?'

'Yes. Or so I'm reliably, or according to you, perhaps not so reliably informed. That's why I wanted to check if you'd had the warrant disclosed to you by now.'

I had. Maybe it was because I was so used to seeing Brechin's signature at the end of a search warrant that it hadn't clicked. I usually just checked to make sure the date and place were accurate and that it had been enforced within the one-month time limit.

'I'll check it when I get into court,' I said. 'I can't do it now. My client's mum is giving me the evil eye.'

'Strange that he'd sign a warrant to allow the police to search his own granddaughter's flat, don't you think?' I had to admit it was surprising. Very surprising. 'And what about the sheer nerve of a cop presenting a warrant for signature to the suspect's grandfather?' That wasn't quite so surprising. When it came to brass necks, if you melted down D.I. Dougie Fleming you'd have had enough raw material to start your own colliery band.

Mrs Brechin was waiting for me when I reached the top of the stairs, her face set like there had been a sudden change in wind direction. 'Who was that you were talking to? She's a newspaper reporter, isn't she? Was she asking about Antonia's case? She was, wasn't she?' Mrs Brechin was doing a fine job of answering her own questions.

'You can't blame the local press for being interested,' I said. 'There's nothing the general public likes to read about more than some prominent figure being disgraced.'

'Even if it's not the prominent figure who suffers, but a young girl?'

Antonia Brechin was not a girl. She was a woman, one who must have known the risk she ran buying cocaine. Now wasn't the time to go into that.

'The Press is just doing its job,' I said. 'What did she want?'

'To know if anything would be happening today. I said that Antonia was pleading not guilty and so she's not interested. They only print a story where there's been a conviction. No-one wants to read about someone being acquitted.'

'But she'll be back?'

'It doesn't matter if she is. Antonia's case will be a headline one day, and a fish and chip wrapper the next.'

'So you think Antonia will be found guilty?' Mrs Brechin was working herself up into quite a state. There was no sign of Mr Brechin. 'I didn't say that.'

'Yes, you did. You said the newspapers only print the convictions and then you said Antonia would be a headline one day and—'

I was saved by the loudspeaker system announcing that proceedings were about to commence. Cutting Mrs Brechin loose, I took off down the corridor for Court 4 where Gail Paton had blown in from Glasgow leaving a trail of expensive perfume. She came over and sat down beside me in the well of the court. 'I hear you've sorted a deal to have the charge reduced to simple possession again. When were you going to tell me?'

'I was keeping it a surprise,' I said.

'I bet you were. And am I to be included in this arrangement?'

'That was the plan.'

'Was the plan?' Hugh Ogilvie looked up from his pile of red folders. 'You've no signed confession for me? Your man not prepared to take the rap? Get it? Take the wrap - with a W?'

'Comedy gold, Hugh,' Gail said, touching up her lipstick by the camera in her phone. 'So, are we simply knocking this case onto trial or what?'

'No, not necessarily.' Ogilvie casually flicked through some papers in one of his case files. 'I've decided that if you plead to simple possession today I'll accept it.'

I was glad to hear he'd come to his senses at last. 'You know what?' I said. 'I think I'll take that plea.'

A smile slithered across Ogilvie's face. 'No,' he said, 'you won't. I wasn't talking to you.' He looked straight at Gail. 'The deal is your girl pleads to the reduced charge, and testifies against Robbie's client at the trial. Interested?'

Gail looked extremely interested.

'Of course she's not interested,' I said, gently pulling Gail to her feet and guiding her a few feet further away so that we had our backs to the PF.

'Don't even think about it, Gail. We're in with a real shout here. All we do is turn the tables on this Freya

Linkwood. Our girls go in, say they knew nothing about the drugs and that it was all down to her. She's the one who's pled guilty to possession of the stuff. We can sell that story, can't we? You and me? I'm telling you, there's a big solid reasonable doubt just waiting for us to parcel up and present to the jury.'

If Gail's client took the deal Antonia was done for. The two co-accused would testify, reluctantly no doubt and there'd probably be tears, but it would all only make their evidence the more credible and reliable.

'Then again,' Ogilvie said, upping the stakes, 'if you don't want to take the deal, Gail, maybe I will offer it to Robbie's client. All I'm looking for is one conviction on the supply charge and two for the possession. I don't really care how it's carved up.'

I put my hands on the shoulders of Gail's black court gown. 'Don't listen to him. You know I'd never stab you in the back.'

'No, he'd do it staring you in the face,' Ogilvie said, enjoying every second.

Gail nipped her lower lip between her teeth and held it while she stared down at the floor and then, pushing past me, returned to her seat. 'How about we knock this First Diet on a week, Hugh, and I'll take instructions?'

37

'I know how it must seem to you, Robbie.'

It wasn't how it seemed that I was bothered about. I was more concerned with how it actually was. It hadn't taken Gail the seven days she'd been allowed to obtain instructions on the Crown's latest offer. It had taken less than ten minutes. I was pacing about in the agents' room when she returned to tell me the news.

'There's not much I can do,' she said, easing out of her gown, folding it a couple of times and cramming it into a big carpetbagger holdall. 'I can only advise and take instructions. I told my client that the deal would be conditional on her giving evidence against Antonia, and that if she did Antonia would likely be found guilty.'

'Only likely? You didn't tell her Antonia would definitely be found guilty?'

Gail smiled. 'I was giving you some credit.'

'So she's really going to plead and let her pal take the blame?'

'I'm afraid so. I even told her that there could be a prison sentence in it for your client. It made no odds. It's guilty and I'm going to draft an affidavit so there'll be no going back.'

I shoved a chair with the sole of my shoe and walked up the other end of the room to collect my own gown and briefcase.

'If it's any consolation, I'd rather go to trial,' Gail

called to me. 'For the money if nothing else. But this deal is best for my client, and her interests have to come first. You'd have done the same thing. Uh-uh,' she said, waving a hand at me, aborting my protests before they'd been conceived far less delivered. 'You would have. I know you would. And if you'd have listened to me and Andy at the beginning, neither you nor your client would be in this mess. It was you who talked me into tendering a not guilty plea in the first place. I shouldn't have listened to you then, I'm not listening to you now.'

'Okay. That's fine. Fair enough. You wheedle your way out if you must,' I said.

Gail marched up to me. 'I'm not wheedling my way out of anywhere. My client is going into the witness box to tell the truth. It was Antonia Brechin who was supplying the coke. The other two knew about it, but she was the one who bought it and was all set to dish it out after winning her stupid award. If you ask me, it's all working out as it should.'

Gail might have been right, but I didn't have to like it.

We cooled down with a reconciliatory hot cup of coffee

in the café downstairs before setting off to our respective offices. Back in Linlithgow I parked my car in its usual place outside Sandy's, and was about to dive in for a bacon roll when a Range Rover Sport with darkened windows pulled up to the edge of the pavement. A rear window lowered. 'Get in.'

I got in. The back seat would have been spacious enough if it hadn't also contained Stan Blandy.

'I want you to settle a bet for me, Robbie,' he said, as

the car pulled away into the early afternoon traffic on Linlithgow High Street. He seemed cheerful enough. It was the way he wasn't looking at me, but straight ahead through dark glasses at the broad neck of his driver that bothered me.

'Oh, yeah? What's that?'

'I was talking to a friend of ours. We spoke about him at the football on Saturday.'

'Toffee?'

'Aye. You see how he was lifted last weekend?'

'What about it?'

'He says everything's all right and he got a PF lib.'

'That's right.'

'Just like that? Off you go, Toffee. You're a free man.'

'That's what happened.'

'And there's going to be no comeback on me?'

I took a little longer to answer that question. 'I don't see why there should be.' I looked at the watch I wasn't wearing. 'I'd like to help, Stan, but I've got a lot of things to do this afternoon. How about we do this some other time?'

'We're doing it now.'

'You haven't even told me what the bet is.'

Stan removed his sunglasses and tucked them into the top pocket of his jacket. 'You're a very impatient man.'

'I'm a busy man.'

'Okay. Here's the bet. I know that Toffee never appeared in Dundee or whatever teuchter court he should have been in. He got taken to Edinburgh Sheriff and then somehow got released. I know you're good, but you're not that good. Toffee's given me his side of the story and he bets that you can back it up.' Stan raised an arm and laid it across my shoulders like a yoke. 'You know me, Robbie. I like a flutter, so I took him up on it. In fact, I've bet his life on it.'

38

Colin 'Toffee' McCowan was sitting bolt upright on an old straight-back dining room chair, ankles secured to the legs by plastic electrical ties, arms behind him bound at the wrists. It's always nice to feel wanted, and I could tell from his eyes that Toffee was extremely pleased to see me, though I could only tell from his eyes, because the rest of his face was wound around with silver duct tape and he was breathing, short and sharp, through a gap at his nostrils.

We weren't alone in the derelict dock warehouse. Besides myself and the man in the chair there was Big Stan, his driver and two other men who had been keeping the captive company until we arrived. As our small party approached, Stan ordered the two men to stand guard at the main door while his driver, short and stocky, shaved head, razor scar and a come-ahead expression, took up position behind Toffee.

Stan clapped his hands together. The sound echoed around the empty building, a reminder that we had the place all to ourselves. 'Here we are then. Time to find out the winner of our wee bet, Toffee.' He put a hand on the small of my back and urged me forward so that I was only a yard or so away from the chair. By now Toffee's eyes were showing mostly white. 'And I don't want you giving Mr Munro any clues, understand?' The driver delivered Toffee a swift punch to the ear, and the old mariner squeezed out a groan of pain, signal- ling his clear understanding with frantic nods of his tape- strapped head.

'Good,' Stan said. 'Over to you, then, Robbie. Explain how come it was that Toffee got arrested by the police and then mysteriously got out again. Maybe I should change his nickname to Houdini.'

There were two ways of explaining things. Unfortunately, the good way for me was the bad way for Toffee. 'Well, it's like this, Stan. Toffee was skimming your quality merchandise, bulking it up with icing sugar and then selling some of the good stuff to his own customers. The cops stopped him and have now got fifty grams of your Aunt Nora in a production cupboard. You could call it disloyalty, I'd prefer to call it business initiative, and the country needs more entrepreneurs.'

The driver scratched his nose with the back of his hand.

A hand that was holding a lock-back blade with a five- inch serrated edge.

I decided to go with the version we'd agreed over a bacon roll two days previously, hoping the prisoner had done the same. 'Toffee had a blow-out on the Queensferry Road. The cops turned up, became suspicious and found some powder in the boot of the car, must have leaked out of a package. Toffee told them he knew nothing about it and the PF had to release him.'

Stan eyed me, like I was trying to sell him a 99p Rolex. 'You know something, Stan? You are one very suspicious individual,' I said, trying to make light of an extremely heavy situation.

After a moment or two, Stan jerked his head at the

driver who cut the plastic ties holding the prisoner's hands together. 'Looks like I've lost another bet,' he said. 'It's getting to be a habit. Just take a finger off him, Rab. One of the knackered ones. He'll not miss it.'

The driver grabbed the hand that Toffee was using to rub circulation back into his wrist and brought the knife to bear.

'Hold on!' I shouted. 'What's that for?'

'Carelessness,' Stan said.

'Carelessness? I hate to say it, Stan, but if anyone's been careless here it has to be you.'

The driver, who had shown no emotion at being asked to remove one of the old sailor's digits, suddenly looked pained. He glanced from me to Stan, blinking rapidly.

Stan's eyes narrowed. He raised his hand, belaying the finger-sawing order. 'I'm...' He had a problem with the word. 'I'm careless, am I?' he just about managed to croak.

'When I say careless...'

'You did say it. You said I was careless. So tell me in what way you think I'm not careful, will you, Robbie?'

I cleared my throat. 'Okay. Who's the registered keeper of Toffee's car?'

Stan didn't know.

Toffee tore his hand out of the driver's grasp and used it to pull duct tape away from his face. 'It's me. The car's registered to me.'

'There you are,' I said. 'What are you doing, Stan? Letting an ex-con drive his own car on a drugs delivery? When the cops saw him broken down at the side of the road, the first thing they'd have done was check the reg to see if the tax and insurance were up to date. The second thing they would have done is check Toffee's record on the PNC for outstanding fines or warrants. Once they saw his previous conviction, they'd have been on the alert for signs of drugs before they came anywhere near the car. To do this sort of delivery properly, you should have—'

'Properly?' Stan winced as though he would have preferred the rough amputation of one of his own fat fingers than have his business practices criticised further. 'You don't think I do things properly?'

I was in too deep to stop now. 'First of all the car should have been registered to someone else, secondly whoever wrapped the stuff should have made a better a job of it so that there were no spillages, thirdly, you shouldn't have used someone with a criminal record to do this kind of work.' I manufactured a smile. 'You said it yourself. You're a big softy.' Stan's eyes narrowed. I pressed on. 'Anyway, the good news is that there's nothing to worry about. Nothing links you to Toffee or the car.'

After an age, he grunted, 'Aye, all right. Let him go.' The driver stooped to snip the ankle ties, allowing

Toffee to climb shakily to his feet.

A barely discernible jerk of Stan's massive head was the only invitation Toffee needed to stumble headlong for the door, ripping tape from his face and not looking back.

On the return trip to Linlithgow we didn't talk any more about Toffee or what had happened in the ware-house, and the Range Rover stopped precisely where I'd been picked up less than an hour before.

'How much am I due you?' Stan asked, as I bid him farewell.

'For what?'

'For Toffee the other day.'

'I never had to do anything. Call it quits for Saturday.'

'The football was on me. How much for going to court?'

If I turned down the offer of money, Stan would think something amiss.

'It was just a couple of hours of my time.'

Stan reached into his jacket pocket and removed some crisp, red fifties from a wallet the size of a suitcase. 'Oh, and, Robbie...' He held the notes out to me. I tried to take them, but he didn't let go at first. 'See, if I find out that you and that wee bastard have been lying to me? We'll see who's a big softy then.'

39

The month of May is a busy month for football. Pretty much like every other month of the year, Joanna would say, but, really, you couldn't ask for more than the chance to watch the finals of all the major competitions: Champions League, Europa Cup, Scottish and English FA Cups, as well as the league play-offs north and south of the border and, of course, pride of place, the Scottish Junior Cup Final.

The last Tuesday of the month would see the second leg of the semi-final between Linlithgow Rose and Irvine Meadow, the tie poised on a knife-edge after a draw in the first leg and home advantage now with the Rose.

I had been going. I wasn't now. Malky and my dad were.

Joanna, not long into her new job and being extra-dedicated, was working late on a cold-case she'd been lumbered with. That left me to look after Tina. Tuesday night was golf lesson night. I was in the garden with Malky, talking football. My dad, a maroon and white scarf knotted about his neck – only football supporters wore woolly scarves in summer – was giving his grand-daughter a few last-minute golf tips.

'That's right, straight back, bend your knees, plant your feet, keep your head still, swing smoothly, right elbow in by your side, don't flap it about like a chicken and shift your balance nice and easy.'

It was a lot for a five-year-old to take in, but at least golf was diverting Tina's mind from other things, like her missing bunny rabbit. I should never have left Tina alone to feed her pet on Sunday night. After feeding it that final carrot, she'd been unable to resist opening the hutch door for a goodnight cuddle. Rosie had jumped out of her arms and disappeared into the undergrowth, and undergrowth, as well as all sorts of different kinds of growth, was something there was a lot of in my dad's back garden. The animal hadn't been seen since, despite us wedging the hutch door open in hope of its return.

'What do you make of the Linlithgow's Rose's chances tonight?' I asked Malky, who, not surprisingly, was confident of a home win and a triumphant stroll to the final for the team he'd played for in his youth – until, that is, a magpie touched down and hopped over to the empty hutch where it began to show interest in the bowl of rabbit food that had been left to lure the missing Rosie.

'Shit!'

'What?'

'You see that magpie?' he said. 'That's one for sorrow.'

'Yeah, sorrow for the Irvine Meadow supporters,' I said. 'Have some faith in your team.'

'No. It was me who saw it, that means I'm the one who'll be sorry. That's how it works.'

I didn't know who drafted the legislation on superstitions, but my brother seemed to be familiar with all the various rules and regulations. 'It's okay. I saw another magpie a wee while ago,' I said. 'That's two for joy and since I'm a Rose supporter too—'

'How do you know it was definitely a different one?' Malky asked.

'A different one?'

'Aye, are you sure you haven't just seen the same magpie twice?'

'It wasn't wearing a name badge, if that's what you mean. It was a magpie, black and white, yellow beak, lots of feathers, wee bit arrogant looking.'

'It won't count if it was the same one. It'll still mean sorrow. You can't just go following the same magpie around all day until you get to the wish you want.'

Two more magpies came in to land next to the first, and saved me from having to put up a defence to the accusation that I was some sort of ornithological stalker. 'There you are, then. That's either three or four magpies we've seen today, depending on whether I saw the same one twice, so that means either—'

'Three for a girl or four for a boy.' Malky was all smiles now. 'We just need one more for silver, like the cup.'

I could almost hear my brain cells pleading for mercy. Meanwhile my dad's golf masterclass continued. 'Pretend that's the ball.' He pointed to an unsuspecting daisy that had mined its way up through the lawn. 'On you go, pet, in your own time. Head up, chest out, chin in and keep your eye on the ball.'

Tina swung like she was killing a cobra. The daisy had never really been in any danger. The first attempt hit fresh air. The second removed three inches of top soil a foot away from the flower and splattered it across the kitchen window.

'I don't bother with all that,' Malky said.

For someone who had taken up golf fairly recently,

and had never had a lesson or practised an hour in his life, my brother was infuriatingly good at the game.

'All what?'

'That keep your head still, bend your knees, stuff. It puts you off. I just go up and hit the thing.'

Maybe that's where I'd gone wrong. I'd listened to my dad too much. If I'd ignored him I'd probably have been on the European Tour by now, instead of an eighteen- handicapper with a swing like an axe-murderer.

'Aye, you don't want to go thinking too much about things,' Malky said. 'Works for me, anyway.'

'That's because not thinking comes easy to you,' I said. It took a second or two for the insult to register. He feinted a punch. Instinctively, I stepped back and stood on something soft. Soft and yet quietly crunchy. Somehow, before I checked under my heel, I knew I'd found the missing rabbit, but not before a fox had.

I kicked a piece of chewed head at Malky. 'Get rid of that before you go, will you?'

Before I could accidentally stumble over any more of Rosie's mortal remains, I gathered Tina's scattered golf clubs, put them in her wee pink golf bag, and, taking her by the hand, half-dragged her to the car and her golf lesson. I shouldn't have bothered.

'Maybe you could have a word with her, Robbie. I don't think Tina's herself tonight. She's a wee bit...crabbit.' Steve the golf instructor was a young man with a lot of dark, sticky-up hair and a gift for understatement.

Despite his best efforts, as well as my own vocal encouragements from the rear of the driving-bay, things had not gone well thus far. Tina had hit fifty golf balls. None had flown remotely straight nor travelled as far as the junior seven-iron she'd hurled in rage after her last attempt, and which now nestled in the lush grass of the golf range.

I knew the reason she was upset. I'd felt the reason crack under my heel. I hadn't told her of course, only mentioned that I didn't think Rosie would be coming home because she'd run off with some other bunnies to live in a field full of dandelions far, far away.

Steve picked up the empty wire-basket. 'I'll get some more balls and we'll have another go. How's that?' He tried to ruffle Tina's hair, but she wasn't having it.

I hunkered down and took her wee hands in mine. 'How about you hit some more golf balls and then we go to Sandy's for ice cream?'

In response to this, Tina pulled herself free, folded her arms and rested her chin on them. As far as my parenting skills went, the weapon of last resort was the ice cream bribe. Seeing it fail so miserably meant I was out of ammo. Joanna would have known what to do. If only she'd been prepared to let her cold case chill a little while longer, she could have taken Tina to her lesson and let me go to the cup semi-final with my dad and Malky. Come to think of it, why wasn't my old man here? Why me? Okay, I was Tina's dad, but the whole golf lessons thing had been his idea.

Thankfully, Tina's bouts of huffiness, though annoyingly frequent, didn't tend to last long, a bit like party political broadcasts. I decided to give her a minute, taking advantage of the lapse in proceedings to phone Joanna. After I'd explained how well things weren't going, I asked her to do me a favour.

'I can't, Robbie, and you shouldn't be asking me.'

'I only want to know what's happening. He's a client of mine who was arrested at the weekend and for some reason it was decided just to release him on a bail under- taking. Can't you look it up on the computer and tell me why? His name is Colin McCowan. I can't remember his date of birth but it's probably nineteen-fifty-something. He's got one previous for being concerned in the supply about eight years ago.'

I signed off when I noticed Tina had changed sports and was now playing football with her golf bag. Watching out for sliced shots from adjacent stalls, like a commando under fire, I went and collected the hurled seven-iron. On the way back I picked up a golf ball, placed it on the rubber tee and handed Tina the club. She wouldn't take it, arms still resolutely folded.

'One last shot and that'll be us,' I said. 'Just one hit and that's it. It doesn't matter where it goes or how far. I don't even mind if you miss. Just do your best and have one more proper try and then we'll go see Sandy for ice cream.' Tina thought about it for a moment. She snatched the club from me. I put a hand on her shoulder. 'Do you know who the best golfer in the world is?' Apparently she did.

It was her Gramps. She had his word on it.

'No, he's second best,' I said. 'The best is your Uncle Malky. And do you know what his secret is? Do you know what he does to make the ball go so far?'

Tina was making a good show of trying not to look interested.

'He just thinks about nothing. He doesn't think about his feet, or keeping his head still, or his elbows or anything. He just steps right up and whacks it.'

I heard Steve, who'd returned with another basket of

balls, mutter something about the importance of squaring up to the line of flight, but I carried on regardless. 'Think of something you're really good at.' I tickled her. 'Come on. What are you really, really good at?'

She thought about it. 'Painting,' she said at last.

It was perhaps fair to say that the world of fine art was divided on Tina's artistic genius. On one side there was my dad and Tina, and on the other side there was the rest of us.

'Okay, then, and when you paint a flower you don't think hard about it, do you? You just think what a flower looks like in your head and paint it.' I wasn't sure if any of this was either making sense or getting through to her five- year-old brain. 'That's what you should do here. Imagine the ball flying through the air for miles and miles and then don't think about anything, just step up and hit it.'

Tina stared down at the end of the seven-iron resting on the green rubber mat.

'Then we'll go for ice cream,' I said.

With a sigh, a roll of the eyes and a deep breath, she steadied herself and looked into the distance, presumably clearing her mind of everything except the vision of a golf ball in flight. Eventually, a determined look on her face, she pulled the club back and up and brought it down again, grunting with the effort.

If my daughter had imagined the ball taking a vicious slice off the toe of her club, striking the driving-bay wall, bouncing back at a tight angle and whacking Steve high on the shin, then she had manufactured the perfect shot. I think we'll leave it there for tonight,' I said and, collecting Tina and her clubs, we left the golf instructor rubbing his leg and not looking forward to next Tuesday night.

Sandy was scooping ice cream onto a cone when Jake Turpie called me. It was urgent. I'd never had a call from Jake that wasn't.

I met him at his cottage on the outskirts of town. The one that he'd bought on Freddy's advice. By the time we arrived it was getting on for Tina's bedtime and, apart from the evidence left behind on the front of her sweat- shirt, the ice cream was but a fond memory.

Jake came to the door. His new mutt was tied to a post in the front garden and, like the rest of Jake's workforce, looking miserable and down-trodden. The dog cheered up as soon as it saw Tina, tail wagging, tongue lolling, straining at the length of clothes line that was cutting into its furry neck.

'How's the latest recruit doing?' I asked. The animal that was supposed to be the replacement for Jake's previous murderous mutt was now rolling on the ground, paws in the air, having Tina rub its tummy.

'It'll no' learn,' he said. 'This one's on borrowed time.

There's plenty more at the pound.'

I untied the dog and gave the end of the clothes line to Tina. 'Just go for a walk about the garden. Don't go far,' I said, and followed Jake inside.

Stepping into that cottage was like stepping back in time. Floral wallpaper, swirly-patterned carpets, dark wood furniture and multi-coloured zig-zag curtains. The whole interior design looked like it was best experienced with the aid of mind-enhancing drugs, and quite possibly had been in the Sixties which, by the look of things, was the last time the place had been dusted.

Such was the assault on my visual senses that it took me a moment or two to realise that there was someone else in the room, sitting on a chintz sofa, sipping gin from a teacup. Ellen acknowledged my presence with no more than a flutter of her eyelashes before turning her gaze once more to the teacup in her lap.

'I'm sending some boys round in the morning to give this place a clean,' Jake said. 'And I'm bringing in some new bedding and that. I've given Ellen money for food and told her she can stay here for as long as she likes or finds somewhere else or until...You know what I mean.'

'Get fed up with all that luxury over at the Balmoral, did you, Ellen?'

'There was a problem with the bill,' she said.

The problem, I strongly suspected, now belonged entirely to the Balmoral. 'Why am I here?' I asked Jake. 'I've got Tina with me and it's past her bedtime. Could this not have waited until the morning?'

Ellen poured herself the last from a green bottle and set it down on the stone tiles in the hearth, eyes fixed on it like it might magically refill itself. 'I'm cutting Freddy out of the will and leaving everything to Jake,' she said.

Ellen still hadn't got it into her head that she didn't have anything to leave to anyone.

'It was you who made me find him and bring him back. Now that he's here it's not possible to cut him out of your will,' I said.

'How come?' Jake wanted to know.

'Because Freddy is Ellen's husband. When she dies, he'll be her widower and he has legal rights to at least some of her estate, and that's not her only problem.'

'What do you mean?' Jake asked.

'Ellen's biggest problem is that she doesn't have any estate.'

'Not yet,' Jake said. 'But you're sorting that out. Remember?' He jabbed a finger at me. 'You're going to see to it that she does have something and that it gets left to me.'

'No, I'm not,' I said.

Jake squinted, as though I hadn't made myself perfectly clear.

'I'm not doing it. I'm out. It's got nothing to do with me. Ellen has told me nothing but a pack of lies from the start. I won half a million on the lottery, no, actually, it was only fifty grand, well, really, I didn't win anything and I borrowed the money from Jake, but all I wanted was to see my husband, but now I don't want to see him again. I've had it. I wanted to help her, but that was when—'

'When you thought I was a lottery winner.' Ellen drained the last from the teacup and put it down by the bottle of gin in the hearth. 'Before that you wouldn't even take my phone calls.'

I walked over to the window to check on Tina. Her bad mood was gone and she and the dog were taking it in turns to chase each other. 'I've already said I'll put you onto somebody that I know who can help, but after that I'm out. Is that understood?'

'Sammy Veitch? That rip-off merchant?' Ellen snorted as though what we were talking about wasn't ripping off an insurance company for half a million.

'He knows what to do,' I said. 'So do you.'

'But he's prepared to do it. I'm not.'

Ellen lowered her head and stared at the gin bottle. It was still empty.

'How much is Veitch wanting to do this?' Jake asked.

'Fifteen grand, something like that. You can sort that out with him yourself,' I said. 'And what about you?'

'What about me?'

'Are you expecting to be paid?'

'What are the chances?'

'Not too good.'

'Then, in that case,' I said, 'I'll settle for something else.'

40

Tina was in bed and asleep, Linlithgow Rose were through to the Scottish Junior Cup Final, my dad was celebrating in the Red Corner Bar and Malky had gone back to Glasgow.

Joanna arrived home around ten looking exhausted. She staggered through to the kitchen and put the kettle on before flopping down beside me on the sofa.

'What are you looking so pensive about?' she asked.

'Nothing.'

'Nothing? You're sitting staring at a blank TV screen. You've either forgotten how to switch it on or you're thinking about something.' She pecked my cheek and snuggled into me. 'Go on. Tell me what you're thinking about.'

Women are always very keen to know what men are thinking about, even though the range of subjects is fairly limited and therefore highly predictable.

'I'm just thinking about stuff. Anyway, how are you getting on with your cold case? Warmed it up yet?' But I wasn't side-tracking Joanna quite so easily. 'All right,' I said, 'I was thinking about another woman.'

Joanna unsnuggled herself.

'Ellen Fletcher,' I said. 'Remember I was telling you about her life insurance plan?'

'The plan I told you to have absolutely nothing to do with? Yes, I remember that very clearly.'

'I was hearing an interesting story about her

tonight.'

'Really?'

'It's more a piece of gossip.'

Joanna sat up. 'Even better. But first I'll go check on Tina.'

'No need,' I said. 'She's only just gone to sleep. If you wake her she'll be up all night.' The kettle boiled and I went through to the kitchen and made tea. 'Do you want some toast with that?' I asked on my return with two steaming mugs.

'Yes, but in a minute. I want to hear the gossip first.' And so I told her what I'd learned.

Ellen and Jake Turpie had been an item years ago when in their teens and early twenties. Jake had been all set to pop the question and then the incident with her brother took place. She and Jake separated. Whether that was to be a permanent arrangement or not was decided by the arrival on the scene of the older and more sophisticated Freddy Fletcher. He swept young Ellen off her feet with promises of travel and riches and not a life counting wrecked cars in and out of a scrapyard.

Until very recently Ellen had not believed Freddy guilty of conning Jake out of his money. She knew Freddy wasn't the brightest, but didn't think even he was stupid enough to pull a stunt like that. Moreover, she knew Jake and that he needed scant excuse to rid the world of the man who'd stolen his true love. Whether that true love was Ellen or the £150k was open to debate.

One night, with her husband off making himself extremely scarce, Ellen had invited Jake round to her house for the evening, hoping to talk him out of doing anything hasty.

'That was brave of her,' Joanna said. 'What made her think he'd listen?'

I wasn't sure, except apparently Ellen had thought removing her clothes would improve Jake's hearing. That was when Freddy had made a surprise appearance, returning home to collect a few things.

Joanna knew the rest of the story. Or thought that she did. Cheated-Freddy had left Ellen and fled to Europe, ending up in Prague.

'It turns out that wasn't quite the whole story,' I said.

'Nothing is with that pair,' Joanna said.

'Freddy had another woman all the time. Whether or not he meant to con Jake, the fact is he cleared out and moved to Prague with the new love of his life. Now that Ellen's found out the truth she isn't happy. She's writing him out of her will.'

'Does Ellen have anything to leave to anyone?'

'You don't want to know,' I said.

She emptied her mug of tea. 'That's right. All I want to know is that you're out of it. Whatever it is.'

I kissed her in confirmation.

'Then I've got some news for you on your drugs man. What was his name again?'

'McCowan. Colin Toffee McCowan.'

The headlights of a taxi bringing my dad home flashed against the curtains of the front window.

'It's good news for him and bad news for you if you needed the business,' Joanna said. 'His bail undertaking has been cancelled and the case is marked for no further proceedings. The cops don't have enough evidence. There was a small bag of cocaine in a toolbox in the boot of the car, but it was well concealed and there's nothing other than his ownership of the car to link it to him. He made no comment during his interview and the vehicle's had lots of previous keepers, some with very shady pasts. The last one, Lee Conway, I think his name was, also had a conviction for dealing coke.'

I remembered Lee. Six feet five, skinny with a daft wee moustache, he'd been one of Stan Blandy's boys too.

'Conway died a couple of months ago. Your client bought the car from his widow. For all anyone knows Conway might have been dealing again and what was found in the car could have been his.'

It was good news. Great news. I sensed the looming presence of Stan Blandy lifting like mist off a mountain.

The front door opened as Joanna continued. 'They also found some fingerprints on the plastic bag the drugs were in. But they weren't your client's, they belonged to a female. I thought I recognised the name. Freda, no Freya. Yeah, Freya someone. I didn't bother to check into her.'

Was she talking about Andy's client? She couldn't be, could she? 'Not Freya Linkwood?'

'Yes, I think that might have been the name. Who is she?'

'I'll explain later.'

'Explain now.'

'I can't,' I said. 'Not right now. Do you know what's going to happen to her?'

'Nothing. There are too many variables to pin the drugs on anyone in particular, Apparently, this Freya person has another case pending anyway, and so the marking depute has just asked for the drugs to be confiscated and otherwise put a red pen through the whole thing. Now do you care to explain why you were so interested in the case?'

'I'd rather not.'

'So, you want me to snoop around trying to find out what's happening to your client, but you won't explain what's so important?'

'I'd like to explain, but I just can't. Not right now.' The living room door opened and my dad entered, maroon and white scarf knotted loosely around his neck, and in less of a celebratory mood that one might have expected. 'Would someone care to explain why there's a dog sleeping on the bairn's bed?'

I got to my feet. Joanna jumped to hers, the empty mug falling out of her lap and onto the floor.

'A dog? Where? In Tina's room?' She glanced about, presumably looking for a weapon. Seeing none she pushed me in the direction of my daughter's bedroom.

'It's okay,' I said, raising my hands in surrender, 'the dog is something I can explain.'

41

Someone else who had a lot of explaining to do was Toffee McCowan. How had the fingerprints of one of Antonia's co-accused been found on a packet of drugs in the boot of his car?

I had no means of tracking him down, and I wasn't sure how helpful he would have been even if I had.

I was in two minds. From one angle the news of Freya's dabs on a bag of drugs was good. It was evidence to support a defence that she, not Antonia Brechin, was responsible for supplying the party cocaine. As reasonable doubts went it was a cracker. The bad news was I couldn't use it in court without fear of implicating Toffee and that would not go down at all well with Stan Blandy; nonetheless, the more I thought about it the more I realised that even if I couldn't use the actual evidence, perhaps just the threat of it might achieve the same result.

Andy and the other legal assistants shared open-plan offices on the first floor of the big glass building up at Quartermile, each workstation separated from the next by a shoulder-height partition. There was a water cooler in one corner, a coffee machine in another, and in between a lot of young, well-dressed people staring at computer screens. Finding a meeting room wasn't easy. Andy didn't get to see clients unless accompanying one of the partners, on which occasions he was expected to input only when outputted to.

'I can give you ten minutes,' he said as, having climbed the stairs to the next floor, he led me along a walkway lined with abstract bronze sculptures, artificial flowers and the occasional David Hockney print. 'I've booked the conference room, but I'll need to release it by three o'clock.'

'I don't need a conference room,' I said. 'I'd be happy enough to discuss your client's drug-dealing activities out here in the corridor. It's just that I wouldn't want her dad, that is your boss, to hear the news before you did.'

'Would you keep your voice down?' Andy said. We came to a door with a small brushed-aluminium sign on it. He slid the sign from 'vacant' to 'engaged' and ushered me into a room. It wasn't all that big. It wouldn't have held the entire population of Linlithgow.

I sat down in one of the many identical chairs ranked around an enormous solid wood table. Andy remained standing. 'Robbie, if you're here to try and make my client admit to something she hasn't done, so that—'

'Hold on,' I said. 'Nobody wants your client to admit to anything she hasn't done.'

'Yes. You do. That was why you came through to see me last time.'

'Well, things change. The reason I've come all this way is to give you some news.'

'Good or bad?'

'That depends.'

'On what?'

'On whether you're me or whether you're you.'

'Okay, what's my news?'

'It's bad. One of my clients, a drugs courier, you don't know him, but he was arrested last Friday.'

'So?'

'The cops found a package containing fifty grams of cocaine in his car.'

Andy checked his watch. 'What's this got to do with me?'

'They can't link the package to my client.'

'It was found in his car. Isn't that a pretty good link?'

'Not as good a link as having someone else's fingerprints all over it.' That elicited no response from Andy. I was going to have to spell it out to him. 'Freya Linkwood's fingerprints.'

Andy emitted a short, throaty laugh. 'I don't believe you.'

'You don't have to take my word for it. Phone Joanna. She's working at the PF's again. It was she who told me about it.'

Andy sat down on a chair next to mine, placed the heels of both hands against his brow and leaned back to stare up at the recessed ceiling lights, groaning softly. This went on for a while until suddenly he removed his hands and sat up straight. 'Why...?' He tapped his forehead and then pointed a finger at me. 'Are you telling me this? Why aren't you using it for your defence? What more do you need? You call Freya as a witness, she's already admitted possession of the coke in her flat. All you need to do is put it to her that, since her fingerprints are on another bag of coke found somewhere else, that it's her and not Antonia Brechin who's the dealer.'

What Andy had suggested was exactly what had first sprung to my mind, until I'd realised that when

Freya was eventually questioned they'd ask for her supplier and she'd put them onto Toffee. That would resurrect the case that had been no pro'd against him and make Stan Blandy a very unhappy man at having been lied to.

'Well? Why not?' Andy asked. 'It's a sound enough defence, isn't it? Why are you telling me?' I'd taught the boy well. If only to be highly suspicious of everything I did. 'What's your angle, Robbie?'

This was quickly developing into a very delicate situation and, as such, no time for me to start dabbling in the truth, at least not the whole truth. 'We're friends, Andy. I wanted to do you a good turn. Tip you off. Do I have to have an angle?'

'Robbie, you've got more angles than medieval Mercia. Out with it. You've got a plan or you wouldn't be here.'

'Has Freya signed the affidavit?'

'Not yet, but it's drafted.'

'Tell her not to sign it. The Crown can't force her to. When she's called to give evidence, I'll put it to her that she was the person who supplied Antonia Brechin with the drugs.'

'And you'd expect her to admit that?'

'All she has to say is that she doesn't want to answer the question in case it incriminates her. That together with her admitted possession should be enough for me to spin a reasonable doubt.'

I didn't think Andy gave that suggestion the consideration it deserved. 'And if she refuses?'

'I'll lodge the drugs and the sandwich bag—'

'Sandwich bag?' Andy scoffed. 'The drugs were in a sandwich bag? Freya could have dropped it in the street. Someone could have picked it up later and used it for keeping drugs in.'

'You could always try that as a defence, Andy. Although you do realise we're talking about an ordinary plastic sandwich bag, not one from the delicatessen department of Harvey Nicks. Once I lodge it and the fingerprint report as defence productions, your girl's going to have a lot of explaining to do.'

There was a knock at the door. Andy got up and went to see who it was. 'Freya...' He opened the door wide and stepped back to allow her in.

'I'm sorry to bother you,' she said. 'It's just that when I saw you and Mr Munro together downstairs I wondered if you were discussing the court case. I've been checking round all the consulting rooms to see where you were.'

If I'd been asked what I expected someone called Freya to look like, I'd have said tall, athletic, blonde hair, quite possibly worn in plaits, and great cheek bones. Freya Linkwood was all of those things, aside from the plaits. Her hair was cut severely short. She looked from Andy to me with an air of suspicion and then glanced casually around the otherwise uninhabited room. 'So what's going on?'

Andy pulled a chair out. 'Robbie's come to bring me some news. He says that on Friday the police stopped and searched a car. They found a sandwich bag full of cocaine. Your fingerprints were on it.'

Freya sank into the chair.

'All you have to do is refuse to testify and no-one need know about the bag or your fingerprints.'

'How can I refuse to testify?'

'Say you don't want to self-incriminate.'

'And let you make it look to the jury like I'm the drug dealer?' she said, face flushed. I'd seen happier Vikings. The young woman took a moment to compose herself before turning to Andy. 'What do you think I should do?'

He shrugged. 'I can only advise you to tell the truth.' For once I agreed.

'Okay then.' Freya shifted in her chair, sat up straight. 'You really want the truth?'

The way she said that, staring defiantly up at me through eyes glazed with tears, made me strongly suspect I perhaps no longer did.

'This man came to the door of the flat one night when I was by myself. He was old with a face like a prune, like he'd fallen asleep under a sun lamp and woken up twenty years later.' Freya attempted a laugh at what was an excellent description of Colin 'Toffee' McCowan. 'He said he had a package for someone and asked if I was Antonia. I told him I wasn't and that she was out, but he handed it to me and stupidly I took it. It was a plastic bag. I suppose it might have been a sandwich bag. There were two other bags inside it, all scrunched up with a knot at one end. I didn't know what it was at first...' Freya reached out into the centre of the table and pulled over a decanter of water and a glass tumbler. 'Then suddenly I realised.' She poured herself a drink and took two or three short sips before continuing. 'I told him to take the drugs and go. He said it was okay, that they'd been paid for, and when I said I wanted nothing to do with it he wasn't very pleased. That's when Antonia arrived. She said we had to take the cocaine because it was a gift. She told me to take one of the small bags and I did. I gave the big bag

253

back to the man. We didn't know what to do with the stuff, so we put it into a box on the coffee table in the living room. Nobody touched it after that, and that's where the cops must have found it.'

Just as Freya had grown less upset and more confident with every word she spoke, Andy looked less worried and a lot more smug.

'That clear enough for you, Robbie?' he asked.

'I don't want to get Antonia in any trouble,' Freya said. 'It wasn't really her fault.'

'You've said enough, Freya,' Andy said.

Not for my purposes she hadn't. 'What do you mean, not really her fault?'

'I'm sure it was all down to a daft discussion we had,' Freya said. 'Quite a few lawyers meet up at the Aspen Lounge on Princes Street on a Friday for an after-work drink.' Freya played with the tumbler, holding it by the rim, turning the heavy base around and around on the polished table. 'Antonia was there with a group from Fraser Forrest and Hawke. We started talking about what we'd do to celebrate if one of us won at the Scotia Awards. We decided we'd have a party at the flat. Someone, I can't even remember who, mentioned cocaine and champagne. It was a joke. I said my dad would lay on the champagne if I won. Antonia's boss heard us and said he'd supply the coke if it was her. It was all a big laugh.'

Antonia's boss? She couldn't mean Ted Hawke. Not Uncle Ted.

She did.

'I thought Ted was joking.' Freya set down the tumbler. 'Evidently he wasn't.'

42

I had a trial on Friday that lasted well into the afternoon and helped distract me from the respective plights of Antonia Brechin and Ellen Fletcher. Over the recent days and weeks I'd spent so much time thinking about their cases that I'd almost forgotten another client who was also extremely worried about her future.

It should have been a big year for Heather Somerville, a graduation in July, followed by a teaching career starting in August, and, before either of those, the small matter of a June wedding. But she hadn't swung by to drop me off an invitation.

'You've lost weight,' I said. A man is usually on safe ground with a statement like that to a member of the opposite sex, especially one who is all set to squeeze into a wedding dress. I hadn't expected it to lead to tears. I pushed a box of tissues across the desk at her and waited a few minutes for Heather to pull herself together. And then a few more.

'I'm sorry,' she said, sniffing. 'I suppose I should be thankful that all the worry has saved me from having to diet.' She smiled a pale, sickly little smile. 'I was wondering if you had any news about my appeal.'

I told her the appeal papers had been lodged the same day she'd given me instructions to proceed, and the hearing on adjustments had taken place nearly two weeks ago. I'd be receiving Brechin's final Stated Case very soon, and it would be sent on to the Summary

Appeals Court. 'An Appeal Sheriff will look at it and decide whether it has merit enough to go forward to a full hearing.'

'What if it doesn't?'

'If it fails the first sift we can try again. If it fails a second time,' I said, anticipating her next question, 'I'm afraid that's pretty much that. The conviction will stand.'

'What do you think my chances are?'

What I thought was that we'd been through all this on her last visit when she'd brought her hard-of-understanding fiancé with her. On this occasion, she'd left him in the waiting room.

'Until I've read the final Stated Case, I can't say with any certainty,' I said, 'but the prospects for a successful appeal aren't good. They never were. You know that.'

Heather closed her eyes, clamped the tissue to her nose and nodded.

'Have you made enquiries with the General Teaching Council about what will happen if the conviction stands?' I asked.

She had. The good news was that the assault hadn't involved a child. The bad news was that it was, nonetheless, a crime of violence and classified as domestic assault. If the conviction remained on her record, she'd have to wait at least two years before she could apply for admission.

'They say the conviction will stay on my record forever,' she said. 'Teaching is an exempt profession under the Rehabilitation of Offenders Act and a conviction is never spent. It's not going to help me find employment, even if I am admitted as a suitable person.'

It was fast approaching five o'clock. I had letters to sign, and Grace-Mary would need to leave soon to catch the last post. No matter how much I sympathised with my client's predicament, she was just another casualty of the Crown's zero tolerance policy and Sheriff Albert Brechin's zero tolerance attitude.

'Where's the wedding going to be?' I asked, hoping to lighten the mood and generally wind up the session.

'St Michael's, a week tomorrow. It's an early start: eleven o'clock.'

'Then that's what your mind should be on,' I said. 'Not a conviction for giving your boyfriend a clip around the ear. Let's wait and see how the appeal goes. Even if it doesn't go well, who knows? Maybe the GTC will understand what you were going through at the time. It might help if you introduce them to your fiancé.'

She managed to smile at my attempt at a joke. With a final dab at each eye, she tossed the tissue in the waste paper basket and rose to her feet.

'Rest assured, I'll let you know as soon as I hear anything,' I said, walking her out of the room.

'If it's good news I want to know right away. If it's bad, wait until after the wedding,' she said, as her fiancé, hearing our voices, came out of the waiting room to meet us in the corridor. 'That way...' on tiptoe she reached up and kissed him on the cheek, 'when I kill Bobby at least I'll get a widow's pension.'

I wished them both all the best. Big Bobby might not have been the brightest, but my client was marrying an honest man, one who knew how to take an oath and stick to it, even if in Sheriff Brechin's witness box had been the worst place to do it.

43

I arrived home to find Bouncer lying in the driveway, rolling around trying to catch his tail and my dad and future father-in-law standing at the front of the cottage, staring up at the roof.

Bouncer stopped trying to bite his tail, started wagging it instead and came over, jumping up at me.

'How's it going, Robbie?' Jim said, shaking my hand. 'Your dad asked me to swing by the first time I was passing and take a look at his flashing. There's been a bit of storm damage over the winter. I suppose Joanna told you all about the problems with your own house plans?' He screwed up his face in sympathy. 'It's a lot of cash to spend on not much house. You'd never get your money back on it if you sold it any time soon. Like in the next twenty years.'

'It was a nice idea,' I said, 'but we'll just have to think again. Lower our sights.'

'Something will come up,' Jim said. 'What's for you will not go by you, and I'm always here to help out in any way I can. Just give me a shout.'

Next up was my dad. 'About this dog.' On cue Jake Turpie's former apprentice guard dog padded over to him, tail wagging, gazing up adoringly at the old man. 'How long is it planning on staying here?' he said, as though Bouncer was considering taking out a lease on the premises.

'I don't know. How long do dogs live?' I replied.

'Oh, no. You can play the Good Samaritan if you like, but don't start thinking you're papping the mutt onto me.'

'The Good Samaritan didn't help dogs,' I said, bending to rub Bouncer's fuzzy head. 'And you've got tons of room for him here.'

'I never asked you to get me it.'

'Consider him a present.'

'No chance. When you go, it goes.'

The roar of an engine heralded Joanna's return from work. She managed to squeeze her sports car past her dad's works van and park up the side of the cottage, blocking my car in. She came around to the front of the house and gave her dad a hug. From inside Tina appeared at the front door, followed by Malky. My brother's football phone-in radio show had finished for the close season and he'd come through early for his tea prior to our regular Friday night five-a-side session.

'It's getting pretty crowded around here,' Jim said.

'Not too crowded that I can't open a home for stray dogs, apparently,' my dad said.

'Come off it.' Malky picked up the dog, jerking his head this way and that as it tried to lick his face. 'Bouncer's brand new. He'll be great company for you when everyone goes and you're left on your own.'

'I don't mind being left on my own. You mix with a better class of person.'

Malky put the dog down and it ran off around the rear of the house with Tina in hot pursuit.

'What's with the dog, anyway?' Jim asked. 'I thought you hated dogs, Jo.'

'I do,' she said.

'Is that right?' Malky asked. 'You're a vegetarian

259

who hates dogs?'

'Just because I don't want to eat something doesn't mean I have to like all its panting and slobbering.'

'That's what all Robbie's girlfriends say,' Malky said.

Jim laughed. 'No, really, were you not thinking about getting Tina a rabbit?'

'We had a rabbit,' Malky said, bumping shoulders with me and Joanna in turn. 'Until this pair allowed it to be torn to pieces by the local fox. We're still finding body parts. It's like a butcher's shop out back.'

That wasn't quite true, but it wasn't easy explaining to a five-year-old that her bunny had gone off to live with some bunny friends when you kept tripping over bits of fur and bone scattered about the back garden.

The two dads and Joanna went inside and Malky and I walked around to the back garden to watch Tina throw a tennis ball for Bouncer. Rather than allow the dog to sleep indoors, my dad had turned the mega-hutch into a kennel by removing the door and putting an old piece of carpet and a blanket inside. Someone had thrown in one of Tina's soft toys.

A magpie swooped down. It landed not far from us and strutted its stuff on the grass until Bouncer chased after it, sending it soaring skywards again, white wing tips spread out like a fan, the bright sunlight of a June late-afternoon bringing out a blue sheen to black plumage and a bright green tint to long tail feathers. I hoped Malky didn't notice and start banging on again about one-for-sorrow.

My phone buzzed. Malky flicked the dog's tennis ball up with his foot and played keepy-uppy while I took the call. It was Sammy Veitch.

'If we're going to do this thing, is there any chance

we can do it soon, Robbie? It's just that the wife's trying to drag me off on a fortnight's holiday before the end of the month when the schools get out and the prices rocket. I'm free tomorrow, if that suits you. How about eight o'clock?'

'I'm not sure what I'm doing tomorrow night,' I said. 'I think I might be trying to have a life.'

'Not tomorrow night. Tomorrow morning. Early start and we can put this thing to bed by noon, no problem.'

I phoned Jake Turpie. He was fine with eight the following morning and we agreed to meet at the cottage that Ellen was to make her home for the time she had remaining. Then I phoned Sammy back to confirm arrangements. It would only take me minutes tomorrow morning to introduce him to his new clients and then I'd be well out of it and back home to a Saturday morning fried breakfast. With one less problem to worry about, I could concentrate on Antonia Brechin's upcoming trial.

Joanna came out of the back door and hooked an arm through mine.

'Tough day?' I asked.

'Yes, and it just got a lot tougher. Somehow it's my turn to make dinner again, and my dad and Malky are staying too, so that's just the six of us. Robbie, we all know I'm not the world's greatest cook.'

'Your soup is getting better,' was the best mitigation I could come up with.

'We can't live on soup and I can't cope with this any longer. We need to get out of here.'

'Go down to Sandy's you mean. The six of us? I suppose—'

'No, me and you and Tina, we need our own place. I'm fed up always cooking and tidying and doing your dad's laundry, then there's the queue for the bathroom...'

'Yes, but—'

'And does your dad have to debrief after every toilet trip? Also I never get to watch my TV programmes. It's always football or golf or one of his old detective shows. And, if I so much as tentatively suggest a veggie meal, he starts coming over all faint or gives me a lecture on the subject of protein and Tina's growing bones. We need our own space if we're going to start a proper married life together. Somewhere we can breathe. It's too claustrophobic here. Sometimes I wish I'd never moved in.'

If you listened to Joanna long enough you'd think she'd been forced to vacate the Palace of Versailles and flit to the Black Hole of Calcutta, as opposed to leaving her pokey wee flat in Glasgow to move into my dad's cottage with me.

'I want to go house hunting tomorrow.' She sounded pretty adamant about that. 'We'll get up first thing and see what's available.'

'Just how first thing are we talking?' I asked, not wanting to share my early morning meeting plans. 'How about if I help make tea tonight and, instead of first thing, we go house hunting in the afternoon?'

Malky was approaching the magic one hundred when the tennis ball came off his foot at an angle and struck Joanna on the side of the head. She picked up the tennis ball and threw it back to him with more force than was strictly necessary to cover the short distance between them. 'No long lies. We're getting up early and going to see what properties are on the market in our price range.' Joanna put her arms around me and pressed her body most agreeably against mine. 'Think how happy that would make me.'

I did think about it, and, when Joanna was this happy I was usually very happy. All I had to do was make a couple of phone calls and shift tomorrow's meeting to Sunday.

'Okay,' I said. 'Let's do it. Me and you, first thing tomorrow, off in search of our new home.'

Joanna took a pace back, holding my hands in hers. 'Promise?'

I preferred it when she was closer. I pulled her against me again. 'Promise.'

44

'Perjurer.'

I didn't recall having actually sworn an oath. Joanna and I were both lawyers, it was important to be legally accurate about those sorts of things.

'Contract-breaker, then. You promised to go house hunting and now you're saying you can't, so that's a breach of contract.'

'Not if the contract is frustrated, by factors that were unknown at the time of its making,' I said, almost sounding like I knew what I was talking about.

'Well, you certainly weren't frustrated last night. You lied to me and then took advantage of the situation.'

I had. Twice.

'Hey, hey, that's enough of that,' my dad said. He was sitting in an armchair, wrapped in his big Paisley-patterned dressing gown, slurping from a cup of tea. I hadn't noticed it until recently, when Joanna had pointed it out to me, but my dad didn't sip, he slurped. It was another thing that annoyed her. She had a list. The old man was trying to read yesterday's newspaper while listening in on our conversation at the same time. 'Will you two try and remember there's a wean in the house?' Tina was outside in the garden and, unlike him, not eavesdropping. She was trying to teach the dog how to sit and beg. I'd have preferred if she'd taught it how to poop in a plastic bag and cut out the middleman.

'Then try and remember that I'm in the house,' he said, when I pointed out his granddaughter's absence.

'How could we forget?' Joanna muttered.

My dad peered over the top of the newspaper. 'What was that?'

I put a hand on Joanna's arm and led her away. 'I'm sorry, but how was I supposed to know this was going to happen? I can't very well not go. We'll house hunt tomorrow.'

'It's always never do today what you can do tomorrow with you, isn't it Robbie?'

Joanna and I had been arguing around in circles since I'd taken the phone call from Bert Brechin that morning. It was almost a relief when my brother arrived carrying a blue carrier bag.

'What's wrong with your face?' he asked me. 'Apart from the obvious. And Joanna, what's with all the mascara? You look like a cat. Or an Egyptian. Or an Egyptian cat.'

'I'll tell you what's up,' Joanna said. 'What's up is that there are no mirrors in this place.'

'There's one on the wall in my room,' my dad called to her.

'Which apparently you think is for hanging dirty shirts over,' she shouted back.

'They're not dirty, they've only been worn the once and don't need to be washed. I can't very well put them in beside the clean ones. I'm actually thinking about you. Saving you extra laundry.'

'And, as for the mirror in the bathroom,' Joanna continued, 'it would be easier for me just to memorise my face than put make-up on using that daft wee shaving thing, all splatted with bits of foam and stubble.'

'Egyptian cat...' Malky laughed, and then tried and failed a serious face. 'Sorry, I'm just in a great mood this morning. No, really, I'm fine. So, Joanna needs a mirror, what's your excuse, Robbie?'

'There's nothing the matter with me,' I said.

'There must be something or you wouldn't be looking like dad does when someone puts ice in his whisky.'

'What Robbie means is that there's nothing the matter that you'd be interested in,' Joanna said. 'It has nothing to do with grown men kicking a ball about a field.'

'I'm interested in other things,' Malky said, not specifying further. 'Come on, try me. Maybe I can help.'

Joanna must have thought it less effort just to tell him. 'Okay. You know this court case Robbie's got?'

'Robbie's always got a court case. That's his job, isn't it?'

'The one with Sheriff Brechin's granddaughter.'

'Never heard of it. Was it in the papers?'

'Not yet, but it'll be all over the front page soon enough.

That's the page on the other side of the back page.'

A rustle of newspaper. 'Strictly speaking, the page on the other side of the back page is the second back page.' My dad wasn't helping.

Malky took a deep breath and exhaled loudly. 'Will you just tell me what the big problem is?'

'The big problem,' Joanna said, 'is that Robbie and I are supposed to be going looking for houses, but Sheriff Brechin has phoned to say he wants to meet him urgently.'

'Antonia will be there, and I have to discuss the case with her sometime anyway,' I told Joanna, not for the first time. 'The continued First Diet is on Tuesday.'

Joanna's eyes flared as she ignored me and continued to address Malky. 'And Robbie's too stupid to realise it's a trap.'

'How can it be a trap if Brechin's insisting I continue to act in his granddaughter's defence?'

Joanna had that covered. 'Pride is blinding you to the obvious, Robbie. Brechin's a sly old fox. Of course he wants to keep you in the case. If you win, great. If you don't, he has Antonia lodge an appeal blaming her conviction on your defective representation. Once the appeal court hears that you ignored your client's instructions to plead guilty to a lesser charge at an early stage, wham, conviction quashed and, bam, you're on the carpet before the Disciplinary Committee being showered with the confetti that used to be your practising certificate. Tell him, Malky. Going to meet Sheriff Brechin is a terrible idea.'

Malky mulled over my predicament for a moment or two, stretching his bottom lip between thumb and forefinger, finally letting it snap back against his teeth. 'You're right,' he said, 'I'm not interested. However, Robbie, you will be interested in this.' He grabbed my arm and dragged me through to the kitchen where he laid the carrier bag back down on the table.

'Malky, I've no time. I've got to go.'

'No, you don't. All you need to do for the next two minutes is sit down and shut up.'

'But—'

'Do you trust me, Robbie?'

'Not an inch.'

'Then you will after this.' With a flourish, he whisked a thin plastic packet from the carrier bag. 'Behold, I give you—'

'It's prosc—'

'Yeah, I know, I can't pronounce it either.'

'Thanks, but I can pronounce it. It's prosciutto.'

'It's easier just to say Parma ham.'

'Malky, what's this about?'

'What did you have for breakfast?'

'Toast and Marmite.'

With a scornful grunt and a shake of the head, Malky walked over to the hob, lit the gas under the perpetually in situ frying pan and poured in a drop of oil. 'I hope your taste buds are limbering up for this.'

There are great moments in history when you'll always remember where you were. I was in the kitchen of my dad's house, one Saturday morning in early June when I had my first bite of a fried prosciutto sandwich.

I took another. How could I have lived this long without realising? It seemed so obvious. It was a universal rule of gastronomy that everything tasted better fried, so why not prosciutto? I gazed into Malky's expectant face, the face of my brother, the brother who had shared this wonderful culinary discovery with me. 'It's...it's...'

'I know,' he said. 'It's bacon but it's better. There's no flubbery fat. It crisps up in thirty seconds and there's none of that white goo squirting out of it, because it's not pumped full of water. It's brilliant on a fried egg roll. I've brought half a dozen with me if you want to give it a try.'

Joanna marched in as I was munching another

morsel of deliciousness. She was dressed for going out, though with less make-up than previously. 'Put the dead pig down and let's go.'

'I told you,' I said, crunching the finest, crispiest cured ham the city of Parma had to offer. 'We'll go looking for houses tomorrow, promise, but for now, right after this sandwich, I'm going to see Sheriff Brechin. Don't you want to know for sure what he's up to?'

'Very much,' Joanna said. 'That's why I'm coming with you.'

45

I'd never given a great deal of thought to where Sheriff Albert Brechin resided, which was surprising given the number of times over the years I'd had an urge to follow him home and pan in his windows.

I suppose I'd imagined him to be proprietor of a sizeable chunk of real estate, perhaps in Murrayfield, Blackford, Barnton or some other prestigious area of Edinburgh, secure behind high gates, with a driveway sweeping up to the grand entrance door of a large sandstone villa. But, no, home to Sheriff Brechin was Torphichen, a village not far from Linlithgow, and a bungalow set in a garden of well-tended trees and shrubs with a lush front lawn that had never suffered the ignominy of a practice shot from a badly swung sand-wedge. I'd already made it clear to the Sheriff when he'd called that I would only discuss the case with him if Antonia consented. For that reason I'd expected her also to be present. What I hadn't counted on was a gathering of Clan Brechin.

Antonia's mother met us at the front door and showed us down a long, dimly lit hallway and into the brightness of a large conservatory. There, sitting on a collection of wicker chairs, Antonia, her father and grandfather awaited us. They remained seated when I entered, only Sheriff Brechin rising to his feet, either out of politeness or surprise, when he realised I had not come alone.

'Miss Jordan, this is most improper,' he said, taking his seat again. For the first time in my life I found myself agreeing with the Sheriff. Maybe he could talk sense into her. 'This is a private and highly confidential discussion concerning the defence in a criminal trial. We can't possibly have a member of the Crown Office and Procurator Fiscal Service present.'

Mrs Brechin hovered at her chair, unsure whether she should offer Joanna a seat. I was permitted to stand.

'I'm not here to listen in to any private discussions about the case,' Joanna said. She smiled at my client. 'Though, I do hope it all goes well for you, Antonia. No, I'm here because if there is to be any threat of a formal complaint against Robbie for failing to follow instructions—'

Brechin was straight in there. 'So you admit that there has been fault on his part?'

'I can't admit anything,' Joanna said. 'I wasn't there, and neither were you, Sheriff. The point I'm making is that if anyone here considers Robbie to have done something wrong, now is the time to say so. Don't wait until after the case is over and start blaming him if things don't go the way you'd have liked. Sack him now, otherwise let him do his job.'

I had to hand it to myself, I knew how to pick a wife. It was true what they said, practice made perfect.

'Let him do his job?' Brechin glowered at Joanna, his complexion that of a boiled ham. 'Miss Jordan, I've watched that man do his job for the last twelve years, and a very unedifying experience it has been, let me tell you.'

'Perhaps...' What did she mean, "perhaps"? 'But you can't deny that he always tries his best for his clients.'

'Oh, I'll give him that,' Brechin scoffed. 'Mr Munro can be extremely trying at times.'

Well intentioned though it was, as pleas in mitigation went, I felt Joanna's was in danger of making things worse. That was the problem with PFs. They were so used to sticking the boot in, they forgot how to accentuate the positive. I walked over to the big glass door and slid it open. 'Joanna, why don't you step outside for a while? I won't be long.'

With a little further encouragement Joanna moved towards the door. Antonia got up from her chair and looked as though she was going to join her.

'Stay where you are, Antonia,' Mrs Brechin said, and the young woman froze.

I slid the door shut behind Joanna, before turning to face the assembled Brechins. 'Right,' I clapped my hands together. 'What's it to be? Am I in or out?'

'That very much depends,' Mrs Brechin said. 'Antonia is back in court on Tuesday, what are you proposing to do?'

'Antonia,' I said, 'are you happy to discuss your case in front of everybody? Because if you'd rather talk about these confidential matters in priv—'

'We're staying,' Mrs Brechin said. 'Everyone here wants what's best for Antonia.'

'Is that right, Antonia?' I asked. She nodded. 'Then that goes for me too, and what's best for Antonia is that she's acquitted. The only way of achieving that, so far as I can see, is to lodge a notice of incrimination against her former co-accused, Freya Linkwood, to say that she acquired the drugs and that she was the person intending to supply them, not Antonia.'

'But that's not true,' Antonia said. Whose side was

272

she on?

'Did you hear that?' Brechin said. 'There's no point going to trial. Antonia won't lie about her role in this, and, in any event, I have it on good authority,' by which I assumed he meant on the word of Hugh Ogilvie, 'that she will be incriminated by both her co-accused. That's two against one,' he added, in case my arithmetic wasn't up to scratch.

'Then I'll challenge their evidence.'

'On what possible basis?'

'On the basis that they've been given a deal by the Crown in exchange for giving evidence against Antonia.'

'Will that work?' Mrs Brechin wanted to know.

It was her father-in-law who answered first. 'No, of course it won't work. The man's clutching at straws.'

'It's a jury trial.' I said. 'You throw enough straws in the air and they cause a distraction. You only need to distract eight out of fifteen jurors for an acquittal.'

'I have never liked your approach to the law, Mr Munro,' Brechin said.

'Then it's just as well you won't be on the jury.'

He snorted, leaned forward in his wicker chair and with a look of annoyance on his face, re-arranged the red velvet cushion at the small of his back. From behind the cushion he removed a large pair of binoculars which, along with me, seemed to be a major cause of discomfort. He looked around for somewhere to put them and opted to lay them on the floor by the side of the chair.

'What if Antonia told the police who'd given the drugs to her? Would that help?' Mrs Brechin asked.

'Of course it would help, but she won't do it,'

Brechin said.

Antonia shifted uncomfortably in her wicker chair, mumbling, 'There are enough people in trouble already because of me.'

Her mother wasn't for letting up. 'But, Antonia, if it might save your career...'

Up until then Quentin Brechin had sat quietly, listening. 'Leave the girl alone. Just because her two so-called friends are prepared to land her in trouble, I don't see why Antonia should try and weasel out by blaming someone else.' He turned to his daughter. 'What do you think, Toni? Would you rather just plead guilty and get the whole thing over and done with?'

Antonia looked to me for help.

'If you're not prepared to reveal your source you really only have two options,' I said. 'Plead guilty or go to trial.'

'Well, I for one think she should plead guilty. Tell the truth and shame the devil,' Quentin said. 'Antonia was a young person looking to celebrate a success.' He shrugged. 'She thought she'd experiment with some recreational drugs and share them with her friends. Is that such a big deal?'

'Yes, of course it's a big deal!' Brechin barked.

'All I'm saying is that she's not going to get the jail for this, is she Mr Munro?'

I thought it possible, though unlikely. While the distinction between commercial and social supply was not one normally recognised by Bert Brechin, with other sheriffs it was often the difference between jail and no jail.

'There you are, Dad. Worst case scenario she gets struck off for something that will probably be made legal in a few years. A career in the law isn't everything. There's a whole world out there. Who wants to sit about a stuffy old legal office all day shuffling papers, anyway?'

'Antonia does,' Mrs Brechin said. 'She's always wanted to be a lawyer, and lawyers don't break the law.' Her eyes began to fill with tears. Antonia was already crying. They hugged each other for a moment, before the older woman stepped back and stared at her father-in-law through red- rimmed, viscous eyes. 'Bert, you've got to do something. You can't just sit there and watch the girl's career go down the drain, everything she's worked so hard for, all because of a few grams of powder. You're a Sheriff. Put pressure on people. Exert your influence. It's really only a small matter of having a charge reduced. Then all three girls can plead guilty and take what's coming to them, but at least they'll still have the chance of a future in the law.'

Brechin sniffed drily. 'I can't. I'd sooner resign my commission than attempt to defeat the ends of justice.'

Mrs Brechin stepped forward, a scowl shrouding her features. 'But what's happening to Antonia isn't justice.' He didn't answer, merely turned his head to stare out of the window at the wild greenness of the Torphichen Hills that lay beyond the manicured boundary of his garden. 'We don't have courts of justice,' I said. 'We have courts of law. Isn't that right, Sheriff?'

Brechin stood and fixed me with eyes set like black rivets in the side of a rusty, old, cast-iron boiler. 'That's right. And it's that system of law that I swore an oath to uphold.'

Joanna had breathed enough fresh air. The glass door slid open. Antonia had been blowing her nose into a paper hanky. When she saw Joanna enter she crumpled it and stuffed it into the pocket of her jeans. 'Joanna,' she said, 'what should I do? Do you think I should go to trial?'

'That's not something Miss Jordan should give you advice on,' Brechin said.

'But I'm going to anyway,' Joanna said. 'Plead guilty and the only thing guaranteed is that you'll be found guilty. Maintain your plea of not guilty, go to trial and, while the odds might be stacked against you, there will always be hope.'

'Is that right?' Mrs Brechin asked me. 'Do you have anything to say that would give us so much as a shred of hope that Antonia might be acquitted?'

I had nothing.

She stood, composing herself, wiping away the tears like she was scraping ice off a frozen windscreen. 'Then Antonia's only hope lies with the appeal court. She strode forward and squared up to me. 'If the best way to save my daughter's career is to have you struck off, so be it.' She gestured to the corridor that led to the front door, in case I'd forgotten the floor plan. 'Mr Munro, please consider your services no longer required.'

46

Just as I preferred never to do today what I could do tomorrow, I thought it best not to worry now about things that could be worried about in the future. Having been sacked from Antonia Brechin's defence, I still had another small matter to deal with.

First thing on Sunday morning while Joanna was only dreaming about house hunting, I was out of bed and off down to Jake's derelict cottage where quite a crowd had gathered. Other than Jake, Ellen, Sammy Veitch and myself, there was a team of men inside the building, stripping out old carpets and furniture and generally giving the place a thorough scrub-up.

The continuing good weather meant that the meeting with Sammy could take place outdoors in the back garden. It was a reasonably sized area of ground with some raised vegetable beds, now rotten with weeds, and a large over- grown lawn with a cast iron clothes pole planted in each corner.

Four wooden chairs had been taken from the kitchen and set out on a slabbed area at the back door surrounding a small felt-topped collapsible card table. Three of them were occupied. I remained standing behind the fourth, keen to get away. There was a chance I could be back home before Joanna even knew I'd gone. Jake had other ideas. 'You're going nowhere. You're staying put till this is sorted.'

'What are you on about?' I said, slowly backing

away. 'It is sorted. Sammy knows what to do. He's brought all the papers with him.' Sammy raised his briefcase, Chancellor of the Exchequer style, to corroborate the position. 'How much more sorted do you want it? He'll talk you through everything and tell you where to sign.'

'Sit,' Jake said. 'You're my lawyer, not him, and I'm signing nothing until you give it the okay.'

It was nice to be so trusted, even by a person I wouldn't have trusted to land on the ground if he fell off his chair. I was about to explain further why my presence was no longer required when Freddy came around the side of the house, looking more chipper than someone who owed Jake Turpie a fortune had any right to be. He saw my empty chair and sat down in it.

'What do you think you're doing?' Jake asked.

'If this is a meeting to divide up my wife's estate I think I should have a say in it.'

'You've got no say. Fact is your wife owes me money and so do you,' Jake said.

'But we don't owe you half a million.' Freddy was obviously unfamiliar with Jake's lending rates of interest.

'You're getting nothing from me, Freddy,' Ellen said. 'You disappeared making me think I was to blame, when you had some bint stashed away all the time. You ripped Jake off for this place and took his money with you to Prague, so why don't you just go back there and leave us alone?'

Sammy made a show of looking at his watch. 'I think I'll come back later when you've all had a chance to talk things over. Robbie can give me a call.' Taking his brief-case, he stood.

'Sit!' Freddy and Jake said in unison.

Sammy brushed dust from the hem of his kilt. 'Look, I came here to sign a life policy. If you still want to do that, I'll stick around. If you're going to waste my time arguing, then I'm leaving.'

'I want half.' Freddy was looking straight at Jake with a courage I didn't know he possessed. 'Ellen's still my wife.'

Jake sprang to his feet. 'Any more from you and she'll be your widow.'

Now we were all standing, with the exception of Ellen who had decided to let the men hammer things out between them. What did she care? She wouldn't be around to witness the aftermath.

'It doesn't matter what you sign, Turpie. When Ellen dies I'll have a claim to her money,' Freddy said. 'She made a will leaving everything to me. Tell him, Robbie.'

Sammy was right in there before I could say anything, 'Makes no difference, Freddy. If Ellen assigns her life policy to Jake now, then when she dies it goes to him. It doesn't matter if there's a will or not. The policy won't form part of her estate. Not you or any other relative or anyone else named in the will can claim on it.'

'Ellen's got no relatives,' Freddy said. 'Just me,'

'No? What about Eric's wean?' Sammy asked. 'A wee girl, wasn't it? Whatever happened to her?'

For the first time in the whole discussion I thought I saw a flicker of interest in Ellen's eye at the mention of her long-lost niece. It was quickly extinguished.

'Who cares what happened to her?' Freddy kicked the chair Sammy had been sitting on seconds before, knocking it over and sending it clattering across the concrete slabs. 'This is my money we're talking about!'

'No, Freddy, I'm afraid it's not,' Sammy said, righting the chair, and sitting down on it again. 'It's whoever's money Ellen says it is.' He laid the briefcase across his tartan lap and popped the locks. 'Of course, any other estate she does have will be all yours,' he added, sweetly, knowing full well that Ellen's only realisable asset was her mortality. 'Now, can we do this?'

Jake smiled, never a good sign for the person on the receiving end. 'You hear that, Freddy-boy? Now beat it before I have Deek find a spare patch of ground and a spade.'

Freddy said nothing for a moment or two, just stared down at Ellen who was making a point of looking in the opposite direction.

'I'll grass,' he said, eventually, in a hushed and yet determined voice. 'When Ellen dies and you try to cash in her policy, I'll go straight to the bizzies and tell them that the whole thing was a set-up from the start.'

'Now, just hold on one minute, son,' Sammy said, clinging to whatever shred of legal ethics he'd failed to shake off during his long career. 'Remember there's lawyers here. Let's keep things professional.'

'The cops would never listen to you,' Jake said.

I begged to differ. If anyone knew what a fraud looked like, it was Freddy Fletcher. It was then I noticed that in response to some invisible signal Deek Pudney had appeared at the corner of the cottage. Arms folded, he blocked the exit and a lot of the morning sunshine.

Freddy showed no sign of backing down. 'I'm having my fair share or no-one's getting anything!'

What was the source of this new-found bravery? Desperation? Greed? So far as I could see his stubbornness was only going to prove right all those people who already thought he was dead.

'We'll buy this house from you, Jake,' Ellen said, suddenly. She got to her feet, holding her side, face tight with pain. 'Me and Freddy. For half a million. We'll make an offer and hold off the purchase date until I'm gone. After that Freddy can pay you from my life policy. That way you get all your money back and Freddy gets the house, which he shouldn't have got you to buy in the first place.'

'But...' Freddy's normally pale features reddened and contorted. Ellen stuck a finger at them.

'But nothing. You can sell this place. Tell the next mug there's oil under it. It's either that or I'm signing no insurance forms, understand? Take or leave it, I don't care. I've nothing to lose.'

'It's actually quite a good idea,' Sammy said. 'Except...' He didn't need to expand. Jake had already spotted the bluebottle floating in that particular batch of snake oil. 'So he inherits half a million and I'm supposed to trust him to use it to buy this dump off me? What's to stop him buggering off back to wherever he came from with all the money?'

'You're right, Jake,' Ellen said. 'You can trust a thief...' She spat the words at Freddy. 'But not a liar.' As a pot- calling-the-kettle-black moment it was one for connoisseurs of charred cookware. 'There's nothing for it, we're all going to have to be in this together.'

Sammy let loose a groan. What he had thought would be a simple morning's work was not going according to plan. He gestured to everyone to sit down. No-one did. 'Listen,' he said, 'Ellen nearly got it right. Here's what we do.'

And so it was agreed that Jake, Freddy and Ellen would form a partnership, purportedly to develop the cottage. There was a good bit of garden ground, so they could pretend they were also going to build another house to the rear of the property. Since Jake owned the land, the profits would be split two-thirds to him with a sixth each to Freddy and Ellen. Sammy would drop a letter to the planning authority advising them of the proposal and approach a few banks for funding. None of this work was necessary, but it would lend an air of credibility as to why the partners of the new firm required to take out a joint life policy for half a million pounds. It would mean that when Ellen died Jake would receive three hundred and thirty-three thousand and Freddy one hundred and sixty-six, which included Ellen's one-sixth share.

As frauds went it was neat and simple and likely to raise very few eyebrows. Even Freddy seemed to realise that he wouldn't get a better offer. So, once the not-so-small matter of Sammy's upfront fees was settled, he opened his briefcase and began sorting out papers on the card table while Jake went off to inspect his workers, Freddy lit up a cigarette and Ellen announced that she was going to make bacon rolls for everyone.

I followed her inside the back door to the kitchen, a large room with an ancient flagstone floor, some free-standing cupboards, a battered old fridge and a small three-burner gas hob by a stainless-steel sink. In the centre of the room was a wooden table and in the middle of that a brown paper bag bulging with morning rolls. 'You up for a bacon roll, Robbie?' Ellen asked, lifting an enormous, cast-iron frying pan down from the wall where it hung on a nail. Scorched black, it looked like it had seen some action in its time. Next, from a well-stocked fridge, she produced a box of eggs, a tray of square sausage and layers of bacon wrapped in greaseproof paper. 'Jake likes a fried breakfast.'

Who didn't? Still, from room service at the Balmoral Hotel to cooking Jake Turpie his most important meal of the day, it had to have come as something of a culture shock.

'Are you going to be comfortable enough here?' I asked her. 'You know there are hospices for when things get bad.'

Ellen smiled and placed a hand on my arm. 'Thanks for caring, Robbie. I'll be fine. I have everything I need here.'

I doubted it. 'Where's your nurse?' I hadn't seen her of the red hair and green trouser-suit in a while.

'Gone. I can't afford private nursing care.' She smiled. 'That's only for lottery winners.'

I didn't know what to say. 'I'm sorry the way things have worked out, you know, between you and Freddy.'

'Really, Robbie, it's fine. At least I know the truth now. For a year I've been torn between blaming myself for making Freddy leave and hating Jake Turpie for killing him.'

'So you and Jake...'

'We're getting along fine.'

There was no easy way to approach the subject, but I felt I had to. 'Sammy was telling me he used to act for your brother. He told me what happened and how it was Jake you blamed for Eric's death.'

'It's true, I did. But it was a long time ago. These things happen. Jake and Eric were just boys. I see Jake differently these days.'

She smiled, and there was a sheen of contentment in her eyes.

'You and Jake? Seriously?'

'Why not?' Ellen took a bread knife from a drawer and began sawing bread rolls in half. 'He's taking care of me now and being the perfect gentleman. What more could a girl ask?'

Gentleman Jake Turpie? It was too much for my breakfast-deprived brain to handle that early on a Sunday morning.

With a farewell to Ellen, my final task was to tell Sammy I was leaving. He was still sitting bent over the card table, filling out an insurance proposal form when I went outside. Freddy was hovering around, smoking nervously.

'How long is all this going to take?' he asked.

'The policy proposal will be ready for the three of you to sign in ten minutes,' Sammy said. 'I wasn't expecting to have to draw up a partnership agreement as well, and it'll need to be done right. We're going to have to meet up again. How about same time next Saturday? You can all sign and then after that...Well...'

'Then after that, what?' Freddy flicked a curl of ash from the end of his cigarette and watched it float to the ground where it drifted and tumbled across the concrete slabs.

I looked at the kitchen door from where the sound of sizzling bacon was music. 'Sammy means that, after that, nature and time will take its toll,' I said.

Freddy took a final drag from his cigarette and pinged the stub at my feet, exploding a shower of orange sparks. 'Then the sooner that bitch is dead, the better.' He turned around to meet Jake's fist full in the face. Freddy stood there for a moment, head pointing at the ground, eyes looking up at the sky. His legs buckled. He reached out to grab hold of something that wasn't there and toppled sideways.

To say he didn't land all that heavily is to say that at least he didn't crack any slabs when gravity eventually brought him to rest. I rolled him over into the recovery position. After a minute or two he groaned and managed to sit up, supporting himself by one hand planted on the ground while with the other he clutched his nose, red oozing between his fingers. If Freddy had known what was good for him, he'd have just sat there and bled. Instead, he glared up at Jake and determinedly, if unsteadily, rolled onto both knees and began to haul himself up on the back of one of the chairs. The moment he was upright Jake would knock him down again. I stepped in between the two. Sammy shifted his chair, pulling the card table along with him. Once out of the danger zone and well away from blood splashes he continued filling out the proposal form. The man was a pro.

'Time to go, Freddy,' I said. 'Be here next Saturday at eight. You can sign the papers and then head back to Prague. Sammy will do the rest.' Keeping Jake-side of him at all times, I led Freddy to the corner of the building, where, with a gentle shove, I sent him, dripping blood, in the direction of his rental car. It took him a while to fumble in his pocket for the keys but soon he had the engine started and I followed him down the track.

And that was that. Job done. I was finally free. Jake would get his money, Freddy would reunite with his woman in Bohemia, Sammy would collect a handsome cash pay-off for his troubles, and all Ellen had to do was die.

As for me? I had a fried prosciutto sandwich to look forward to. Somehow, at that precise moment, it was enough.

47

'What happened to that Parma ham that Malky brought yesterday?' I asked, removing my head from the fridge after a brief fact-finding mission.

My dad was at the big Belfast sink, scrubbing at a set of golf irons. Tina was kneeling on a chair at the kitchen table, swirling a paintbrush around and around in a jam jar of murky water with Bouncer looking on, a splash of bright blue paint on one of his ears.

'Eaten,' my dad said, taking a pitching wedge and drying it on an old tea towel. 'No-one knew where you were. Up and away at the crack of dawn. Sorry if we were supposed to know you'd be back and looking for breakfast.'

'Joanna and me had fried egg on a roll,' Tina said, not looking up. 'I had crispy bacon on mine. There's none left for you,' she added for the avoidance of doubt.

'Where is Joanna?'

'House hunting,' my dad said. 'And I've a game of golf to get to.'

'When did she leave?'

'Twenty minutes ago. She tried to phone you, but you'd left your phone on the kitchen table.' He dropped the club into his golf bag and started on an eight-iron. 'I think you should know that she's not best pleased.'

'Joanna wants to kill you,' Tina said. 'Will she get into trouble for that?'

'No, pet,' my dad said. 'We'll see she gets herself a proper lawyer.'

My phone buzzed. Bouncer jumped onto all fours, ears cocked. I checked the display. Six missed calls, one from Joanna and five from a number I didn't recognise. It wasn't unusual for the police to call with news of an arrest, but if I didn't answer they always left a message.

'It's been doing that for the past ten minutes,' my dad said. 'I answered it once, but whoever it was hung up.'

I dialled the number. It was answered immediately. 'Hello Robbie? Is that you?'

I couldn't quite place the voice. 'It's Ted. Ted Hawke. Joanna's—'

'Hi Ted. I'd been thinking about giving you a call. Looks like you beat me to it.'

'Robbie, it's very important we talk.'

'I know it is.'

'Don't say anything over the phone. When can we meet up?'

My dad checked his watch, threw the tea towel over the heads of the remaining irons and gave the bunch a quick rub before ramming them into his golf bag. 'I've a tee-time in half an hour at Kingsfield and I've still got Davie to pick up in Philpstoun. I don't know when Joanna's coming back, so the bairn's all yours. Why don't you take her and the hound out for some exercise?' Giggling, Tina tried in vain to fend off his bristly kiss. 'It's not good for the pair of them to be cooped up on a day like this.'

He grabbed a blue windcheater from a coat hook on the back door, then he, his fourteen golf clubs and one highly dubious handicap, were gone.

'It's difficult at the moment, Ted. I'm childminding. How about we—'

'It's okay. I'll come to you. Today. Now.'

Tina came over carrying an A3 piece of paper, dripping a rainbow of paint across the kitchen floor and the dog that was padding by her side. She held it up to me for evaluation. 'Very nice,' I said.

'What?' Ted said.

'I was talking to Tina.'

'Who's Tina? What have you told her?'

'She's my daughter and I've told her she's just painted a lovely picture.'

I could hear the sound of exasperation on the other end of the line. 'Look, Robbie, I need to speak to you urgently. Where are you? Just give me your postcode and I'll punch it into the Sat Nav. I can leave right now.'

'I'm at home. The postcode is—'

'Hold on. Is Joanna there? I can't meet you if Joanna's going to be around.'

I didn't bother to say that Joanna wasn't with me, because she could return at any time. In any case, I could guess what Ted wanted to see me about and I was as keen as he obviously was to ensure that his niece remained blissfully unaware.

'Okay,' I said. 'How about I meet you at the Kelpies? If you're leaving from Edinburgh, just batter down the M9 until you come across a couple of thirty-metre-high horses' heads. You can't miss them. I'll meet you there in an hour. How's that?'

It was fine. So anxious was Ted to see me, I had the feeling I could have asked to meet him abseiling from the Falkirk Wheel and he'd have arrived with rope and harness.

I hung Tina's latest creation on the kitchen wall over the top of the last one she'd painted which was now a crinkly sheet of streaks and faded brush strokes. Ten minutes later the three of us were in the car heading west. Leaving the motorway at Grangemouth, we continued along the bypass road and parked in the overflow car park at Falkirk Stadium. From there we walked through the Helix Park, the journey being temporarily diverted while Tina and Bouncer took a detour to the splash zone, where nozzles sunk into the ground randomly spurted jets of water here and there, but mostly onto my daughter and her dog.

After that, I walked with wet dog and soaking child a further kilometre, past the great lawn, across the wetland boardwalk, following the Forth and Clyde Canal to its eastern end where it met the River Carron. Ted was already waiting for us in a checked shirt and slacks, a finger through the loop in the collar of a tan corduroy jacket that was slung over his shoulder.

He and I shook hands beneath the two enormous stainless steel structures, each shining brightly in the sunlight of a June midday, one rearing its mighty head skywards, the other staring down at us disapprovingly.

For all his obvious concern, Ted managed a smile. 'Is this your daughter, the artist?' he asked, and, before I could say yes, the smile was gone, replaced by a worried expression stretched tightly across his broad features. 'I understand you've been talking to Freya Linkwood. What did she tell you?'

'That it was you who arranged the supply of cocaine to Antonia Brechin.' The Bush and How Not to Beat About It by Robert A. Munro.

Ted pursed his lips and nodded his head a few

times, slowly. 'What else?'

What else? What else could there be? A tug at my elbow. It had taken Tina precisely thirty seconds to admire the Kelpies and a further thirty to locate an ice cream outlet. I told her we'd get some on the way back, gave her Bouncer's lead to hold and she squelched off in her sodden sandals with me yelling after her to keep well away from the water.

Ted drew closer. The park was busy with tourists, but there was no-one in our immediate vicinity, certainly no-one who would have been interested to listen in on our discussion when they were standing metres away from the world's largest equine sculptures. 'What has Antonia said about me so far?'

'Absolutely nothing,' I said.

Tina had lost the end of Bouncer's lead and the dog had thought it should come over and stand by me before giving itself a shake. I could tell that Ted was growing more and more frustrated with each interruption.

'What about Joanna? What does she know?'

'I haven't told her, and I'm not planning to.'

'It'll come out in court, though, won't it?'

'I don't think so. Antonia is refusing to reveal who gave her the drugs.'

'But she could?'

'It's possible she could,' I said, though not if I had anything to do with it.

'And if she does?'

'If she reveals her supplier there's a good chance the Crown would drop the prosecution.'

'They would do that? Drop the charge if she told them who her supplier was?'

Was he kidding? If Hugh Ogilvie discovered who Antonia's supplier was, he'd bite my hand off for a deal. In fact, Ogilvie would probably be happy to bin the case against all three trainees if he thought he could take the scalp of a partner at one of Scotland's top corporate law firms.

'Then that's what she should do,' Ted said. 'It was stupid. I don't know what came over me. I suppose I was showing off, not acting my age.'

It was honourable of him to offer to sacrifice himself, but I couldn't let him do it. The person who had physically delivered the drugs was Toffee McCowan. I couldn't let word of his involvement escape. Antonia Brechin might be looking at the loss of her career. Some people would be set to lose a lot more, and without anaesthetic.

'What if I told them who my supplier was? Would they do me the same kind of deal?' Ted asked.

'I don't know if it's such a great idea going up the chain of suppliers,' I said. 'The links at the top don't like it.'

Ted frowned. 'I understand. Don't worry, I'll keep my mouth shut.' So he said. I preferred not to run the risk of the cops prising it open. 'My contact is an old friend. He knows that I'd never give them his name.'

An old friend? I hardly thought the managing partner of Fraser Forrest & Hawke and a rum-soaked old sea dog would navigate the same social circles.

'Your contact for the cocaine?' I said. 'Can I take it he's not a wee weather-beaten guy who looks like he might know how to crack open a bottle of Navy Rum?'

Tina held onto the crook of my arm and swung on it. 'Can we get ice cream yet?'

Ted unslung his jacket and pulled out a calfskin wallet. He extracted a twenty-pound note and handed it down to Tina. 'Get us all one,' he said. 'The dog too.'

The cash was out of Ted's hand in a flash and Tina was off and running. You couldn't teach that. It was all in the genes.

'That's not quite how I'd describe him,' Ted said, getting back to the subject at hand and the identity of his drug dealer. 'Quentin's an old school chum. I'd describe him as more of a—'

'Quentin?' I didn't know anything of Uncle Ted-to-be's schooldays but, during my own, Quentins had been pretty thin on the ground.

'Yes,' he said. 'Ironic, isn't it. Antonia's father. Quentin Brechin.'

48

Suddenly I felt a lot better. Quentin Brechin, drug dealer. Who'd have thought it? It was the quiet ones you had to watch out for. Sitting there in his dad's conservatory yesterday morning, giving it, 'Plead guilty, Antonia. Tell the truth and shame the devil,' when all the time the drugs his daughter had been caught with had come, albeit circuitously, from him. I'd see how Sheriff Brechin and his daughter-in-law liked those apples. Complain about me for defective representation, would they?

It was a long, wet journey back to the car for some of us. Tina, now wearing my jumper, sat chittering in the back seat with a damp dog across her lap.

Back at the cottage the front door was ajar. I was sure I'd locked up before leaving and my dad wouldn't be home yet. Even if he'd holed out at the eighteenth he'd still have a few more to sink at the nineteenth. It had to be Joanna returned from a hard day's house hunting. It wasn't. It was Stan Blandy. He was sitting in my dad's favourite armchair, a folded newspaper across his lap, tapping his teeth with a pen and making a show of studying the racing pages. Toffee McCowan stood nearby, a hand shoved in his trouser pocket. He looked pale and weak and struggled to arrange his features into an apologetic grimace when I entered the room. I retreated back into the small hallway to shepherd Tina into her room before she started asking a lot of awkward questions. I retrieved a towel from the bathroom and told her to dry herself and put on some fresh clothes. After that I shoved the dog in beside her and closed the door.

Back in the living room the scene hadn't changed. 'Hope you don't mind, Robbie, we let ourselves in,' Stan said, looking up from the newspaper. 'Very trusting of you to leave a key under the plant pot.' He set the paper down on the arm of the chair and balanced the pen on top of it. 'While we've been waiting, Toffee's been telling me a few things. Isn't that right Toffee?'

Tina reappeared with Bouncer by her side. She wasn't looking very dry, and was dressed in a random assortment of clothes. When she saw the two strange men she caught her breath. Every fibre in the wee dog's body tensed, and a warning rumble escaped between its bared teeth. Perhaps Jake had taught it something after all.

Another figure appeared in the doorway leading through from the kitchen. I recognised him from our warehouse meeting. Same shaved scalp, same razor scar, same come- ahead expression. When he saw Tina he lunged forward with a growl to give her a fright. It was too much for Bouncer. The dog leapt through the air straight at the man's neck. He wasn't a big dog, but he was solid and compact and struck scar-face square-on, catching him off balance. The man clutched for the frame of the door. Fingers slipping, he stumbled and fell backwards. Bouncer was all over him in an instant, snarling and snapping. Scar-face scrambled along the kitchen floor aiming blows at the dog, none of them seeming to connect or at least not sufficiently so to make blind bit of difference. One arm shielding his face the man reached into his pocket. I knew what he was likely to find in there.

Tina ran forward. 'Bouncer!' she yelled, 'Come here!' With one bound the animal jumped off the man and ran to my daughter's side, tail wagging, tongue hanging out the side of its mouth like it had all been a game.

On his feet now, lock-back in hand, the scar on his face showing white against red, the man shuffled forward. Growling, Bouncer planted his paws. Teeth like knives, ears pinned back, the dog showed no signs of retreat. I stepped between them.

'Tina, take Bouncer to your room and don't come out until I tell you.' The tone of my voice was enough for her not to need telling again.

Meanwhile, Stan was finding the whole violent episode mildly amusing. 'Put the chib away and wait outside,' he told his associate.

'Sorry about that, Stan,' I said, trying to match the big man's casual approach to the situation. 'Now, do you want to tell me why you're here? My dad will be back soon and, if you think his dog's crabbit, wait until he finds you've been sitting in his favourite chair reading his paper.'

Stan stood up. 'This is a friendly visit, Robbie. I'm not here to lean on anybody,' he said in the quiet, reassuring way dentists tell you, "this won't hurt a bit". 'It's just that I've been hearing things. Things that I don't like.'

'And what would that be?'

'I got a call from somebody this morning. Somebody I haven't heard from in a long time.'

'Is this twenty questions or are you going to tell me

who you're talking about?'

'You're his daughter's lawyer.'

'Quentin Brechin?'

Stan's big face relaxed into a smile. 'Me and Quentin go way back. He was working on the docks when I set up my little import, export business. He helped me with some legal stuff when I was getting started. Years later after he decided he was going to be an artist, he got himself into debt and came looking for a loan and so, naturally, I helped him out. Things took off, and when he started exhibiting across Europe, I asked him to help me out and we came to an arrangement.'

'Exporting art, importing cocaine?'

'Only until he'd paid me back. I don't like long-term business associations. It's dangerous to tread the same water. You need to swim about or you end up in a net.'

'I still don't understand,' I said.

'Quentin was quite fond of my product and I used to send him a thank you every so often via Toffee. Before today, I'd not spoken to Quentin in two or three years, but it turns out that Toffee has been continuing the service by dipping into what belongs to me.'

A sheen of sweat had distilled across Toffee's forehead, lining each crease like rain in a gutter. There was no colour in his face and I thought he might throw up. I told him to sit down.

'He's fine standing,' Stan said. 'Me and Toffee have had a chat. He's no longer in my employ. I've given him a severance package. Isn't that right, Toffee?'

Toffee pulled the hand out of his pocket. What was left of it was wrapped in a cloth that may once have been white but was now soaked in blood.

'Are you threatening me, Stan?' If he was, he was

doing an excellent job of it.

He strode forward and put a hand on my shoulder. 'Not at all. I like you, Robbie. I like your wee girl. I even like her mad dog. I don't threaten people I like. I'm asking you as a friend. Keep Quentin Brechin's name out of whatever you're doing. Don't mention his name to anyone. The man's weak. If people start asking him questions, he might think he should answer them and, if he does, then my name might be mentioned. If that happened...' He lifted his hand off my shoulder and patted my cheek with it. 'I'm sure you understand.'

I peered past him to see Toffee, grimacing in pain and cradling his injured hand. I did understand. I understood perfectly.

49

Stan Blandy shipped out, cutting me adrift from any chance of using Quentin Brechin's drug involvement to my advantage and leaving me marooned with Toffee McCowan. The old sailor was finishing the day two deformed fingers short of what he'd started with, but still thinking he'd got off lightly. I gave him money for a taxi to hospital and swore Tina to secrecy about what had happened, explaining that it had all been part of Bouncer's training to teach him to be a good guard dog.

Later that Sunday afternoon, Joanna returned home with a bundle of property schedules wrapped in a copy of the Edinburgh Solicitors' Property Centre newspaper. By the sheer volume of paper it seemed everyone in East/ Central Scotland had a house up for sale. She dropped the lot onto the kitchen table.

'There were some bad men here and Bouncer chased them away,' Tina said, and then skipped out of the door with the dog trotting after her.

I laughed. 'Really. That girl. What an imagination. She's going to make a great fiction writer.'

'Or a defence lawyer,' Joanna said.

I tried to give her a kiss, but she repelled my advances. 'And where were you off to so bright and breezy this morning?' I asked.

'I can't tell you.'

If anyone wanted to know ways guaranteed to annoy their fiancée, I was thinking of writing a book.

Joanna stared through dangerously narrowed eyes. 'You can't tell me?'

'All I can say is that I had important legal business to attend to.'

'So?'

'So, you're a PF. I can't tell you for professional reasons.'

'Then tell me for unprofessional reasons. That shouldn't be too difficult for you.'

I rose above that remark. Joanna moved closer and began to toy with the collar of my shirt. 'Can't you even tell me...hypothetically?'

'Your attempts to seduce the information out of me won't work,' I said.

She stepped back giving my shirt collar a parting flick. 'Don't think I couldn't have you singing like a choirboy if I wanted to, but, as it happens, I'm going home.'

'Home? This is your home.'

She lifted the pile of paperwork from the table and waggled it at me. 'Robbie, my home, our future home, is somewhere in amongst this little lot. And, if you're not interested in finding it...'

'I am. Of course I am. We can go house hunting next weekend.'

'No, I think I'll go home next weekend, and see if my mum and dad will come with me to view some properties.' That sounded like a great idea to me. If house hunting with Joanna was anything like shopping, I'd just be going along to make up the numbers; however, I couldn't let Joanna think I was trying to duck out of it.

'There's no need to bother your parents. I'll go with

you next weekend. Today was a one-off. I had some business to settle and now it's all sorted, so I'm completely free.'

She put the paperwork down on the table more gently this time and approached me again. She placed her arms around my neck and kissed me. 'Okay, next weekend it is.'

My bluff had been called. That was why I never played poker with women.

'I've singled out a few houses and most of them have open days Saturday and Sunday. We can make an early start both days and see how many we can fit in,' she said.

I laughed. 'Of course, when I say next weekend, I mean next Saturday.'

Joanna let me go and stepped back. 'Last time I checked we had two days at the weekend.'

'But Sunday's the Scottish Junior Cup Final. You can't expect—'

'Yes, I can, Robbie. This is our future. It's more important than some game of football.'

I laughed. Obviously, she didn't realise it was the Scottish Junior Cup Final. I thought it would help if I explained, but Joanna was already marching towards the back door. I went to the kitchen window to see her standing outside, arms crossed, staring down to the far end of the garden where Tina was playing with the dog. Two magpies, sorrow and joy, were perched on top of the former hutch, now kennel, Bouncer jumping about, barking up at them. A sun that had been cavorting in a clear blue sky all day, now had a dark cloud threatening to gate-crash the party. A few drops of rain hit the glass. Tina had already changed her clothes once, following her soaking at the Helix Park. I opened the door and called to her to come inside before the rain came on any heavier. She pretended not to hear me. I tried again. No response. I went out and took Joanna's hand, although it took three attempts. 'Next Saturday for certain,' I said. 'Who knows? We might like the first house we see.'

Joanna was rubbish at being in the huff. That was one of the things I liked best about her, because I gave her plenty to be huffy about. We walked together down the garden hand in hand. The magpies that had been sitting on the hutch roof, ignoring Bouncer's yelps and probably wondering when rabbit would be back on the menu, took off in close formation as we approached. The sun gave a farewell performance before bowing out under a curtain of grey, and its last rays caught the birds' iridescent plumage. Magpies got such a bad press that I'd never stopped to think how beautiful they were.

'If this was a tropical rainforest and not Scotland, they'd be called birds of paradise,' Joanna said. 'Makes you wonder why a birdwatcher like Bert Brechin needs to go all the way to Madeira.'

It wasn't Brechin's leaving the country that I minded. It was his coming back again that I objected to. Especially when he returned early and convicted one of my clients of a politically-correct crime that now threatened to ruin her career.

The first drops of rain started to fall. I grabbed Bouncer and put him inside the kennel. 'Stay,' I commanded. He did. For about five seconds and then jumped out again. I pretended to make a grab for Tina. Squealing, she ran off inside. Joanna and I turned and walked after her.

'And look what he came back to find,' Joanna said. 'His granddaughter arrested for drug dealing.'

'All because of a search warrant he'd signed personally,' I said.

Joanna stopped in her tracks. 'No way.'

'Very much way. Kaye Mitchell is all over the story like batter on a Mars bar. Puts a nice angle on it, doesn't it? Sheriff helps convict his own granddaughter. Bound to be picked up by all the dailies.'

'The whole thing has been a disaster,' Joanna said.

I agreed. Talk about Mayday, Mayday? It had been a calamitous first of May for both Antonia Brechin and Heather Somerville.

It could all have been so different if only Brechin had stayed in Madeira birdwatching and not come back to convict my client or sign that search warrant.

Sign the search warrant?

The magpies had circled around. Swooping down they came in to land atop the hutch again.

'They're amazing creatures, aren't they?' Joanna said. 'Yes, they are.' I planted a firm kiss on her lips. 'But not

as amazing as you.'

50

Antonia Brechin shared the upper floor of a subdivided old stone-built house that had ivy climbing the walls and starlings roosting in the eaves. It was situated on Royal Terrace, a five-minute walk to Linlithgow train station, from where a further twenty minutes would take you into the centre of Edinburgh. There were people living in Edinburgh who couldn't get to the centre of Edinburgh that quickly.

This was the best day of the summer so far, which, since we were in Scotland, wasn't saying much; however, the three young women were taking full advantage, catching the late afternoon rays of a sun that had risen early and wouldn't be thinking of setting for another five hours or so.

I'd wanted to come earlier, but it was Monday, usually my busiest day in court, and I did still have a business to run.

'You'll have to leave.' Freya Linkwood reached for her iPhone. 'Andy said I was to call him if you came anywhere near me.'

'There's no need to phone anyone. I only want a quick word with Antonia and then I'll be gone.'

'Go away, Antonia doesn't want to speak to you.' I'd never paid much attention to Gail Paton's client before. Gail had made very sure of that. I couldn't even remember her name, although it was right there on the indictment next to Antonia's. She was a small woman, her hair, black and sort of frizzy, was pulled tightly and tied in bunches high on each side, dropping down to her shoulders. She wore a lot of make-up for a sunbather and was making the most of her small breasts, which were pushed up and squashed inside a tight-fitting, low-cut T-shirt, like a couple of pink marshmallows in a vice. 'If you don't leave right now we'll have you done for trespassing.' She'd obviously been spending too much time reading up on the type of law that paid, and neglecting her studies in crime. 'Not in Scotland, you won't,' I said, 'and since I'm not here to commit a theft or cause damage to property, I think you might struggle to have me arrested.'

'We could say you were causing a breach of the peace and threatening us,' she said huffily.

'You could,' I said, 'but you lot are so bad at sticking to the same story you'd only end up with a charge of wasting the time of the police to add to the supplying cocaine on your indictment.'

'Stop it, now!'

Antonia, halter-neck top, cut-off denims and pink sandals, pulled herself out of a padded sunlounger.

'I'm surprised you're still hanging out with this pair,' I said to her, as she flip-flopped her way over to me. 'Are you not scared they'll stab you when you turn over to tan your back?'

Antonia took a firm hold of my elbow. 'I'll give you as long as it takes to walk back to your car, and that's it,' she said. 'So, if you've got something to say, you'd better make it quick.'

I stopped walking, removed her hand from my arm and looked at her. 'Re-instruct me to act for you and I'll have you acquitted. That quick enough?'

The other two were on their feet, Freya with a mobile phone to her ear.

'Don't listen to him,' Crinkly-hair said. 'Have the case put off tomorrow, lodge a complaint against him and see if the prosecution will lower the charges. That way we can all plead guilty to the same thing.'

'Like we were going to, before you got him involved,' Freya Linkwood added, just so I knew that their verdict on my incompetence was unanimous.

I didn't look at them. I looked at Antonia. 'You can do that if you like, but I don't think it will work. Should I have followed your instructions and pled guilty right at the start? Probably. You know what the appeal court will ask? They'll ask if you knew the difference between guilty and not guilty and that, if you did, why didn't you say something at the time? You're a lawyer too, remember? Complain against me and I'll get into trouble, but you're the one charged with supplying a Class A drug and so guilty that even your best friends are prepared to testify against you. The appeal court isn't going to throw a conviction like that out in a hurry.'

Freya's face was red to the roots of her flaxen hair, and it wasn't sunburn. She handed me her phone. I didn't have to put it anywhere near my head to recognise the voice shouting at me. 'Robbie, what do you think you are doing? Leave my client and get out of there right now, or—'

'Or what, Andy?'

'Or...'

I pressed the red button and tossed the phone back to Freya. 'I'm not here to talk to you or your lawyer,' I said. 'It's too late for you. You've pled guilty and will

306

just have to take what's coming.' I turned to Frizzy-hair. 'As for you, there's still time.'

'I'm having nothing to do with you.'

'Then go back to your deckchair and leave us alone.' I took Antonia's hand and pulled her into the shadow of the building.

'It's no good, Robbie,' she said. 'Granddad has already spoken to another lawyer. I'm supposed to meet him at court tomorrow. He insists that I say who gave the drugs to me. If I do, he guarantees the prosecution will drop the charge back down to simple possession.'

Grass on Uncle Ted? That was all I needed. Never mind the distress to Joanna, what if he in turn ratted on his pal, Quentin Brechin? Did Antonia know that her father was on the next rung up the drug-dealing ladder? It was all getting very near to the top where sat the very large, highly vindictive Stan Blandy. Witnesses would lose more than fingers before he went anywhere near prison.

'You're really going to testify against your boss?'

She closed her eyes and nodded. 'How long have you known?'

'Not long,' I said, 'and I can understand why you'd want to go down that line, but what if I told you we could leave Ted out of this, and be acquitted, not just of supplying, but of possession too?'

She laughed disbelievingly. 'How?'

'I have some very important evidence.'

'What evidence?'

'I can't tell you.'

'Why not?'

'I don't trust you with it. No offence, I don't trust

anyone with it.'

'You don't trust me, but I'm supposed to trust you?' She had her grandfather's knack of raising one eyebrow. It looked better on her. 'That doesn't seem fair.'

'I don't do fair,' I said. 'I do what is best for my client and that's you, if you'll take me on again as your solicitor.' She stepped back into the sunlight. 'Why should I, after all that's happened? How do I know this is not just some attempt to get yourself out of trouble?' The look of contempt on her face reminded me so much, too much, of her grandfather.

'You know what?' I said. 'Why don't you just do what you like? Plead guilty, lose your career, go to prison. Your grandfather does his best to make my life a misery. Why should I care what happens to you?'

'If you hate us all so much, why did you agree to take the case on?'

'Because I asked him to.' Joanna appeared from the shadows at the side of the big house. 'I felt sorry for you and thought you needed help.'

Antonia scuffed the sole of a flip-flop along the ground. 'Yeah, well, thanks a lot for that.'

There were tears in the young woman's eyes when she turned and walked towards her friends. As Antonia approached they reached out to console her.

Joanna pinched the arm of my shirt and gave it a gentle tug. 'Come on. Let's go.'

I didn't move. 'Don't do this,' I called to Antonia. 'Give me another chance and I promise everything will be all right.'

'You should really stop making promises you can't keep,' Joanna said.

But I really thought I could keep this one.

Head bowed, her back to us, Antonia stood with her friends, their arms around one another. I was about to leave, when, suddenly, she straightened, extricated herself from the huddle and strode over to us. She wasn't crying anymore, the determined expression on her face now less contemptuous and more determined, reminiscent of Sheriff Brechin doing his best not to be persuaded of a reasonable doubt.

Ignoring me, she turned to Joanna. 'What do you think?

Should I trust Robbie to keep his promise?'

Joanna looked at Antonia as though she was mad. 'Trust him? Trust Robbie?' Then she smiled and placed a hand on the worried young woman's shoulder. 'Of course you should trust him.'

51

There were a number of First Diets on the court roll that Tuesday morning. Five minutes before the start of court, Antonia Brechin and she of the frizzy-hair were sitting side by side in the public gallery with Gail Paton yet to arrive.

Earlier, I'd noticed Andy sneak in ungowned to take a back seat. No doubt he'd been sent to keep a watching brief. His own client, Freya Linkwood, would be a witness if the trial went ahead and sentenced once proceedings were over. If she played her part and put the blame on Antonia, she was looking at an admonition, possibly even an absolute discharge, as a thank you from the court for her early plea of guilty and co-operation in convicting her friend.

'A preliminary issue?' Hugh Ogilvie said, taking the sheet of paper from me. 'You've got to be kidding. You know this should have been intimated three days ago?'

'You're not going to object to late-lodging are you?

You don't need three days to read three lines.'

Ogilvie stared at the piece of paper I'd handed him, turning it this way and that as though it were some alien artefact.

Anyone whose knowledge of criminal trials is based on TV courtroom dramas or crime thrillers will be well used to the surprise witnesses and other evidential bombshells that are sprung on an unsuspecting prosecution and which, accompanied by gasps of shock from the assembled jurors, invariably lead to an acquittal. It all makes for excellent television. It also makes real lawyers laugh. There had been a day, way back in the mists of history, long before I first put on a black gown, sometime around the time the oceans drank Atlantis and the last hike in Legal Aid rates, when it had been perfectly feasible to ambush the Crown. An unheralded attack on the validity of some vital piece of evidence or highlighting of a procedural error by the police or Procurator Fiscal, was common-place mid-trial, and it was not unusual for someone to take a walk from the dock on what the newspapers liked to call 'a technicality.'

Recently, however, there had been a change in the law requiring the defence to tell the Crown, before the trial, of any errors it had discovered in the prosecution case. This was done by raising what was known as a preliminary issue. Understandably, the Crown found this extremely helpful, allowing as it did the remedy of any awkward, defence-favouring blunders before the jury got to hear about them.

'You're challenging the search?' Ogilvie waved the Minute at me. 'You haven't exactly gone overboard on detail, have you?' He was right about that. The real art in drafting a preliminary issue was to fulfil one's statutory obligation to provide notice, while giving the opposition as little clue as possible to what it was really all about and, hence, no time to prepare a counter-argument.

'This vague nonsense is just a stalling tactic. You're looking for an excuse to delay the trial, aren't you?'

If he expected me to answer, he was going to be disappointed. I wasn't about to tell him the basis of my

311

challenge to the admissibility of the search evidence. He'd learn that soon enough.

Gail arrived seconds before the start of court. She had her own sheet of paper with her. An affidavit signed by her client that, once handed to the PF, would guarantee the acceptance of her guilty plea to the lesser charge of possession. By agreeing to testify against Antonia, Gail's client's reward would be the saving of her career. Some people settled for thirty pieces of silver.

I stepped in front of Gail as she tried to walk past me and go around the big table in the well of the court to where Hugh Ogilvie was seated.

'I've something for you,' I said, giving her an intimation copy of my Minute.

'Ooh, Robbie, a section seventy-one Minute, and look, it's raising a preliminary issue. It's not like you to get bogged down with unnecessary stuff - like the law. What are you challenging, the flammability of the Crown witnesses' underwear?'

'Tell your client to maintain her plea of not guilty,' I said.

She pinched my cheek and gave it a waggle. 'No, Robbie, I won't do that. I can understand why you'd prefer a two- pronged attack on the Crown case but, sadly, my client is not prepared to take that risk.' Gail placed a hand on each of my arms and moved me to the side. 'Sorry you didn't get a deal, but what's bad news for your client is, I'm pleased to say, good news for mine.'

'I'm challenging the search,' I said. 'No search, no drugs; no drugs, no case to answer.'

'Yes, thanks, Robbie, I know how evidence works;

however, I can detect one tiny flaw in your plan.'

'What's that?'

'It's crap.' She pushed past me. 'Seriously, Gail—'

'Nope. My client wants the case over and done with. She's not going along with any scheme of yours to drag things out in the hope that tomorrow will be a better day.' Gail and I were friends. I'd tried to help. I didn't see what more I could do. She had her client to look out for,

I had mine.

Ogilvie took the affidavit from her. 'If you won't listen to me, listen to Miss Paton,' he said. 'You're not seriously going ahead with this preliminary issue thing, are you? It's a blatant attempt to delay proceedings and if you try to move for an adjournment, I'm going to have to strongly object.'

The Sheriff came on. I hadn't come across her before in my travels. The merest hint of eye shadow and smudge of red lipstick, she was no more than forty-five, with long, dark hair descending from beneath a snowy-white horsehair wig to the shoulders of her pristine black robes. I guessed she'd been recently appointed and allocated Antonia Brechin's trial to avoid any suggestion of partiality that might have followed had one of the other local sheriffs or a contemporary of Sheriff Brechin been asked to preside.

Everyone stood. The Sheriff bowed and sat down. Eleanor, the Sheriff Clerk, announced to the public that this was a court of First Diet and called the first case. 'Her Majesty's Advocate against Antonia Alberta Brechin and Emily Leigh Harris.'

The two young women took the dock. Antonia was dressed plainly in a cream blouse and dark skirt.

Frizzy-haired Emily, whose hair was not quite so frizzy today, wore a light summer frock. Pretty and demure, they both looked like butter wouldn't melt in their mouths, far less cocaine dissolve up their noses.

I stood and confirmed my client's plea of not guilty. 'As your ladyship will see, I have a preliminary issue I'd like to draw to the court's attention.'

'And are you seeking an evidential hearing on it?'

'I am.'

The Sheriff looked down at Eleanor. 'There seems to be quite a busy morning ahead, Sheriff Clerk. What days do we have available before the trial for a hearing on Mr Munro's Minute?' Before Eleanor could answer, Hugh Ogilvie was on his feet. 'M'Lady, this Minute is, in my opinion, a delaying tactic by the defence. If Mr Munro is so keen on it, then why don't we hold the hearing this afternoon.'

The Sheriff didn't seem terribly enthusiastic about that suggestion, but then all sheriffs hated afternoons. It was almost as though judging things after lunch wasn't part of their job description.

'Very well,' she said, with a sigh. 'I trust it won't take too long.'

'Not long at all,' I said.

I sat down, Gail stood up. 'M'Lady, I appear for the second-named accused. You'll find that she is now pleading...' Gail looked down at me. 'You're not asking for an adjournment?'

I smiled and shook my head.

'And you're going ahead with this preliminary issue thing this afternoon?' I smiled and nodded my head. Gail studied me for a moment and then in turn looked to the PF, to her client and back up at the bench. 'My client is pleading not guilty, M'Lady.'

'No, I'm pleading guilty!' Crinkly-hair called from the dock.

'I think your client wishes to give you some new instructions, Miss Paton,' the Sheriff said.

Coolly, Gail walked around the table, lifted her client's affidavit from the top of Hugh Ogilvie's pile of papers and tore it once, straight down the middle, all the time staring at me. 'No, M'Lady, she doesn't.'

52

Hearings on preliminary issues were dealt with by the sheriff in the absence of a jury.

The first witness to be called was Detective Inspector Douglas Fleming. He had been sitting in Police HQ, catching up on his foot-dangling, when unexpectedly summoned to take the stand, and was none too happy about it. After the oath had been administered, I rose to question him.

'Please have before you Crown production one,' I said. 'Do you recognise that?'

'Yes.'

'What is it?'

'It's a warrant.'

'Could you tell me the procedure for obtaining a search warrant?'

'That depends on the type of warrant.' Sometimes I thought I should have been a dentist.

'Let's assume Mr Munro is talking about the search warrant you have in your hand, Inspector,' the Sheriff said, already sensing the witness's lack of motivation. 'It's seeking authority to search premises for illegal drugs, is it not?'

Fleming gave the two-page document the briefest of glances. 'So it would seem.'

'And would it also seem to have been signed by you, Inspector Fleming?' I asked.

'That's correct.'

'Would you be so good as to talk us through the procedure for obtaining this warrant, please?'

Ogilvie climbed to his feet. 'Is this really necessary? I'm sure the Inspector seeks warrants all the time. I don't know how he's supposed to remember them all.'

'Nonetheless, I'd like Inspector Fleming to explain the procedure,' I told the Sheriff.

Ogilvie was out of his seat again. 'M'Lady, everyone is well aware of the procedure. We are all lawyers, after all...' He smiled. 'Even the accused.'

The Sheriff looked at me enquiringly. 'If your Ladyship would indulge me.'

Generally speaking, sheriffs just want whatever is calling before them to be over and done with as quickly as possible. This particular sheriff had come to the conclusion that engaging in a debate with me and the PF over my question would take longer than just having the witness answer it.

Fleming released an enormous sigh when told to proceed. 'First of all, a police officer—'

'And in this case that police officer was you?' I said. 'Yes. That's correct. The police officer was me. I've already said so. That's my signature beside Sheriff Brechin's on the warrant. I'd have contacted the on-call Procurator Fiscal to say I needed a search warrant. They'd have drafted the petition for me - that's the first page...' Fleming's voice was now monotone and bordering on the impertinent. 'I'd have collected it, called in at the Sheriff Clerk's office and been shown up to the Sheriff's chambers.'

'Carry on,' I said.

'Next I would have presented the petition to the Sheriff, advised him of my suspicions—'

317

'Under oath?'

'Yes, I would have sworn an oath, explained the reasons for the search and we'd both have signed.'

'Did the Sheriff date the warrant?'

'He did.'

'And the date is very important with a drugs search warrant, is it not?'

'It is.'

'Why is that?'

'Because the search has to be carried out within one month.'

'And when was this warrant granted?'

Fleming checked. 'Twenty-seventh April this year.'

'And on what date was the search actually carried out?'

Fleming received permission from the bench to refer to his notebook. 'The first of May.' He snapped the notebook shut and shoved it inside his jacket.

'How certain are you of that search date?'

Fleming tapped the breast of his jacket. 'I have it noted right here.' He turned his head to look at Antonia who was sitting in the dock, ashen faced. 'I remember the first of May very well. I'm sure it's a date that sticks in your client's memory too.'

The first of May was a date that stuck in a lot of people's memories, boyfriend-slapping Heather Somerville's included.

Ogilvie made a show of looking at his watch. 'M'Lady, time is marching on, and Mr Munro hasn't led the Inspector to the premises yet, far less searched them.' The Sheriff stared down at me. 'Obviously, it's been interesting to be reminded how one goes about obtaining a search warrant, Mr Munro, but I think we should cut to the chase.' She looked up at the clock on the far wall of the courtroom. 'I understand you have another witness still to call. How much longer do you expect to be with Inspector Fleming?'

'Thank you, M'Lady, I'm finished with this witness,' I said.

As I sat down beside Gail Paton she leaned into me and whispered, 'Devastating stuff, Robbie. Any chance you could tell me what the hell is going on?'

I couldn't. Not yet.

Hugh Ogilvie saw no need to cross-examine, and so I was asked to call my second and final witness.

'What's the name of your witness, Mr Munro?' the Sheriff asked, pen poised over notepad.

'Sheriff Albert Brechin,' I said.

Gail grabbed her nose between thumb and forefinger and failed to stifle a snort.

Ogilvie jumped to his feet, the blue worm of a vein proud on his scarlet scalp. 'This is outrageous.'

'Explain yourself,' the Sheriff said.

'Like it says in the Minute, I'm challenging the search. Perhaps I should have been more specific and said I was challenging the search warrant. It was signed by two people. Inspector Fleming was one, Sheriff Brechin the other.'

The Sheriff took time to think that over, then spoke down to the clerk. 'Is Sheriff Brechin available?'

I knew he was. He was rattling through the custody court next door so that he could come in and watch his granddaughter's case. Well, he was about to get a closer view of proceedings than he'd expected.

53

Sheriff Brechin took the stand having removed gown and wig but still clad in his blacks. A white fall spilled over the brass collar stud of his wing-collared shirt and onto the top buttons of his waistcoat. He took the oath without the need for the presiding sheriff to recite it, and, when given the nod, I stood and asked him to provide his name, address, age and occupation.

'You know perfectly well who I am, where I live and what I do for a living, Mr Munro. How old I am is none of your business. Get on with it.'

Clearly he wasn't going to let a minor matter, like the fact that I was representing the interests of his grand- daughter, mellow his usual hostile attitude towards me. He was only making the whole thing more fun.

'Do you recognise this?' I asked, lifting production one from the ledge of the witness box and holding it up to him.

'It's a search warrant by the looks of things,' he said.

'Very good. Now, I wonder if you could talk us through—'

Ogilvie leapt out of his seat to address the Bench. 'M'Lady, we are now all very familiar, if we weren't already, with the procedure for obtaining a drugs search warrant.' If he looked at his watch again, he would wear the face of it. 'I'm inviting your Ladyship—
'

'I'm way ahead of you, Procurator Fiscal,' the Sheriff said. 'Mr Munro, get on with it. We know the procedure for granting a search warrant. Move along.'

'Sheriff Brechin, do you see two signatures on this warrant?'

From a waistcoat pocket, Brechin produced the pair of half-moons that every sheriff seemed to come supplied with along with a horsehair wig and an air of superiority. He lifted the document to eye level. 'Yes, I see two signatures.'

'Inspector Fleming has told us that one is his and the other yours.'

'It would seem so,' Brechin said, setting the warrant down and tucking his spectacles away in his waistcoat pocket again.

'Detective Inspector Fleming told us that he'd sworn an oath, told you his suspicions for obtaining a warrant and then you both signed.'

'Is that a question?' Ogilvie was spending nearly as much time on his feet as I was.

'Perhaps we'd find out, if you stopped objecting and let Mr Munro get to the point,' the Sheriff replied.

'If there is a point,' Ogilvie muttered under his breath, so quietly that there may have been some people in the courtroom next door who didn't quite catch it.

Her ladyship looked down sympathetically at the witness and then at me. 'Do we need to delay Sheriff Brechin any longer, Mr Munro?'

Indeed we did.

'Sheriff Brechin, there are certain laws and procedures governing the granting of a warrant are there not?'

'Patently so.'

'And these must be followed?'

Hugh Ogilvie and the lady sheriff sighed in tandem. 'It's not as though,' I said, 'you keep a stash of pre-signed warrants on your desk to dish out to any old copper who swings by, looking to turn over somebody's flat on a fishing expedition – is it?'

Eleanor Hammond, the clerk who had been listening intently, suddenly found something on her computer monitor that required her immediate and undivided attention.

'Mr Munro, that's quite enough,' said the Sheriff. 'Remember where you are and whom you are addressing.' I picked up the warrant, flipped it over to the second page and handed it to Brechin. 'Tell me. On what date did you sign this?'

Hugh Ogilvie bounced to his feet. 'M'Lady, we've already heard the date of signing was the twenty-seventh of April. It's written right there on the warrant.'

The woman in the wig did not reply to Ogilvie's objection. Clearly sensing something, she leaned forward, arms folded on the bench in front of her, forehead furrowed. 'Continue, Mr Munro.'

As the Procurator Fiscal took his seat again, I poked the search warrant at Brechin. 'Read and tell me the date that you put Detective Inspector Fleming under oath and granted him this search warrant.'

I heard the sound of someone in the public benches stand up and leave the courtroom. I didn't have to take my eyes off the witness to know it was Dougie Fleming.

'I'm afraid the handwriting's not very clear.'

'It's a date and your signature, I'm not asking you to translate the Dead Sea scrolls,' I said.

'That's enough, Mr Munro.' The lady Sheriff looked down at the witness and he gazed up at her, appealingly, seeking the sort of mercy so many had sought from him in the past.

'Please answer the question,' she said, coldly.

Holding the warrant in his right hand, Brechin patted himself with his left. 'I'm sorry, I'm not sure what I've done with my glasses.'

'Maybe you'd rather use binoculars,' I said. 'I believe you keep a pair for birdwatching. How was Madeira?'

Sun Tzu, author of The Art of War, advises that one should always leave the enemy a golden bridge over which to retreat. The art of cross-examination is no different; except the bridge one lays for a witness to retreat across should always lead to exactly where the cross-examiner wants the witness to end up.

'Is the date on that warrant the twenty-seventh of April?' I asked, when at last Brechin had located and donned his spectacles.

He screwed up his eyes and peered closely through his half-moons at the piece of paper he held in his hand. 'Hard to say, really, but no, it's definitely not twenty-seventh April.' Having decided the matter, he whipped off his spectacles and laid the warrant down on the edge of the witness box. 'Though I can see why Inspector Fleming might have been mistaken.'

'How so?' asked the Sheriff, who had her own copy of the production. 'It looks like twenty-seventh April to me.'

'Yes, my handwriting can be quite poor at times.'

Brechin manufactured a little laugh. 'It certainly says the twenty-seventh, but it must be March not April.'

I could do no other than agree with the witness's

deciphering of his own handwriting, and so I sat down.

By now the lady Sheriff's mouth was a thin, grim line of red. 'Procurator Fiscal, do you have any questions for this witness?'

Not rising, Hugh Ogilvie shook his head.

Her ladyship turned to me again. 'Then, if Sheriff Brechin's evidence is to be believed, the search was not carried out timeously, rendering the findings inadmissible,' she said, summing up my position precisely. 'Do you agree, Mr Munro?'

How could I not? There was no way Sheriff Brechin could have signed a search warrant on the twenty-seventh of April. Not when on that day he'd been birdwatching in Madeira. 'I do, M'Lady. The only other explanation is that Sheriff Brechin pre-signed a pro forma search warrant and left it behind like some kind of blank cheque for the police to cash in on any search they fancied.' I fabricated my own little laugh. 'But that would mean that both his Lordship and D.I. Fleming have stood before the court this very afternoon and lied under oath.'

The Sheriff stared down to her right at Hugh Ogilvie. He looked like a man who just wanted to go home, lie down in a darkened room and dab his temples with cologne. 'Do you agree, Procurator Fiscal?'

Ogilvie's responses were now restricted to head movements. He nodded.

The Sheriff picked up her copy of the warrant again and made a show of studying it very carefully. 'I suppose it must all have been a terrible mistake,' she said. 'Unless, of course, anyone thinks I should consider the other possibility...' Now she was staring directly at the man in the witness box. 'That what we have here is evidence of a blatant abuse of power, compounded by perjury. What are your views on that, Mr Munro?'

What a darling. She was leaving it to me. I could almost taste the pleasure. It was win-win. The warrant was either out of date in which case invalid, or it had been pre-signed by Brechin in which case equally invalid, but with a criminal investigation to follow and heads to roll — one quite possibly with a horsehair wig on it. I looked at him standing there in his black suit and white shirt, like a great, big, sullen magpie. What was it to be? Sorrow or joy? Good news or bad? It was all down to me.

'Stick it to him, Robbie,' Gail whispered, hand covering her mouth.

'Don't, Robbie, please,' Eleanor the clerk mouthed at me. She knew that all I had to do was call her to take the stand and the career of Albert Brechin would be shredded like a bird flying into a jet engine.

From behind me I heard the sound of someone crying. It was Antonia. Silence fell in court like a feather falling on water. Eventually, having savoured every last beautiful moment, I heard a voice that sounded very much like my own, say, 'I'm sure, M'Lady, it has all been a most unfortunate misunderstanding.'

54

No valid search warrant, no lawful search. No lawful search, no drugs. No drugs, no case to answer - just two very happy clients.

I tidied up my papers and left the courtroom to see Gail Paton outside in the corridor being hugged by her frizzy-haired client.

Further along the corridor, there was more embracing, Antonia Brechin and her mother standing, arms wrapped around each other, crying, while Quentin smiled and stroked his daughter's head.

'You can't beat getting a guilty person off, can you?' Gail said, cheerily, once she'd disentangled herself and followed me into the agent's room.

I knew what she meant. Where was the fun in having an innocent person acquitted? It was like a doctor curing someone who had nothing wrong with them in the first place.

'My client's delighted she took my advice to plead not guilty,' Gail said. 'I knew it was the right thing to do when I saw you meant business with that search warrant challenge.'

I hadn't noticed Crinkly-hair actually accepting Gail's advice. In fact, by the way she'd yelled from the dock, I'd formed the completely opposite opinion. It was funny how clients never complained when you didn't follow their instructions, so long as everything worked out well. It was only when things didn't go to plan that fingers were pointed.

Andy came in to collect his coat. He didn't acknowledge us. His client had pled guilty. She'd be sentenced in course. There was no going back for her, dodgy search warrant or not.

'Cheer up,' I called to him. 'You did the right thing. Played the odds.'

'Don't patronise me, Robbie,' he said, taking his rain- coat off a hook without looking round.

'I'm not. You did what you thought was in your client's best interests. I only got a result because I was forced to gamble. Some you win, some you lose. You can't be blamed because I had a lucky win.'

He grunted. 'Somehow I don't think Freya Linkwood's father will see it that way.'

'You know that Joanna's gone back to the Fiscal Service,' I said as, putting on his coat, Andy walked past us. 'If you get kicked out of the Halls of Valhalla, there's a place for you in Munro and Co. Just name your starting salary, we'll all have a good laugh and then I'll tell you what it really is.'

But even that attempt at humour, such as it was, failed to lift my ex-assistant's spirits.

As he stomped off into the sunset, I sat down at one of the tables, swung back and put my feet up for ten minutes, content to give the Brechins time to leave the building before I returned to the office.

'Not going out to face the adoration of your client and her family?' Gail asked.

Of course, I was pleased for Antonia and would have liked to have passed on my best wishes, but I wanted to hear no words of gratitude from her drug-dealing father, nor any lame excuses for the threats made by her mother. Gail packed up her papers and stowed them alongside her court gown in her holdall. 'I've got to hand it to you, Robbie, it was a very neat piece of work. I'd let you buy me a coffee if I wasn't in such a hurry. You'll just have to make do with helping me carry my stuff to the car.'

Usually you can tell when it's summer in Scotland: the rain gets warmer. Unusually, the last few days had been wall to wall sunshine. It had to end sometime, and it did. Gail and I were standing in the foyer, waiting for a heavy burst of rain to exhaust itself, when the automatic doors opened and Sammy Veitch came scampering through them, holding a plastic carrier bag over his head, kilt flapping in the breeze.

For a man who'd had a sudden soaking, he seemed pretty upbeat about the weather. 'Great, isn't it?' he said, once the glass doors had swished shut behind him. 'After that wee spell of dry weather a spot of rain'll make the roads nice and greasy.'

But Sammy hadn't popped into court just to spread the good news about the treacherous driving conditions. He was there to hand something into the planning department. I took him aside on his return. 'How's that thing going with you-know-who?'

'It's going fine,' he said. 'I've just lodged a bogus planning application, the life policy proposal has been submitted and the first premium is paid. It's just a matter of time.'

'And no comebacks? Ellen's not got that long. You don't think someone will be suspicious?'

'Not a chance. It's all as neat as you like.' Sammy shook water from the carrier bag across the stone floor. 'Nice piece of business. I'm telling you, you should have wet your beak a little on this one, Robbie.'

He seemed happy enough and yet I couldn't help feeling guilty for getting Sammy into it.

'No reason to be concerned about me, son,' Sammy said. 'No-one knows about Ellen's big C. It's a straightforward term insurance policy. If she dies, they have to pay out.'

'And if the insurers make some enquiries...?'

'Robbie, is there something you've not told me?' There was. It had been preying on me for a day or two. I confessed it to Sammy.

'She had a private nurse! Now you tell me. What was her name? Who did she work for?'

All I could remember was long auburn hair, even longer legs and a lime green uniform with some kind of red-cross logo on the collar.

'A long-legged redhead?' Sammy said. 'Well, I suppose if you've got to have a nurse you might as well... No, Mrs Veitch would never stand for it. Not even if I was dying. But, Robbie, d'you realise that if word gets out that Ellen knew the score before signing that policy, it's going to blow the whole thing wide open.' He stared down at his ox-blood ghillie brogues, and shook his head sadly. 'Why did I let you get me into this?'

Get him into it? Sammy had got into it like a La Quebrada cliff-diver gets into the Pacific Ocean.

'What'd do you think we should do?' I asked.

'We?' Sammy said. 'We should do nothing. But you, you're going to have to go see Ellen and get things sorted.'

55

I tried to contact Ellen over the next couple of days but she was never available, always off somewhere with Jake who seemed determined to show her a few last good times. Eventually, I phoned Sammy to say he'd just have to keep his fingers crossed that Ellen's nurse had either been unaware of the nature of her employer's illness or sworn to secrecy.

Come Friday afternoon I was in an excellent mood. The very fact it was Friday was a pretty good start in itself, and then Joanna had phoned me at lunchtime to say that the threatened weekend of house hunting might be curtailed because she'd seen a property she liked.

I told her to note interest and we'd make an offer when a closing date was fixed. I didn't think there was a need for me to view it. If Joanna liked it, then, so long as she was going to live there with me, and my dad wasn't, I felt sure I'd like it too.

As I walked down the stairs from the court and into the atrium of the Civic Centre at three thirty that mid-June afternoon, with an unsullied weekend spread out before me, I heard someone call my name and turned around to see Eleanor Hammond, the Sheriff Clerk, at the top of the stairs waving a brown envelope. I could tell it wasn't my favourite type of brown envelope because it was thin and A4-sized and also by the way that, when I'd climbed the stairs to meet Eleanor on the top landing, she tried to hit me over the head with it.

'What were you trying to do the other day?' I knew there had to be a reason she was personally delivering something that could easily have been stuck in the post. 'I don't see what the big fuss was about,' she said huffily. 'It's not like the Sheriff wouldn't have granted the warrant if he'd been here. I've been clerking for Sheriff Brechin for twenty-five years and he's never refused to sign a warrant yet.' She thrust the envelope at me.

'What's this?'

'The final stated case in your appeal.' The final nail in the coffin of Heather Somerville's teaching career more like. 'You'll need to lodge it with the summary appeal court. Also...' she jabbed a thumb at the ceiling. 'Sheriff Brechin wants a word before you go.'

Sheriff Brechin had his back to me when I was shown into chambers. He had changed from his formal black suit into a more informal, slightly less black suit, and was busy knotting a tie about the collar of a fresh white shirt. Without turning around, he asked me to take a seat and Eleanor to close the door on her way out.

'About Antonia's court case, I haven't had a note of your fee yet,' he said, once he'd taken up position in the chair opposite.

'There are a lot of numbers to add up,' I said.

His smile was as thin as an honest alibi. 'I see you have Miss Somerville's stated case.'

'For what it's worth.'

He kept smiling, apparently waiting for me to say

some- thing more. Was he wanting an assurance that I wouldn't seek an investigation into the pre-signed warrant and his obvious perjury?

'There's one thing I don't understand,' I said, when the silence grew uncomfortable.

'Oh come now, Mr Munro. I'm sure there are very many things you don't understand.'

'Remember the first meeting we had about Antonia's case? It was in here after the pleading diet, when I'd made her...advised her...to plead not guilty. You didn't want me to act. What made you change your mind? Was it purely in the hope that she might win a defective representation appeal? That would have been a bit of a long shot, wouldn't it?'

Hands clasped on the desk in front of him, Brechin leaned forward. The sunlight from the window behind him bounced off the shiny bald patch where his comb-over had gone AWOL. 'After the initial shock of realising that Antonia had pled not guilty,' he said, 'I also realised that you, being you, would be intent on taking the matter to trial. I suppose...' he cleared his throat, 'I had faith in you, Mr Munro. Faith in you to be as irritatingly persistent as you usually are in seeking out a defence where it seemed none existed.'

'Then if you had so much faith in me, why did you let your daughter-in-law sack me from Antonia's case last Saturday?'

'You were asked to set out your plans for Antonia's defence, and it was clear you didn't have any. I thought that my faith had been misplaced. I have to say I was surprised. Over the years there has not been a legal barrel you have not scraped. You probably have wood-shavings under your fingernails.'

'I didn't have to scrape too deep this time,' I said. 'It was at that same meeting I saw you give the Sheriff Clerk a pre-signed warrant.' I looked to my left. The wire basket was gone.

'And it took you long enough to appreciate the significance of that,' he said.

'What do you mean?'

'How many times have you been in chambers with me over the years, Mr Munro? Dozens of times. Certainly far too many, and, usually arguing some point of law — or at least your version of the law. Had you ever noticed that basket of pre-signed warrants before?' He answered his question for me. 'Of course you hadn't. Never mind the dishonesty of such an arrangement, do you actually think I would be so stupid as to pre-sign a warrant and then hand it over in front of a defence solicitor?'

I found questions along the lines of, 'How stupid do you think I am?' were usually best left unanswered.

'There was no policeman wanting a search warrant that day,' Brechin said. 'It was a put-up job. You were supposed to notice. You were supposed to start scraping around in those barrels of yours. You certainly took your time about it.'

I stood up. 'I'm sorry, Sheriff, but it's Friday afternoon and I've better things to do than listen to you try and cover up the truth that you pre-signed a warrant and that you committed perjury, not to save your granddaughter's career, but to save your own. That warrant didn't sign itself. And it wasn't signed on the twenty-seventh of April.'

'You're correct about one thing, Mr Munro.' Brechin rose to his feet. 'There were indeed two careers at stake, but mine was never one of them.' He turned again and looked out of the window. 'I've been here since this place was built. Before that I was seventeen years at Linlithgow Sheriff Court. For every single one of those years, my clerk has been Eleanor Hammond. Over that time, including my wife's illness and subsequent death, she has been a great comfort and support. Yes, Eleanor knows me very well and is a true friend. As for the warrant, I have to disagree. It was signed on the twenty-seventh of April; however, it wasn't signed by me.'

It took me a moment or two to absorb what he was trying to tell me. I sat down again and stared at the green leather surface of the massive solid teak desk. 'Eleanor signed your name on the warrant when you were in Madeira?'

He didn't admit it, but neither did he object.

'Why didn't you just say so? If you had, Antonia's case would never have got off the ground.'

'If I had said something, Eleanor's career would have been over. Forging a sheriff's signature on a legal document? Without doubt she would have been summarily dismissed and goodness knows what might have happened to her pension. She could very well have gone to prison.'

'But your granddaughter's future was at stake.'

'I was left with a terrible choice. Whatever I did could not help them both.'

I could see that. What was good news for one was bad news for the other.

'I had to make a decision. I did so on the basis of what I thought was the most just course of action.'

'You risked your own granddaughter's career for the

sake of your clerk?'

'Antonia was guilty of possessing drugs. Drugs that she intended to share with others – that is the very definition of possession with the intent to supply, whether those others are friends or not. All Eleanor was guilty of was oiling the wheels of justice by granting a warrant that she knew would have been granted anyway, had I been there. Where was the justice in ruining her life over that?'

'But you do not preside over a court of justice,' I said. 'Yours is a court of law. Remember?'

'I do, and I allowed you to use that law to achieve justice.'

'By making it look to the Sheriff that you had pre-signed the warrant, without you actually admitting it?'

'It would have been a lie for me to say that I had signed the warrant on the twenty-seventh of April, and yet neither could I say, truthfully or otherwise, that it had been pre-signed. You, on the other hand, Mr Munro, could raise such a doubt, and the raising of reasonable doubts is your job, is it not? I knew I couldn't save both careers, but I believed, together, we could.'

He walked past me and stopped, his hand on the door knob. 'Thanks to you my granddaughter will go on to be a fine lawyer and, thanks to me, in due course Eleanor will enjoy a well-deserved retirement.'

'So you are quite happy that both have broken the law without penalty?'

'Not happy, Mr Munro, but content that each has learned a very valuable lesson.'

'Have it your way,' I said. 'I might call what's happened a great result, but I never thought I'd hear you call it justice.'

Brechin threw the door wide open for me. 'Pass on my best wishes to Miss Somerville,' he said, as I walked by. 'Tell her you were right. Sometimes a good slap is justice enough.'

56

I had the brown envelope ripped open before I'd taken more than three paces down the corridor. From it I pulled a single sheet of paper, not the six or seven page stated case that had been adjusted two weeks before. 'Erred' is a small word, but it leapt off the page and hit me in the face like a frying pan in a Warner Bros. animation.

Erred? I could sense the sheer, excruciating pain that emanated from each of those five letters. Sheriff Albert Brechin had erred in law?

In hindsight and having reflected upon the highly persuasive closing submissions of the Appellant's learned solicitor...'

Learned? He meant me. It was no good, I was going to have to find a seat before reading on. In a daze, I found my way out of the court building, down the stairs to the atrium where I sat down hard on one of the benches.

'...I have come to the conclusion that the case as led before me by the Prosecution was driven not due to the serious nature of the alleged conduct, but by a pedantic and, in this instance, oppressive politically induced policy of zero-tolerance. It should not have been required of this court to adjudicate on such a trifling affair. The time and money already spent by the Crown in bringing this case amounts to a waste of resources. I would not expect your Lordships to be part of further squandering, and ask that the matter be deemed de minimis and the appeal upheld. To answer the* *question put by the Appellant for a finding: I concede that in convicting her I erred and reached a verdict that should not have been returned by a reasonable sheriff.'*

Both the signature and date looked genuine enough. I folded the paper and replaced it in the brown envelope as carefully as though it were a winning lottery ticket. Brechin had really done a number on himself. The only things missing were sackcloth, ashes and a spot of self-flagellation.

I couldn't wait to pass on the good news to Heather Somerville. What better wedding present could there be?

And then I had a thought. If Bert Brechin was able to reconsider his opinion, why not certain others? The Civic Centre not only housed the Sheriff Court, it was home to West Lothian's planning department and the people who'd rejected the original proposals for Joanna and my cottage. Perhaps they could be persuaded otherwise. It was Friday, after all.

After a short wait while they dug out my papers I was taken to a desk in an open plan office where I was introduced to a middle-aged man with a bushy, grey beard and dressed in a checked suit, stripy shirt, spotted tie combo that was painful to the eye.

'Good old dress-down-Friday,' I said, as an opening pleasantry.

'We don't do that here,' he replied. 'The boss doesn't like it.'

I cleared my throat. 'So… Anyway… About my planning application. The proposed changes…' I laughed lightly. 'A bit drastic, aren't they?'

No, apparently they weren't, and it took him ten minutes to explain why they weren't.

'Is there anybody else around I might have a word with, do you think?' I asked as he reached the end of his sermon on sewer systems, safe vehicular access and environmental impact assessments.

'Like who?'

'Like your boss.'

'I am the boss. When I said the boss didn't like dress- down-Friday, I was talking about myself. It was a joke.'

'Is that a joke beard too?' I asked, 'because you seem very hairy for a woman.'

'Mr Munro, we usually try to finish up at four on a Friday. Feel free to have your architect amend anything he thinks appropriate and re-submit. Not that it will—'

'Your boss...?' I reminded him. 'I've told you that's me.'

'You're the boss? As in you're the head of planning?'

He swivelled in his chair, pulled open a drawer and pretended to rummage about inside it. 'I've got a badge somewhere. I can put it on if you like.'

'But I thought...Isn't the head of planning a woman?' That was what my conversations with both Jake and Freddy had led me to believe.

He stood up, the better to stare down at me. 'No Mr Munro, I've been called a lot of things in my time, but never a woman. Like you say, I think it may have something to do with the beard. Now is there anything else you'd like to know?' he enquired, in a there-had-better-not-be kind of a way.

I thanked him for his time. There was plenty more I'd like to have known but, I was equally sure, it was nothing he could have helped me with. I really needed to find Ellen Fletcher.

57

'The good news is that it's within our budget,' Joanna said, as the three of us and dog, piled into the car and headed for the High Street. 'But I've got to warn you, it is quite small.' I'd been kidding myself. There was no danger of me getting away with not viewing the flat Joanna had chosen for us. 'And the other thing is the garden. It's tiny. Practically non-existent.'

Now I knew why my fiancée had never become an estate agent; however, I had the feeling that the garden could have been alligator-infested and she wouldn't have minded so long as it meant we were at last going to have a place of our own. The fact that my attendance at the Scottish Junior Cup final on Sunday was now assured, was also a nice little bonus.

'One other slight problem...' Joanna leaned closer and whispered. 'There are no dogs allowed in the block.'

That was more than a slight problem. My dad had already rejected the suggestion that he look after Bouncer and I couldn't blame him. He was spending enough of his retirement child-minding, without a dog to add to the mix. Malky? He didn't have a garden either. No, finding Bouncer a good home wouldn't be easy. It wasn't like the pound wasn't already full of dogs, most of which, I was sure, could boast at least some resemblance to a recognised breed, unlike

Bouncer's distinctly cosmopolitan appearance.

'Who's going to tell...' I jerked my head backwards to where Tina was sitting on a booster-seat with Bouncer beside her.

It was at times like these that Joanna liked to remind me who Tina's father was.

'But it's you who wants us to move into this new flat,' I said.

'Don't get me started, Robbie. You brought the you-know-what into our lives. You never consulted me, you just arrived with it in the dead of night. Well, you caused the problem and now you're going to have to solve it.'

'But—'

'No buts. It's got to go. Take it back where it came from.'

Return Bouncer to Jake Turpie? What chance would the animal have if I did? Assuming Jake did take it back, unless the dog bucked up its ideas and endeared itself to Jake by tearing the leg off some scrapyard intruder, it would likely face euthanasia by torque wrench.

Joanna twisted in her seat and looked over her shoulder at Tina. 'This place we're going to see is nice and handy for your new school.'

'I don't like it.' Tina said.

'You've not seen it yet,' I said. 'It'll be great. You'll have a nice room all to yourself, much bigger than your wee box room at Gramps'.'

'Not all that much bigger,' Joanna said, 'but it'll be lovely and new and you'll be able to get all your toys in it.' Tina wasn't falling for the sales pitch. 'Bouncer won't like it if the garden is wee and he can't play in it properly.'

The girl had inherited her grandfather's gift for eavesdropping.

'Never mind that just now,' I said, bumping the car over the kerb and into my usual space outside Sandy's café. 'First of all we're going to St Michael's.'

'Are you sure you want to go through with this?' Joanna asked. 'It's the girl's wedding. She's not going to want you barging into the church on the happiest day of her life with news from the courts.'

I'd tried to get hold of Heather Somerville on Friday night with no success. Earlier that morning I'd phoned again to be told that she was at the hairdresser's and could be some time. Later attempts had gone onto an answering service. I could have left a message or sent a text, but preferred the personal touch. I also wanted to see her face when she heard what I had to say.

'It's bound to be hanging over her head. Think how even happier she'll be when she finds out the good news,' I said.

'Why can't it wait until Monday?' Joanna said. 'Why do you have to go charging in like the pony express? Look at you. You're not exactly dressed for the occasion.'

'All I'm doing is handing over a letter and then leaving.'

Tina was becoming impatient, struggling against her safety straps. 'Are we going to the wedding or not?'

'See?' I said. 'Tina's dying to go.'

'Okay, Robbie,' Joanna relented. 'Have it your way. Just so long as you know what you're dealing with here. Heather Somerville will have been planning this day for months, years, possibly since she was a little girl. She might look all calm and sedate in her wedding dress, but she'll be a cauldron of emotions, a mixture of excitement and worry, there will be a thousand things going through her head—'

'Well this will only be one more,' I said, as we all climbed out of the car. 'And it's a nice thing.'

I rolled down a window to let some air in for Bouncer, then unstrapped Tina, took her hand and us humans set off in the direction of the Cross Well.

'And there will be tears.' Joanna was not willing to let up.

'Not necessarily.'

When we came to the foot of Kirkgate, the cobbled brae leading to St Michael's Church, Joanna stopped. 'Imagine it. Heather comes out of the Church, a newlywed, there's organ music, cameras going off, people cheering, confetti being thrown. You suddenly appear in jeans and T-shirt. She's confused and upset, the happy moment is gone. What's my lawyer doing here? He must be bringing bad news. That's what lawyers do isn't it? You give her the letter. She rips it open, no, it's not bad news, it's good news, it's great news, it's all too much. She's just married and now her career has been saved.' Joanna put a hand firmly on each of my shoulders and looked me straight in the eye. 'Trust me, Robbie. There will be an ocean of tears.'

'D'you think?'

Joanna nodded. 'And hugging.'

'Well, if you put it like that...'

'Lots and lots of hugging. At first people gathering around, wondering why the bride is crying. What has the man in the T-shirt and jeans said to her? They all want to know what's going on. They're angry at first and then they find out, and everyone wants to hug and kiss you: the bride's mother, the bride's father, then there's the groom and the rest of the in-laws and friends, all wanting a piece of you, all—'

'Take this.' I gave the envelope to Tina. 'Go with Joanna up to the church and give it to the lady in the big white dress—'

'You mean the bride, Dad?'

'Give the letter to her and I'll meet you back at Sandy's later for ice cream and then we'll go see the new house. How's that sound?'

The ice cream part sounded fine to Tina. She started to trot up the brae, clutching the letter and dragging Joanna along.

I walked back to the car. Bouncer stared excitedly through the window at me as though I'd been gone for a fortnight. What was I to do? Give the dog back to Jake and tell Tina Bouncer had been missing his old master? Missed being kicked about the place? With just a little more time I was sure I could persuade my dad to take him. The problem was I didn't have time. Which was perhaps why I thought of Ellen Fletcher, someone else with very little time, but right now she didn't have Freddy, and Jake's business dealings meant that he wouldn't be around all that much either. Maybe, living out in the wilds, she'd appreciate some canine company, and by the time she'd reached the stage she could no longer cope, I was sure I'd have my dad talked into appreciating the benefits of dog ownership. I tapped the glass. Bouncer barked, jumping about on the back seat, wagging his tail. That was it settled. I'd break the news to Tina over ice cream that Bouncer had gone on holiday for a couple of months. Worst case, to tide us over, I'd buy another grey bunny and tell her that Rosie had come back.

I was opening the front door when Sammy Veitch approached, munching a roll on square sausage.

'Have you been where I think you've been?' I asked him.

'The deed is done,' he confirmed, patting a sporran that hung a little lower than normal. 'All signed, sealed and very much delivered. Now I'm off to the sun with the missus for a few weeks.'

There was still one thing bothering me.

Sammy read my mind. 'No need to speak to Ellen,' he said. 'I asked her about the nurse, the redhead. It was just a temporary agency job. She never asked about Ellen's condition.' He bit off a hunk of roll and began to chew.

'That's good,' I said. 'You think the whole scheme will actually work then?'

'Why wouldn't it?' He chewed some more and swallowed. 'They're working like a real team those three. Building work underway to the cottage, applications made to the banks for loan funds they'll never need. It would fool me if I didn't know the real story.' He took another bite. 'Freddy even brought along the head of the planning department to go over the plans.'

'Oh, him,' I said. 'I thought the fashion police might have a warrant out on him by now.'

'Him? No, she's a woman. Tall girl, red hair, great legs.' He winked. 'Seems to be a lot of them about these days.'

'No, Sammy,' I said, wrenching the car keys from my pocket. 'I think there may only be one.'

'Where you going?' he called after me, as I hurried off. 'Business,' I yelled back at him. 'I've got to go and see a woman about a dog.'

58

There were two vehicles parked outside Jake's cottage; a grubby, white Ford Transit van and a small hatchback that I recognised as Freddy's hire car.

With Bouncer following, I walked around the side of the house, dodging in and out through a forest of shoogly-looking scaffolding poles, to the rear. When I took the time to step back and look, it was actually a nice, solid, sandstone building. The previously sagging roof had been worked on over the past few days and was now partially stripped with a pallet laden with new slates waiting, precariously balanced on a makeshift wooden platform above the kitchen door. Jake, Freddy and Ellen were certainly giving the impression of a redevelopment exercise to cover any later questions about an insurance claim. It was a fine example of the unifying power of greed in action.

I knocked and walked through the back door to find Jake and Freddy sitting at opposite ends of the big kitchen table, separated by a half-eaten packet of chocolate digestives, each with a steaming mug in front of them.

Freddy was casually dressed for him, and Jake had for once discarded his oil-stained boiler suit and was clad in clean jeans and a new, bright red shirt that I guessed someone not a million miles away had bought for him.

It was a homely scene, Freddy and Jake sitting at the table waiting to be fed, Ellen standing by the cooker in a floral apron. There was a carton of eggs to her left and a chopping board to her right on which was stacked slices of haggis, black pudding, a saucer of button mushrooms and some tomatoes.

'What do you want?' Jake asked me. 'I need to ask Ellen something,' I said.

'She's busy and I'm hungry. Come back after I've eaten, if you've got to.' Now that the transaction was complete and Jake's money safe, I was surplus to requirements and a mere annoyance.

'That's no way to speak to Robbie,' Ellen said, draping rashers of bacon into a large cast iron frying pan. 'You want something to eat, Robbie?' Breakfast seemed a long time ago. It had been porridge. Fry-ups weren't quite a thing of the past in the Munro household, but Joanna had introduced a certain degree of rationing. 'Go on, there's plenty.'

'Maybe a bit of bacon, then,' I said. 'Perhaps a sausage.

Or two.'

'Black pudding and haggis?'

'Twist my arm.'

'Fried egg?'

'Just give him the works,' Freddy said. 'Someone's going to have to eat the stuff. I can't. Not with my IBS. I'll be lucky to keep an omelette inside me for five minutes. I've had the lavvy door swinging like the Count Basie Orchestra all morning.'

'What is it you want to talk to me about?' Ellen said, poking some link sausages with a fork. 'You can speak here. We're all friends now.'

The looks Freddy and Jake gave each other made a lie of her words.

'Aye, just tell her here or wait until after I've eaten,' Jake said.

Should I just come out with it and say I thought it strange how Ellen's former nurse fitted the description of the non-existent female head of West Lothian's planning department? Surely Jake wasn't being conned again. Not over the same piece of land. And, yet, without a great deal of effort, or parting with any money, the husband and wife team were now partners with Jake and had a legally binding agreement to prove it. Fictitious though those development proposals were supposed to be - what if the land wasn't green belt? What if it was suitable for development? If the whole thing was a triple bluff by Freddy, he and Ellen now owned a one-third share in a million-pound development site.

It was almost surreal. There was Freddy, so terrified of Jake that for the past year he'd put a thousand miles between them, now sitting at the same table having breakfast with the man who wanted to kill him. And then there was Ellen, once desperate for Freddy's return, now shacked up with Jake, the man who'd not only wanted to kill her husband, but was at least partly responsible for the death of her brother.

The only constant factors in the whole business were Ellen's lies. She'd lied to me from day one. Did she really have blood cancer? She was the healthiest leukaemia victim I'd ever seen. If she truly had only three months to live I'd have expected more symptoms than the occasional cough, holding of her side and pained expression.

'It's about Bouncer,' I said.

'Who?' said Jake. 'The dog.'

'What about it?'

'I wondered if Ellen might like to keep him. Just for...a while.'

'What's the matter with the dog, Robbie?' Ellen asked.

She tossed Bouncer a scrap of sausage

'Nothing,' I said. 'He's great, but I'm not going to have any room for him in my new place. I thought he might be company for you.'

'I'm company for her,' Jake said. 'I mean for when you're not here.'

Jake made Ellen's mind up for her. 'It's not happening.'

'Come on, Jake,' I said. 'It's only for a few weeks until

I can make other arrangements.'

'Not even for a day. If you want me to get rid of it, leave it. If not, take it with you.'

Whether Jake was being conned again was fast becoming a matter of complete indifference to me.

Bouncer padded through the back door and over to Ellen. What should I do? Let him take his chances at the pound? There was no way I was leaving him for Jake to deal with.

'He's a lovely wee dog, right enough,' Ellen said, patting Bouncer's head.

'Munro, you've already been told about the dog,' Jake said. Ellen pulled the sleeve of my shirt. 'Come on, Robbie. I'm needing a fag break anyway.' Leaving the frying pan sizzling, she walked to the back door. I followed, Bouncer tagging along. Once outside, Ellen put her hand into the big pocket in the front of the apron and removed a single cigarette and a match. She gave the latter to me. I sparked it off the door post and held it to the end of her cigarette.

She took a couple of quick puffs. 'The food will be ready in two minutes.'

'When did you start smoking?' I asked.

'I've got cancer. I thought I might as well see what all the fuss is about,' she laughed. 'It can't do much harm and I shouldn't have any trouble stopping.'

'Everything okay, between you and Jake, is it?' I asked. Ellen took another quick puff and then threw the cigarette away. It lay smouldering on the slabs, a thin ribbon of smoke spiralling upwards. Bouncer went over to investigate. Three draws from a cigarette? She hadn't come out for a smoke.

'Why are you here?' she asked.

'The dog.'

'That so?'

'And to find out what you and Freddy are really up to. Please tell me you're not trying to con Jake. Not again.'

'What makes you think that?'

'Are you?'

She looked at her feet for a second or two. 'What do you know?'

'I know that Jake has signed over to you and Freddy one-third of the development rights to what he thinks is a piece of worthless land. I also know that the head of planning isn't a tall redhead with great legs. However, your former nurse is.' I walked over, squashed the still burning cigarette with the sole of my shoe and came back. 'What I don't know for certain is if this land is worthless, or if there's anything actually the matter with you.'

351

She went to put a hand on her side. I took a hold of her wrist. 'Don't bother for my sake.'

She stood up straight. No sign of pain in her face. 'You won't say anything, will you?'

'Why shouldn't I?'

'Do you trust me?' I laughed.

'Just this once, Robbie. Trust me, everything will be made clear later.' She bent down to scratch Bouncer's head. 'I'll even look after your wee dog for as long as you like.'

I released my grip on her arm. 'I'm warning you, Ellen, Jake's a dangerous man. He would have killed Freddy if he'd managed to find him the last time. Don't think he'll have forgotten all about that, and don't think you're bomb-proof either. You might have him besotted for now with your long-lost love routine, but Jake's first love was, and always will be, money.'

Ellen replied with a smile and a wink. She patted my cheek, and, drawn by the smell of fried food, and with Bouncer at my heels, I followed her into the kitchen.

59

It was only about twenty minutes since I'd left Joanna and Tina. Definitely no more than half an hour. They'd be ages at the wedding. Women loved that sort of thing; even five-year-old ones. There was plenty of time for me to stay and have brunch, just so long as in doing so I didn't give Jake the impression that I was in on whatever plan Ellen was hatching. I didn't want any repercussions later.

I looked to my right at Freddy. I didn't know what to make of him. Was Ellen's rejection of him for real? How had she found out about his woman in Prague? Did he have a woman in Prague? I'd never told anyone after he'd confessed to me. The whole thing between Ellen and Freddy and Jake was built on layer upon layer of lies and deceit, so much so that I wanted to cut through it all with the knife Jake was spinning around on the table top.

Ellen brought over two plates of food, set one in front of me, the other in front of Jake and stepped back to accept our praise. Bacon, sausage, black pudding, a slice of haggis, fried mushrooms, a grilled tomato and a round of buttered toast cut in triangles. Ellen had already offered to open a tin of beans, but it was Jake's opinion, with which I wholly concurred, that the baked bean like the hash-brown had no place on a Scotsman's breakfast plate.

I started in on mine straight away. Jake sat back,

knife and fork at the ready, while Ellen refilled his mug from a big brown teapot. Having done so she whisked up a couple of eggs in a bowl, poured the mixture into the frying pan and, bringing her own mug of tea with her, took a seat at the table while Freddy's omelette cooked.

'How do you fancy a wee dog to keep you company, Ellen?' I asked. 'Plenty of room for it here.'

Jake answered for her. 'She's got company, and you've been told. Now shut it.' He cut the end off a link sausage, dipped it into the yolk of a fried egg and, balancing the morsel on the corner of a slice of toast, shoved the whole lot into his mouth.

Ellen watched him, admiring him eat. 'Jake likes a fry-up,' she said. 'Never starts the day with anything else.'

Up until then I'd always assumed Jake Turpie ran on ill-will and red diesel.

'How's my omelette doing?' Freddy asked.

Ellen got up and prodded the edges of the egg mixture with a fish slice. 'Won't be long. Do you want anything in it?'

'How can I have anything in it?' he asked. 'My IBS is bad enough without stuffing my gut with slices of fried offal.'

'There are some mushrooms there. Full of goodness, as you well know,' I said, harking back to his lecture on the nutritional benefits of fungus, as delivered to Joanna and me in Prague.

Freddy glanced over at the few remaining mushrooms on the chopping board. 'No, thanks, I've gone off mushrooms.'

Freddy took out a pack of cigarettes and put one in

his mouth.

'You're not smoking in here,' Jake said, mouth full of sausage, egg and toast.

Without a word Freddy and his cigarette went outside. Bouncer came over and sat beside my chair, looking patiently up at me, not begging but happy to deal with anything that might happen to fall from the table.

There was a scraping sound somewhere above my head. Ellen looked up at the ceiling. 'Birds on the roof again.'

'Sounds like they're wearing hiking boots,' I said.

Bouncer started to bark. Ellen came across and patted his head. 'I know. You hear everything through the felt. Sooner it's finished and all the slates are on the better. Go on, Robbie,' she said. 'Give the dog one of your sausages.' From what little knowledge on dog training I possessed, I knew it wasn't good to teach a dog to beg at the table. And, apart from that, the sausages were excellent.

Ellen removed a chocolate digestive from the pack. She broke it in half and threw a piece to Bouncer who devoured it in an instant. She was about to throw him the other half, when I remembered Joanna's warning about the dangers of giving chocolate to dogs. The words weren't out of my bacon-filled mouth before the rest of the biscuit was mid-air, snapped up and gone. Oh, well. It was just a bit of chocolate. How poisonous could it be? Did it matter for a dog whose days were numbered anyway? I speared a mushroom, lifted it to my mouth and stopped. I pulled it away and looked at it. Freddy was off mushrooms? What happened to mushroom omelettes being as much fun as food got for him? What about Ellen not having cancer, that Jake had taken out a joint life policy with the Fletchers, and that a lot of mushrooms were highly poisonous?

'What's wrong with you?' Jake demanded, clearly wondering why I was sitting staring at the button mush- room on the end of my fork.

I reached across and, with a sweep of my arm, propelled his breakfast plate off the side of the table and across the room. It smashed, scattering food everywhere.

Jake, knife and fork in hand, stared down in disbelief at where his food had once been and then up at me with a face that matched his nice red shirt.

Ellen folded Freddy's omelette expertly, laid it on a plate and brought it over to the table. 'What was all that about, Robbie?' she asked, calmly.

I ignored her, not taking my eyes off Jake, talking slowly to him as I backed my way out of his immediate strike-zone. 'You need to listen to me, Jake,' I said, when I thought I'd reached a safe distance. 'I've got some good news and some bad news.'

Slowly and deliberately, Jake set down his cutlery. 'The good news is that there's nothing the matter with Ellen...'

He closed his eyes, shook his head and opened them again. 'What?'

'She's not got cancer, it's all a con. The bad news is that she just tried to kill you for the insurance money.'

Another 'What?' though louder, was all Jake could manage.

'The mushrooms,' I said. 'Ellen was trying to poison you...' Even more worrying was that she'd also tried to poison me.

Ellen set down the omelette where Freddy had been sitting. Jake was standing now, white knuckles pressing down on the table, and looking very much as though he was ready to leap across it at me.

Ellen showed Jake the palm of her hand, as though she were stopping traffic. Staring straight at me she used her other hand to pick up my fork with the mushroom still impaled on its prongs. She ate it. Then one by one she picked up every single mushroom from my plate and ate those too. Jake edged his way around the table towards me.

Bouncer, who had been making a good job of clearing the mess on the floor, sensed something was amiss and started to growl; almost as loudly as Jake.

Ellen's raised hand was now firmly in the centre of Jake's chest. 'Sit down,' she said to him. 'Robbie just made a mistake.'

'A mistake!' Clenched fists by his sides, Jake's eyes measured me for a coffin.

Ellen laughed. 'I think he's been watching too much telly. Now, go outside and cool off and tell Freddy his omelette's on the table. I'll sweep up in here and make you some more food. There's plenty left. I can cook it up in no time. Go on, Jake,' she said, when he showed no intention of moving. 'I want a word with Robbie, in private.'

How did she do it? I'd seen brave men quake in the face of Jake Turpie's anger, and yet Ellen treated him like a misbehaving schoolboy.

Jake grunted and eventually sauntered grudgingly towards the kitchen door. Sneering viciously, he feigned a kick at Bouncer. The dog had a good memory. It bolted, but once at the door, it turned to face him, snarling, blocking Jake's exit.

'There's a lot of things you don't know,' I called to Jake.

He stopped in the doorway. 'I know all I want to know.

Now move the mutt before I kick its head in.'

A single flake of slate fell from the roof and landed beside Bouncer. The dog lowered its head to sniff it.

'Bouncer!' I yelled, and, cautiously, man and dog passed each other in the doorway.

'Oh, Jake...' Ellen called sweetly.

Now outside the kitchen door, Jake turned around, cracking a smile at the sound of her voice. 'Yeah?' Two more flakes of slate, larger than the last, floated down like black snow and landed on the shoulder of his bright red shirt. Sometimes X marks the spot. This time I was certain red was intended to spot the mark.

If I'd thought about what I was going to do next more carefully, I might never have done it. I'd already riled a man who really did not like being riled and, if I was wrong, he was going to like what I was about to do even less.

Stamping on one of Bouncer's paws as I did, I sprinted forward. The dog yelped as I yelled and hurled myself at Jake, hitting him dead centre of his nice new shirt.

As I lay sprawled on the ground, trying to catch my breath, what stunned me most was not my body having thudded first into Jake and then onto the concrete slabs, not even the searing pain in my left ankle, but the noise of half a ton of finest Welsh slate exploding beside me. I tried to move. The pain in my ankle was excruciating. Somehow I climbed to my feet, the bottom of my jeans soaked with blood, I'd lost a shoe and one of my socks felt horribly squishy and warm.

Whatever Jake was made of, it was resilient stuff. While I'd been rolling in agony, coughing amidst the clouds of slate-dust, he'd already leapt up and, having tramped over the hill of broken slates, was now standing in the kitchen doorway, confronting Ellen, blocking her exit, his face inches from hers.

Ellen held his gaze defiantly and then, for the first time ever, I saw fear in her eyes. Her expression, previously so relaxed and confident, began to weaken and then crumble. Lowering her chin onto her chest, she began to shake and whimper.

From the front of the house came the sound of a car ignition turning over, catching. I hopped to the side of the building to see Freddy in the driver's seat of the hired hatchback, revving the engine. A woman alighted, holding a back door open. I recognised her, though she wasn't wearing a green trouser-suit today. No, today her dress was different: a dark suit and blouse and stout sensible shoes. Only the hair was the same. Auburn. Who she was I didn't know. Only that she was neither a nurse nor the head of West Lothian planning department.

'Come on, Aunt Ellen!' she yelled.

Jake raised a hand. Ellen flinched. He put the hand on her cheek. Eyes squeezed tightly, she cowered from his touch.

'Is that right, Ellen,' he said softly. 'Do you not have the cancer?'

Ellen could only reply with a tiny, terrified shake of the head.

Jake removed his hand. 'Good.'

Ellen raised her head, daring to look at him. 'Jake...'
Jake spat in the black dust and stepped back.
'Just go,' he said.
And she did.

60

When it came to treating gaping leg wounds, Jake's first aid training didn't take him much beyond wrapping a tea towel around the bloody bit and making a cup of sweet tea.

His considered opinion was that the laceration would scab over. Mine was that it needed immediate treatment at whichever hospital bred the fewest flesh-eating bugs.

My phone was a shattered collection of plastic, glass and silicon chips. I managed to wring a call out of it and phoned Joanna to ask if she'd jump in a taxi, come to the cottage and drive me to A&E.

No answer. She was on another call. I really hoped it wasn't to her mother or I'd have as much chance of dying from old age as from my injuries.

I put the phone down, and gently, very gently, removed the tea towel that was starting to adhere to the wound. Maybe it wasn't as bad as it looked. The pain was gradually easing as my leg grew numb. I wasn't convinced the creeping numbness was a particularly good sign; nonetheless, it did give me the chance to mull something over.

I looked across the big oak table at the despondent figure sitting opposite. I'd never seen Jake this way before, and I'd known him for a lot of years. He was a cruel man, a man who lived by his own set of rules and who thought nothing of dispensing his own twisted, self-serving brand of justice upon those who broke those laws. Yes, Jake was a selfish, quick-tempered, irrational, violent individual, and yet to see him sitting, hunched over an ignored mug of tea, broken-hearted and emotionally traumatised, no more than a shell of a man, it made me think - what a perfect time to take advantage of the evil bastard.

'How much do you want for this place?'

He looked up at me as though coming out of a deep sleep. 'Eh?'

'This place. The cottage. How much?' Short sentences seemed to work best.

'You want to buy it?'

'If the price is right.'

'How right?'

'Seventy-five.'

He sat up straight. 'I paid a hundred and fifty for it.'

'No, Jake. You paid one hundred thousand and only because you thought you were going to make a million. You gave the other fifty thousand to Freddy for a finder's fee – remember?'

Jake stood up, came around the table and stared down at me. 'Try again.'

'How much are you enjoying being alive?' I asked.

He had to think about that. 'It's yours for a hundred grand.'

'Seventy-five,' I said. Grimacing in pain, I laid a hand on the bloody tea towel.

There was a long pause before Jake spoke again. 'How long does that life insurance on Freddy last for?'

'As long as someone keeps paying the monthly premium, I suppose.'

Jake sighed. 'Eighty.' He held out a hand and I

shook it. He didn't let go. 'Plus the three grand you owe me for the new motor.' He let go and nudged my smashed phone along the table at me. 'I'm a busy man. I can't sit about here all day watching you bleed.'

I got through to Joanna on my second attempt. She arrived ten minutes later, flustered and worried, to find a scene of devastation.

'Nothing to do with me,' Jake said to her, as, having traversed the mountain of broken slates, my fiancée burst in through the kitchen door, glowering at the man in the filthy red shirt. 'It was a pure accident.'

Joanna looked at me for confirmation.

'Just one of those things,' I said. 'How'd it go with Heather Somerville?'

'Fine.'

'Tears?'

'Floods.'

'Hugs?'

'You think your leg's bad? My ribs are killing me.' Tina bounded into the kitchen with Bouncer alongside, trailing shards of broken slate. Hands on hips, head to one side, she looked at me sitting there on a kitchen chair, leg resting on the table, the leg of my jeans rolled up past my knee, blood oozing through the tea towel that was wrapped around my lower leg, and forensically assessed the situation. 'Have you hurt your leg, Dad?'

'Yes I have, and now I'm going to see the doctor to make it better.'

Using the back of the chair for support, I hoisted myself onto my uninjured leg and hopped to the back door, Tina leading the way, Bouncer by her side.

'What about the dog?' Joanna asked, when my

daughter disappeared out of sight. 'Did you manage to speak to Jake about it before the house fell on you? Is he going to take it back?'

Tina and Bouncer reappeared with instructions for us to hurry up.

'Jake's not keen,' I said. 'How not keen?'

'It's not happening,' Jake said, following us out of the door.

'Well, that's a shame,' Joanna took my arm and laid it across her shoulder to support me,' but you know we can't keep a dog at the new flat, and while that's good news for me, it looks like you've got some bad news to give Tina.'

'No,' I said, as together we hobbled our way to the car. 'For you, Tina, and especially Bouncer, I have some very good news indeed.'

Author's Note

Some readers may notice a similarity in the names of the fictional Sheriff Albert Vincent Brechin and the entirely non-fictional Sheriff Albert Vincent Sheehan, erstwhile of Falkirk Sheriff Court, and before whom I appeared on an almost daily basis for around twenty years. I'd like to put the record straight on this.

While I do occasionally merge fact with fiction, so far as the Sheriff Brechin/Sheehan situation is concerned, other than certain shared mannerisms, such as the notorious eyebrow, which the non-fictional Sheriff could raise to dizzying heights during moments of extreme incredulity (most often when being addressed by the defence), that is where any similarity ends. It is true that Sheriff Sheehan, like his fictional counterpart, was not one to, as we say, miss-and-hit-the-wall when it came to sentencing, but a fairer trial judge it would be difficult to find, and one more prone than many of his brother and sister sheriffs to reasonable doubts.

Furthermore, unlike Sheriff Brechin, Sheriff Sheehan had a sympathetic side – some would say just as the Nile has a source. However, many will remember his high regard for the military. Certainly we defence lawyers were well aware of it, and whenever faced with a particularly hopeless case the first line of enquiry made was whether the accused had any connection, no matter how loose, with Her Majesty's armed forces.

I remember appearing for an elderly gentleman in

the late 1990s. He had been charged with driving without a valid licence or insurance. Unlike today, such cases were treated seriously and merited an appearance in the Sheriff Court where, unless one had an exceptionally good reason, Sheriff Sheehan was apt to follow the now largely disregarded opinion of the Appeal Court that such offenders should be heavily fined and disqualified.

Assuming that my client, an elderly man, had merely forgotten to renew his three-yearly driving licence, I asked him when he had last held a licence or insurance.

'1945,' came the reply. 'When we were demobbed, they told us to report to the Town Hall where they gave us a green card and said we could drive.'

I fastened onto the word 'demobbed' like a limpet mine to the hull of a Panzer IV. Further interrogation revealed that this little grey-haired man had served in the 3rd Battalion of the Scots Guards and on D-Day landed at Juno beach where, as a tank driver, he'd taken part in Operation Bluecoat, which saw the most concentrated infantry tank action of WWII.

When his case was called before Sheriff Sheehan, and doing my best to ignore the reason we were there, namely the half-century or so my client had been driving without either a valid licence or motor insurance, I proceeded to narrate his war record, while Sheriff Sheehan listened, head bowed and solemn, staring at the bench, usually a sign of impending doom.

When I'd completed my plea-in-mitigation, such as it was, and fearing the worst, I was surprised to see the Sheriff look over my head to the man in the dock and smile.

'Well now,' he said, jovially, and with a cock of the infamous eyebrow, 'fifty years and you haven't applied for a licence yet? It's not like a Scots Guard to be forgetful...' as though he were a school teacher scolding a favourite pupil for overdue homework, and not a judge addressing a driver who had just admitted flouting the Road Traffic laws for most of the twentieth century. 'Whatever, you're admonished.'

He thereon, despite a complete lack of any mitigation to support it, went on to make a finding that there were 'special reasons' why neither a disqualification nor even the imposition of the minimum number of penalty points was merited in the circumstances.

Continuing with #9 in the Best Defence Series

Stitch Up

Newly-wed and happy, surely criminal lawyer Robbie Munro can stay out of trouble. But a notorious child-murderer might soon be free because prosecution evidence was fabricated – and it was Robbie's dad who secured the conviction. With time running out, can Robbie uncover the truth?

'A deft slice of Caledonian crime... rings viscerally true, thanks no doubt to McIntyre's lifelong experience in criminal law.'
The Times

'Nail-biting, dark-humoured writing, with twists and gut-wrenching surprises that leave you thinking, "just one more page please".'
Scottish Field

'A compelling, well-plotted mystery.'
The Herald

'A cracking read: cleverly plotted, engaging characters, humorous and McIntyre knows his subject matter well.'
Grab This Book blog

Printed in Great Britain
by Amazon

34434659R00209